LAND OF DREAMS

Frances mande

LAND OF DREAMS

by

Jacob Jaffe

Mahr yum dreams come trne Jack

ISBN 1-58500-774-9

1stbooks - rev.02/09/00

About the Book

Land of Dreams is a coming-of-age novel about a ten-year-old boy in 1938-1939, the year America was struggling out of the Depression and Europe was staggering into war. Al, the adult narrator, relives that fateful year. He is witness to the struggles of his immigrant family: his father risking his life to oust the gangsters from the painters union and avoiding deportation because he falsified his immigration papers; his mother trying to smuggle her sister's family out of Soviet Russia and worrying about her own family as well. Al has his own conflicts: being accepted by his Irish-American fourth grade teacher, dealing with the class bully who dislikes him because he's fat and Jewish, escaping his mother's overprotectivness and trying to make sense of his family and the world. While he daydreams about Native Americans in nearby Crotona Park, he meets a black classmate whose grandfather is an Apache survivor of his tribe's 1890 Florida imprisonment. Another classmate, whose father is a physician, introduces him to the middle-class. His triumph in being chosen Santa Claus in the school play is turned into disaster when his mother forbids him to portray "that Christian saint"; only his older brother's intervention resolves the crisis. In Hebrew School, his rabbi rejects a Chanukah play as too militant and fires the teacher who selected it; but Al and his "Maccabee" classmates plan their own rebellion.

Besides the serious themes, we witness the mishaps at the Christmas and Chanukah plays; the 1938 World Series in which the *Bronx Bombers* win their third victory. In his struggles, Al enlists the help of the 1930's comic strip and radio heroes (e.g., Superman, Flash Gordon, Buck Rogers, Tom Mix) as well as Biblical characters (e.g., Noah, Abraham, Moses and God) to confront formidable enemies: the school bully, the immigration police, the autocratic rabbi, Adolph Hitler, the Evil Eye, Death and the Brooklyn Dodgers. When his father considers pursuing the American dream by going into business with the help of a wealthy Atlanta brother, Al is devastated by the possibility of moving from the Bronx. Yet Al resonates to his father's conflicts about abandoning his union principles and to his mother's fears. He learns how a decision that brings joy to one family member makes another miserable. He resonates to his grandfather's Orthodox morality (and mortality), his brother's dedication to science, his father's principles, his mother's possessiveness and fears, one uncle's humor and another's ruthless pursuit of wealth. When everything is on the verge of working out, Al's world collapses with the death of his grandfather. His parents, who fled Europe and moved numerous times in America, assume responsibility for the grandmother and must again move.

During that fateful year, many of Al's childhood beliefs are demolished: the Good Guys are not always the victors as in the radio and movie serials; threats come not only from outsiders but also from family members; stability and order are not the laws of the universe or his family; transience and capriciousness play crucial roles in life. Yet despite the disappointments and conflicts, Al has the security that only family can provide. While Al was involved in his child's moment-to-moment existence, as an adult he realizes that his father was a hero and his mother dauntless, both trying to protect their family in a world where security is illusory.

Comments from editors who read the novel included, "You're certainly a competent writer" "evocative...interesting, admirable" and "the author captured the protagonist's point of view with sensitivity and warmth." A literary agent wrote, "a strong piece of writing and an important examination of the immigration situation in the late 30's and as it largely remains today. You have a talent for portraying characters and making them surprisingly knowable and real. The protagonist, his parents (especially the mother), his older brother and his teacher were all strongly rendered and profoundly human characterizations."

To my parents and brother, alive in memory

Contents

Ah, love, let us be true
To one another! for the world, which seems
To lie before us like a land of dreams,
So various, so beautiful, so new,
Hath really neither joy, nor love, nor light,
Nor certitude, nor peace, nor help for pain;
And we are here as on a darkling plain
Swept with confused alarms of struggle and flight,
Where ignorant armies clash by night.
    Dover Beach   Matthew Arnold

...But soon we shall die and all memory...will have left
the earth, and we ourselves shall   be loved for a while
and forgotten. But the love will have been enough...Even
memory is not necessary for love. There is a land of the
living and a land of the dead and the bridge is love, the
only survival, the only meaning.
    The Bridge of San Luis Rey   Thornton Wilder.

Prologue

The falling snowflakes speckled the field, gently blanching the earth's grays and browns. I barely felt the cold as I stared at the double tombstone under which my parents lay. At least they had a known resting place, not like my brother Morris, who had wandered far from home. Beyond them stretched an endless field of tombstones. At first I saw them as solemn markers, then as the finger-tips of their occupants trying to claw their way out . Finally they were accusing fingers pointing heavenwards, wanting justice for their earthly days. No living person was within sight, but the buzzing traffic on the nearby expressway was a reminder of the world outside. As I stood there, the landscape slowly transformed itself into images of my parents, not the time-worn persons they had become, but the spirited couple of my childhood. I found myself staring into memories that flashed across the screen of my mind like unedited film clips, until the scenes slowed down to September of 1938.

Death, the Great Depression, Trade Unions, Gangsters, War, and Pogroms were abstractions; I lived in the moment-to-moment details of my child's life. I heard but barely understood my parents, who had survived pogroms and revolution in Russia to escape to their Land of Dreams. Their initial struggles were rewarded in the prosperity of the '20's, but the Great Depression wiped out those gains. They suffered with millions of others, but they survived with Poppa's working and Momma's frugality. I did not know the dangers we faced that year: the gangsters that Poppa challenged in the painters union, the naturalization investigators who could discover Poppa's falsified birth date and his participation in the Russian Revolution. Momma was always worried, if not about us, her family in Russia. I played detective to uncover family secrets that I would not, even under torture, reveal. I had the murkiest impression of a world tottering on the brink of destruction yet keenly felt the triumphs and disappointments of my small, yet all-encompassing universe. I faced a class bully, a stern Irish-American teacher, a pretty Hebrew teacher and an authoritarian rabbi. I had as allies a brother who was often my savior and sometimes my nemesis, a pious grandfather, an overprotective mother and a father who tried to toughen me for an unjust world. I also enlisted the help of Superman, Buck Rogers, Jack Armstrong, Dick Tracy, Moses, Abraham and God. I was convinced of our inevitable triumph-- weren't the Good Guys supposed to win? They did in the radio serials and comics. Sickness was a temporary aberration curable by the presence and medications of Dr. Astrakhan. Death was nebulous and the sun was supposed to shine for family outings. I did not yet know that the laws of the universe were transience, capriciousness and chaos. The vortex of my existence was the intersection of Fulton Avenue and 174th Street in the Bronx, bordered by Public School # 4, Crotona Park and the Bathgate Avenue market. Beyond those boundaries lay a world I was beginning to discover. As the cold snowflakes dissolved on my cheeks, merging with my tears, I was snugly in bed...

One

September Evening, 1938

"Where can they go? We waited two years in Warsaw for visas."

Momma's plaintive voice pierced my sleep with its mixture of entreaty and indictment.

"If America and Europe sent soldiers, they'd take Hitler by the throat-"

I stirred, responding to Poppa's anger, which I was familiar with from his right hand as well as his voice. I hadn't yet learned that his anger shielded him from his fears.

"Why should they care about the Jews?"

That was Momma sounding hopeless.

"But millions of Christians will be destroyed along with the Jews-"

Poppa was sometimes optimistic about Christians helping Jews.

"Who cared about the Jews in the Big War?"

Uncle Sol! Poppa's older brother, sometimes serious, often funny.

I stopped listening until Momma mentioned the *contrabondist,* whom she said could get her sister's family out of Russia. Poppa said that would be like throwing money out the window. Uncle Sol, usually neutral in such disputes between Momma and Poppa, said, "Even a mouse couldn't escape Stalin's police." I made a mental note to discover who was this *contrabondist.* I didn't understand all of their talk, but not caring to go to sleep, I used the shaft of light from the kitchen to make shadow animals on the wall. Morris, six years older than me, had a menagerie that danced on the wall. If he was home now--and in the mood--he could answer my questions. He could also be as vengeful as the Dragon Lady in Terry and the Pirates. Above his bed was a poster of Lindbergh and the *Spirit of St. Louis.* Morris made model airplanes and fantasized that he would fly some day. How could I--or even he--imagine where his dreams would take him? He and Poppa argued about the poster: Poppa wanted to take it down because Lindbergh was an anti-Semite; Morris said he still was first to fly the Atlantic. Poppa no longer slapped Morris for being fresh. I was not sure whether it was because Morris was in high school or Momma standing between them and saying he was too big to be hit. Since I was much younger, I wasn't as lucky. If I misbehaved, I could still risk getting a smack. But I must admit, Poppa no longer hit very hard.

"Experience is the name people give to their mistakes."

I was amazed at how long grown-ups could talk about the same subject. Where did they get all those things to say? One or two sentences was all I could think on any topic.

"But if necessary, a bear can learn to dance!"

Uncle Sol said funny things!

"There'll be bloodshed, war-"

Momma again. Even if I didn't understand her, I resonated to her worries, which hovered about her like an invisible cloak.

"They let this madman take Austria and now he wants Czechoslovakia! Give a bear honey and you'll only whet his appetite."

That was Poppa, but he sounded like Uncle Sol. My mind reeled trying to understand them. Where was the Ruhr? What was the *Anschluss?* Who would dare get close enough to a bear to give him honey? Some things I understood, like Momma wanting to rescue her sister's family in Russia. What I knew of war was from the illustrated cards that came with chewing gum, including one of Japanese soldiers bayoneting Chinese. I knew who the Bad Guys were: the Germans and Japanese. The Good Guys were us, along with the English, the French and Chinese. Who was this madman--the *meshugener*-- who aroused their anger but also terrified them?

I sat up and the springs of my fold-away bed squeaked. My feet searched for the slippers Momma insisted I wear to keep from catching a cold. When Momma noticed me in the kitchen doorway, she asked, "Did we wake you?"

Uncle Sol said, "God should waken the world as easily!"

"Yalkala," said Momma, "go back to bed."

"Al," I muttered. "You don't call Morris *Moshe* anymore!"

"Oh, pardon me," said Momma, sarcastically. "I gave you life--with the help of God--so I can give you your name. "

"Max helped too, I hope," said Uncle Sol.

From behind his tea glass, Poppa whispered, "I gave a little push."

They laughed, while Momma clucked her disapproval. I was too young to appreciate the risqué meaning of *shtup*, but knew that was something I wasn't supposed to hear. Momma turned to me. "You are Alvah on your Jewish birth certificate, in memory of my dead father--may he rest in peace--but I did name you Al for public school."

I was grateful for that small favor.

"In America, don't fool around with names on official papers," warned my uncle. I frowned, knowing that cheating was not right. Uncle Sol saw my expression and grabbed me. I winced, not from pain but fearful that he'd comment about my being fat. I felt insecure even with him, although it was other relatives who embarrassed me by reminding me that I was "chubby" or "healthy-looking."

"How come you're not asleep?" asked Poppa. His face was stern, darkened with a stubble grown only since his morning shave. Often his face or words made me wonder if I did something wrong. It didn't occur to me then that his severity, which I feared, was his way of toughening me.

Sol answered, "He wanted to see his Uncle Sol--heh, heh." I was grateful for the rescue and didn't notice his "heh, heh" mannerism.

"Danish with some milk?" asked Momma enticingly. Sitting with the men, she seemed less overpowering than when alone.

"Early breakfast or late supper?" asked Uncle Sol.

Momma did not appreciate his humor. "In Russia we never had enough to eat!" Despite our always having enough food, starvation still stalked Momma. Sol smiled uncomfortably--he recognized that his joke had crossed the boundary of discretion.

"I'm not thirsty," I answered, but did reach for a Danish.

"I knew you'd pick prunes!" said Sol. He popped his eyes and blinked them shut, his eyebrows shifting wildly, like Groucho Marx. I laughed. He was the only adult I knew, besides movie comics, who acted silly. His antics made Momma and Poppa uncomfortable, so he asked, "Studying hard?" He knew I was a good pupil, but my parents looked pleased. Then, "You'll be a doctor?"

I was flattered that relatives thought I was old enough to consider a profession. They held doctors in awe. Although I liked Doctor Astrakhan, our family physician, I didn't want to visit sick people. I shook my head and Uncle Sol frowned. "Then an engineer, like your brother. The world needs more building and less destruction." He winked. "You'll go to the Holy Land and build a homeland for the Jews? Balfour promised us that."

I said, "We're going to be pilots."

"Airplanes?" asked Sol. "The newest weapon of death. The Germans used them in Spain and the Japanese in China."

Poppa explained, "Morris' newest *mishigas*."

My heart beat faster. Morris would be furious with me for tattling about his plans. And why did Poppa call it "crazy"?

Sol pointed to a letter on the table and said to Momma, "Surah! That's how we can get your family out of Russia-- in an airplane!" He was pleased with his joke, but Momma was close to crying.

Poppa said, "Surah's sister wants to come here, but can't, and your wife's brother can, but won't."

"How Yakov can believe the Germans will get tired of Hitler-" Sol shook his head and then picked up the letter in the funny-looking Yiddish script. "I wish I could lead a band of Cossacks into Berlin. They have a natural hatred for Prussians-"

"Cossacks?" interrupted Poppa. "A natural hatred for the Jews is more like it." He shook a finger at his brother. "They'll go after a Jew quicker than a German." He tapped his left biceps. "I still carry this Cossack bullet as a souvenir." This time he didn't mention his murdered cousin Shmuel. I asked what

4

aundenk meant--while I understood most of their Yiddish, I didn't know "souvenir." Sol told me. Then he glanced toward the door and whispered to Poppa, "Advertise you were in the Red Army. Let Herbert Hoover and the F.B.I. find out."

Momma whispered, "You signed for your Citizenship papers!"

Poppa ignored Momma and said to Sol, "I was fifteen and a half. You were already six years in America." Poppa pointed at me. "I was his age when you left and Morris' age when I joined the only army fighting the *bonditan.*"

How often as a boy did I hear of these supposed brief partings that lengthened into years, leaving scars of recrimination and guilt that time refused to heal. Sol repeated a story that I had heard. "Our father wanted to make sure they wouldn't cut off his beard in America before he sent for you and *Muter.* Remember what the emigrant leaving Russia for the 'Land of Dreams' said?" He mimicked, "And now, dear God, farewell--I'm going to America." Poppa and Momma smiled but Sol, serious, said, "Should we have known a World War would drop like a wall to cut you off?"

Poppa, after a sip of tea, said, "You didn't make the war." They took turns apologizing: Sol for leaving, Poppa for being angry.

"Don't be loudmouthed about your adventures with Trotsky!" Sol spoke as the older brother, the same tone I recognized in Morris. "Before you came, Palmer's spies sent greenhorns back to Europe."

Momma glanced at the door, as if Palmer's spies were outside.

Poppa said, "Who wants to remember the War and Revolution?"

Malchuma-und-revolutzia! In those days I thought they were one word. Momma nodded toward me and said in idiomatic Yiddish the English equivalent of "Little pitchers have big ears." Their secret past was to be guarded even from me! Sol had not completed his finger-waving and warning: "The ink on your naturalization application hasn't dried yet!"

5

"How can they find out?" asked Poppa. "Besides, I was a boy."

"They have informers. And being in diapers is no excuse!"

"I warn him," said Momma. "About the union, too!"

Poppa glowered at Momma. I recognized it as saying, *Don't bring that up!*   Sol said, "If it wasn't for Borinka." He shook his head sadly and put down his tea. "Had he lived, we'd have left in 1913 and you and *Muter* would never have seen the war." Besides accusations and apologies, there were the "if only's."

Momma's face darkened and in a harsh whisper, "There is no Borinka in America." The two fingers pressed against her lips was meant for me! Over the years I had pieced together the story: Borinka, their youngest brother, had been too sick for the family to travel. He delayed Grandpa and my uncles' departure by six months, which would have enabled Poppa and Grandma to leave before the outbreak of the War. While that was unfortunate, it was not the secret. Borinka died of tuberculosis! Regardless of how healthy you were, if United States health authorities discovered you had tubercular relatives, they'd refuse the hapless immigrants entrance. "Ellis Island was as far as they got," said Sol with a hand gesture that whisked the family back across the ocean. "Their wailing could be heard as far away as Siberia." Sol shook his head--"If only someone had warned them not to mention their son." After all those years, they still seemed afraid. I had taken a personal oath never to reveal to anyone the existence of a Borinka, even if tortured by the Dragon Lady.

Poppa said, "He suffered so," and Sol, "May he rest in peace." They paid their respects to Borinka with a brief silence. Then Momma picked up the letter to remind them of current dangers. She squinted at the tiny script through her thick lenses, reading, "There's trouble--the Jews are hated more than ever. We can be enveloped in the flames at any moment. What's to become of the children?" Her eye glasses magnified her tears. She asked, "How can we bring them out?" The past had its tragedies, the present its dangers, the future its perils. Poppa looked uncomfortable at being unable to protect Momma's family. All he could say was "Hitler should be in his grave before the year's end."

Momma seconded that with, "God grant that for the Jews--*Halevai!*" "God grant" was a favorite appeal of hers. While her lips curled in a hopeful smile, she rapped her knuckles on the table, another of her many ways of warding off the Evil Eye. "Our family should be together in 1939 and our children shouldn't see pogroms--Amen!" Her glance caught Poppa's. Often I'd catch their eye messages recalling the past. She rapped again on the table and her lips moved in a silent prayer. From my earliest years I had heard about the pogrom in which the *bonditen* killed six Jews in Momma's home, miraculously overlooking Momma and her mother. Once, I had naively asked why they killed Jews. Momma looked at me as if it was self-evident, yet she explained, "Because we were Jews." Afterwards, I had nightmares.

"Why does God permit these troubles?" asked Momma. She looked upwards, but the answer came from Sol: "There are many evil people and only one God." My parents didn't join his laughter.

Momma picked up the letter and shook it, as if loosening some secret. "The *contrabondist* may get them out." She looked pleadingly at Poppa. "It's worth the money."

Poppa looked exasperated and turned to his brother. "The swindler will line his pockets with our money!"

Momma turned to me and asked, "Can we look at Yalkala knowing his cousin Avrum will be consumed in the flames?" I marveled at how skillfully they could prove their point. Momma's desperation made her believe in the impractical, if not impossible. Poppa was the realist, if not the cynic. Now they were looking at me as if my face held the answer. Poppa said, "Surah, we'll talk about this later." Just then there was a knock on the door. Fright flicked across Poppa's and Sol's faces, while Momma's remained frozen in terror. She expected pogromists or the F.B.I. Poppa whisked the fear off his face, patted Momma's hand, and went to the door. When we heard ordinary conversation, Sol said, "Only a doorbell!"

It was the Deutsch. In my eyes, he was a giant, over six feet tall and with hands the size of my head and a handlebar mustache that was the width of a six inch paintbrush. He had six children, one my age, whom I enjoyed playing with. He was also a non-Jew and fellow union reformer whom Poppa trusted like a member of the family.

"I'm sorry to barge in like this," he said to Momma, sounding truly sorry. He and Poppa disappeared into the bedroom.

"Why did he come tonight?" Momma asked Sol, as if he knew. Why a scowl on her face? She was delighted to see him on summer Sundays when he came with his family to take us on picnics. She whispered, "Union" and *"Tsuris,"* the first in English and the second in Yiddish. "Union," I knew, meant something Good to Poppa while for Momma it was Trouble. She poured another glass of tea for Sol, despite his protesting, "My bladder will burst!" She placed another Danish on his plate and he exclaimed, "One more bite and I'll bust!" Momma used food as a sedative. Not only did she eat when she was upset, but she got pleasure from watching others eat. Momma said, "Reform the world is what he wants. His suffering in the War-and-Revolution taught him nothing." Now Momma was the cynic! Yet her voice had a trace of compassion. I was amazed at how they could instantly supplant emotions. Momma cut a Danish in half--a rare treat since she usually had bread and jam--and said, "Trying to make things better can bring new troubles." Momma didn't say that about what she did to make things better.

I left their speculations to go to the bathroom. I had discovered that by pressing my ear against the wall, I could sometimes hear what was said in my parents' bedroom. Tonight I was rewarded with inaudible mumblings until I heard Poppa's, "They wouldn't!" The Deutsch, to convince Poppa of the possibility, loudly said, "Murder isn't new to them." Then Poppa whispered--curiosity had sharpened my hearing--"Treasurer," "Dumped into the East River" and "Feet in cement." That happened only in movies starring Edward G. Robinson or George Raft. My eavesdropping was interrupted by a pounding on the door. Morris burst in saying, "Stop hogging the place!" He left no uncertainty as to who had priority. I stepped aside and he splashed into the toilet bowl. I asked, "Where were you?" It was way past his bedtime.

8

He answered, "You playing detective?"

For a moment I thought he had discovered my eavesdropping. I answered, "Poppa doesn't let you stay out late on school days." I had learned from my parents how to divert accusations. Morris took it as a threat and poked me. We left the bathroom together just as Poppa and the Deutsch walked into the foyer. Poppa frowned at Morris, who busied himself greeting the Deutsch and asking about Carl, the son who was his age.

Momma asked the Deutsch if he cared for tea, but he said, "No thanks," and again apologized for coming so late. After he left, Momma asked Poppa, "What new troubles are you planning with your union?"

Poppa didn't answer; instead he turned to Morris. "It's ten o'clock! Where were you?" Morris' curfew was nine on school days. Poppa's jaw jutted out but his anger was not really toward Morris.

"Downstairs," answered Morris. "And it's only a quarter to ten." Poppa didn't like excuses or being corrected, but Morris tried to divert him by greeting Sol more enthusiastically than usual--including a kiss! Momma frowned at Poppa and said, "We have a guest." Poppa took care of the serious offenses; Momma decided this was minor. When I misbehaved, I hoped it was in Momma's province. Poppa thought she let us "get away with murder" and I suspected his harsh punishments were attempts to balance the scales of justice. But Poppa wouldn't let the matter drop. "You said you'd be up by nine."

Momma interjected, "He's not the only one who doesn't keep his word." Poppa glared at her. His disciplining Morris had turned into Momma's censuring him. That was not only "interfering," but also embarrassing. Poppa was now angrier at Momma but said, "We'll settle *It* later." The *It* was Poppa's most feared punishment, the delay worse than the actual punishment. Morris hoped Poppa was referring to my parents' quarrel, not his transgression. Meanwhile I was thinking, "How come I go to bed so early?" I resented Morris' privileges earned merely because he was six years older. Fortunately, I didn't say it aloud.

Sol, rescuing us from disaster, asked Morris, "How do you

like your special high school?" Morris was going to Stuyvesant.

Poppa said, "Morris hopes to get a college scholarship when he graduates." He was smiling now--a minute ago his neck artery nearly popped! I had trouble fathoming the inconsistencies of grown-ups.

Sol said, "I wish my boys were interested in school. Ben's working in the garment district more days than he's in high school and Simon's 'dropping out.' He says, 'College graduates can't get jobs.'" Sometimes Sol valued education while at other times joked that the only purpose of a college degree was to let you know in what field you were unemployed. He stood up. "Look at the hour! I'll soon be opening the store." As he put on his jacket, Momma said, "Tell your brother the naturalization police believe his union reformers are Communists." Even I knew she was talking to Poppa." She continued, "Talking to your brother is talking to the wall."

Sol said, "I keep telling you Mordcha, stop being a poor worker and get yourself a business. I'm not a millionaire, but I'd never give up my tailor shop. Let Yitzchok help, he owes you." That was my rich uncle who lived in Atlanta.

Poppa answered, "No one owes me!" Then sarcastically, "You got stung in your partnership with him." I heard that story of brotherly betrayal, but rather than complain, Sol said, "A little hurt from a brother is worse than a big hurt from a stranger."

Poppa asked, " A little hurt?"

"We couldn't get along," said Sol. "I was born a year after him--*Muter* said we fought in the cradle. *You* were the baby."

"He lent us money when I was sick," said Momma, giving her rich brother-in-law the benefit of the doubt.

Poppa answered, "I paid back every penny!"

Sol guiltily said, "I couldn't help you then." I had heard about Sol's failed candy store. Sol warned, "I tell my sons: learn a trade or find a business." Then, addressing Morris, "I hear flying is your business." Morris looked sharply at me. If they missed it, I didn't. I had promised not to tell. Poppa ended the discussion with, "Enough from the two of you! To bed!" I wondered what had taken him so long.

"Why do brothers fight so?" asked Momma. Sol, walking

into the foyer, answered, "Because it's safer than with strangers--heh, heh." He continued, "If you want to see a Louis-Schmeling fight, you should see Ben and Simon! Like Cain and Abel." I knew about the World Champion Boxing Match and would soon learn about Cain and Abel in Hebrew School.

When I got into bed, Morris muttered, "Stool pigeon--you broke your oath!" and smacked my arm. I shouted, "Morris hit me!" He shouted, "No, I didn't!" From the foyer came an ominous, "Another sound and both of you are going to get *It.*" Momma appeared in the doorway and went, "Shh!" If we cooperated, she could still rescue us. She kissed me and whispered into my ear what she often did when tucking me in, "Sleep is the best doctor. My mother told me that." I marveled at how many things her mother told her that she remembered. Then, in the direction of Morris' bed, "Goodnight." I liked her kissing me but wanted to be old enough for her just to say, "Goodnight." Before she disappeared, she warned, "No more arguing."

"You'll never learn to fly!" hissed Morris across the chasm separating our beds. He had shown me a summer camp snapshot of him standing next to a pilot, a Piper Cub behind them. Morris claimed the pilot took him for a ride *and* let him fly! He promised to take me up in a plane--if I kept his secrets. I was skeptical, but didn't want to risk losing a chance to fly. Would he get revenge by never taking me up in an airplane? He had just opened up the door of his fourteen-year-old world to me. Close to tears, I pleaded, "I didn't mean to." Not only wouldn't I fly, but I'd never do other things as well. All because of my big mouth!

From the adjoining bedroom, I heard Momma's raised voice. "How many times do I have to tell you the union will bring trouble?" Poppa angrily replied, "That's not your business!" Momma, sounding angry and worried, said, "The racketeers are murderers and you talk about running for Treasurer. The last one had his legs broken and was lucky. Do your buddies want you to run because the Deutsch's wife won't let him?" Poppa said, "You always think the worst." Momma replied, "Worst is if you get murdered, God-forbid! Or if the immigration police take you away!" There were more exchanges before Momma said, "Shh, the boys are sleeping."

I wondered how Momma knew so much without eavesdropping. But there was something else I wanted to find out. I asked, "Will Hitler come to the Bronx?" Not only was I hearing about him at home, but I clipped articles about him for school Current Events lessons. Morris finally whispered, "Hitler's in Europe. Forget about him, he's a crackpot." I took advantage of his talking to me to ask, "Will there be a war?"

"A war? Je-sus!" Since starting high school, he'd say 'Je-sus' when he was annoyed. Then, "Not after the last war. Too many people got killed. Now go to sleep!" He sounded like a grown-up, but I was relieved he was still explaining things to me. I asked, "Who puts peoples' feet in cement?" I was sorry he answered. "Murder Incorporated. They put stool pigeon's feet in a bucket of wet cement, let it dry and dump them into the East River." I gasped and he chuckled. Were the union gangsters in Murder Incorporated? I was too afraid to tell Morris what I'd overheard. Wanted desperately to fall asleep, I did what I hadn't done in a long time: I imagined the Sandman sprinkling sand into my eyes.

That night, I dreamt that Edward G. Robinson, the chief of Murder Incorporated, and his men were looking for Poppa and the Deutsch. I woke up terrified. When I fell asleep again, I had one of my recurring childhood dreams: I was Superman. Recently, a distant buzz and dot became a plane. Inside the cockpit, wearing flying regalia was Morris. I flew alongside, matching his rolling and looping. Of course, he wouldn't let me into the cockpit--he said I was too young! But he waved a friendly farewell. I watched his plane become a speck, the engine a hum, before vanishing into nothingness and silence. I felt an uneasy fear.

Two

The New World

The next morning, I played my game: with eyes closed, I figured out what everyone was doing. The rhythmic slapping of a straight-edge razor on a sharpening strop meant that Poppa's face was lathered a clownish white. When the trickling of water stopped, I knew Poppa was wiping his face. That's when I went to the bathroom.

"You're up early," said Poppa.

As I peed, I said, "Be careful of the gangsters."

He glared at me as if I were Momma, but then grinned, tousled my hair and asked, "One of your dreams?"

"Dreams can tell what's going to happen," I protested.

Poppa nodded and said, "Like Joseph's dreams in the Bible." Then, as he slapped after-shave alcohol on his face--I smell its pungency to this day--he said, "I think you've been listening to your mother."

I went back to bed, unhappy that Poppa dismissed my warning. I awakened again when Morris frantically shouted, "My button!" From the spitting sounds I knew Momma was sewing the button on while Morris wore his shirt. Shrouds were sewn on the dead and it was necessary for a living person to take off his garment before it was sewed. But Morris didn't have time, so Momma compromised: by emitting spitting sounds, she could ward off the Evil Eye. When the outer door closed, Momma had only me to get off.

"Yalka, wake up," she called, more out of habit than for its effectiveness. Next came a shoulder nudge followed by a shout of, "I don't have all day!" With eyes closed, I guided myself to the kitchen, peeking to find my chair and spooning the soft-boiled egg into my mouth.

"You'll poke your eye out," said Momma. When that had no

effect, "Next time, you won't stay up when your Uncle Sol visits."

My eyes popped open! Momma used arguments in shotgun fashion until she hit her target. To distract her, I pointed to my aunt's letter on the table. "Soon I'll be able to read Yiddish."

Momma said, "Before you learn our *mamalushin,* I hope my family will be in this country--*Halevai!*" She rapped her knuckles on the table. "This is Avrum's writing-" she pointed to a script larger and not as neat as the lines above it. "He's your cousin, my sister's boy." She often repeated things that I knew, but I listened as if hearing them for the first time. A photo in an earlier letter showed a round-faced smiling boy wearing dark velvet shorts and a silken white Cossack blouse, similar to the costume Momma had sewn for me in first grade. He stood proudly in front of a garden backdrop. Momma said we could be twins, but he was much thinner. I also envied his smile. When I smiled for a photo, my teeth didn't show.

Momma whispered, "Your father's stubborn, but we'll convince him to pay the agent! How can we not take the chance?" She pressed her fingers against my lips and whispered, "Don't tell your father!" A month ago the agent visited when Poppa wasn't home--this was a secret I had to keep from him.

I looked at the clock. "I'll be late!" I rushed back to the living room and as I dressed, Momma transformed our bedroom into a living room. Years later I realized the dexterity and strength required to lift both ends of our folding beds and latch them together. She could do that while lecturing me. "You stretched the rubber on your knickers more in two weeks than your brother did in two years." I resented wearing hand-me-downs, but asked, "When can I wear long pants?" Momma knew that complaint and I her answers, but I didn't mind engaging in a familiar though futile argument.

"Your brother wore knickers until this year, when he began high school." My answer was, "Why do *I* have to wait?" Her reply, "There are two good pairs Sol gave Morris, who kept them like new."

Why couldn't Morris have worn them out? And why didn't Uncle Sol stop giving Momma knickers that customers left in his cleaning store? I suspected that boys my age brought their knickers to his store and tore up the receipts so their mothers couldn't claim them. I didn't appreciate Sol's generosity and said, "Only babies wear them." I was an amateur in refuting Momma's logic, but this morning she abandoned reasoning and flung at me, "*Moishe Kapoyr!* " -- "Moshe, the Backward One." The term, more denigrating in Yiddish than its English translation, left no doubt about how hopeless I was. "Look how he dresses?" she asked, glancing up at her Invisible Audience, whom she often addressed for support in her arguments with me. Today, they were experts on the art of dressing. After rolling the beds against the wall and camouflaging them with a bedspread, she warned, "Don't blame me if you're late." How could I continue arguing if I'd have to face an angry Miss Cleary?

I hurriedly finished dressing, sticking my tongue out at the high-top shoes worn only by overweight or handicapped boys. I frowned at the knee-socks, which bunched around my thick calves no matter how I pulled them up. I glared at my protruding stomach, another source of misery. If Momma's Invisible Audience was still in the room, I hoped they felt sorry for me. Momma glanced through the doorway to see how I was doing when the doorbell rang. Fright flashed across her face. I was amazed at how instantly her self-assurance was replaced with fear--even terror--at anything unexpected. I followed as she called through the door, "Who's there?" She recognized the muffled response and unlocked the door. The visitor was Mrs. Chernow, our neighbor and mother of my best friend. Momma asked, "Anything wrong?"

"Harold's stomach is upset. Could Al tell their teacher?" Although I was behind her, Momma repeated the message. I nodded and while getting my books heard Mrs. Chernow say, "Investigators just asking routine questions," translating *routine* into Yiddish. She didn't speak like a greenhorn, having been brought to this country when a baby. Momma cautiously asked, "Why should they ask questions?" Mrs. Chernow asked, "Could it be your husband's wanting to become a citizen?" Momma shrugged noncommittally. Poppa called Harold's mother a yenta who could, in their candy store on Bathgate Avenue, broadcast "our business" to our neighbors.

Mrs. Chernow said, "They had badges and said, 'Don't tell anyone--confidential.' But don't worry, I said only nice things about him, that he'd make George Washington and Abraham Lincoln proud of them." Momma thanked her and Mrs. Chernow asked, "What are neighbors for?" She lingered as if waiting for Momma to tell her more, but Momma thanked her again and closed the door.

When Momma turned to me, panic had returned. "Your father's having a union meeting here tonight! If the investigators find out-" She clutched her brow and said, "I'll need two extra-strength headache powders!" Then, "Miss Cory will like you being late." My teacher's name was *Cleary*, but I didn't correct her. Besides Momma giving me the usual good-by kiss, she gave me a smothering hug and whispered, "Yalkala, you don't know how lucky you are to be young and not have worries--they eat you alive." She released me and I rushed out.

Fortunately, I could walk to school in three minutes--less if I ran. While relieved to escape, I resonated to Momma's upset about the "men with badges." Were they the ones who whisked immigrants back to Europe? Or encased union workers' feet in cement? Troubled as I was, the sight of the school--127 steps from home--transferred me to another world. There I was learning to become a good American and preparing for a Profession. I had no idea as to what that would be, except that I'd not have to work with my hands--like Poppa--work steadily, make lots of money and wear a suit. I rushed to school with mixed feelings: eager to become Americanized but insecure about achieving that goal. Only last year did Momma let me walk to school by myself--fear fluttered about her, having followed her across the Atlantic and now included kidnappers and automobiles for me, gangsters and immigration police for Poppa. Her fear was contagious; I struggled to escape it but it pursued me. I first saw her as others did when she enrolled me in kindergarten: a short, overweight woman in an inappropriate floral-pattern dress that she wore to dinners at Poppa's Russian hometown burial society. I was also embarrassed by her accent, which sounded more foreign than those of other immigrant mothers. I knew from the movies how American mothers were supposed to look and talk. I stood next to her in my hand-me-down knickers, carefully selected from Uncle Sol's unclaimed clothes with the waist let out. Standing with her while waiting to register for school, I felt shame while she beamed with pride, enrolling her second son in public school. She was a greenhorn while we were American citizens!

Those memories and confused feelings were often wordlessly evoked as I anxiously approached the red-brick building that resembled a medieval Christian castle. Even the hallways smelled strange, not the familiar *CN* disinfectant Momma used. 174th Street might as well have been the Atlantic Ocean separating the *Old* from the *New World.*

The school crossing guard greeted me with a, "Hey Fatso, don't you see my hand?" He was a mean eighth grader, broadcasting my humiliation and reminding me that I was leaving the safety of home. I was sure that the guard, wearing an impressive red "Crossing Guard" sash across his chest, was an anti-Semite having connections with the Russian *bonditan.* He was policeman, United States Consul, and Ellis Island Official all rolled into one. More enamored with arbitrary power than his assigned mission, he enjoyed making us wait even when there were no cars.

Harold came running up to me. I wondered if his mother made up the story of his not feeling well in order to make her early morning announcement about the investigators. I was as suspicious as Momma until he explained, "I had to go to the bathroom again." He suffered from diarrhea, especially on school day mornings. We were inseparable: born in the same week, attending the same classes since kindergarten, and spending much of our free time together. Yet in later years, I remembered him not from memory, but from a crinkled photo of us holding each other around the shoulders and mugging at the camera. The photo also reminded me of how I envied his slimness.

"Hey, Tubby, can't you *move?"* The guard had finally decided to let us cross. Safely on the other side, Harold asked,

"Why does he pick on you?" I ran on, not answering him. When we entered the courtyard filled with hundreds of noisy children, Willie, our classmate, was wrestling a fifth grade boy. He had defeated every challenger in our fourth grade. Strong and wiry, he had no trouble throwing the larger boy down. The children cheered, relishing displays of brutality even at that early hour.

"Hey!" said Willie, spying me. "Wanna wrestle?"

Of course I didn't accept his challenge, but I did not want to be a coward in front of the others. Although we'd never fought, I felt a hair's-breadth away from provoking him. He depended on me for homework and not reporting his misbehavior when I was monitor--that helped our fragile truce. Fortunately, the bell rang and we ran to our assigned places. Harold whispered, "Someone should beat him up." I hoped he didn't mean me. We lined up by class, boys and girls in separate, adjacent size-place lines. Being the shortest as well as the fattest boy in class 4-1, I had the honor of being first. Behind me was Willie. Miss Cleary descended the stairs; our pushing and talking lessened as she advanced. When she was within ten yards, two straight and silent lines awaited her. Miss Cleary was an immense woman who walked on ponderous but quick-moving legs. She wore a no-nonsense expression and had a rolled-up bun of brown hair set firmly on her head.

Years later I realized that seniority was why Miss Cleary was assigned the brightest class in the fourth grade. She was more a severe disciplinarian than a creative teacher. Harold's diarrhea and vomiting worsened last spring when he realized he would be promoted. Each 3-1 class prayed for her retirement and were successively disappointed. Although I didn't throw up-- food was too precious in our family--I had upset stomachs. On our first day in fourth grade, she had led us through the yard, up the narrow staircase to our classroom, seated us and called the roll. Then she recited our misbehavior from the moment she lined us up, identifying transgressors by name! Had she walked across a tightrope from the roof of the apartment building opposite P.S. #4 to a school turret, we wouldn't have been as impressed. Only Willie, who sat behind me, dared whisper, and was promptly made the first example of her tightly enforced disciplinary code. Today, before she reached us, Willie whispered, "Fatso, Al." When she reached us, she asked me, "Was everyone quiet on line?" I lied, "Yes," despite the eyes directed at Willie.

She smiled at her trustworthy monitor, not realizing at that moment I was more afraid of Willie. As she led us up the stairs, she turned her head slightly to scan the two lines that snakelike trailed behind her. Several pupils in last year's 4-1 class swore she could see from the back of her head. Our class didn't believe *that,* but we knew she had a sixth sense for detecting misbehavior and excellent peripheral vision.

After entering our classroom, we hung up our sweaters and jackets and started the morning routine. Since desks were screwed into the floor, there was no scraping of chairs--Miss Cleary had the custodian oil the seat hinges. Our presence was revealed only through the faint sound of footsteps and opening books. We dutifully copied spelling words from the blackboard while Miss Cleary took attendance. No one misbehaved--except Willie, who waited until she went to the blackboard and had her back to us. He whispered, "The sentences." Why hadn't he copied them in the school yard instead of fighting? I wondered how he had ever gotten into our class or why he was allowed to remain. Years later I realized that by punishing him, the rest of us were kept on our toes. His presence exemplified the proverb, "Talk to the door so the walls will hear."

Willie commanded, "Give me the homework!" He risked talking to being unprepared. Miss Cleary, without turning, warned, "Someone is whispering." Willie poked me. I wasn't sure what to do. If I gave him the homework, Miss Cleary could catch me; if I didn't, I risked his fury. The decision was made when Miss Cleary turned around and started her inspection. She stopped behind me and I heard the rustle of paper. "Stand up!" She walked to her desk and picked up her Delaney book. "You'll write each word this week *twenty* times." Willie sat down with such force that I was bounced about in my seat. Miss Cleary sternly continued, "And for showing me yesterday's homework-" *How could he be so stupid?* "Next time you do *anything*

19

wrong, your mother comes in." When she resumed checking the homework, Willie spat, "I'll get you!"

I didn't learn much that morning and Willie didn't have to kick my seat to remind me as to why. I hoped Miss Cleary would keep him in that afternoon, her usual punishment, but I didn't yet realize teachers could have personal obligations after school. My only reprieve was his eating lunch in school. Our classmates were anticipating an after-school fight that would be the highlight of their day, despite there being no suspense in a Willie-Al fight. I never shared their enthusiasm for *any* fight, leastwise this one. As we lined up for lunch, Miss Cleary noticed the class' restlessness. At lunch time, before our class separated, Willie muttered, "I'll get you at three o'clock, *Bronx* Fatso!" Willie, who couldn't remember a fact two minutes after studying it, remembered my fiasco of the previous week, when I mistakenly believed Russia was near the Bronx.

As we walked home, Harold said, "You're not going back-- he'll smash you to a *pulp.*" He explained that was "mashed up meat." Harold proved again that his mother's graduating from high school gave him a vocabulary edge. He was not being cruel- -he believed I wouldn't return. Before we parted in our building, he suggested, "Throw up. My mother never lets me go to school after that." He demonstrated by sticking a finger down his throat and gagging. Since Momma was traumatized by starvation, I vomited on the rarest of occasions. Still, I was grateful Harold believed there was a way out.

Halfway through lunch, Momma kissed my forehead to see if I had a fever. I had washed my face with the hot water, but Momma shook her head. My forehead had cooled off. I didn't press the issue, not wanting Momma to use a rectal thermometer. Besides the humiliation, the more reliable indicator would show no fever. Momma sensed something was wrong. She asked if something was wrong. I shook my head. She was a cracker-jack at reading my mind. "Anything in school?" Like Sherlock Holmes, she checked every clue. "Not having your living room tonight because of your father's union meeting?" I didn't fall for that one. Finally, she returned to her own worries. "I don't like your father having those union buddies here tonight."

Disapproval was evident in the way she said *buddies,* not *friends.*

Outside, I stared into Crotona Park, where there was supposed to be an Indian Cave. I could hide there, except I never found the cave. I thought of telling Miss Cleary that Grandpa was in the hospital with a heart attack and leave early, but that excuse risked provoking the Evil Eye. I tried imagining myself Superman and beating up Willie, but I couldn't. Where was Harold? Perhaps he could think of something besides vomiting. The sunny park was made gray by my fears. I walked slowly toward the school, unable to think of any alternative. My legs made the final decision. I envied Willie and the simplicity of his world: he seemed fearless and was looking forward to three o'clock.

My only recollection of that afternoon was Willie whispering his threats and kicking my seat when Miss Cleary wasn't looking. The afternoon dragged on with an excruciating slowness but ended too soon. At two minutes to three, we sat waiting for Miss Cleary to line us up. Couldn't someone misbehave so that she'd have no choice but to keep us in? No one did. Could I do something outrageous? Willie made it seem so easy. When she waited for us show her we were ready, she was amazed at how perfectly straight Willie sat. She didn't know why he was so eager to be dismissed.

Outside, my legs were leaden, but an attempt at running wouldn't have done any good--Willie was right behind me. We were not alone. Word of the fight had spread throughout the school and the crowd ranged from kindergarten babies to 8th grade seniors. Willie's boasting in the lunchroom and the school grapevine did their work. Everyone pushed to get the best spots, but respected our 4-1 classmates' right to get the best view. I didn't appreciate the attention, but Willie did. I felt like John Garfield awaiting execution.

My classmates, who showed no interest when I got an Achievement Award in the Third Grade Assembly--some even hissed--relished my being in the limelight now. You could bounce a ball off the excitement surrounding Willie and me. Why were they so interested in a fight whose outcome was certain and my performance disappointing? Willie started jumping and waving his fists. My attention turned to him. He was clearing a space for us as well as showing off. Scared as I was, I couldn't help but admire his agility. The spectators were appreciative as well--their mouths were open wide enough to swallow whole sandwiches and their eyes were popping. Willie pranced about and shadow-boxed, just like fights in the newsreels. While I usually never watched fights, today I longed to be a spectator rather than a participant. Willie's acrobatics had everyone cheering, including Harold. Willie pirouetted around me in case I had forgotten what role I was to play. He was in no rush for the kill--he enjoyed the attention in what promised to be the highlight of his elementary school career. But his audience became impatient and shouted, "Hit him" and "Fight!" Willie took their cue and danced a tighter circle around me. The children shrieked. Willie, his fierce face inches away, whispered, "Put your books down." He knew the audience wouldn't appreciate his attacking me if I didn't defend myself and he expected my cooperation. I closed my eyes and held my breath, wishing for the strength to knock him down or the ability to fly away. "Up-and-away!" I thought and blinked. When I opened my eyes, Willie was grinning and mimicked, "Up-and-away!" The words had escaped me!

Willie jeered, "He thinks he's Superman!" The audience chanted, "Up-and-away!" Willie pulled at my book bag and we fell. Voices shouted, "Fight!" They were dissatisfied with a book bag-pulling contest. When we got up, Willie growled, "Fat Bronx Jew-boy!" When I just stood there he whispered, "Kike!" and struck me in the cheek. I pushed with all my strength and Willie, surprised, went backwards. Recovering, he came swinging, connecting with my face, shoulder and stomach. I swung wildly, mostly missing and ineffectively blocking his blows. As his rained on me, I become an observer. Earlier, I believed I'd be overwhelmed by fright and suffer excruciating pain. After the first blows, I wasn't that afraid or felt much pain. I observed our audience cheer when I was hit and taunt me with "Up-and-away." Soon Willie's blows weren't as hard and his breathing became labored. Occasionally, I connected, but without much of effect. I lost track of time and had given up hope of the fight ending when two teachers from our school separated us.

While grateful to be rescued, I resented their interference. Willie, more indignant than me, struggled with the stronger teacher. I twisted in the grip of the smaller teacher, but it was more for show. Our audience shouted disapproval at the termination of their entertainment, but the teachers ignored them and escorted us in opposite directions. I tried to look angry and disappointed.

"Are you all right?" the teacher asked when we turned the corner. Although I was too numb to know, I said, "Yes." I pointed to my apartment building and said, "That's where I live." He watched me walk on before he left.

"Some fight! You okay?" The voice behind me was Harold's. I had felt betrayed when he cheered Willie, but also thought that he had the right to cheer the winner. He handed me my book bag and asked, "Are you hurt?" His concern sounded genuine. He added, "You stood up to him!" He was now my friend again and I thought, *I survived a fight with the biggest bully in school!* Inconceivable--except in a Superman fantasy! I was exhilarated and wondered if Harold noticed, but he was staring at my knickers. I looked down. They were torn! My left knee burned, but that was minor compared to the tell-tale tear. My eagerness to reach the safety of home vanished. I walked at a snail's pace. The tear of my knickers looked like the tongue of a dog. Earlier, I had been apprehensive about surviving an encounter with Willie. Now Momma seemed more formidable.

Three

I Join the Rank-and-File

Long after the echo of Harold's closing door faded into silence, I continued staring at my doorknob, noticing for the first time its discolored brass. I blinked, held my breath, said, "Up-and-away," but wished for the invisibility of the Shadow.

"What's wrong?" asked Momma, who had an uncanny way of knowing. I hadn't made it past the kitchen doorway. I stood with my head down, but the scratches on my forehead gave me away. "Your face!" she said and led me to the bathroom. Looking down, she added, "Your knickers!" The rip seemed to wag at her. "You were fighting!" She took peroxide and cotton out the medicine cabinet and sponged my cheeks and forehead. I didn't dare make a sound or even flinch. Then she commanded, "Your knee!" I lowered my knickers and she wiped that bruise. With first aid taken care of, I knew what was next.

"Why did you fight?" she asked.

"I didn't start it! And it's not *that* bad."

"Not that bad?" she repeated. Her thick eye glasses had magnified the bruises. Then "You're a doctor?" She didn't wait for my answer. "You nearly lost your eye." I didn't argue or tell her that *she* wasn't a doctor.

Momma picked up my knickers and shoved her fist down the leg. She wiggled her fingers through the hole. If they weren't my knickers, I would have found that funny. She said, "Your new knickers!" They were hand-me-downs, but I didn't correct her.

Then she said what I was most afraid of: "Your father will hear about this!" I was not ready for *three* battles today! She disappeared and I ran after her. In the kitchen, she ignored me and lifted a pot cover. I begged, "Please don't tell Poppa!" As frightened as I'd been of Willie and Momma, I was most afraid of Poppa.

Momma turned to me. "I shouldn't tell your father you were nearly killed in a fight and your new knickers got torn to pieces?"

Momma was not asking a question. Poppa, who didn't like stool pigeons would listen to her. I said, "He doesn't have to know."

"He doesn't have to know?" She made it sound impossible.

I said, *"You* don't tell him everything." Momma stared at me in disbelief and I begged, "Don't tell him tonight--he has the meeting!"

Momma thought differently. "Tonight he *should* know! He's always busy with his union, and tonight, when he can be with his family, he brings his union *shleppers."* Poppa's reformers were demoted to "Bums." I was not only getting myself into more trouble, but Poppa as well! *That* would not help my case with him.

Momma asked, "I fool you?" I turned to where she was looking, but Poppa wasn't there. That didn't stop her from answering her question. *"You* fooled me by saying you wouldn't run for Treasurer. If you *think* of running, I'll go to the fabric shop to buy material for a mourning dress."

I was relieved that she was angry at Poppa rather than me, until she said, "Instead of risking your life for others, you should be home making life better for your children!" I did not have to be as old and as smart as Morris to figure out what was coming next. "If you were home more, they wouldn't act like hoodlums and fight!"

If I lived to be twice 120, which was how long Momma wished, I could have never thought that up. Poppa, not Willie, was responsible for the fight! By my staying in the kitchen and listening to her, she'd think up more reasons. I turned to leave, but she shouted, "Yalka!" She grabbed me and burst into tears. "You could have gotten hurt even worse." Her tears stung my cheek but then she switched moods and held me at arm's length. "Who hit you? Why did you fight?" No explanation could help and none was necessary because she continued, "Our troubles come not only from Hitler. We neglect our own. Your father has to know." With that, she turned back to the stove, as if I wasn't there.

If Momma was upset about Willie beating me, why tell Poppa? Had I survived Willie's blows only to face Poppa's? He would be angry not only about my fighting, but Momma accusing him of being a bigger culprit than Willie. I was too dejected to sneak my *Superman* comic out of its hiding place behind the living room couch. I sat on the couch as George Raft had in his cell on death row. My only hope, if I dared believe in a miracle, was Morris. When he finally arrived, Momma must have told him, because he rushed in and asked, "Who did you fight?" I liked his question and told him. He asked what happened and I answered, "I didn't lend him my spelling homework." He asked, "Why should you do his work?" How could I explain my having lent him my homework for weeks because I was afraid of him and that this morning Miss Cleary was watching. I said, "Willie called me, 'Fat Bronx Jew-boy" and "kike."

Until then, I had forgotten Willie's mutterings. Morris' jaw dropped. "Willie's an anti-Semite, like Hitler! No wonder you had to fight him." Then, "How did it end?"

I answered, "Two teachers broke it up."

Morris said, "Good!" I thought he meant something different until he said, "Willie will be waiting----you can beat him up tomorrow!"

The room darkened. Up until then I thought the fight was over, not "interrupted," a vocabulary word I learned the previous week. Morris said, "I'll show you how to box." He held up his hands, trying to look like Joe Louis. Morris was smart, but I never imagined him a boxing expert. Morris said, "Jab, jab, swing," showing me how. He shadow-boxed around the room. I joined him, leading with my left. Morris said, "Give it to the Jew-hater! Swing at Willie--make believe he's Hitler." He gestured for me to hit him. My touch sent him across the room. Then he landed a blow that made me drop. He stood over me and said, "He's down for the count of one, two, three-" He stopped suddenly. Momma was in the doorway.

"What's going on here?" We froze. "Are the two of you

meshuga?" To Morris she said, "I thought you'd talk sense into him. Instead you nearly killed him.

"I'm teaching Al to defend himself," said Morris.

"You'll get him killed!" shouted Momma. "An older brother should have more sense! " She turned to me, no longer caring that I was knocked down. "You'll never learn!" Then to both of us, *"Shkutzim!"* That was one of her worse insults, its closest meaning *non-Jewish hoodlums.* "Your father will hear about this! Right after supper, but before his meeting." She walked away, but her anger remained suspended in the room.

Morris dropped into his desk chair. I felt sorry for him. He was only trying to help me. But I felt sorrier for me. By not lending Willie the homework, I had started a chain of troubles. At least Momma wouldn't tell Poppa until after we ate. A strict rule in our family was that Poppa was never told bad news before supper. Spoiling his appetite was forbidden. That rule didn't apply to me.

Despite Momma's rule, when Poppa came home, she shouted, "Run for Treasurer--you'll get deported, if not killed!" Then she told him about the investigators who visited Mrs. Chernow. He shouted back, "Mrs. Chernow is a yenta! I won't live in fear the rest of my life!" She replied, "Be brave and leave me a widow and your sons orphans." Poppa went to their bedroom and slammed the door. I walked into the kitchen to get Poppa's *Daily News.* Momma lamented, "Why should my sons respect me if my husband doesn't?" Then, sarcastically, "You're going to read the funnies?" She had not forgotten my transgression. I said, "I need an article for Current Events. If you don't want me to do my homework-" Actually, I was going to read the comics. Without turning from the stove, she said, "Don't think I'm going to forget your fight."

With Momma and Poppa in such bad moods, I dreaded what could happen to me. I sat on the couch reading the front page article to prove Momma wrong and then brought it to Morris, asking him why "London Opposes Chamberlain." Morris skimmed the article. "Chamberlain's cabinet--that's his party leaders--doesn't want to give Hitler part of Czechoslovakia." He looked at me and said, "This mess could start a war." I went back to the couch thinking of how much Morris knew by having a six year head start: politics, unions, airplanes, planets, flying, how fish breathed and even boxing.

During supper, my parents' expressions of anger said more than words. Then, several minutes into the meal, Momma asked, "How can you think of running for office if the Deutsch's wife won't let him?"

Poppa took a deep breath. "If you *listen*, I'll explain." They were talking as if Morris and I weren't there. "Most of the gangsters are Jewish," he said calmly, "and many New York painters are Jewish. If only Christian Rank-and-Filers run against them, the gangsters will say the Christians want to get the Jews out of the union." He raised his hand so Momma would let him finish. "We're just *talking,* nothing's decided." Momma asked, "And you'll still have the meeting tonight?" Poppa's silence was his answer. Momma said, "If you don't listen to me, remember what your brother said at this very table last night." Momma first noticed Morris and me and said, "The boys are here and I'll say only one word: when the Messiah comes, the sick will be healed, but fools will remain fools." She said nothing else during the meal. Neither did Poppa.

After supper, I pretended to study, pleased that my parents were preoccupied with this new twist in their conflict over the union. In an hour and a half, the union meeting would start and I hoped Momma wouldn't have a chance to tell him about the fight. I wasn't that lucky--an hour later, when Momma decided Poppa's meal was digested, Poppa called me. I walked slowly to the bedroom, my heart pounding. He was sitting in his armchair. "Your mother says you were fighting." He lowered his *Forward* and let it rest on his lap, as he did when a conversation required his full attention. Momma was sitting on the bed and sewing his torn work shirt. She looked like Madame Defarge. If I had one wish, it was that she leave. Justice would have been better served.

Without looking up, Momma said, "Show him your wounds." In case he didn't notice, she said, "His eye and cheek." Then, "Remember our oath in Warsaw?" She paused to give him time to recall, if it had slipped his mind. Another pause. "Morris learned his lesson. I never dreamed Yalka-" She shook her head sadly and picked up the section of the paper with the *Bintel Brief.* That was a letters-to-the-editor column in which readers wrote of their troubles and asked for advice. Momma read aloud, "My husband gives his whole life to his union. He fights for the working class but neglects his own family. He is seldom home. I'm like a widow and my three children are fatherless. Should I ask him to leave and find a father for our children?" Poppa raised his newspaper, but Momma looked right through it. From behind the paper, Poppa asked, "Who wrote the letter?"

She read, "A Union Widow--but it could have been me."

Poppa lowered his paper. "What does the wise editor answer?"

Momma read, "Your husband's concern for the downtrodden shows he has a good heart-" Poppa smiled at that, but Momma continued, "-that shouldn't excuse him from being a good husband and father. Sit down and have a talk about family responsibilities." Momma muttered, "If she has a husband like mine, he'll talk but not listen." I thought they had forgotten about me, but Momma said, "The apple doesn't fall far from the tree." Before I could leave, Poppa looked at me sternly and said, "I'll see you later and decide what *It* should be." I shuddered at the mention of *It.*

Morris asked, "What did Poppa do?"

"He'll see me after the meeting."

Morris' expression confirmed what I already knew: I was in *deep* trouble. I asked, "What was their oath in Warsaw?"

Morris shook his head. "When Mom and Pop were waiting for their visas after the new Immigration Act was passed by Congress-" Morris, usually deaf to my questions, was giving me a History lesson! I knew better than to be annoyed. "-they had lived through the War-and-Revolution. Pop was a soldier-" I was half-listening, like sometimes in school, until, "They swore that their children would never fight in America." Morris saw my mouth drop yet said, "Pop sometimes hit me with the razor strop." Morris saw my face and said, "Mom made him stop using it before you were born." Yet I thought, *Poppa still has the strop!* Momma could forgive, not Poppa.

I asked, "Did you ever fight?"

Morris answered, "First grade. This kid picked on me for no reason. I was scratched, but Mom told Pop and he used the strop- -two swings on my behind before Momma stopped him." I winced. I was too terrified to ask if my offense was serious enough for that leather belt hanging in the bathroom. Would Momma stop him in time?

When I went into the kitchen for a drink of water, Momma muttered, "He throws his children out of their room to have his buddies over. If the gangsters don't break down our door, the police will." Momma had used those arguments with Poppa. He said there were too many men for the gangsters to show their faces and that regarding the police, they were not Cossacks. Momma reminded him one gun is stronger than a roomful of men and that he thought differently about the police when they beat up painters during strikes. I didn't hear her consenting to the meeting and don't know what made her change her mind. Yet with the meeting to start in less than half an hour, she was still arguing with an imaginary Poppa.

About twenty men came, singly and in pairs. I knew only the Deutsch. He dwarfed Poppa, who seemed giant enough for me. As he shook my hand, he had a big smile below his handle-bar mustache. He said, "If the weather's nice, we picnic this Sunday." How could I forget? Our families went on picnics in his big black car since I was a baby. I wondered how Momma would greet him but he hugged her and she asked about his family. As the men streamed in, Poppa introduced them to Momma. She surprised me by greeting them with polite "Hello's." Poppa proudly introduced Morris and me as "My sons." The men shook our hands and some said, "What nice boys." One of the workers was a tall black man. The only other black person who had been in our house was Eunice, who took care of me years ago when Momma was sick. A few minutes after 7:30, Poppa closed the door to the living room. Morris had left to study at a friend's. I carried my school books to the kitchen, but the table was covered with all of our cups, including the china ones used for company. On the stove was our biggest pot, filled with boiling water. Momma muttered, "Your father

31

said only a *few* men were coming--they're packed in like Madison Square Garden." She was complaining but preparing tea! She was also cutting up a honey cake! I offered to help.

When I entered the living room, Poppa was surprised to see me. The Deutsch was talking as I carried the cake around the room. The men were squeezed together on the couch and every regular and folding chair we had. They took slices and said, "Thanks." There was one piece left and Poppa said I could have it. Then Momma came in with cups of tea and two men went into the kitchen to bring the rest. One man said, "You shouldn't have bothered, Mrs. Segal." Momma replied, "What's the bother? With all the talking, you must be thirsty." She gave Poppa a funny look but no one else noticed. The men thanked her and she left. I remained behind.

The Deutsch continued as if he weren't interrupted. "The men know they've more to gain joining us than staying with the gangsters." A thin man opposite him said, "The men are still afraid." Poppa answered, "The *gangsters* are running scared!" Several men nodded but the thin man said, "Scared men with guns are more dangerous than brave men with paint brushes. Remember what happened to Ben." Poppa answered, "Only some of the men deserted when they tried to shoot him." The thin man said, "Bolton in Chicago wasn't as lucky." There was a buzz of whispering. I was the only one who didn't know.

A heavy-set man in a rough voice asked, "How long can we be intimidated by the bosses on one side and the gangsters on the other?" He didn't wait for an answer. "We've had seven years of the Depression and millions of workers are still looking for work. The CIO-" Someone interrupted, "Get off your soap box! We're a craft union, part of the Federation, not a bunch of Communists." The heavy-set man answered, "I'm not arguing about industrial unions. It helps our men to know that they have allies, that the country is on the march-" Someone interrupted, "We're here to clean our own house, to get our slate elected, one that puts our interests first." A man asked the black worker if Negroes would support the Rank and File. He answered, "If the Rank and File proves it's on their side. Look at me." A man said, "Don't take it personally, but there are too few Negro painters in the union to make a difference." The Deutsch said, "If we bring them in, the contractors can't use them as scabs." They couldn't agree on *anything!* Poppa asked the men to lower their voices or all the neighbors would hear. It was a mild September night and the windows were open. Most of the men had taken off their jackets and loosened their ties. They kept interrupting each other and I realized for the first time why Miss Cleary had us raise our hands.

I sat in the corner, hoping no one would notice me. Nothing that I had overheard in adult conversations sounded as interesting. They talked about the elections. Someone repeated what Poppa had said at the supper table. "We've got to have Jewish Rank-and-Filers on the slate to win." He asked Poppa if he would consider running instead of the Deutsch. Before he could answer someone said, "Whoever's least afraid of his old lady will run." The men laughed. One man said, "I told my wife I'm down at the saloon." There was more laughter. Someone asked, "Should we hold off having the election? Remember Chicago." There was a buzz of whispering. I tried to imagine what had happened there. Poppa said, "We've already waited too long. We've got to stick together and act now!" There was a buzz of approval. The heavy-set man said, "Sticking together is what it's all about. Let's remember the bosses are our enemies, the gangsters their tools, like the police and courts-" Someone muttered, "He's on his soapbox again," but the heavy-set man continued, "-we've got to see ourselves part of a movement, workers on the march-"

The next thing I heard was the scraping of chairs. I opened my eyes-- the meeting was over! A dozen conversations were going on at once. I was surprised to see men who were arguing now acting friendly. If Harold and I argued, we wouldn't speak to each other for days. I overheard one of the men ask Poppa, "If you run for Treasurer, will your wife make a fuss?" Someone said, "Max will first take on the gangsters, then his wife." Several men thought that funny. The Deutsch came over to me and said, "Our meeting put you to sleep." He easily lifted me off the floor and said, "I didn't hear your vote."

Morris was surprised to see me coming out of the living

room. The Deutsch said, "Your brother's a card-carrying Rank-and-Filer." Poppa and several of the men nearby laughed. I like the expression on Morris' face. As the men walked past the kitchen, they thanked Momma for the tea and cake. The Deutsch balanced a pile of cups and saucers in his hands and told Momma, "I was a waiter in Bavaria and would have been one in this country if your husband didn't get me into painting." The Deutsch was the last to leave. He and Poppa were in the foyer, out of earshot of Momma in the kitchen. Poppa whispered, "It went well." When the Deutsch left, he patted my head and said, "Let's hope we have nice weather Sunday."

Although it was late, Momma served us leftover honey cake. Poppa drank tea with a lump of sugar in his mouth, though he hadn't at the meeting. He said, "That was nice, your serving tea." Momma, washing cups, didn't answer. Poppa said, "I didn't think of cake or serving tea."

Momma, her back to him, said, "Men don't think of those things."

Poppa, after a noisy sip, said, "I'm glad you did."

She turned around and faced him. "Don't get any wrong ideas," she said, wiping her hands on her apron. "I'm still against your getting into trouble with gangsters."

Poppa said, "There are many men behind the Rank and File."

Momma turned to the sink. Above the noise of running water, she said, "Having a lot of fools for friends doesn't make you wise or protect you from gangsters." Poppa didn't answer. Momma said, "How you dragged the Deutsch into this I'll never understand. His wife and children will never forgive you."

Poppa tried not to answer, but finally said, "If the painters don't stick together-"

Momma interrupted with, "No speeches!" She faced him. "Workers should take care of their families. My mother--may she rest in peace-" she rapped her knuckles on the wooden table to ward off the Evil Eye--"My Mother used to say, 'No one needs help from others to get into trouble." She looked at me. "You haven't finished with Yalka."

I had completely forgotten! I swallowed the cake and gulped

down the milk. Before I escaped, Poppa said, "I'll be in to see you."

I got into bed in record time. While I waited, Morris asked what happened at the meeting. I told him what I remembered. Then Poppa came in. He sat down on my bed. I was never so scared. His words were serious but his voice calm. "Your mother is very upset about your fighting."

Morris, on the other bed, sat up. "This kid called Al a 'kike!' Should Al let the anti-Semite get away with it?"

Poppa got angry when anyone got in the way of his punishing us, but he answered Morris. "You want your little brother to fight *every* anti-Semite?"

"He's not that little and better learn quick. With Hitler in Europe and Father Coughlin in this country-" He stopped when he saw Poppa's expression.

Poppa said, "Don't *you* give me a speech about anti-Semitism. When I-"

Morris did something he'd never done--he interrupted Poppa. "You joined the Red Militia to fight the anti-Semites after the Cossack killed your cousin. You were fifteen--you risked your life when you were younger than me!"

"That was Russia," answered Poppa, "during a revolution-" Although he could end any argument in his favor, he was silent. I knew Morris had the better of him.

Morris asked, "Are you going to run for Treasurer?"

I saw Poppa's face. Rather than me being in the hot seat, Poppa was. I could have hugged Morris--he was a genius!

Poppa sounded very controlled. "I don't have to answer to you or *anyone* else." Then, softly, "I love your mother, but I have to do what's right." He stood up. "There are big ears in this house and I hope not as loose tongues." He paused in front of me and said, "You're young Al, but you will have to make your own decisions. Even if you don't have the experience." That was the closest he ever admitted that Morris was right. He kissed me on the forehead and patted Morris on the shoulder. He rarely displayed affection. At the doorway, he turned. "I love you both more than anything." Then he disappeared.

It took a while for me to realize his visit was over. Morris turned off the light. I whispered across the darkness what I rarely said, "Thanks, Morris."

He whispered back, "Don't thank me, thank that Cossack and Hitler." He added, "And the gangsters."

I didn't understand what he meant. Neither did I try--it had been a long day. When I turned over and closed my eyes, I first realized that I'd escaped Poppa's *It.* "

Four

Up-and-Away!

While I went to bed at peace with Poppa, my dream mind was busily engaged with Willie. I was leaving the *Daily Planet,* but despite being Clark Kent, Willie recognized me. I ran, looking for a telephone booth, but my high-top shoes slowed me down. Then I wasn't even Clark Kent. Willie, gaining on me, shouted, "Fatso, Al, Bronx Jew-boy! Kike!" On both sides were all the children of P. S. # 4, forming barriers preventing my escape. I woke up, sweating and breathing hard. It was dark outside and Morris was still in bed. Poppa and Momma were in the bedroom, arguing about the union. It was the middle of the night. When I opened my eyes again, it was light. Momma greeted my entrance into the kitchen with, "I hope you're not up early for another fight."

I didn't need any reminder--my body ached more than yesterday. I went to the bathroom and looked in the mirror. I had a black eye--I looked worse than yesterday! I kept my head down while eating, but Momma said, "With your eye black and blue, you look like a real hoodlum." Her thick-lenses could make a fly look like an elephant. "Your eye could have been knocked out--God forbid!" She rapped her knuckles on the table. Then her face hardened. "I won't be able to sew your knickers." To make sure I understood, she held them up, sticking her fist through the hole again. "Lucky, you have another pair for school." She shook her head. "Your father let you get away with murder! I'll talk to him tonight."

What a switch--that was what he said about her. She looked at me severely and paused to heighten the suspense in case I thought I'd heard the worst. "I'm going to your teacher, Miss Cory."

I no longer saw my spoon suspended in mid-air. Instead, Momma in the brightly colored dress she wore to register me for kindergarten. She walks into my class. All eyes are on her as she greets "Miss Cory." The boys and girls laugh, while Miss Cleary frowns. If that wasn't bad enough, Momma speaks in the English that she pronounces like Yiddish. Willie smirks and says to everyone around him, "Momma's boy! Fatso had to bring his mother to school 'cause he's scared of me!" Momma, after explaining her mission, raps her knuckles on Miss Cleary's desk to protect us from the Evil Eye--the class bursts into laughter. Every previous embarrassment of mine--real and imagined--pale in comparison. When I returned from the movie in my mind, Momma was pleased with my expression. I shouted, "I'll never fight again! I promise!" Momma pointed a stubby forefinger towards the ceiling. I knew she was not calling my attention to the crack-line that Poppa's paint job failed to conceal. I said, "I swear to God-" and looked at where Momma imagined Him to be "-that I will never fight again." I was more concerned about persuading Momma than God. To seal my vow, I kissed my pinkie and tossed the sacred kiss to the ceiling. While I was certain God was convinced, Momma asked, "You're sure?" Momma was not letting me off easy. I shouted the oath again, in case Momma thought God was hard of hearing. Momma still looked more skeptical than God and said, "We'll see."

I quickly left for school before she could say another word, grateful for even this reprieve. Harold caught up to me, surprised that I was going to school. I walked slowly, trying to figure a way out. God and Momma had my sworn oath not to fight, but at this very moment Willie was waiting to finish me off. Today I wouldn't be lucky to have rescuers. More frightening than Willie's blows was the prospect of Momma's coming to school. God was the least of my worries. Harold asked, "You're not afraid?" I slowed to a snail's pace. If I couldn't avoid disaster, I could at least delay it. Harold again suggested throwing up, but I considered other options: escaping to the farthest end of the Bathgate market that Momma and I had never yet reached; doubling back to Crotona Park to find the Indian Cave. When we reached the school crossing guard, I stopped. Was I being brave to face Willie, or a coward afraid to run away? My legs again made the decision, reluctantly to be sure--my knee still hurt--obeying the crossing guard's hand-wave. I was relieved that he made no comment.

I had a perfect punctuality record but I debated, forty steps from the school yard, to get to school late. But then, rather than getting my beating over with this morning, I'd only postpone it until the afternoon. If I was really unlucky, Willie could beat me up this morning *and* this afternoon! Would Momma pay *two* visits to Miss Cory? My only hope was my dream-- Willie had not caught me.

I scanned the school yard: hundreds of children were playing as usual while the teachers were talking with each other on the school steps. I had two minutes before the bell. If Willie appeared suddenly, how badly could he beat me? My thoughts were interrupted by the sight of a crowd. Curiosity overcame fear and we wedged our way through.

I didn't believe my eyes! In the center was Willie. I carefully looked at the face and banged my book bag against my leg to make sure I wasn't dreaming. I turned to Harold--his open-mouth expression mirrored mine. If it was a mirage, both of us were seeing it.

It was Willie, no doubt about that. And there was no mistaking what he had on his right arm. Its whiteness glistened in the sunlight: a cast from his shoulder to his wrist! Even if it was a dream--or a trick--I'd have enjoyed the spectacle. But the reality was undeniable. My classmates saw me and someone called out, "Al got you yesterday, Willie." Other voices joined in, "Willie got a beating!" and "Al knows the 'Up-and-away' Superman punch." Moments ago I didn't believe my eyes; now I didn't believe my ears. Those were the same voices that yesterday were taunting me and cheering Willie. *The tables are turned,* I thought, a phrase from the *Shadow* radio show.

"I fell," Willie shouted menacingly. I stared at the cast and the protruding fingers, skinny and helpless. "I can beat Fatso with one arm!" He ran towards me and everyone leapt out of the way. My heart pounded, I blinked and said, "Up-and-away" to myself three times and then heard the fourth as a shout! I raised my arms like Superman preparing for flight, except my book bag swung from one hand. The onlookers' gasps sounded like helium escaping a dirigible. Besides my shout surprising him, he was thrown off balance by his cast when he swung his left arm. He missed me and hit my book bag. The children heard only the resounding wallop and gasped. When I remained upright, they "Ooh'd" Willie's eyes were all rage, his body trembled--fury cloaked his helplessness. Several boys pulled him away, one saying, "Al hurt you enough." Another, "Al's not going to fight you in a cast." I dropped my bag and stood in my best boxing posture. Willie roared more like an animal than a boy. I didn't flinch, ready to defend myself but gallantly refraining from attacking a helpless opponent.

The bell rang and everyone rushed to their line. I felt taller than usual and not even fat. As we followed Miss Cleary up the stairs, my classmates gave me admiring glances. She stopped and asked, "What's gotten into you this morning?" She'd never have guessed! When we were seated, she noticed Willie's cast. He explained, "I fell." When she finally quieted down the derisive laughter, someone called out, "Up-and-away!" Fresh laughter erupted. "I'll get you!" Willie shouted at the class and when he finally could be heard, he explained, "I tripped in my yard." Miss Cleary was pleased that he had come to school--he stayed out for *any* reason. I felt sorry for him until he muttered, "I came back to get you."

During Current Events, I reported on Hitler's demands for the *Sudetenland* in Czechoslovakia. Morris told me how to pronounced the name. Miss Cleary shook her head and asked, "Do bullies always get what they want?" I wanted to answer, "Not always," but kept silent. She looked around the room, until her gaze settled on me. "Al, since Willie can't write, would you copy the words for him?" Without waiting for my reply, she handed me a sheet of paper. I copied the words slowly and carefully, not because I wanted them legible. I was thinking that yesterday I didn't give Willie the spelling homework because I was afraid of getting into trouble with Miss Cleary and he beat me up. Today, Miss Cleary says I'll get credit in Citizenship *because* I'm copying the words for him!

When I finished, I handed him the neat list. Miss Cleary didn't see or hear him crumple and tear the sheet, an awkward and difficult feat with just his left hand. Then he muttered curses at me. He didn't realize how pleased I was. I felt good until I remembered Poppa's telling me to make my own decisions. How could I when *everyone* tells me what to do? Miss Cleary, Willie, Momma, Poppa, Morris--even in *shul* I was trying to figure out what God wanted me to do. Then I thought about Luck. If Willie hadn't broken his arm, Momma would probably be coming to school. Last night I had expected Poppa to give *It* to me--even hit me with the strop.

When we went to lunch, Willie muttered threats behind me, but as he walked to the lunch room line, his right arm swung forlornly. I felt a mixture of pleasure and pity, but I must admit, mostly pleasure. Out in the yard, boys and girls I didn't know congratulated me and said Willie deserved it. Yesterday they had been cheering him! I felt proud of my black eye, which everyone thought was the result of the "second" encounter. Even eighth graders came over to ask about my Superman blows. I told them Superman made me take an oath not to tell. Several times I was on the verge of admitting that I never saw Willie after the teachers separated us, but with each congratulation it became more difficult. Soon, I was tempted to tell them in detail about the fight. I lingered in the school yard to hear the plaudits, Harold at my side, wanting everyone to know he was my best friend and telling them I gave the "bully" what he deserved.

When I got home, Momma looked me over carefully. She had expected the worst and even seemed disappointed. "You didn't fight this morning," she said, "Let's see about this afternoon." Did she think I didn't learn my lesson? Or was she disappointed not to go to school? Or was it just her general pessimism. On the way back to school, Crotona Park looked more cheerful than this morning. Everything worked out, better than with a Superman rescue.

Five

American *Bonditan!*

That Sunday, I was awakened from a dream about the Deutsch by my parents arguing. Momma was still upset about the Naturalization police and Poppa asked, "Should I be a greenhorn all my life? I'm no longer a Russian so why can't I be an American?" Momma warned, "Not everyone is Mrs. Chernow, saying nice things about you. Remember Subotsky." Poppa said, "He had enemies." Momma answered, "You don't with your union *mishigas?*" Poppa shouted, "We've lived in fear all our lives!" Momma shouted back, "So *now* we're safe? When you hear a dog barking, you walk *away.* You don't need to be bitten. Those papers-"

My ears perked up. I had never heard about them. Poppa said, "They burned in the Town Hall during the Revolution. You were afraid that the Ellis Island doctors would find out about Borinka. Only family knows." Momma's replied, "Lucky once doesn't mean lucky twice." I marveled how deftly they argued. Momma dug her point home with, "You're only a paper away from being sent back. At least keep away from the union." Poppa replied, "I know what I'm doing!" Momma said, "The biggest foolishness of the fool is to think he's smart." If Momma had the last word, Poppa made the last noise. He left and slammed the door, waking Morris.

"Who's Subotsky?" I whispered.

He stopped stretching. "Who told you about him?"

"Who is he? *Please!*"

He sensed my desperation. "Subotsky was Pop's friend. He was arrested because he lied on his visa."

"About what?"

He gave me his quizzical stare. "That was years ago. I haven't heard his name in years. How did you hear?"

43

"Momma and Poppa--just before."

He sat up. "They told me to forget him." He whispered, "Big ears! You training for the F.B.I. or Dick Tracy's Secret Service?"

I did get a Dick Tracy detective badge with Quaker Oats box tops, but didn't remind him. "I dreamed the Deutsch got hurt."

Morris looked at me. "Think you're Joseph?"

Morris would say no more and I knew it was useless to ask any more questions: what happened to Subotsky's family and to him. Distressed as I was, the aromas from the kitchen got me up.

The table was loaded with bowls and jars of chopped liver, eggs, salami, corned beef, pickles, potato salad, a package of Wonder bread, sauerkraut and other foods hidden from view. Momma, busily at work, finally noticed me. Without interrupting her sandwich-making, she asked, "You're excited about the picnic." I certainly was but said, "I had this dream about the Deutsch--that he fell off his horse-" She stopped what she was doing and faced me. Her brow furrowed. I quickly said, "He wasn't hurt bad," although the dream ended before I found out. Momma shook her head. "I know there's trouble without your dream-- tell your father about it. He doesn't listen to me." She hugged me. "For a little love, you pay with your whole life." Then, holding me with one arm, she wiped her eyes and said, "You're young--don't worry. Enjoy today's picnic." She attempted a smile.

As far back as I could remember, I couldn't wait for the Sunday picnics with the Deutsch's family. We'd all squeeze into his car, the largest and shiniest I'd ever been in. By the time I was dressed, Poppa returned with the Sunday *News,* the *Jewish Daily Forward,* and a bag of jelly rolls. That was a Sunday ritual nothing interfered with. Poppa, surprised to see me up, handed me the comics, saying, "They'll be here soon." To Momma, "You can feed an army with all that food. The Deutsch's wife will make as much as you." Momma answered, "You and the Deutsch said that last year, but ate everything, like hungry horses." Poppa took a deep breath and explained, "The country air." Momma, squeezing pickles into a jar, said, "It'll be nice going to the country." She poured him a glass of tea. He sat down and said, "People were meant to live where there's plenty of trees and fresh air." They had declared a truce. So did Morris and me with the comics. We divided them in half. If we fought over them, Poppa would take them away and threaten to throw them into the garbage. He had to do that only once.

After breakfast, I waited impatiently downstairs until I saw the car in the distance. I ran upstairs, shouted, "They're here!" and ran back down. The Deutsch got out of the car and asked me, "How's the Rank-and-Filer?" Poppa came down and they shook hands as if they hadn't seen each other for years. Poppa waved to the Deutsch's wife while the children clamored to be let out. The Deutsch asked Poppa, "What can I do with them?" With a magnanimous sweep of his arm, he signaled their release. The six of them came tumbling out, a girl and five boys. Herman, my age, grabbed my shoulders to show how pleased he was to see me. We all helped bring down the food and drink. When the Deutsch's children argued about who would carry what, he said something in German that quieted them. I tried to speed up Momma's departure--she always had to check the gas jets a half dozen times to make sure they were "Off." She asked me to check to make "doubly sure." Then she did the same with the door locks. I wondered how Momma got out of the apartment when I wasn't around.

When we were ready, Morris got to sit in front with Carl. I resented sitting in the back on Momma's lap, but decided to make a fuss to sit in front on the way back. Little did I know how the day would end.

The Deutsch was proud of his model A Ford that no longer required cranking. He started the engine and the children beat him in saying, "A-1 engine!" Momma asked if they took *all* the food and Poppa assured her they had. When she wondered if the gas was turned off and the door locked., I shouted, "Yes!" and the Deutsch drove off. Going through the Bronx streets, I thought of how nice it would be if we had a car. Poppa talked about it and Momma told him to get his driver's license; Poppa would answer, "If I had a car, I'd get a driver's license." But he never got either one.

I watched in fascination as the city's apartment buildings disappeared and we reached the trees and grass of Van

Courtland Park. I was enjoying myself until the Deutsch showed Morris how to change gears. Morris shifted the "stick" while the Deutsch stepped on the clutch. That settled it! On the way back, I'd have to sit in front! The Deutsch children, seasoned travelers, played car games, like identifying States from car license plates. We finally arrived at the parking lot of Tibbets Brook in lower Westchester County, where carloads of New Yorkers drove for a Sunday "in the country"--until non-residents were excluded.

When the Deutsch parked, pulled up the brake and said, "OK," we children popped out. Our fathers called us back and we helped carry *everything* so we'd make only one trip. We were ready to pick any table but our parents were fussy and approved our third choice. The boys tried to get our fathers to play baseball. The Deutsch said, "We work all week," but the boys pleaded until they relented. When we got to the field, the older boys didn't want to let us younger children play. Poppa said, "If they're too young, we're too old." He and the Deutsch laughed. Poppa laughed more with the Deutsch than with anyone else, including Uncle Sol.

At the field, Morris and Carl chose up sides. The boys coached our fathers and after a few innings, they caught on, playing so well that they played as if they were born in this country. I got on base when the first baseman dropped the ball, but struck out the rest of the time. "You got a hole in your bat," Morris taunted, but the other children were too polite to say anything. Herman got on base twice and Katie hit a home run. The boys resented our mothers' announcement that it was lunch time but the Deutsch said, "Even the bosses let you eat."

Back at the food-laden table, we ate with as much enthusiasm as we had played. Sandwiches, potato salad, sauerkraut, pickles--everything--disappeared into our hungry mouths, washed down with cupfuls of juice. Momma pointed to the empty containers and said to Poppa, "You said we made too much." The Deutsch's wife nodded. The Deutsch explained. "We worked up big appetites. Besides, you're both good cooks!" Poppa added, "Our stomachs are bigger than our eyes." Even the mothers laughed at that. The Deutsch put one arm around Momma's shoulder and the other around his wife, whom he hugged. Poppa hesitated before giving Momma a hug. Then all the children joined in a huddle, which turned into a free-for-all until we children started chanting, "Let's play ball!" We were unsuccessful in getting our fathers to return. While everyone went off to play, I remained behind, near Poppa and the Deutsch. They were lying on a blanket at a distance from the wives, who were at the table. The Deutsch brought schnapps in a small bottle and Poppa vodka in a metal hip flask from Prohibition days. They didn't notice me several feet away.

Poppa said, "He warned the men not to vote Rank and File," and the Deutsch said, "Leon asked me if I was running for Secretary-Treasurer." Poppa asked, "The gangsters hear things before we get the word around. Who's the stool-pigeon? " The Deutsch shrugged. "There's always a rotten apple." Then, "If I didn't see a gun bulging under Leon's jacket, I'd have kicked his ass."

I remained mouse-quiet. They wouldn't have talked like that if they knew I was listening. The Deutsch continued, "I told him, 'Try to scare someone else,' and he said, 'You're getting too big for your britches.' I answered, 'I got more in my britches than you got in your head." The Deutsch laughed, but Poppa didn't. The Deutsch said, "The men are afraid of the gangsters *and* a strike."

Poppa whispered, "What does your wife think about your running?"

The Deutsch glanced in his wife's direction. Although she couldn't hear, he whispered, "She doesn't like it and complains about my spending too much time at meetings."

Poppa glanced at Momma and said, "My wife's too smart for her own good." I knew he was thinking of what Momma might tell the Deutsch's wife about the agents or what she thought of their union activity. Poppa sipped from the flask, wiped his mouth and said, "The gangsters and bosses always talk of strikes at election time." He handed the flask to the Deutsch and said, "The gangsters want the men scared so they won't vote them out."

The Deutsch said, "With all these mouths to feed-" he pointed toward the baseball field-- "and the car to pay for, a layoff or a strike will be hard." Then he laughed. Poppa looked at him strangely and the Deutsch said, "The bank will take back the car but they'll leave me with the *kinder!*" He laughed so hard he nearly knocked over his schnapps. Poppa frowned, but then burst out laughing. Then the Deutsch said, "I got a visit from the Naturalization investigators."

Poppa asked, "What did they want?" He tried to sound casual.

The Deutsch answered, "I didn't want to tell you today, with the picnic." Poppa looked as if he wanted to know more and the Deutsch said, "I told them only good things about you." He laughed, trying to make light of the visit.

Poppa glanced at Momma. "They asked a neighbor--why you?"

The Deutsch replied, "That's how they make their living--but don't worry, the questions were whether you were a steady worker, things like that. I went through that too. Three people told me they were questioned when I applied." Poppa's face asked, *And?* The Deutsch said, "I'm a citizen--see, they don't find out everything." He meant it as a joke and laughed again, but Poppa took a drink from the flask, looked at the women and said, "I bet they're figuring out ways to get us to drop the union."

They didn't just talk about the union. The Deutsch told the story about visiting his uncle's farm in Bavaria and getting thrown from a horse called *Vilder* and breaking his leg. He said, "I've never been on a horse since." I wondered if that was what this morning's dream was about. Then Poppa said, "I never had much to do with horses until the war came to our town in the Ukraine." Maybe he would not have told the story if he had not had the second swig. Poppa was only fifteen and walking with his cousin Shmuel when a Cossack rode toward them, waving a saber. Poppa pulled his cousin down, but when he got up, "Shmuel lay like a crumpled bag of clothes. Only when his shirt turned red did I know what happened." The Deutsch looked shocked and touched Poppa's arm. Poppa continued, "I went to the Red Army militia outside our town. They were the only ones fighting the bandits and let Jews join them. I found the commander, a tall man with a mustache bigger than yours. I lied

48

and told him I was sixteen. He said I could join if I brought my own horse." Poppa smiled. "He was trying to get rid of me." But Poppa knew a peasant for whom he picked apples in the Fall. "Of his three horses, one was taken by the Reds, another by the Cossacks, leaving only a horse so skinny only a starving soldier would take him." The farmer let Poppa take the horse! "I walked him to the commander's camp because I didn't want to wear him out--he was not like your uncle's *Vilder*. I mounted him just before I reached their camp. The commander couldn't believe his eyes! But he let us join, an old horse and a boy whose face never felt a razor." The Deutsch shook his head and said, "God was looking after you."

I learned a lot by listening to grown-ups when they didn't know I was around. There was much I didn't understand, but I didn't dare ask questions. Since Poppa and the Deutsch stopped talking, I slipped away to the bench. Momma was telling the Deutsch's wife her recipe for the potato salad. Poppa was wrong, but I couldn't tell him that.

Herman came over and asked me to play. Before we could leave, his mother made us take along his sister Katie, two years younger than us. Herman and I protested we didn't want a "baby" tagging along. Herman's mother gave him a stern look and Momma said to me, "Now you know how Morris feels when *you* want to go with him." Of course I didn't see the similarity--after all, she was a girl.

Herman and I decided to race in order to get rid of her. He easily took the lead, but Katie was beating me! I swore at my high-top shoes. Herman let us catch up with him and we traipsed through the woods. I thought nothing of the popping sounds in the distance--they were not like gun shots in the movies--but when we heard screams, we raced back.

A crowd had formed and we squeezed through. In the inner circle I saw my parents, Morris, the Deutsch's wife and children. My relief at seeing that Poppa was all right was replaced with the horror of recognizing who lay on the ground. The Deutsch's wife was screaming her husband's name as she leaned over him.

The rest of that afternoon was a nightmare. I can still hear the screams and see the Deutsch sprawled out with blood darkening his shirt. It seemed like an eternity before an ambulance came--it rode right through the picnic area. I have the vaguest recollection of how we got home, but remember that I was home alone with Morris until Momma came back from the hospital late that night. She said he was "alive," and cursed the "American *bonditan.*" I reminded her that in my dream he was "only hurt." Momma just nodded and Morris frowned.

Poppa came home in the morning--he had stayed at the hospital and given blood. He told us that the doctors said the Deutsch was in "critical, but stable condition." Momma said she couldn't imagine a "just God not saving the Deutsch," although on other occasions I heard her mutter her doubts about His compassion. Nevertheless, she was praying to Him as she would for a family member. Poppa regretted being unable to pursue the two men who had shot the Deutsch--he had run to the Deutsch. Momma, in her only unsympathetic reaction that morning, glared at Poppa and said, "So there'd be two of you in the hospital--or worse!" Poppa said nothing. A little while later, two men whom I recognized from the union meeting picked Poppa up--they were going to the hospital to give blood. Morris wanted to go but Poppa said, "No!" Morris and I left for school and Momma was going to look after the Deutsch's younger children.

I wasn't interested in school that morning and resented Miss Cleary asking me to give Willie a spelling test. She seated us at a table in the back of the room. I read the first word, "Stove," and made up a sentence, just like Miss Cleary. Willie's thin lips tightened and since he couldn't write, I started writing before I realized he had spelled, "f-u-c-k-y-o-u." He grinned, showing a missing upper tooth. That was how he spelled the rest of the words. When I gave Miss Cleary the paper, she smiled at Willie and said, "Seventy." I enjoyed Willie's shocked expression. Miss Cleary said to Willie, "You did better than when you study by yourself." She looked at me. "Be sure to teach Willie the rule about doubling the consonant after the vowel." I had purposefully misspelled "tipped," as "tiped," along with two other words. Had he gotten a higher score, she would have been suspicious; I couldn't give him a zero because that would have shown how poor a teacher I was. Afterwards, I barely paid attention to Miss Cleary, thinking about the Deutsch. I was roused from my worrying only when Miss Cleary called on me for Current Events with, "I'm sure Al will bring us up-to-date on Europe."

Despite my worrying about the Deutsch, I was relieved to be prepared. Luckily, I had clipped an article on Saturday. My classmates weren't pleased. They weren't interested in the topic of my first Current Events article, which resulted in Miss Cleary dubbing me the "Expert" on Europe. The others selected sports and crime stories, the favorite gangland murders. As I summarized my article on President Benes of Czechoslovakia complaining that the British were forcing him to give the Germans the Sudetenland, the class looked bored. I mentioned the Polish and Hungarian demands on Czechoslovakia without saying their unpronounceable regional names. Miss Cleary said, "Leave it to the British to decide how to carve up the turkey."

Harold's article was as predictable as mine. He reported, "The Yanks are picking up steam"--I wondered if my clipping trembled as obviously as his. The class listened with enthusiasm. "After their slow start"--even I knew that meant they had lost a lot of games--"they'll win the pennant." When he mentioned Joe DiMaggio's batting average, his enthusiasm overcame stage fright and he concluded with a flourish: "The Yankees will win their third pennant!" The class cheered. Miss Cleary smiled-- even she respected our reverence for the *Bronx Bombers.* Then I returned to worries about the Deutsch--was he still alive?

At lunch time, as usual I walked home with Harold. His mother greeted me at our apartment door. Momma had arranged for me to eat with Harold. That happened once before, in second grade, when Grandpa had a heart attack and Momma rushed to Bronx Hospital.

Mrs. Chernow said, "Your mother said a friend of your father's was hurt on the job." She asked it more as a question, but I would reveal no more than Terry did to the Dragon Lady in the comic strip. While I wondered how the Deutsch was doing, I learned one thing eating with Harold: he had made up having ice-cream and chocolate milkshakes for lunch. He had a tuna fish sandwich, just like mine.

When we returned to school that afternoon, Mr. O'Hare, the assistant principal, entered the room and whispered to Miss Cleary. After he left, she asked Ronald to clean the papers out of a vacant desk. I knew something was up from the way she kept glancing at the door. During the term, whenever a new pupil would be transferred to our class, a monitor would bring him. Today, Mr. O'Hare stepped into the room with the newcomer. Miss Cleary said, "This is Clarence Harlow, he'll be joining our class." All eyes were already on the new boy. Willie muttered, *"Melanzane,"* whose meaning I'd find out later.

Clarence Harlow was tall for a fourth grader, neatly dressed in long pants, a white shirt, tie and jacket. His skin was closest in color to cinnamon, his nose broad and hair curly. He looked over our heads, as if unconcerned about our inquisitive stares, but his right hand tightly gripped a notebook. Mr. O'Hare was uncertain how to complete the transfer until, with a forced smile, he walked out. Miss Cleary, pointing to the vacant desk and scanned the class as if we were on the verge of becoming disorderly. Then she asked Harold to go to the book room for a set of books. The only noise was made by Harold. On his way out he couldn't keep his eyes off Clarence and tripped over a desk. Miss Cleary "Ah-hemm'd" for order and pointed to the assignment on the blackboard. Clarence was first to start writing. We sneaked glances at him while also pretending he wasn't there. Clarence wrote busily, as if he'd been with us since the beginning of the term. A casual observer wouldn't have noticed anything unusual, except a black pupil in an all white class.

Harold returned empty-handed, explaining that the book room monitor wasn't there. At dismissal, Clarence walked quickly out the gate toward Third Avenue. Harold, at my side, watched him disappear. It was no secret that you had to have an above average I.Q.--*Intelligence Quotient*--to get into the "1" classes. But we'd never had a black pupil in our class. In fact, there were no more than four or five black pupils in our entire school. I had been to a black community in the Bronx when Eunice took me to her home. Her son, my age, was as curious about me as I was about him, but all we said was "Hi." Our older boys warned us not to wander off to their neighborhoods, where "gangs" were ready to pounce on any white boy. Yet I never remembered any fights.

That afternoon, Momma still wasn't home but she had left my Yankee Doodle Cupcake with Mrs. Chernow. She left one for Harold, whose eyes nearly popped. He claimed he had ice-cream sodas for snacks! Mrs. Chernow asked, "I wonder how that friend of your father's is doing?" My reply was to busily eat my snack. Momma left my Hebrew books and instructions to go to my grandparents after Hebrew School.

Six

The Garden of Eden

If Family was one pillar of my life and Public School another, Judaism was becoming the third. My introduction was through Grandpa and shul, which whetted my appetite for Hebrew School. Momma said, "Morris didn't go until a year before his Bar Mitzvah." Just as with knickers and high-top shoes, I'd have to wait. Morris joined my cause by arguing, "I didn't want to go, but Al *wants* to go." Grandma also supported my going, but since she and Momma didn't get along, that didn't help. Poppa refused to intervene--he left educational matters to Momma. Grandpa was too wise to say anything and antagonize his daughter-in-law. I pestered Momma for weeks until she grudgingly gave in, "If only so you'll stop giving me terrible headaches." When Momma appointed Morris to walk me to Hebrew School, he claimed my interest in religion was "phony." Just as with public school, I talked Momma into letting me go by myself.

On the first day, I had waited for a carbon copy of the gray-bearded rabbi in Grandpa's shul. I thought Mrs. Schwartz was the secretary. She was young, pretty and shapely, with raven-colored hair and friendly eyes. She was the prettiest woman I'd seen. When she told us she was our teacher, I thought of Uncle Sol's saying, "You could have knocked me over with a feather." I was shocked--even jealous--that she was married. Another shock was how much Hebrew she knew. Mastering Hebrew was doubly hard-I concentrated on her rather than the strange alphabet.

Today, when the bell rang, I forgot about the Deutsch. Despite her smile and sweet *"Shalom,"* Lenny was blowing through a comb. I couldn't understand how any boy could misbehave, especially someone Jewish. It seemed every class had its troublemaker. I glared at him, having appointed myself

55

unofficial monitor to protect her from rudeness. On that first day, she gave us a preview of the Bible, like the coming attractions in the movies. And she always ended with a suspenseful story, which was how the adventure serials in the movies and on the radio ended. Of course, we also learned Hebrew. Today, she reviewed how God made all living things, lastly Adam and Eve. I asked questions out of curiosity as well as to show how smart I was, but when I asked how God got the rib out without Adam's bleeding, the class laughed. She looked embarrassed but said God made miracles in those days, but they were rare now. I made a mental note to tell Momma why her prayers for her sister's family in Russia didn't come true. Today she told us about the Garden of Eden and its Tree of Knowledge. She mentioned the snake just when the bell rang. I was so absorbed in the story--and Mrs. Schwartz, who resembled the drawing of Queen Esther in my Jewish Holiday Book--that I didn't notice the trees in Crotona Park tinged with their autumn colors or that I was walking home. From the way she mentioned the snake, I figured he'd get Adam and Eve into trouble. Momma said "Good Times" don't last and what could be more perfect than this beautiful place where they paid no rent, didn't have to work, had no wars and all the animals got along. Then I remembered that I was supposed to go to my grandparents. I doubled back, their apartment being only three blocks from Hebrew School.

Until the past summer, Grandpa was a remote figure in my life. He was the respected patriarch of the family and resembled the bearded Moses in the Passover *Haggadah,* but I was one of many grandchildren. I didn't believe he noticed me until I started going to *shul* with him. I reached my grandparents' apartment building on St. Paul's Place, one of the row of attached gray brick buildings that were old in those days. It had no courtyard or lobby, only a small hallway with rows of mail boxes on either side. I ran up the stairway not stopping on the dimly lit half-landings and was panting when I reached the fourth floor. I turned the door key and the clapper jingled the bell.

Grandma was surprised to see me. I told her what happened but had trouble convincing her it was a friend and not Poppa who was in the hospital. Grandpa had to repeat what I'd said in a more fluent Yiddish. He was lying in bed and explained that he had "only a cold." Grandma thought it more serious and said he should listen to his sons and retire--"the heart isn't made of stone." He reassured her he would be "fine and working tomorrow." When Grandpa and I were alone, he asked for details and I told him all I knew. He shook his head. "Terrible! Gangsters taking over unions and shooting honest workers."

Grandpa ate with us, almost as if to prove he was all right. He said, "Roosevelt should get rid of the gangsters, like he did the bootleggers." My parents also believed Roosevelt could solve most problems, no matter how troublesome. Grandma shook her head and said, "Shooting like in a war." She asked if he was Jewish and Grandpa asked, "Does that matter?" Momma also asked that question, not that she wasn't concerned about the person but only to know if he was one of "ours."

When they were drinking tea and I was sipping my seltzer-- they observed the dietary laws and I couldn't have milk after meat--Grandpa said, "Last year, we voted for a union in our factory and they gave us a retirement plan." Of course Grandma asked, "So why don't you retire?" Grandpa replied, "I have to find out more about the new Social Security." After the meal, I followed Grandpa into the living room. When he was settled in his armchair, I asked, "How do I pray for the Deutsch?" He opened the prayer book on the table next to him. I moved my cane bottom chair closer.

"There's the *gomel* prayer," he said, "to thank God that the Deutsch is alive. And this prayer asks God to give us more years of life."

I said, "But I don't know the Hebrew words."

He smiled. "You don't have to pray in Hebrew, Yalkala, or use the *siddur*." To prove his point, he closed it. "The *Midrash Haggadah* says you can pray in any language."

I asked, "What do I say?"

He looked at me thoughtfully. "What do you want to say?"

I said, "I want God to make the Deutsch well."

He rapped the table. "That's the prayer! Just start, 'Dear God' to get His attention--and say what you said."

I couldn't believe it was that simple. "In English?"

"In English, Yiddish, Hebrew-any language." He leaned over and put his arm around my shoulder. "God understands *every* language. You can *think* prayers or let feelings come straight from your heart."

I asked, "Children, too?"

He nodded. "Children, grown-ups--God listens to everyone."

"Do I have to pray in *shul?*"

"Some prayers have to be said in *shul,* but you can pray for the Deutsch *anywhere."*

I hesitated. "But the Deutsch isn't Jewish."

The sun had gone down over the apartment buildings across the street and the room had become dark and Grandpa's face was in a shadow. "God cares for *everyone* who's upright. We're are all his children--Jew or Christian. After all, we're all children of Adam and Eve."

I was pleased that I knew the story. "The Deutsch is upright."

Grandpa said, "Then God will hear your prayer." He spoke with such certainty that I *knew* the Deutsch would live. I told him about my dream and he said, "That's a good sign." The shadow of worries that had enveloped me lifted. Sitting next to Grandpa, listening to his voice and looking at him, I felt secure. Even the room brightened. In a world where I was discovering perplexity and disappointment, Grandpa's conviction was comforting. He didn't make the world simplistic, but he provided buoys I could hold onto. We sat in silence for a while before he turned on the radio and listened to an English news program. The newscaster said that "German troops were mobilizing on the border of Czechoslovakia." Then he tuned to a Yiddish program. I understood the newscaster talking about German Jews trying to leave. Grandpa, as if talking to the newscaster, said, "There are too many Hamans and only one Mordechai."

When Grandma finished cleaning up in the kitchen, she joined us with her sewing basket. Grandpa threaded the needle for her and while she sewed, he read his Yiddish newspaper. Then the clapper rang. It was Morris. "He's a lot better," was Morris' answer to our questions. "All bandaged up, but talking."

Grandma clasped her hands together and said, "Thank God!"

Grandpa and I smiled at each other. Grandma asked Morris if he'd eaten and he replied, "We ate out." Then, "I'd better take Al home." I kissed them. Grandpa's beard soothingly brushed my cheek as he whispered, "Remember, *shul* is in your heart."

As we walked home, I asked questions and got most of the story. Morris had gone to the hospital from school; the Deutsch had been shot in the back, the bullet going out his shoulder; ten workers gave blood, but he didn't need all of it; his wife cried in the waiting room but was quiet in his room; Momma brought the children but only the older ones were allowed to see him; despite being bandaged and looking weak, he was able to joke. Morris concluded with, "The bullet missed his heart by that much." He pressed his thumb and forefinger together. I didn't ask, but he didn't spare me the details about eating out with Momma and Poppa. "Franks with mustard, sauerkraut, pickle and a big glass of soda." I tried to hide my jealousy, but my expression gave me away. He added, "The hot dog was so long it stuck out both ends of the roll!" I didn't know how much to believe.

When we got home, Momma asked me a hundred questions, from, "Did you get to your grandparents all right?" to "What did your grandmother give you for supper?" For the last question she wanted the *whole* menu. Poppa asked, "When did anyone ever leave my mother's table hungry?" He quickly added, "Or yours?" They looked tired, Momma in her house dress and Poppa in his undershirt. Although I told her Grandma gave me milk before supper, Momma poured a glass. During my turn to ask questions, Poppa answered, "The Deutsch will be all right. By shooting him, the gangsters shot themselves in the foot."

Momma glared at him. "The Deutsch is in the hospital--who's next?"

Poppa, addressing Morris and me, explained, "Mark my words: with the police hunting for the gunmen, those they don't put in jail will leave town. The men are angry and will vote for-"

Momma interrupted with, "Why are you telling them fairy tales?" She called them *bubba mayses.*

Poppa ignored her and continued about "a better day for the painters-"

Momma interrupted, "A dog's barking doesn't catch a thief.

Talk is cheap and the gangsters have guns." She didn't give Poppa a chance to answer. "Yalka, to bed! You've been up since six this morning." Then she delivered the *coup de grace:* "The boaster and the fool don't know when to keep quiet."

Poppa's belch was anti-climactic. He muttered, "That hot dog is coming up on me.

Momma said, "I told you not to put on all that sauerkraut and mustard." *Morris had told the truth about eating out.*

After putting on my pajamas, I returned to the kitchen. Poppa put down the newspaper and said, "Everything will be all right." He kissed me on the forehead, the second time in 24 hours! Momma said, "God was looking out for us-" To make sure there was no misunderstanding, she added, "-this time." To Poppa, she said, "I don't want you leaving me with two orphans." I went to the living room and soon they went to their bedroom. I expected an argument, but they were quiet. Morris turned off the light and got into bed. I asked, "How did you get in to see the Deutsch?"

Morris waited before saying, "I told the nurse I was eighteen." He paused. "She didn't believe me." He laughed. "I told her I lied, but that I was the Deutsch's sixteen-year-old son. She let me in."

While that sounded ingenious, I said, "*Poppa* said you couldn't go!"

Morris said, "With the Deutsch lying in bed, they couldn't say anything. Later Pop didn't mention it."

He not only won the nurse over, but he disobeyed Poppa and got away with it! "And the hot-dog," I asked, "how long was it?"

He was silent before admitting, "It was skinny. Mom's Zion hot-dogs are bigger." I felt better until he said, "I had two of them."

My next question surprised me. "Did you pray for the Deutsch?"

"Medicine and science help people get well."

I asked, "What about God?"

There was silence before, "You don't need God to explain things." Another pause. "How do you explain God?"

When I was with Grandpa, I didn't question the existence of God, but Morris' scientific certainty burrowed doubts into my beliefs. Did I have to choose? I felt God and Science were helpful. Remembering Grandpa's words, but not wanting Morris to hear, I silently prayed, "Dear God, *please* make the Deutsch well." Morris already breathed heavily. I envied him.

Soon I was eating a foot-long hot dog with mustard, sauerkraut, and pickle. Morris begged me to give him a bite but I ignored him. I drank *two* bottles of cherry soda. When I woke up, my stomach hurt.

Seven

The Suspect

The next morning, I slept through Poppa's and Morris' departures. I was awakened by the doorbell and Momma padding to the door. I heard a man's voice followed by Momma calling, "Yalka!" I rushed to the door.. Momma turned to me, her face ashen. She asked, "What do they want?" Through the door, open as far as the chain allowed, were two men in suits and fedoras.

"Sonny," said the man closer to the door, "your name Segal?" I nodded. "And the lady, your mother?" I nodded again. "Is your father home?" Although I knew, I turned to Momma. She shook her head. "No," I said. He said, "Tell your mother we want to ask her a few questions." Before I could translate, the man behind him asked, "What's the sense if the husband isn't home?" My heart pounded--I had seen enough movies to know they were either detectives or gangsters. I translated their wanting to ask her a few questions. She whispered, "Who are they?" As if he understood, the man held out a wallet with a badge and said, "Detectives." I'm sure Momma understood, but I whispered, "Police." The one closer to the door asked, "Could you let us in?" I didn't hear it as a question. To his partner, he said, "We're here--might as well have a look." I don't know what frightened me more, the expression on Momma's face or them. We *had* to let them in. I unlocked the chain. Only when Momma released my arm did I realize her painful grip.

They walked in as if they owned the place--just like in the movies. The first detective was taller and sharp-nosed, the other had finer features. Neither was as handsome as James Cagney, or as truculent as Edward G. Robinson. We retreated. They looked into the living room and bedroom and the shorter one said, "I told you." His partner asked, "Where's your husband?" Momma understood, but I translated anyway. She said, "Tell them he's at work," and under her breath, "What do they want?"

The tall one took out a small pad, opened it and asked, "English Painting Company?" *He knew where Poppa worked!* The shorter one chided, "I told you we should have gone there, Frank." The taller one, annoyed, said, "If he's not there we'd have to explain why we didn't check here first." Then to me, "When did he leave?" Momma said to me in Yiddish, "When he always does," and under her breath, "What's wrong?" I translated, "My mother wants to know what's wrong." The taller one said, "Just some questions we want to ask him. When do you expect him home?" The shorter one said, "We'd better check his job. If he's on the lamb, we'll have to explain what took us so long." Then to me, "Tell your mother we're sorry to bother her." He stepped to the door. The taller one said to us, "A routine investigation." To his partner, "Their women are high-strung and skittery." When I closed the door, Momma said, "I should call Mordcha."

"Do you have his phone number?" How I wished Morris was here.

Her brow furrowed. "When your grandfather had his second heart attack, your father was at work. I called him from a candy store."

I said, "You can call him from Mrs. Stone."

I don't know if she had thought of that but she rushed to the bedroom to look for the number. While I dressed, she called, "I found it!" We were nearly out the door when she remembered. "You didn't have breakfast." I was about to protest, but she poured a glass of milk and took out a cupcake. "I'll go upstairs," she said.

I gulped down the milk, grabbed my book bag and cupcake, and ran up the stairway. Momma was explaining to a surprised Mrs. Stone that she had to call Poppa. Momma seemed glad to see me. Mrs. Stone asked, "No one's sick, God forbid?" Momma shook her head and handed our neighbor the number, which was on a crumpled slip. As Mrs. Stone dialed, Momma said, "Tell him not to worry." Mrs. Stone spoke into the phone, "I'm trying to reach Mr. Max Segal." She covered the mouthpiece with her hand. "He's in another building." After a wait, she gave her number and hung up. "It may take a while, but you can wait here." Momma turned to me. "Go to school--don't worry." Mrs. Stone said, "I'll be here." I hesitated but kissed Momma and left. The crossing guard was gone and I ran to the front entrance.

A boy on the late line called out, "Teacher's Pet is late." Willie! I tried to look unconcerned about my first lateness. He asked, "Doesn't your mother feed you at home?" I looked down-- I was still clutching the cupcake. I casually ate it before we got our late passes. When we walked into the classroom, everyone turned. Miss Cleary asked, "Were you studying together?" Pupils giggled and Willie shouted, "No!"

After Willie and I sat down at the table in the back that was becoming our regular seats, Miss Cleary said she was so pleased with the improvement in Willie's work that she wanted me to help Clarence catch up with his. As Clarence walked to our table, Willie's nostrils flared, his jaw jutted out and his eyes narrowed. Clarence looked warily at him, but sat down next to me. I wanted to tell Miss Cleary that I didn't like her assigning me responsibilities without asking. Nevertheless, I gave Clarence my notebook. Meanwhile Willie went through a whole repertoire of threatening expressions. Clarence ignored him and started copying my notes.

While I was still uneasy with Willie--he frequently reminded me that his cast wasn't going to be on forever--I saw him less and less through the haze of my fears. The closeness of his eyes made his squint threatening. Adding to his ferocious expression were pencil-thin lips jutting out, nostrils that flared menacingly and unruly hair. When he didn't think I was watching, his expression flattened and he picked inflamed blackheads. The medallion hanging from his neck suggested dependence on powers beyond himself. The greatest evidence of his vulnerability was his fingers helpless protruding from the cast, which he swung off the table when he saw me staring at them. The longer I observed him, the less frightening he became.

During Current Events, Harold reported our team's loss to Detroit. Though the headline read "Tigers Bite Yanks," Harold was confident the Yanks would clinch the Pennant. I reported on

Chamberlain's meeting with Hitler to prevent a war over Czechoslovakia. Only Miss Cleary appeared interested. The well-behaved pupils made believe they were listening; others stirred restlessly or looked out the window. To get their attention, I held up a photo of Chamberlain standing in front of a twin-engine plane, "the first plane the British Prime Minister flew in." Miss Cleary had the last word: "The English and Germans are forever meddling in other peoples' business. God knew what he was doing when He separated us from Europe with the Atlantic Ocean."

At lunch time, I ran home worrying more about Poppa than listening to Harold bring me up-to-date on the feats of Joe DiMaggio. From our kitchen doorway, I asked Momma if she had talked to Poppa. She made me wash up first and as I sat eating my sandwich, she told me Poppa called and told her that the police were questioning *everyone.* She said, "Your father said not to worry-" and muttered, "The world could be coming to an end and he'd say that." Saying she had a headache, Momma wrapped a wet towel around her head and lay down.

Back in school, I joined the others sitting rigidly. I had forgotten that Miss Cleary would announce her choices for the class play. Long before I started kindergarten, Miss Cleary was in charge of the Christmas play, performed by her fourth grade class for *all* the assemblies. The carrot of her disciplinary repertoire was, "I'm watching to see who'll be in the play." She ended the suspense by announcing, "Al will be Santa Claus." The class "Oh'd" and "Ah'd." My triumph was short lived-- Willie whispered, "She picked Al because he won't need a pillow in his pants." The class went into paroxysms of laughter. When she read off the rest of the cast, I had the last laugh: Willie was *Blitzen,* one of my reindeer. Then we had to write a composition on "1) Should *all* children get presents at Christmas" and "2) Different ways to celebrate the Christ Child's birthday." On the way home, I could tell Harold was disappointed-- he was the *Toy Soldier With the Wooden Leg.*

That evening, Momma read Poppa another *Bintel Brief* letter from an "Abandoned Wife." Poppa, with the newspaper in front of him, muttered, "Read the *Gallery of Disappearing*

Men." That was a column listing men who deserted their wives and families. I had wandered into their bedroom to overhear news about the detectives, but before I could leave Momma said, "Your father's done nothing to fix your knickers."

I was the lightning rod of their conflict and the knickers the symbol of paternal neglect. She told Poppa to take the knickers to Uncle Sol. I was to accompany him, Momma reminding him, "Make sure your brother gives Al 'what-for' for making extra work and nearly getting killed."

I didn't dare reveal that what Momma considered punishment was a treat. Perhaps she thought Poppa would view it that way as well because she warned, "Don't gossip with your brother so you forget the clock."

Traveling to Uncle Sol was a glamorous adventure. We were the only ones at the corner of the trolley stop, when we saw the small flickering headlight grow larger. Poppa waved frantically before it screeched to a stop. He paid the nickel fares and got transfers. The evening rush-hour was over and we found seats together. I slid onto the cane-covered seat near the window and had a full view of the traffic. I imagined myself at the controls as we sped down the tracks, the trolley swaying dangerously on curves. The driver barely gave passengers time to step on or off and clanged threateningly at jay-walking pedestrians or cars in his way. The electric power rod slipped off the overhead cable and the driver got out to re-connect it. At Tremont Avenue our driver gave several sharp clangs to either ask our transfer trolley driver to wait or just in greeting. Poppa held my hand as we ran across the street. This driver went more leisurely, especially up the snaking hill. I asked Poppa who was going to run for Treasurer now that the Deutsch was shot. He took a while before answering, "The men want me to run, but the way your mother feels-" He shook his head, but said no more. Still, I felt privileged that he said even that. When we got near our stop, Poppa let me pull the signal cord. He stepped off first and offered me his hand, but I managed the tall steps by myself. We walked briskly along Featherbed Lane, the dusk and nearness to our destination speeding us up. After passing two blocks of apartment buildings, we reached a store whose window lights--

the brightest on the block--flickered, *Sol's Cleaning & Tailor Shop*.

My uncle's greeting was, "What brings you to this part of the Bronx?"

Poppa asked, "Can't I visit my brother?"

Sol grinned and gave us big hugs. Poppa said, "You're awfully cheerful."

Sol grinned. "Don't open a store unless you know how to smile-" He gestured to the front "-and have bright lights." We followed him to the back, dodging clothes that hung on both sides. We sat down at a table and he inspected the knickers. Then, looking at me, "Some fall."

Poppa said, "He was in a fight."

Sol rolled his eyes and shifted his mustache. "What's the world coming to when a pacifist fights?"

Poppa said, "A bully in his school called him a kike."

"He's in the hospital!" He looked serious, but I knew he was joking.

I replied, "No, but his arm is broken."

Sol's mouth dropped. "Another Joe Louis!" When I explained, he said, "God works in mysterious ways. I'm sure this boy would have two good arms if he didn't call you names." He made a fist. "Nothing's too bad for an anti-Semite." He winked at me and said to Poppa, "Should we send Al to Berlin to beat up you-know who?"

Poppa wasn't amused. "Surah was upset."

"Wives," said Sol, dismissing them with a hand gesture. "The world steps on your throat and they want you to be polite." With mock seriousness he said to his imaginary adversary, "Pardon me for dirtying your boot with my blood." I couldn't help but laugh. Even Poppa smiled. Sol waved his finger at me- "As long as the police are not after you-"

Poppa interrupted with, "The police questioned *me.*"

The timing couldn't have been better. Sol, alarmed, turned to Poppa. "The citizenship application?"

"No, the shooting."

"Why question you?" From Sol's expression I knew Poppa told him about the Deutsch. Before Poppa could reply, he shook his head and said, "When the ball of wool unravels-" He regretted saying that and patted Poppa's shoulder. "We'll figure a way out." Then, "Surah knows?"

"The detectives also came to the house-" Poppa looked at me.

"This morning," I said. "They said it was 'routine.' *Two* detectives, one mean, the other nice."

Sol patted me on the back. "Good you're on our side." Then to Poppa, "Who else are they questioning?" When Poppa told him other Rank-and- Filers, Sol asked, "You sure those detectives aren't Pinkertons?" I told them about the badge and Sol said, "Everybody has a badge. What questions did they ask?"

Poppa told him: how long he knew the Deutsch, where he was when he was shot-"

Sol interrupted, "That sounds bad enough, but nothing about-" He looked over his shoulder before whispering and pausing after each one, "The Bolsheviks, Borinka, the Subotskys, your birth date?"

Poppa shook his head at each of them." I was proud that they talked so openly in front of me, though I'd heard most of it. Except Poppa's birthday.

Sol asked, "Just the shooting?"

As if just remembering, Poppa said, "Where I was born, when I came to this country-"

Sol looked worried. *"That* is not 'routine'!"

Poppa saw the expression on my face and tousled my hair. "They said, 'routine." When he turned to Sol, his smile vanished. "Don't worry, I answered matter-of-factly."

"The Palmer raids were a long time ago. Thank God we have a different president." He again patted Poppa's shoulder. "Don't worry, lots of immigrants changed their birth dates." Then, "Your election! You think-"

Poppa nodded. "The men believe they're trying to scare us."

"Gangsters have connections-" He pressed his thumb and forefinger together- "with the police." Then, "Maybe you should visit Yitzchok."

"Leave town? Wouldn't that be suspicious?"

Sol raised his hand. "I'm thinking out loud." He rapped his

knuckles against his head and shifted his mustache thoughtfully. "Leave for a good reason like checking on business opportunities. That's as American as apple pie. *Everyone* dreams of being his own boss, the biggest dream in the *Land of Dreams*. Entrepreneurs come out of the woodwork when times are good-" his eyes twinkled "-and when times are bad." Poppa frowned and Sol asked, "When's the elections?"

Poppa answered, "Two weeks."

"If you left before the elections, the police will stop bothering you."

Poppa asked, "Wouldn't the police be suspicious?"

"If my hunch is right," said Sol, "they'll give up the investigation after the election."

Poppa's look of disbelief matched his words. "Not find the gunman?"

Sol explained, "If they're questioning the Rank-and-File now, do you think they *want* to find the gunman? After the elections, the coast will be clear for you." A customer entered and Sol called, "I'll be right with you." While getting up, he whispered, "I think I've figured it out." As he walked to the front, Poppa smiled, but said, "Maybe I shouldn't have brought you."

When Sol returned, he said, "The gangsters and painting bosses don't want to lose their sweetheart contracts. Why not say the shooting is a disagreement in the Rank-and-File and have *them* run for cover?"

Poppa frowned. "The men wanted *me* to run for Treasurer."

Sol slapped his forehead. "Dear God, help me get up; I can fall down by myself." He whispered to Poppa, "Mordcha, how foolish can you be? There are four reasons for you not run." He raised a finger. "The gangsters don't like you." He raised a second finger. "If you take your friend's place, you've given the police a motive for wanting the Deutsch out of the way." He raised a third finger. "The Naturalization people think reformers are anarchists or communists. *Everyone* will be after you like bloodhounds." Then, "You don't need another reason." He shook his head. "When the wind blows, the garbage flies."

Poppa took a deep breath, about to say something, but didn't.

"Leaving town seems better by the minute," said Sol. "Who knows, you may become your own boss." He gestured at the clothes around him. "I'm not Yitzchok, but I make a living. Listen to an older brother. I know you say he doesn't owe you for taking care of our mother in Russia while he was safe here making money hand over fist-"

"But look what Yitzchok did to you when-"

Sol interrupted, "If I've told you once, I've told you a hundred times, *we* don't get along. Sure, a stab in the heart leaves a hole, especially from a brother, but I've made my life-- and peace." Then, "You have enough money for the trip and for expenses at home?"

Poppa nodded. "We've saved since the bank crash. I can always swing a paintbrush. Thanks, anyway."

"What are brothers for?" Noticing me, he winked. "Or uncles?" I knew what he was going to say- "If I need money and God doesn't help me, I'll ask my uncle in America." He laughed and Poppa smiled. Sol tickled my stomach and even though I didn't want to, I burst out laughing.

Poppa looked at his watch. "Your mother will be worried." To Sol, "I came just to bring the knickers."

Sol stood up. "Tell Surah her brother-in-law talked you an earful." He put the knickers on the table and said to me, "Next time don't wait until God punishes an anti-Semite." To Poppa, "We'll train Al for the ring. We could use a World Champion Jewish boxer." His eyes brightened. "We'll be his promoters! You can give up painting and me tailoring!" He patted me on the back. "In the ring, a Jew can beat up a Christian in front of *everybody* and not only get away with it, but make a fortune."

Poppa said, "Surah wanted you to give him what-for for fighting."

Sol patted me on the head. "When you fight, don't get hurt and don't kill anybody-heh, heh." He lifted the counter board and we walked through. "You'll need a fancy name for the ring." He snapped his fingers. "I got it! Yalkah, the Boxah!" He exploded with laughter. Despite Poppa's protest, he drove us home. He switched off the store lights and turned the sign on the door around so that it read, *Be Right Back.* "See the advantage of being boss?" He muttered, "Of course I was here six this morning."

I sat between them as they silently drove through the dark streets. We were home in ten minutes. I marveled at how quickly that contrasted with the two trolley rides. As we left, Sol said to me, "Tell your mother an expert tailor will fix the knickers. A five dollar reward for anyone able to find the tear." Then to Poppa, "See how charming I am? The women bring their clothes just because I treat them nice." Then seriously, "Listen to me--go South young man." As we walked up the courtyard steps, the street light made our shadows dance wildly in front of us. I reached for Poppa's hand and felt a moist grip.

Momma greeted us with, "I thought you got lost-tomorrow's school."

Poppa replied, "You know my brother. Once he starts talking-"

Momma interrupted with, "A woman is nine times more talkative than a man-" and Poppa joined her to say, "but Uncle Sol is twice as talkative as a woman." I heard their private joke before. Poppa laughed first and easily, Momma tried not to, but couldn't help herself. I joined them, but Momma stopped laughing and looked at me sternly. "I hope your Uncle gave you what-for, making extra work for him." To Poppa, "I hope he talked you into getting out of this union business." A disapproving head shake was directed at both of us. "Neither of you listen to *me.*"

I said, "Uncle Sol will give five dollars to anyone finding the tear."

Momma didn't find that amusing. She said, *"I* don't need to see it to remind me of your fight. I'll remember for a long time."

Poppa, his back to her, winked at me and said, "Al won't forget."

In the living room, Morris asked what Poppa and Sol discussed. I told him: Sol believed the police want to scare--or blame--the Rank and File, particularly Poppa, for shooting the Deutsch; Poppa *may* run for Treasurer but Sol thought he should go to Yitzchok in Atlanta. Morris looked very thoughtful and said, "You'd make a good detective." I wasn't sure if that was a compliment. If I was a good detective, I'd have kept that to myself. I had kept from him Poppa's not giving his right birth date. That was so scary, I didn't want Morris to explain its consequences.

We went to bed early and there was no conversation from my parents bedroom. I was sure Poppa wouldn't tell Momma what I'd heard. It was a while before I fell asleep.

I was on a large steamship with two smokestacks. Poppa was wearing his Red Army uniform and I the Cossack velvet shorts and white silk blouse. I ran to Poppa, not noticing that next to him was a man in an American suit and a fedora--the tall detective! Poppa tried to reassure me. "Don't be scared-" The detective interrupted, "Might as well tell him--he'll find out soon enough." Poppa hesitated and the detective continued, "Your father's going on a little trip." Although I dreaded the answer, I asked, "Where?" The detective grinned. "Russia! A country far from the Bronx." Poppa put his hand on my shoulder. "I owe the immigration people three years, but everything'll be all right." His smile was not reassuring. The detective scowled. "Don't fool him or yourself. There are penalties. You'll be as old as Al's grandfather before you can return." My first thought was, *How did he know about Grandpa?* Then, *As old as Grandpa!* I looked from the detective to Poppa. The ship's whistle shrieked and I jumped.

It was a while before I fell back asleep. I was awakened by Momma's raised voice. "How can you even *think* of that, especially now."

Had he told her? I wondered.

"It's not decided, just thinking about it."

"When you tell me *think*, you've already decided to *do*. I thought you gave up that foolishness *before* the Deutsch was shot."

Poppa said, "Don't yell like that. You'll wake Al."

"You're worried about waking Al while you're ready to leave him without a father. Twenty men I counted at your meeting and you're the only one who can take the Deutsch's place?"

I thought Sol had convinced Poppa not to run and to leave

73

town. I wondered what made him change his mind as they continued arguing, Momma even saying, "If you asked Sol, he'd tell you not to run!"

Poppa didn't have the last word, but he again made the last sound by slamming the front door.

At breakfast, Momma asked, "You heard an earful last night." I stuffed my mouth with cereal. She shook her head and used a Yiddish expression that I understood as, "With your silence, you've joined your father's conspiracy." Then, as I was getting dressed, she asked, "Did you dream anything that I should know?"

I shook my head. How could I tell her?

Willie must have noticed my upset because he thought I'd fail him in spelling. He got half the words right, an improvement and I gave him eighty, ten points higher than the last test. Clarence overheard Willie's misspelling, but kept copying from my notebook.

My Current Events article was about the fall of the Czech government and its replacement by a "government headed by General Sirovy." I didn't have a chance to ask Morris how the name was pronounced, but Miss Cleary didn't correct me. "He doesn't want to give in to Hitler and the people are getting ready to fight the Germans," was how I summarized the strikes and mass protests that brought the popular General to power and the mobilization of the army that was more than a match for Hitler's. The class stared blank-eyed, as usual, but Miss Cleary said, "If the English had any backbone they'd help the Czechs stop Hitler now."

Harold reported that the "The Yanks won their third pennant in a row without having to play a game!" Miss Cleary let the class cheer for ten seconds before asking him to explain. He said, "The two games scheduled between the Red Sox and the White Sox were postponed because of rain and the Red Sox will play two less games-" He went on, but it didn't help me. I wondered if Miss Cleary or our classmates, despite their nodding, understood. Harold held up the headline so we'd know he wasn't making it up. Morris would have to explain how the Yankees, as miraculous a team as they were, could win a pennant without playing a game. Then, my mind, like a steel ball, was drawn back to the magnet of Poppa's troubles. I didn't notice Miss Cleary write *Melting Pot* on the blackboard, but perked up when she said, "Europe, which Al keeps us up-to-date on, is where most of our families came from." We were to ask our parents--or grandparents--which country they came from. Willie whispered, "That's because of Al's articles," and the others looked at me accusingly. Willie muttered, "I'm not telling *anyone* where my family came from. Not the class, not Miss Cleary, not *you!*" I sympathized with him. I didn't want to tell everyone the funny names of the towns Momma and Poppa came from.

At lunch time, Momma still looked as if Poppa had just slammed the door. Before I left, she wrapped the wet towel around her head and muttered, "I should never have left Chernobyl." I memorized the name in case I needed it. That afternoon, when we had a reading rehearsal of the play, I remembered I had forgotten to tell Momma that I had the biggest part.

In Hebrew School, Mrs. Schwartz told us about Antiochus, who was going to kill the Jews who didn't want to give up their religion. Even though I was worried about Poppa, I half-listened to her explain that the Hasideans wanted to keep our religion while Jason, a Hebrew priest, betrayed his people by siding with the Assyrians. I thought of what Uncle Sol sometimes said about the Jews: though always surrounded by enemies, they couldn't get along among themselves. Before dismissal, she said, "Our class will give a play for Chanukah." Deborah, one of the star pupils, looked pleased. I thought, *Oh, no, not another play!*

Eight

Grandpa and Grandma

Despite the upset of the past week, Poppa brought back daily reports on the Deutsch's improvement. That Friday, we ate at my grandparents, a tradition that went back as far as I could remember. While Morris once enjoyed going, he now preferred being with his high school friends. He couldn't convince Momma and didn't dare ask Poppa about not visiting Poppa's parents. Tonight, he said he doubted if our cousins Ben and Simon would be there, but that didn't sway Momma. He complained to me that he *never* had time for himself. I didn't remind him that he saw his friends afternoons and week-ends. I still hoped he'd teach me to use the slide rule, which he said would revolutionize arithmetic. When Poppa came home, he poured his usual *schnapps.* I liked to watch him gulp half the drink, go, "Ahh, helps clean out the paint," and then down the rest. Today, as he poured his drink, he asked, "Why are you always getting a drink of water when I come home?" I never thought he noticed and nearly choked. I waited in the foyer and heard, "Ahh, that cleans out the paint." He said that when no one was around! Then Poppa helped Momma into her corset. Once, as he struggled to pull in the laces after Momma exhaled *all* the air in her lungs, he said, "If women ate less, they wouldn't suffer so." Momma was angry, although he claimed he wasn't talking about her and never said that again. When we were all dressed, Momma went through her ritual of twisting all the gas jets and asking me to check. While Poppa and Morris waited outside, we rechecked the door until Poppa said, "Surah, we're going!" She tried twice more as Poppa muttered, "What would happen if there was a fire?" I again wondered how Momma got out of the apartment when I wasn't around to check.

Downstairs, Momma told Poppa the big news in our apartment building: 4-A was robbed. Momma called some neighbors by name, others by their apartment number. Then she asked me, "Did I lock the door?" I shouted, "Yes!" Once she walked home from the Third Avenue train station to check, leaving me on the platform. We turned off Fulton Avenue onto 172nd Street. As usual, Momma and I fell behind. Momma said, "He'd reach Siberia before he'd notice I wasn't behind him." She said that often when we all went walking.

Soon we approached the building that traumatized her. Abandoned now, it was once a bank. Momma repeated the story every time; I knew it by heart. She started with, "If that building could talk, it would tell a story to make you cry. Money was supposed to be safe there; it even made more money." I had the vaguest idea of money making more money but knew why that building made her cry. "Your father and I had *all* our savings there, money I put away each week. He worked hard, sometimes on the outsides of buildings-" she looked knowingly at me, "-before I learned he nearly fell five stories." That was another story and she continued with the bank. "Each week I put away fifty cents or a dollar. One afternoon, Mrs. Slatsky knocked on my door." She imitated Mrs. Slatsky: "Mrs. Segal, you've got to hurry-' She was so excited I thought the building was on fire. 'Take your money out of the bank!' I asked, 'Why?' She answered, 'The bank's failing.' She left, but greenhorn that I was, I didn't know what 'bank failing' meant. I waited for your father. Without eating supper, he rushed us to the bank--we walked faster than when I escaped from Chernobyl with the bandits behind us." Momma walked faster *now*. "But when we got here-" She turned and pointed to the red-brick building we had passed--her timing was off "-the street was filled with people and the bank was closed!" Disbelief was still in her voice and she sadly shook her head. "How could that happen here, in the *Land of Dreams,* a United States Bank?" She looked at me for the answer and then continued. "I couldn't stop repeating, 'Why didn't I listen to Mrs. Slatsky? If I went with her, I'd have saved our money.' Your father--God bless him!--didn't say a word." Her eyes gleamed with grateful tears. "Not a word from his mouth. Ten years' savings gone like that!" She sighed, as if it had happened yesterday. Then, "That money could help get my sister out of Russia." Only recently had she started mentioning that up-to-date use of the money. "The next morning, I was sick in bed for six weeks! Doctor Astrakhan tried everything, even *bankas,* but nothing helped. That's when your brother found Eunice to take care of you. "

Familiar as I was with the story, I heard *bankas* for the first time. Later, I learned they were suction cups, but I didn't ask just then--when Momma explained anything, she slowed down and we were already two blocks behind Poppa and Morris. I also learned, many years later, that it wasn't only Momma's bank that failed--9,000 did nationwide. I don't believe she ever discovered that despite the bank's name, it was privately owned.

When we saw the apartment building, I left Momma and raced Morris up the stairs. I kissed Grandma, whose wrinkled skin and hard cheek bone were so different from Momma's softness. Morris, Poppa and Momma appeared in that order. When Momma handed Grandma a jar, Grandma asked, "You have to bring your own food?" Momma answered, "Just a little *comput,.* Grandma said, "Don't I have dessert? Your father-in-law bought a strudel." Momma answered, "You'll have for tomorrow." They went through that routine every visit, including Momma's saying, "These stairs!" Grandma's reply was, "Even an old lady like me gets used to it." I wondered which contributed more to Momma's panting: the stairs or the corset. Since Grandpa was still in *shul,* I followed Momma into the kitchen. With the pretext of putting her *comput* into the icebox, she peeked into a pot on the stove. Grandma, whose vision was very poor, heard the muffled clang and said, "No kitchen-work for guests." Momma left, looking offended. Morris entered and asked if he could fix the radio. Grandma said, "It's almost *Shabbes,"* but Morris reassured her, "It's still light outside." I had told Morris about the radio and he brought his screwdriver and pliers. He turned on the radio and it crackled with static. He unplugged the electric cord, warning me, "Do that *first!"* He was often my teacher and I his appreciative pupil. Poppa, sitting in the living room and reading Grandpa's Yiddish newspaper, warned, "Don't break your grandfather's radio." Momma, uneasy when she wasn't doing housework, sat on a cane-bottom chair. She asked, "Why can't they move to a first floor apartment? Your mother doesn't mind the climb, but your father's heart doesn't need the strain." At home they could have gotten into an argument, but Poppa kept reading.

Morris peered into the innards of the radio--his crooked smile, almost a smirk, meant he was trying to figure something out. "A loose connection." He didn't sound certain. Poppa, without looking up, warned, "Don't blow a fuse." Morris' squint of concentration directed the screw driver. He whispered, "It should be soldered." He was preparing an excuse. When he put the radio together, I held my breath but didn't blink. While I wanted the radio fixed, I wouldn't have minded seeing Morris' expression if it didn't work. The crackling sound started again but then a voice came clearly through the speaker. I followed Morris into the kitchen, where Grandma rewarded him with a kiss. She said, "Grandpa will hear his Yiddish programs again!" I was jealous not getting any credit.

Momma came to the kitchen doorway. She couldn't stay away for more than fifteen minutes. Although she had seen what Grandma was preparing, she asked, "Stewed chicken?" Grandma replied "Like every Friday," positioning herself between Momma and the stove. Then Grandma said to me, "You'll be going to *shul* with your grandfather tomorrow." I said, "I'm going by myself." I was as elated as I'd been about going alone to Public and Hebrew Schools. Momma said, "My heart will be in my mouth." Grandma replied, "You shouldn't worry so." Momma replied, "I'm not a mother that I shouldn't worry?" Grandma, offended, replied, "I'm not a mother? I have three living sons and if it wasn't for sickness and the war, I'd have *nine* children." I wondered why they kept repeating things the other knew. Momma persisted, "You can't be too careful. My mother used to say, 'God couldn't be everywhere, so he invented mothers." Grandma said, "My mother said, 'A horse has a big head--let him worry." Momma said, "Not all trouble comes from heaven," and Grandma answered, "Worms eat you when you're dead; worries when you're alive." Momma returned to the living room. I chalked up this verbal duel to Grandma, who turned to me and said, "You're the only grandchild who goes to *shul.* Your grandfather says you'll know more Torah before your Bar-Mitzvah than a Yeshiva boy." I kissed her, pleased at the compliment but regretted that my family wasn't there to hear. I sniffed loud enough for Grandma to offer me a piece of *kugel*--with two warnings: "It's hot" and "Don't spoil your appetite." Momma disapproved of my snacking before meals, so I knew she meant for me to eat it in the kitchen. I did, burning the roof of my mouth. I left wondering why Momma and Grandma argued so much. Momma said, "Time enough for you to find out." I didn't want to ask Grandma and Morris wouldn't tell me.

I returned to the living room to hear Poppa tell Morris to turn up the radio. It was a news bulletin: Chamberlain was meeting with his ministers and the French ambassador to discuss Hitler's demands. Poppa said, "Chamberlain will make himself dizzy flying back and forth to Hitler." Morris asked, "Think Hitler will keep his word?" Poppa shook his head and said, "Giving Hitler the Ruhr and his taking Austria only whetted his appetite. Your Uncle is right-" I thought he'd repeat the saying about the bear and honey, but instead, "Show a dog a finger, and he bites your hand." I said, "Chamberlain doesn't want to go to war over Czechoslovakia." Poppa answered me with, "Their deals won't make for peace." I was pleased to make a contribution to their discussion--Miss Cleary was right, Current Events was useful.

Poppa glanced out the window and said, "It's *Shabbes!* Turn off the radio." Morris said, "They haven't lit the candles." Poppa's sharp look ended the debate as to when the Sabbath began. Morris turned off the radio. He once asked Poppa not only why we listened to the radio at *our* house, but also why Poppa worked on the Sabbath. Poppa nearly hit him.

I went to the hallway and watched Grandma and Momma lighting the candles. All through my childhood I was fascinated with the ritual at Friday sundown. Momma kept an extra pair of candle holders at my grandparents. Grandma had a tall brass-plated pair with decorative bases, similar in their stateliness, if not design, to the pair Momma had at home. Momma lit her candles and offered to light Grandma's, but she refused and finally succeeded after two tries. They covered their heads with their shawls and whispered their prayers in a sing-song mumble whose words I couldn't make out no matter how carefully I listened. Momma held her cupped hands over her eyes, as if to keep from peeking. Grandma's eyes were shut while she made circular motions over the candles, almost touching the flames. Both swayed back and forth, Grandma more than Momma, and their shadows danced along the wall and ceiling. I watched in awe, believing that God was listening to their prayers. Grandma finished first tonight, with a flourishing wave of her hands and a *"Gut Shabbes!"* I replied first to her and then to Momma. Just then the bell rang. I ran to the door, but instead of Grandpa, there stood Uncle Sol and Aunt Becky.

"You weren't expecting your Uncle and Aunt--heh, heh." He started to lift me, but then shook his head. "What did your mother feed you since last night?" Noticing Momma, he kissed her and said, "I was only joking." To me, he winked and said, "Eat until you're 120." I couldn't avoid getting kissed by Aunt Becky, whose lipstick stuck to my cheek like indelible paint and whose perfume was strong enough to taste. Morris hoped she wouldn't notice him, but he suffered my fate. In the confusion, I was first to notice Grandpa and responded instantly to his *"Gut Shabbes,"* believing that brought good luck since his greeting came directly from *shul.* I kissed him and felt the reassuring brush of his beard against my cheek.

When Grandma announced "Dinner!" there was a big discussion about who'd sit where, although everybody ended up in their usual place. Aunt Becky seated herself where she'd have difficulty getting out and then asked if she could help. Momma, as usual, appointed herself assistant hostess and said to Becky, "Be a guest." At home, Momma complained to Poppa that Aunt Becky sat in her starched dress "like a Queen without hands." Grandma served a lavish Friday dinner: chicken soup with matzo balls (I hungrily slurped it up and ignored Morris making faces at me); gefilte fish with horseradish (which I skipped); the entree of chicken, mashed potatoes, *tsimus-* (sweetened carrots) and *kugel* (noodles with spices and sugar baked into a pie). When I asked for more *kugel* (Grandma's tasted better than Momma's, though I never dared tell her), Momma made me finish my chicken and potatoes. Busy as she was helping Grandma, who no longer protested, Momma kept an eye on me. We ate ravenously, but that didn't keep the grown-ups from talking all the while. I listened to whichever conversation sounded most interesting. Morris asked Sol where Ben and Simon were and he answered, "Those two *shleppers* don't go with us. They 'go out dancing." That was a Yiddish idiom meaning they went out with their friends. Morris looked at Momma, hoping she overheard. Even if she did, he'd be sure to remind her.

What they didn't talk about was more significant than what they did. Either everyone knew the latest news about the Deutsch or were afraid to ask. Sol said, "I'm glad I don't have a boss over me. The garment shops were worse than slavery when we came in 1914, only three years after the fire." Even I knew they were referring to the Triangle Shirtwaist Factory tragedy, but Uncle Sol reminded them. "Girls jumping from the tenth floor to their deaths because the boss locked the fire exits." He shook his head sadly. "I'm not a Rockefeller, but now I'm my boss." Poppa, glancing at Momma, said, "Someday I'll have my own shop." Momma made a face and said, "You talk, but never do." Sol prevented an argument by joking, "God must love the poor, he made so many of us." Even Grandpa smiled. Then Sol joked, "It's not that money makes everything good, it's that no money makes everything bad!" He laughed the loudest. Then, "You know what my new presser told me? If the rich could hire others to die for them, the poor would make a nice living." That was a joke I hadn't heard and the others appreciated it as well. When the laughter died down, Grandma asked, "Why did Yitzchok move to Atlanta?" She voiced that complaint since I was small.

Sol said, "Labor's cheaper." He turned to Poppa, "He'd help get you started in a business." Momma said, "See--listen to your brother. Get away from the gangsters before it's too late!" She glared at Poppa.

Becky said to Sol, "If you weren't so stubborn, Yitzchok could have made you a millionaire." Sol replied, "We had a falling out." Everybody knew what that was--except me--so Sol

83

didn't go into that. He said, "That was years ago. Besides, envy's a sickness that destroys you. But we were talking about a business for Mordcha so he doesn't have to swing a paint brush the rest of his life." He turned to his wife. "My store makes a living." Becky answered, "You could have been a boss in Atlanta and I could have had a mansion like Yitzchok's wife." They glared at each other, but like Momma and Poppa, kept their tongues.

Sol turned to his father and asked, "What does the Talmud say about workers?" Grandpa, who was more a listener at such gatherings, said, "Work brings dignity. The Talmud also says that a worker's rights are more important than those of his employer." Sol exclaimed, "The Talmud sounds like the *Freiheit!*" referring to the Yiddish Communist newspaper. Sol laughed and said to Poppa, "Maybe you should have a rabbi talk to the bosses and gangsters." Then to Grandpa, "You've been a worker long enough--you should retire." Grandma rapped her knuckles on the table. *"Halevai!"*

That could have started an argument between my grandparents, but Grandpa said, "The summer after this one, I'll retire." Poppa asked, "Why not sooner? You've done enough hard work." Sol added, "We'll help." Grandpa said, "I don't need help from my sons. Use your money for your children or to help family in Europe." Momma heard that and said, "Your son doesn't want to spend a couple of hundred dollars to get my sister's family out." Poppa corrected her, "Three hundred." Momma countered, "If my family was in Europe and my sister here, she would-" Poppa interrupted with, "I don't want them out? We'll just be throwing money out the window." Sol told Becky, "Your brother-in-law, who can still leave Germany, is too thick-headed." Becky said, "He doesn't want to lose his business." Before Sol and Becky got into their argument, Poppa blurted to Momma, "Give the thief the money--you'll nag me to my grave!" I was as shocked as everyone. Momma glanced around the table. "Everyone is my witness!" Poppa said, "My word isn't good enough?" Momma kissed him. They hadn't done that in a while.

Becky said, "Don't give up hope. Stalin's not an anti-Semite like Hitler." Sol replied, "The person with his back to a fire is last to find out he's burning." Becky asked, "It's safe in the *Land of Dreams*? The Bund is in Yorkville and American Nazis fill Madison Square Garden. Millions of people listen to that anti-Semitic priest-" Morris supplied, "Coughlin." Sol turned to his father-"You took care of that American anti-Semite!" He told about the man who pulled Grandpa's beard. "Grandpa knocked him unconscious. I don't know if was the *zetz* or seeing a bearded Jew hitting back." Momma frowned, but I liked that story.

Though everyone was "ready to bust," we had dessert: strudel, *comput* and sponge cake washed down with glasses of tea. In the kitchen, where my grandparents couldn't see, Momma poured me milk. I protested it wasn't kosher after eating meat, a stronger argument than my being stuffed, but it didn't help.

With the dessert eaten, Sol asked, "What about some songs, Surah?" That was a request he always made, but which Momma invariably declined with a shake of her head and a flutter of her eyelashes. Grandpa said, "A song will cheer us up." Others voiced their agreement. Sol banged a spoon against his glass, but Momma modestly shook her head again. That only increased the coaxing until Momma started singing the lullaby, *Sleep My Child,* the words by Sholom Aleichem. That song that was my companion in infancy and haunts me to this day.

"Sleep, my child, my sweet, my pretty one,
    Sleep, my darling, sleep.
Sleep, my life, my sweet, my pretty one,
    Sleep, my darling son.

Verses told of the sad story of a father's leaving for "that far-off land" but not forgetting his family ("Daddy will send us twenty dollars, And his picture too") but there's doubt ("If he's living...he'll fetch us") and hope ("we wait his happy message") and reassurance ("Sleep my darling, since you're little, And I watch over you.")

85

Momma had a sweet untutored soprano voice, all the more moving because of its ingenuousness. When she finished, Sol led a gentle hand-clapping. Next, she sang *This Golden Land,* which resoundingly described America as the dream and hope of every Jew, where there was no suffering or persecution. When she finished, she said, "It's getting late," signaling the end of the performance. Everyone applauded loudly and made appreciative comments. Sol shouted, "Encore! Encore! You sing like Bertha Kalish." He always said that, but Momma blushed as if hearing it for the first time.

Poppa said to Sol, "I first noticed her when she sang at a party in Warsaw." Then to Momma, "You remember?" Momma smiled and said, "How could I forget? That was at Manya's. I thought you were only sixteen." Poppa repeated, "Sixteen!" as if he'd heard that for the first time. "I was a two-year veteran of the Third International Army!" Momma replied, "You looked like a boy who needed his first shave." Their glances sparkled and I was pleased as well as jealous.

After Sol went to the bathroom, Poppa left the room. I went into the dark hallway and saw they had gone into my grandparents' bedroom. I stood near the closed door and heard Sol ask, "Have you made up your mind?" I didn't hear Poppa's reply and left when the doorknob turned.

Sol and Becky left first. Sol kissed me and said, "If I tried lifting you now, I'd get a hernia." I wasn't offended--I really ate a lot. Poppa told Grandpa that the new Social Security law should help him retire." Grandpa, with Grandma out of earshot, whispered, "I'm not ready to sit around like an old man." Poppa said, "You have your *shul.* You can read and listen to your radio, now that Morris fixed it." Morris looked pleased until Poppa said, "Morris will find out your benefits with the new law."

Outside it was dark, but the street lamps cast shimmering patches of light. The buildings were shadows and I knew I'd have been scared if I were alone. For a change, I was walking with Poppa and leaving behind Morris and Momma. Morris complained, "Benny and Simon didn't come!" Now I knew why he was walking with her. Momma's reply, "You've got me for a mother, not Becky!" left no doubt as to who had the better deal.

Poppa walked slowly; I wasn't sure if it was because he had eaten a lot or was letting me keep up with him. I wanted to talk to him the way Morris did, but when I tried too hard to think of something to say, my mind went blank. I finally asked, "What was the name of your horse?" Poppa frowned. "You overheard us?" Then, "Grizha--that means 'dirty gray'. I can trust you." He imitated Sol--"Heh, heh!" I laughed so hard I nearly fell down. From behind, Morris shouted, "What's so funny?" I didn't answer. He never told me what he and Poppa talked about.

At home, I quickly got ready for bed. Nevertheless, Momma said, "It's late. You'll go to *shul* next week? Morris can take you then." I shouted, "No!" Morris muttered from his bed, "Je-sus! He's not a baby." When she bent over to kiss me, she whispered, "I don't want anything to happen." I whispered back, "I'll take care. I promise." I had to say that despite Morris hearing me, but I didn't swear, "So help me, God." After Momma left, I asked, "What's Social Security?" Morris' "Je-sus!" was followed by fifteen seconds of silence and then, "I'll tell you if it's the last question." I promised. "It's for when you get old and retire. You stop working and get checks from the government. It's really your money--you pay into it. The boss also pays--oh, you won't understand! Go to sleep!" A half minute later, I asked, "Will Poppa run for Treasurer?" Morris responded with, "Je-sus!" Then, across the darkness, "You're the eavesdropping G-Man."

That was the last thing either of us said. If we argued, Momma would come in and I knew what her punishment would be. For the first night in a long time my parents weren't arguing. Their recalling their meeting at Manya's must have made them nostalgic. I enjoyed the silence.

Next thing, I was on Buck Rogers' rocket ship. With us were Wilma, his pretty co-pilot, Jack Armstrong, and Superman. I looked down at the Earth becoming a small ball, black and white, not like the later photos of the astronauts. Jack Armstrong repeated what the Tibetan Monk had told him: that the world belonged to the boys and girls of America, providing we were honest and had hearts of gold. We'd save the world and become rich as well. The monk's message was on boxes of Wheaties, the cereal advertised on his radio show and which I insisted Momma buy so that I could get his Whistle Ring and Secret Code. Our mission was to save Momma's and Aunt Becky's families and as many other Jews as could fit in our rocket. Wilma was afraid Ming would intercept us. She meant Killer Kane and Ardala-- Ming was in the Flash Gordon comics. I didn't correct her. Anyway, it was Hitler who would try to stop us. I wasn't afraid-- Buck had his Rocket Pistols and Disintegrator Guns. I tried to get radio contact with Earth, but there was too much static. "I'll fix it!" said a familiar voice. Morris! The radio was more complicated than Grandpa's, but Morris took out his pliers and screwdriver. That's when I woke up. Just like with the serials in the movies or on the radio, interrupted at the most exciting part. That left me hanging as to whether Momma's family could be saved.

Nine

Shul

The next morning, while Morris ate breakfast, I pretended to be asleep. That way, he'd escape to his friend's before Momma could ask him to take me to shul. I extracted for my end of the bargain Morris' promise to teach me the Morse Code. I lay in bed counting the different kinds of flowers on the wallpaper. Poppa protested to Momma that he was a "paintner"--which was the Yiddish pronunciation of "painter"--"and not a paper-hanger." To please Momma, he had hung up the multi-colored floral pattern. When the outer door closed, I went to the kitchen.

"You missed your brother," said Momma. "Still want to go alone?"

I ate *all* my cereal and dressed quickly. Momma inspected me in the foyer. "You look nice in that new jacket." That *new* jacket was left in Uncle Sol's store for more than thirty days, which was how long he was responsible for keeping unclaimed clothes. He told Momma the lady wouldn't recognize it because he had to let it out ("A good ten inches!") I didn't appreciate that, nor his saying if the lady did recognize her son's jacket, she could have me arrested for *klayna ganeyve* --petty larceny.

I didn't complain about my knickers and high-top shoes, but instead repeated how carefully I'd be crossing the streets. She asked if I remembered the little girl run over by a car. How could I forget? Momma reminded me at least twice a week. "If you get hurt-- God forbid!--I'll remind your grandmother and father that they said you could go." She sighed. "Yalkala, extra-strength headache powders won't help." She closed her eyes and moved her lips in prayer and when she opened them said, "Go, before I change my mind."

I was instantly out the door. For the entire week I'd been waiting for this moment. The red lights seemed never to change, but I waited and looked both ways, something Morris didn't always do when he took me. I was out of breath when I reached St. Paul's Place and panicked at the wild thought that the *shul* had vanished. Then it came into view. I was not waylaid by anti-Semitic gangs, kidnapped by evil men or came close to a moving car. It was an anxious but uneventful trip, not at all what Momma anticipated and I imagined. I was disappointed.

I paused in front of the *shul's* large wooden doors. Above them were stained-glass windows with a blue Star of David. I entered and put on my *yarmulka,* which I was too embarrassed to wear in the street. I hoped God understood. In the high-ceilinged vestibule, I was dazzled by the multi-colored shafts of light that streaked through the stained-glass windows and flickered on the floating specks of dust. The vestibule was saturated with an amalgam of odors--old prayer books, musty clothing, perspiration, aging wood, furniture polish, soap-washed floor tiles and others that were unidentifiable. I heard the cantor's singing and the congregation's murmuring responses through the thin doors of the adjoining worship chamber. Awesome sensations seeped through me as I stood there. Mrs. Schwartz said *shul* was the Temple of God and the Sabbath holier than the most important holiday. No one could see God; He was a spirit, invisible and everywhere. I couldn't understand that, but I felt His presence there as I didn't elsewhere. The Invisible Man on the radio program also couldn't be seen, but he was make-believe. I looked up at the oak-beam ceiling, hoping to see a sign of God's presence. Even a stirring in the colored shafts of light would have been sufficient. I waited, but nothing happened.

Impatient to join Grandpa, I pushed the small wooden vestibule door, which swung open effortlessly, in contrast to the more formidable one behind me, as if once inside the building, one could easily enter the holy prayer chamber. The cantor had his back to the congregation and sang to the Torah Ark. Below him stood the congregation, their striped shawls forming a swaying wall of rhythmic patterns. They chanted refrains to remind the cantor and God of their presence, while their synchronized "Amens" affirmed the prayers. I barely breathed; I could see and hear everything but remained invisible. I searched among the backs of the prayer shawls, indistinguishable except for their different heights and girths, but I recognized Grandpa's. I squeezed through the men and joined him. Without taking his eyes from the *siddur,* his lips still moving and his fingers following the prayer, he bent over and kissed me.

The congregation was mostly older men who came from the ghettoes of Russia. A sprinkling of teen-age boys were wedged in among their fathers or grandfathers, waiting patiently. Part of the Sabbath service was reading a portion of the Torah, which took about a half hour. Regardless of who the reader was, he recited in an inaudible monotone and the boys left by the side door into the adjoining lot. There they played softball, an activity forbidden on the Sabbath. On my first service, I wondered if the earth would swallow them up, but they returned after the Torah reading looking cheerful. I expected something dreadful to happen to them during the week, figuring God wasn't in a hurry, but they returned very much alive and eagerly awaiting the Torah reading. Some members of the congregation muttered "sacrilege," but Grandpa said the important thing was the boys coming to *shul.* I regretted being too young to join them, but was relieved at not offending God.

Near the end of the service, the man who complained loudest about the boys' playing fell asleep. Grandpa leaned over and tied the threaded strings of his prayer shawl to those of an unsuspecting neighbor. When the congregation rose for the final prayer, the sleeping man's prayer shawl was swept off his shoulders. We laughed. The man glared at Grandpa, who was innocently looking in his *siddur.* When the man left, Grandpa and the others laughed again. If Willie went to *shul,* he would have played a prank like that.

We stopped with the other men to have the *Gut Shabbes* schnapps and cake. Outside, walking home, I asked, "Why can't we look at what the men are doing with the Torah?" Grandpa chose his words carefully. "Only the *Kohanim,* the descendants of the ancient priests, do that." I asked, "Are we *Kohanim?"* Grandpa replied, "No. We're also not Levites, their assistants. We're Israelites, the common people." I asked, "Can you *ever* say those prayers?" When Grandpa shook his head, I shouted,

"That's not fair!" Grandpa said, "They're traditions from ancient times." We walked in silence until he said, "Belief is not always something we can see or understand. But no man is less than another because of who he is or what he does." Then, "If we believe, there are no impossible questions; without belief, there are no complete answers." I was pleased he wasn't unhappy being a common Israelite, but I still thought it unfair.

Grandpa walked slowly and that gave us more time to talk. I said, "My Hebrew teacher tells us stories from Genesis, and I got another hundred in a spelling test in public school." If Morris heard me, he'd have called me "A show-off," but Grandpa said, "You'll be a scholar in both Cheder and the American school." We walked around three girls noisily playing jacks on the sidewalk and continued for a while not talking, comfortable just being together. When we crossed the street, I searched for his hand, which was large and callused from years of working in a factory. Poppa said Grandpa was a Hebrew scholar in Russia but when he came to this country with my uncles, he didn't speak English and had to work as a laborer. But he continued studying the Torah.

We walked into the hallway of his building and the sunlight was extinguished as if someone had thrown a switch. The dim light bulbs were not on during the day. Last night I had rushed up the stairs, but now I stopped on each half-landing for Grandpa. He'd hold the banister and breathe heavily before we'd start up again. The center of each step had a worn groove from the many people who had walked up over the years. I smelled Grandma's cooking before we reached the front door. After exchanging *"Gut Shabbes,"* she invited me for·lunch. I enjoyed not only her food, but also the tender way they got along.

After the meal, I followed Grandpa into the living room. He sat in his armchair and I pulled over a cane-bottom chair. I told him about the Bible stories in Mrs. Schwartz' class and the play my class would give in public school. Eager as I was to hear him, I could go on and on. When I finally paused, he nodded and commented on my question about a young woman being our Hebrew teacher instead of a rabbi. "Anyone who studies can become learned. Even the rabbi's servant girl can interpret the law." He sounded as if he was talking to one of the men in *shul*. "The *shtetl* in Russia is different from here." His eyes slowly glazed over and I wondered if I looked like that when I had my daytime fantasies. Although I was very curious, I respected his not explaining certain things. I tried to imagine him back in the *shtetl* as a boy studying Torah, but couldn't imagine him a boy. He forever remained in my memory as then--a wise old man with a gray beard. I went to the bathroom. It had a water tank near the ceiling, old-fashioned even in those days. The water noisily ran down the pipe, whirred around the bowl and threatened to splash onto the floor, but it never did.

Grandma cut a piece of *kugel* for me to take home. "Have more for yourself. You earned it by going to *shul.*" The kugel warmed my hands and its savory aroma accompanied me home. I hurried, eager to prove to Momma that I had gone to *shul* safely, but crossed over to the Crotona Park side of Fulton Avenue and saw the black and white cat that lived in the park. It stopped to return my stare, its body poised to run. "*Gut Shabbes,*" I said, tossing it a crumb of *kugel.* The cat crouched suspiciously, then grabbed the morsel and ran off.

Momma greeted me as if I were Admiral Perry returning from the North Pole. After nearly crushing me, she held me at arms' length and said, "When you have children, you'll understand." I thought I'd never treat children the way she did. But I didn't say it out loud.

When Poppa came home--he worked overtime-- he patted my head and said, "You're getting to be a big boy." Poppa wasn't glib with compliments. I felt prouder that evening when he called me into the bedroom and handed me the large soft-covered book *Our American Way of Life, Book I* and said, Page forty-eight." I turned to the page and asked, "Why did the English come to America?" He answered, "They wanted freedom." He answered my other questions: the Revolutionary War "was also called the War for Independence"; George Washington "was the father of our country."; "To become a citizen you must understand English, know the history of the country, be loyal to the United States, and know how to sign your name." He got the answers right, although he didn't pronounce some of the words correctly, but I told him how only when he asked. Finally, he said, "It's late--you must be tired." I was but would have continued anyway. He squeezed my shoulder and returned to the bedroom. I went to bed feeling pleased that I was helping him become an American citizen.

Monday morning, after Poppa and Morris left, the doorbell rang. Momma wasn't panicked. She wore a street dress, rather than a house dress. She led the man into the kitchen. I recognized the overweight man in baggy pants and worn jacket from a visit a month ago. I had hid in the foyer and overheard them talking about Momma's family in Russia. I suspected something was up and after he left, Momma said to me, "You don't have to tell your father *everything.*" Another secret! This morning I was prepared to sneak into the foyer to eavesdrop but Momma invited me into the kitchen. She served me my bowl of cereal, saying, "Eat your breakfast or you'll be late for school. I knew better than to say that it was a half hour before my wake-up time. Momma served him tea and he said, "You have a nice son." I wanted to say, "How do you know?" I had taken an instant dislike to him. Besides his insincere voice, he had squinty eyes whose glances darted about the room. Momma said, "Yalka's a good pupil," said Momma, "in public school and *Cheder.*" The man smiled and replied, "He looks smart." Momma offered him a dish of cake.

I slowed down my eating--I'd finish before I found out why he came. He reached for the "cake." Rather than the miniature Danish Momma served for company, I recognized it as a cut-up Yankee Doodle Cupcake. Nevertheless, he chewed it appreciatively and said, "Nice vanilla filling." Then he looked at me funny-like and Momma said, "He's no *yenta.*" He licked the cake off his fingers. "The tongue has no bones, it's loose." He laughed, but Momma frowned. "Yalka wants to see his cousin Avrum." I figured it out: the *contrabandist!* She saw him *before* Poppa agreed to pay! She wanted me there as a witness as she took a roll of bills from her apron pocket, slipped off the rubber band, and slowly counted them twice before handing them to him. She said, "One-hundred and fifty," but he frowned and said, *"Three* hundred." Momma's jaw jutted out. "The rest

94

when you find them." The agent looked unhappy but wet his thumb as he counted the roll. Then he took a small notebook from his battered briefcase. "Our contacts will do all they can to reach them in Kiev."

Momma asked, "How soon?"

"Our next trip." He glanced over his shoulder, "The rest I'm not at liberty to talk about. Let me make sure I have the correct information." He read the address from his book and Momma corrected," 124 *A* Zitomsky Prospect, not 24." He wet the tip of his pencil and made the correction. He tried to make light of the error by saying, "Our contact would have asked neighbors." He put the pad back into his briefcase and the money into a worn billfold.

Momma watched the money disappear. "My husband said I was throwing away money." He got up too quickly and Momma stood up, blocking his way.

He sat down. "It's easy to doubt and not trust." Then he drew out the billfold. "If you don't want us to try-"

Momma frowned, then nodded. "How can I not try?"

He stood up again but this time Momma let him pass. As he walked leisurely to the door, he said, "How can we live without hope and trust?"

Momma asked, "When will I hear?"

He edged toward the door. "As soon as possible. You have my word we'll do our best." He glanced at me. "Let's pray *Yalka* sees his cousin *Avrum* soon."

Momma looked pleased that he remembered our names. She said, *"Halevai!"* as he walked out. Even with her back to me, I knew she was crying. When I touched her shoulder, she turned and held me. She looked up at the crack-line in the ceiling. "Why do You test us so?"

In school, I explained to Clarence my notes while Willie stared belligerently at us. Clarence had gotten used to Willie and ignored him. Later that morning Miss Cleary picked me to be Mr. O'Hare's monitor. I thought his office small for an assistant principal. He had only a worn desk, his swivel chair, a chair for visiting parents, and a two-seater wooden bench for misbehaving pupils. The room needed a paint job. I stared at his balding head until he finally looked up and handed me an envelope to take to Miss Cleary.

I went to the upper landing of a rarely used stairway and opened the envelope. That was the perk in being a monitor: reading messages if the envelopes weren't sealed. I developed speed reading and race walking in order to discover school policies and personal scoops about teachers and pupils. Inside this envelope was a booklet entitled, *The Intellectually Gifted Program--Lesson Plans for Committee Work--Grades 4-6.* A note clipped to the cover read, "*From the Desk of Dr. O'Hare,* Dear Kathleen, Here's the new syllabus," It was signed, "Don." I didn't bother opening the syllabus, satisfied to have discovered that Mr. O'Hare was a Doctor, which made no sense, since I knew doctors took care of sick people. "Don" was an intriguing discovery and more surprising was Miss Cleary's being Kathleen. I quickly slid the syllabus and note back into the envelope, looped the string around the tab and went to my classroom. If I took too long, I'd arouse suspicions.

Miss Cleary--I couldn't imagine her Kathleen--read the note, muttered to herself and then wrote a reply. The envelope was unsealed, so I discovered what made her angry. I read, "Dr. Donald O'Hare!! Livingston Street's crazy if they think my fourth graders can do committee work! I won't do it either! Kathy. "I thought, *She wrote "crazy" to Dr. Donald O'Hare!* and reread, with disbelief, her defying our assistant principal. Of course I didn't miss that she was also "Kathy." A minute later, as Doctor Donald O'Hare read her note, I was furtively watching him. I expected him to be angry, but he surprised me by smiling and muttering, "Kathy, Kathy! I thought the dinosaurs were extinct. Why do you insist on teaching the Gifted class?" He glanced at me, but I was staring blankly over his head. He handed me a large envelope. "It's important--a transfer record." While his concern was for its safe delivery, mine was with its contents. I dashed straight to my staircase sanctuary. It was Clarence Harlow's school record. I skimmed his achievement scores: "3.1 grade reading level" in the first grade. The most recent, in third grade, was 5.8. Religion was "Christian"; Race, "negro"; with parentheses enclosing "grandfather on maternal side Apache Indian"; the last school, "Montana Reservation School."

When I returned, Miss Cleary placed the envelope on her desk without opening it. I casually glanced at Clarence, who, like everyone else, was writing. I felt special, possessing knowledge about him that no one else in the class knew. Numerous times that morning, I stared at him. When he caught me, I turned away quickly. One of my earliest fantasies, before Superman, was being an Indian. I had spent many hours roaming through the pre-Columbian forests of Crotona Park and earned my name Running Bear by killing a Grisly. Now, sitting opposite me in Miss Cleary's class, was a real Indian. Yet I was puzzled by his skin color. Although a lighter shade of brown than Eunice's, I had trouble reconciling his ancestry. I was to discover how his grandfather, an Apache imprisoned in Florida, met his grandmother, the descendent of an escaped slave.

When no longer distracted by Clarence's color, I observed his facial expressions. They contrasted with those of Willie, whose emotional reactions instantly played across his face. Clarence's were harder to read--he kept his feelings under control. Yet I was learning to read his brown eyes and the flicker of his lips. When Miss Cleary told him how quickly he was catching up on his work, his lips and eyes revealed appreciation, despite a controlled, "Thank you, Miss Cleary." After she left, Willie muttered, "Teacher's pet!" Clarence glance warned, "Watch yourself!" Willie went through his grimaces, but Clarence ignored them.

During lunch, Momma looked more worried than usual. I asked if it was the *contrabandist* and she replied, "Trouble doesn't come alone." That's all she would say.

During play rehearsal that afternoon, I was repairing the *Wooden Soldier with the Missing Leg.* Harold whispered, "Hurry!" which was not in the script. In my haste, I hit him with my hammer. The class thought that funny, except Harold, who no longer pretended to hop. That ended the rehearsal and Harold wouldn't speak to me.

When I came home for my snack, Momma had a towel wrapped around her head. I couldn't guess what the new trouble was. I left for Hebrew School early and waited in the principal's office, where Rabbi Weiss was warning a boy that if he didn't behave, he'd throw him out of the Bar Mitzvah class. The rabbi spoke sharply despite the secretary and three pupils being in the office. His threats, accentuated by his pointed goatee and angry eyes, nearly brought the thin boy to tears. I was relieved when Mrs. Schwartz arrived. During the story period, I found it hard to understand how the first couple on Earth managed to get into so much trouble. Lenny asked why Adam got the same punishment as Eve, since she was first to bite the apple and talked Adam into eating it. Deborah came to Eve's defense, claiming that the snake was the culprit. Besides, she explained that God couldn't just throw Eve out--"They *had* to be together, otherwise there wouldn't have been children." Classmates giggled, but I kept a straight-face, not wanting Deborah to think me silly. I asked why God hadn't put a fence around the Tree, one with barbed wire on top, like the one protecting Public School #4. Mrs. Schwartz thought it a good question, though she had no answer. I also asked why God didn't give them another chance--even Miss Cleary usually gave us a second chance. Mrs. Schwartz had no answer for that either. She did explain that the knowledge they gained included shame at being naked. The class was in Pandemonium. Rabbi Weiss entered! He had been listening at the door. He admonished the class with, "Hebrew School's for learning, not laughing or talking." He glance at Mrs. Schwartz when he said, "Children should memorize the Bible-" and then at me to conclude, "and not ask foolish questions." He threatened not to let us be in the Chanukah play and left.

Ten

Everything Will Be All Right

I sensed something was wrong at supper. Momma looked more worried than usual and Poppa more preoccupied. Morris asked for the ketchup and Poppa turned on him--"Don't you have feet? Your mother cooks and cleans-" Morris leapt up and searched through the refrigerator but Momma had to find it for him. She *always* got the ketchup and her frown told Poppa she didn't appreciate his newly discovered concern. Poppa let the matter drop, but the bottle trembled in Morris' hand. I felt sorry for him but was glad I hadn't asked.

An hour later, when Sol arrived, everything became clear. His visit was unusual on a week-day evening and when Morris and I greeted him, Poppa shooed us back to the living room. Momma lay in bed with a towel around her head. Poppa and Sol whispered in the kitchen. I stood in the hallway darkness and heard Sol say, "Leave tonight!"

I told Morris, "Poppa's going to Atlanta--tonight!"

Morris looked up from his desk. "Just had a dream?" With that, he returned to studying. Fifteen minutes later, Momma called us. Next to our glasses of milk were large wedges of pie. Momma said, "See what your uncle brought." Sol said lifted a forkful and said, *"American* apple pie." None of us smiled. Momma asked, "You can leave the store for so long?"

Sol answered, "I have this new presser, Yussie, a jewel of a worker, really a skilled tailor." He kissed his finger tips and looked around conspiratorially. "He's a refugee-" I was unsure whether he said *plit,* meaning refugee, or *blat,* meaning illegal "-who wants to bring his family here. If I say his wife is my sister, they'd come under the family immigration quota."

Momma's brows furrowed. "You can get into trouble!"

"You sound like Becky," said Sol. "If we don't look after our own, who will? Anyway, Yussie's becoming more than a brother. Kindness is better appreciated by a stranger. If that's not in the Talmud, it should be."

Now Poppa frowned. "And you're sending me to Yitzchok?"

Morris' mouth dropped and he looked from Poppa to me.

"Didn't Yitzchok agree?" asked Sol.

They spoke to Yitzchok on the phone!

Sol put down his tea. "I've thought about that. 'A meowing cat doesn't catch mice." I wasn't the only one who looked at him quizzically. He explained, "If they think Mordcha did it, they'd watch carefully until they had evidence, not warn him--that's number one." Sol raised a second finger. "Two! It's 100 percent American to look for a business. Workers drop their union like a hot potato.." He raised a third finger. "He's visiting a brother to talk over a business deal." Sol had raised a fourth finger, but then shrugged. "We don't need more reasons." Momma asked, "How long?" She glanced at Poppa, who looked away. She turned to Sol, who shrugged.

I ate my pie but don't remember tasting it. Poppa told Morris and me, "If anyone asks where I am, I'm visiting my brother."

"There's no law against that," said Sol.

Poppa said, "The Rank-and-File want me out-of-town."

"That's the smartest thing for them too," said Sol. "In the meantime, the police may trip over the gangsters who shot your friend." Then, in a lowered voice, "Remember, the Naturalization police asking questions doesn't mean they know anything."

The Naturalization police were asking questions!

Poppa avoided looking at Momma, whose expression and towel said enough. Yet she couldn't help but say, "You didn't listen to *me.*"

Sol said, "Look for the rainbow and silver lining, Surah. Soon you'll sing, 'He goes away a paintner and comes back a businessman."

Momma didn't appreciate his paraphrasing the nonsense song about a rabbi who goes into water and comes out wet. She

100

said, "Mordcha will just get soaked. You need a boss' head to become a boss." Then to Poppa, "What will you take?"

I couldn't restrain myself. "Will *we* be moving to Atlanta?"

Sol said, "Be adventurous! You wouldn't exist if your parents weren't. Your mother would have never left Chernobyl and your father Radomysl." Seeing my expression, he patted my arm. "Don't worry, you're such a good boy, you'd be eating delicious apple pie somewhere else. Of course you may not have such a delightful an uncle!"

Any other time, we'd have laughed. But we sat quietly, the yellowish glow from the ceiling light giving everyone a waxen pallor. Sol looked at his wrist watch and said, "You should be packing."

Tonight!

The three of them went into the bedroom, leaving Morris and me staring at each other. I tiptoed to the foyer.

"You're taking *that* suitcase?" exclaimed Sol.

Momma said, "I told him it was a shame carrying that to America."

Sol said, "I'd have lent you one of mine."

Poppa said, "It was supposed to be Borinka's." There was silence. Then Poppa continued, "I'd show Borinka the suitcase every night and say, 'That's what you'll carry off the boat at Ellis Island.' Sick as he was, he'd smile when I said that. Borinka didn't come here, but at least the suitcase could." Momma cried often, but not Poppa. His back was to them and they may not have noticed, but I saw him cry for the first time.

Momma held a pile of underwear and Poppa said, "That's too many." Momma dropped the underwear on the bed and covered her face with her apron. Poppa said, "Okay, I'll take them." He stuffed them into the suitcase. Momma took Poppa's winter coat from the closet and Poppa said, "I won't have room for anything else." Before Momma cried again, Sol said, "Max will carry it!" Then, after putting in other clothes, Poppa, said, "A handkerchief won't fit in." Sol sat on the suitcase so Poppa could snap it shut. He then tied a belt around it. He went over to Momma. I couldn't see them but heard Momma sobbing and then say, "I should be so angry with you, but like a fool I help you pack. If you had listened to me about the union-"

Poppa asked, "Who could know-" and Momma interrupted, "You don't have to *look* for trouble. After escaping the revolution, you still try to be a hero, but stumble like a *schlimazel.* "

"Mordcha didn't invent the world," said Sol. "You stare straight ahead and only later smell what you've stepped into."

Momma said, "If you smell trouble, you walk the other way, not into it. You should have listened to Yalkala's dream."

I almost stepped into the room to take credit as Sol said, "With a smart wife and Joseph for a son, how come you step into *drek?"*

I stepped closer to the door and saw Poppa take something out of his pocket and hand it to Momma. She said, "You already gave me money for the agent and the house--you need some for yourself." Poppa replied, "I have for me. Soon I'll be working." Sol said, "I'll be here to help." Then, "It's getting late." Poppa picked up the bulging suitcase and said, "It'll hold" Sol said, "If not, the railroad station will be wearing your underclothes." Only Sol thought that funny. He looked at his wristwatch. "To catch that train, we'll have to leave at eight."

I went back to the living room and told Morris, "Poppa's leaves at eight." He was no longer skeptical about what I told him.

The hour passed slowly. Morris studied, or pretended to. I kept looking at the window to see the faint light smothered by darkness. I went back to the hallway and overheard Poppa ask, "What I should say to the boys?" Sol said, "I think they know." Momma said, "Even Yalka understands."

When Poppa stepped into our room, before he could say a word, I ran over and grabbed him. Morris also rushed over. Poppa said, "I want you to be good while I'm gone." He moved us toward the couch and the three of us sat down, Poppa in the middle. "It won't be long before we're together again." He looked at Momma in the doorway. "Listen to your mother. Remember, I'm just going to visit my brother."

"Mordcha," said Sol, "it's eight-ten."

Poppa said to Morris, "I want you to take care of your brother-" We walked with Poppa into the hallway, where he hugged Momma. She held him and whispered, "All the good-bys were on the other side--there were to be no good-bys in the *Land of Dreams.*"

"Everything will be all right," said Poppa, patting her on the back.

Momma said, "You always say that."

Poppa replied, "We're still here."

Sol said, "You'll still be here when your train leaves!"

Poppa kissed Morris and me again, while Sol said, "What is a Jew without hope?" Then worriedly, "Do you think anyone's outside, watching?" He and Poppa exchanged glances. Sol turned to us. "Quick!"

We were practically out the door when Momma called, "Wear your jackets." We grabbed them from the closet and rushed out. We casually walked up Fulton Avenue, looking in all directions as well as into the parked cars. When we returned, they were waiting near the door. Morris gasped, "The coast is clear!" Momma was crying and Poppa hugged her. He asked her not to cry and she wiped her eyes.

Sol glanced at the suitcase Poppa was carrying. "I'd give a hundred dollars to be there when Yitzchok sees that." It was a discolored brown, worn through in spots. Sol turned to us before he followed Poppa out. "I'll stop by." Morris turned off the kitchen light so we could look out the window. It was too dark to see anything. All we heard was the slam of a car door. Momma, behind us, said, "I didn't think you'd ever see this."

When Momma kissed me goodnight, she whispered, "Sleep is the best doctor." She hadn't told me her mother's saying in a long time. As usual she told Morris, "Don't stay up late." Instead of ignoring her, he answered, "I won't."

When Momma left, I asked, "Will *they* follow Poppa?"

Morris asked, "Who?"

I hesitated. "The detectives and Naturalization police."

Morris said, "Pop's visiting Uncle Yitzchok and he's looking for a business. Nothing's wrong with that."

I kept repeating to myself, "Nothing's wrong," until I fell asleep.

The next morning, I strained to hear the trickling water and the stropping of the razor. Their absence confirmed what I didn't want to believe--that last evening was not a nightmare. Though Momma called, "Yalka!" I pretended not to hear. When she finally shook me, I got up but avoided looking at her. I followed her into the kitchen and was surprised to find cereal waiting for me like on any other morning. I was even more surprised that I ate as if nothing was wrong. I pretended nothing was wrong although a voice in my head echoed, *Poppa's gone!* When I kissed Momma good-by, her cheeks were wet. She pretended she wasn't crying until I couldn't hide my tears. We didn't mention the other's crying or we couldn't have gone on with the day. Momma held me longer than usual and I clung to her. Finally, she said, "Be careful--everything will be all right." I usually left saying, "I will," to whatever she said. But I didn't trust my voice and simply nodded.

Willie's narrow-set eyes observed me. He asked, "You sick?" I wondered what he'd noticed and continued with our spelling. I said, "Journey," and made up a sentence, not knowing what it was until after I'd said it: "The father went on a *journey*." Willie frowned and said, "Your father went on journey!" I quickly said, "*Journey* is the spelling word." Willie was weak in academic skills, but I was discovering that he shrewdly read people. He spelled, "J-e-r-n-y." Later, Miss Cleary walked over and picked up his test paper. She nodded. "Good. You spelled 'journey' correctly." Clarence tried to hide his frown.

I had selected an article before Uncle Sol came over and in Current Events brought the class up-to-date on Europe: "German soldiers marched into the Sudetenland." Miss Cleary asked, "Now that Chamberlain gave Hitler what he wanted, that should settle things." Poppa and Uncle Sol weren't optimistic. Then Harold surprised us by giving the Chicago Cubs credit for winning the National League Pennant. Of course they had no chance against our Yankees. When he sat down I realized I had forgotten about Poppa! I felt guilty enough for that, but what bothered me more was the thought reminded me: *Who'd bring home the newspaper for Current Events articles?*

At lunch time, my sandwich was waiting on the table. Momma had surrendered to her headache and was lying in bed. I ate everything and put the dish and glass into the sink. On my return to class, we had a rehearsal. A storm had wrecked my North Pole workshop and I hammered the wings back on an angel. Clarence raised his hand. "Al should screw the wings on Pat instead of using nails." He bolstered his case by adding, "If he used a screw driver to fix Harold's leg, he wouldn't have hurt him." When Miss Cleary asked him how he knew about woodwork, he said his grandfather did carpentry work. He was speaking up more in class and to Miss Cleary's credit, she asked me to use a screwdriver. On the way home, Harold said I should have known not to use a hammer. He was talking to me again.

That afternoon the Hebrew class was as talkative as ever. The class quieted down and I was roused only when Mrs. Schwartz distributed the scripts for the play--*Chanukah, the Glory of the Maccabees--The Eternal Struggle for Freedom.* Mrs. Schwartz reviewed the story of Mattathias Maccabee killing the traitor and Antiochus' soldiers and then fleeing to the mountains with his sons. The playwright, Lev Litofsky, was not only an "inspiring" writer, but an "anti-fascist." His friends were trying to get the United States government to let him come here. With the dismissal bell, the class left noisily. I stayed behind and told her that we were trying to get my aunt's family out of Russia." She smiled and said, "I hope you do--before there's a war." She looked as if she regretted saying that. I wanted to ask if Lev Litofsky's friends knew about the smuggler, but my tongue froze. I managed to say, "I like the play." She smiled and handed me the script. "I'll make copies for the class." I thanked her, feeling privileged.

With Poppa gone, time passed slowly and was punctuated with reminders of his absence. Of course I could never forget the World Series, the only acceptable topic of conversation that week. Although I believed myself a loyal Yankee fan, my enthusiasm was negligible compared to Harold's and the other boys. I feared they might discover I didn't know Selkirk's home run record, although I knew DiMaggio's (32). Harold was not the only one with a seemingly total recall of batting averages and countless other statistics. Willie, whose knowledge of world events was Columbus in 1492 and July 4th in 1776, rattled off endless *AB's, BA's, HR's,* and *RBI's..* I discovered later that I was a Baseball Laodicean--having only a lukewarm interest in the sport.

If educators respected what children cherished, that week would have been a national holiday. In Current Events, Harold crowed, "The Yankees have the best batters--DiMaggio, Dickey and Gehrig," as if he had personally signed them up. "The Yankees mightiest siege guns," he waxed eloquently, evoking images that were obviously plagiarized from baseball columnists. The Yankees were "absolutely invincible" and he changed his opinion of the Cubs--"a nondescript outfit that won its pennant through a fluke." He mentioned the two starting pitchers, Charlie Ruffing for "our Bronx Bombers" and "Lefty Lee" for *their* team, concluding with who would win. The class responded with cheers for the Yankees and *Bronx cheers* for the Cubs. Miss Cleary extended liberties to us that no one thought possible.

I remember the final game--after the Yankees won the first three. Miserable as I felt, we sat in our socks in Harold's living room--his mother didn't permit us to walk on her rug with shoes--following each play as dramatically described by the broadcaster, the crowd roaring in response. In the second inning, Harold's mother came in to quiet us. The Yankees, with two out, scored three runs because of an error by Jurges. She said, "They'll hear you in Yankee Stadium!" We didn't bother telling her that today's game was in Chicago. We also reserved the right to shout when necessary, one occasion being O'Dea's homer in the top of the eighth, which brought the Cubs to within one run of a tie. Harold shrieked and rolled from one end of the room to the other. His mother, whose interest in baseball didn't match Harold's, asked, "Why don't you listen like Al?" I wasn't quiet, except in comparison to Harold. I respected his right to yell louder and carry on more because it was his apartment. Besides, Harold was such an avid fan, it would have been hypocritical for me to be as boisterous. Pandemonium broke out in the stadium and in Harold's living room when the Yankees scored four more runs in the eighth inning. Harold screamed and jumped, ignoring his mother's threat not to let him listen to another game. She didn't know that with this victory the series was over. Afterwards, Harold strutted about as if his allegiance was as important to the Yankee's victory as Rugging's, the pitcher for all nine innings. Harold didn't have to say, "Wait until I tell the class!"

I remember more vividly than the World Series, our calling Poppa. Momma told us after supper, so we wouldn't be too excited to eat. Since we didn't have a telephone, we'd have to go out to call him. She dressed as carefully as if she were going visiting, including lipstick and rouge, but not her corset. She belted her coat tightly and she asked, "I hope I look all right." Then she rushed through her gas and doorknob-checking. Once outside, Morris and I raced down Fulton Avenue, leaving her behind. Her high heel shoes slowed her down and we waited impatiently. When she caught up, she gasped, "You'll reach Siberia and not know you left me behind--like your father." As we walked ten paces ahead--as if that would speed her up-- Morris muttered, "We could have called from home if we had a phone." He had pestered our parents to get a phone but his pleas went unheeded to frugal Momma. He must have been embarrassed not to have one while his Stuyvesant High School friends did.

Of course we couldn't call from Harold's parents' store-- they'd learn all our business--and continued to a Washington Avenue candy store. The public telephone was on a back wall surrounded by racks of toys and cartons of syrup bottles. Morris said, "Everybody can hear us." Momma said, "No one's here," ignoring the owner in front. She handed Morris a nickel from a purse bulging with coins. Morris, whom I doubted ever made a long distance call, skimmed the directions on the phone box. He asked the operator, "Atlanta, Georgia," and looked surprised when the coin was returned. He listened to the operator and deposited coins, each one clanging loudly. We heard a "bah-bah" noise and the operator told him the line was busy. He hung up and gave Momma a *If-we-had-our-own-phone!* look. Her look said, *Don't-start-with-me, Morris!* The store owner walked over and asked, "Can I help you?" Morris shook his head and called again, dropping in the coins more quickly. Then, "Uncle Yitzchok? Morris... Fine... How are you?... Is my father there?... Pop? Hello!" Momma gratefully raised her hands, as pleased as Alexander Graham Bell when Watson came running to him. Morris said, "Fine... Okay... Here's Mom." He handed her the receiver. Despite her familiarity with Mrs. Stone's phone, Momma squinted at this wall phone's ear piece. Morris pointed to the mouthpiece. She stood on her toes and shouted, "Hello? Mordcha? This is Surah." Then, "I can't hear--talk louder!" Morris went, "Shh-not so loud," but Momma ignored him as she said, "I'm all right, the children are all right... You taking care of yourself?... Is it cold?... Take care--here's Morris." Morris said, "It's Morris again... School's okay..."

I pulled desperately on Morris' arm but he shook my hand off. Only when he said to Poppa, "Yeah, he's here," did he thrust the receiver into my hands. I froze and Morris commanded, "Talk, it's long distance!" I managed to say, "Hello? Poppa?" His "Hello, Yalka" sounded unfamiliar and distant. I was grateful that he asked, "How are you?" but after answering, "I'm fine," didn't know what else to say. Morris said, "Hurry up!" I asked, "How are you?" Morris muttered, "He said he's all right!" prevented me from hearing Poppa's answer. But Poppa went on to say. "Take care of yourself." I said, "Good-by and handed the ear piece back to Morris. He gave it to Momma, who repeated several versions of, "Good-by, take care."

We walked home in silence. The familiar streets looked strange in the dim glow of the street lights. When we were in bed, Momma said, "I forgot to tell your father that I miss him."

Eleven

Dyed Morozh

The next major event was the Christmas play. We rehearsed the scene when Jane, Mrs. Santa, comes on stage and I tell her, "With all these toys to fix, Mrs. Santa, I don't think I'll have them ready for Christmas." Jane answered, "Santa, you say that every year and you're always ready." She was much taller than me and had a round, cheerful face, framed with long blond hair. She was overweight and Willie didn't fail to whisper at least once during a rehearsal--if Miss Cleary couldn't overhear--"Fat Santa has a fat wife." With the rehearsal over, Miss Cleary reminded us that we should give our mothers enough time to make our costumes. With all the excitement, I'd forgotten to tell Momma about the play!

On the way home, Harold said, "My Mom is using crepe paper to make my costume." Momma, I knew, would use material. After entering the apartment, I stood in the kitchen doorway and watched her prepare supper. Finally, I asked, "Remember the play, Momma?" She turned. "The Chanukah play?" I *had* remembered to tell her about that one. "No--the one in public school. It's 'A Special Christmas Story.' I've got the biggest part--Santa Claus!"

Her expression changed. Did she knew who he was? I explained, "He gives children presents and wears a red suit."

"Dyed Morozh?" she asked.

I nodded, figuring that was Santa Claus in Russian.

She asked, "The holiday for the Christian God?" She never referred to Christ by name. I ignored her shocked expression and told her that parents would be invited. She asked, "How could Miss Cory ask *you* to be *their* saint?"

I shouted, "It's an American play!"

Her jaw tightened. "The worst pogroms were on that holiday!"

Morris entered and walked past us with a "Hi." Momma said, "Not another word! Tell Morris we'll be eating in ten minutes." The discussion was over.

"You look sick," said Morris. I was too dumbfounded to explain. When we sat down at the table, Morris suspected something and asked, "Is Pop okay?" Momma said, "Your father's fine," and gave me a sharp look. Half-way through the meal, I perked up, thinking, just because she didn't *like* the play didn't mean she'd *prevent* me from being in it. She was really angry at the anti-Semites in Russia. I finished everything on my plate not because I had an appetite. Morris noticed and said, "For someone who looks sick, you sure were hungry."

After supper, Morris went to a friend's. I built up my courage to return to the kitchen, where Momma was strangely calm. She made me sit and said, "On that holiday the peasants would beat and kill Jews. It was terrible under the Czar and worse during the revolution." She concluded, "Your teacher will understand why you can't be in the play."

I gave my arguments: It's a *play*-- an *American* play; Christmas is a public school holiday; Miss Cleary expects me to be Santa Claus. I paused after each reason, but realized they were lightweight compared to hers. Besides, Momma wasn't listening. She put her fingers to my lips and said, "You can't be in this play!" I fled to the living room. Tears stung my eyes. I was sitting in the dark when Morris returned. He switched on the light. "What's wrong?" I blurted it out. To my relief he said, "That doesn't make sense." I followed him to the kitchen. If anyone could convince Momma, it was Morris.

Momma was drinking tea--she rarely took breaks from her chores. Morris hesitated, but said, *"Everybody* celebrates Christmas in public school." He didn't pause for Momma to do more than look up. "It's an *American* holiday-" His explanation and tone left no doubt as to the disloyalty of anyone, particularly the foreign born, to object. He gave one convincing argument after another, bolstering my cause and soothing my distress. When he finished, Momma said, "If *they* celebrate Christmas, it's *their* business. We're Jews." She told Morris what she'd told me with new rhetorical flourishes, including, "The part the Jews played in the celebration was being victims in pogroms." She had honed her arguments to dagger-point sharpness. When Morris interrupted with, "Al's playing Santa Claus isn't going to start a pogrom-" my rapid heartbeat signaled that Morris was losing not only the argument, but his cool as well. He seemed unaware he was adding fuel to the flame of her anger. She asked, "Only a play? Pogroms are *play?*" She didn't need to look upward for support from Him or her Invisible Audience. Morris' "Ma, that was Europe, not here," resulted in Momma asking, "Christians here are different from those in Europe? What about the boy who beat up your brother?" She marshaled more anti-Semites by mentioning the German Bund parades in New York! Whatever hope I had completely vanished. Morris' "We have the Bill of Rights-" were eloquent but wasted on her. She recounted the 1920 pogrom, in which everyone in her house was killed except her and her mother. She even added an argument I had not heard before: "You think the Christian mothers want a Jewish Santa Claus?"

"Oh, Ma," said Morris, throwing up his hands. His gesture of despair looked more like a surrender. He walked out and I followed. He had tried his best, but only made things worse. My situation, bleak enough before, was now hopeless.

Later, Momma appeared in the living room doorway. "I have enough worries with your father! If *he* had listened to me, he wouldn't have had to run away!" If it wasn't bad enough to link the play to the union, she concluded with, "You've given me another headache!"

That night, I dreamt I was in Chernobyl. I ran frantically through the muddy streets until I found the thatched-roof house and knocked on the door. Momma drew back in terror. I shouted, "It's me, Al--Yalka," but her eyes showed disbelief. I reached out and noticed my sleeves were red. I was wearing a Santa costume: a pillow puffing out my pants, a red cap on my head and a cotton beard pasted to my face. Momma turned to her mother, whom I recognized from a photo, and yelled, "That's not Yalka! That's the man who celebrates the birth of the *goyisha* God!" Momma

111

and her mother pushed me out the door. When I heard hoof beats behind me, I knew it was the Cossack who killed Poppa's cousin. When he rode closer, I shouted, "I'm Santa Claus!" Willie came out of an alley and shouted, "No! He's the Bronx Jew-boy!"

"Another nightmare!" It took Morris a while to convince me where I was.

On the way to school the next morning, Harold asked, "Is your mother going to sew a Santa outfit?" The bright morning sun light dimmed: how would I tell Miss Cleary? Whenever Miss Cleary looked at me, I thought my expression gave me away. That was especially true during the rehearsal. I trembled whenever she interrupted to make a comment, thinking she'd reveal my secret to the class.

On Friday night, I had an idea and the next morning, couldn't wait for the service in shul to end. For the first time, I was impatient as Grandpa lingered in the vestibule when we had *Shabbes* cake and drinks. One of the men, patting his ample stomach, said his doctor told him to lose weight. Grandpa said, "What a fat belly costs, I wish I had; what it does, I wish on my enemies." They laughed. Another man said, "Doctors can cure anything, except poverty." More laughter. Grandpa said, "Show me a doctor who can cure old age." They laughed even louder.

Outside, Grandpa closed the collar of his coat against the cold. "It's a shame your father being away." That reminder made me feel guilty--here I was worrying about the play and Poppa was gone. I asked, "Think Poppa will find a business in Atlanta?" Grandpa was silent for a while and then, "I know my sons. Yitzchok has the head for business. Sol is *charming-*" he used the word *bachant-* "and makes a living from his store. Your father is a worker and idealist. The Midrash says a trade is as important as studying the Torah." Silence again before, "I still would have loved spending more time studying." He sighed. "One has to make a living, whether in Russia or America." I was pleased that he talked to me as if I were an adult, yet he patted my back and said, "You listen patiently to an old man's ramblings." Then, "Let's hope there's an end soon to the gangster and immigration troubles." As we walked up the dark stairs of the apartment building, he stopped for longer pauses than usual on each half flight. I thought it was his winter coat.

After our *Shabbes* meal, when we sat down in the living room, I asked, "Do you know about Santa Claus?" His thick eyebrows came close together and I was about to translate when he said, *"Dyed Morozh."* I burst out, "I'm *Dyed Morozh* in a public school play--my teacher picked me--but Momma says Christmas is a Christian holiday, that they killed Jews in Russia-"

Grandma entered. "What's this about *Dyed Morozh?"* Grandpa told her. She frowned. "What could be bad about Yalka being in a play? I don't understand her." Grandpa answered, "Surah remembers the pogroms on that holiday." Grandma frowned. *"I* don't? But that was *there."*

I said, "The teacher is *depending* on me! Morris told Momma Christmas was an American holiday."

Grandma said, "Anshul, talk to her--she'll listen to you."

I looked hopefully at Grandpa. He sighed and said to Grandma, "I can't tell her what to do." Then to me, "I'll try to talk to her." When I left, Grandma gave me a piece of *kugel* and said, "Have a big piece--you earned extra by going to *shul."*

As I walked home, I kept repeating *Dyed Morozh,* and held my breath and blinked, hoping Grandpa could change Momma's mind. When I got home I ran straight to the bedroom and above the noise of the sewing machine shouted, "Grandpa said there's nothing wrong with my being *Dyed Morozh!'""*

Momma let the whirring slow down before she turned to me. Her expression revealed my miscalculation. "Is that what your grandfather said?" Her lips pursed and her brow furrowed. "Or your grandmother?" Then, "Don't drag your grandparents into this! That play is not for a Jewish boy." As she started the treadle, "There'll be other plays."

I shouted, "I don't want to be in any other play!" I was angrier at myself than Momma. After supper, I told Morris what happened. He said what I already knew, "You should have let Grandpa do the talking. When Mom makes up her mind-" He shook his head. That was something I also knew. Almost as an afterthought, he asked, "Where's your play?" I took it out of my book bag and handed it to him. He put it on the side of his desk.

Sunday night, Uncle Sol came for a visit. He greeted me with "How's the boxer?" Momma looked at him sternly. He gripped my shoulders and said, "Peace is important! God's word is *Shalom*." When she went to the bedroom, he whispered, "But if an anti-Semite starts anything, hit him in the *kishkas*." Downcast as I was, I couldn't help laughing.

When Momma returned, he waved my knickers, saying, "You can't find where it was torn with a magnifying glass." He picked up the Chanukah script on the couch and grinned. "Lev Litofsky's a fiery writer whose heroes give it to those bastards." The Yiddish word *momzer* doesn't have the harsh connotations of its English translation, but Momma gave him a sharp look. He shifted his mustache skittishly and said, "We Jews could use Maccabees to teach Hitler a lesson!"

Momma asked, "More fighting? We didn't come across the ocean to fight another war."

Sol said, "We don't make wars, but we have to defend ourselves."

Momma said, "Better a dog in peacetime, than a soldier in a war."

Sol countered, "I heard that, too, but with a Hitler-"

Momma looked at the ceiling. "Why does God permit such troubles?"

Sol followed her gaze and said, "It's a good thing God's in heaven. If He lived on earth, people would knock out all His windows." He laughed and Momma smiled. "Fortunately, God lets us defend ourselves."

I said, "God let the Maccabees fight the Assyrians on the Sabbath."

Sol patted me on the head. "You're a lawyer, too." He put the script down. "Don't give up school to become an actor. It's not something you make a living from, unless you're a Maurice Schwartz or Molly Picon."

I was about to ask him if he thought I should play Santa Claus, but Momma's expression said, *Don't-bring-up-that-goyisheh-play!* She asked about his helper, Yussie, and he answered, "Not only can't he bring his family over, he's having trouble himself." He whispered *omlegal,* meaning "illegal." Momma shook her head. "Where can the Jews escape to?" Sol whispered, "Shanghai." Momma frowned and he explained, "Shanghai, China, is the only place in the whole world that lets Jews in without a passport and no questions asked. That's the truth, so help me, God!"

Momma asked, "How can they make a living in China?"

He shrugged. "At least they live. Roosevelt's afraid to help us because of all the anti-Semites in Congress." Then, "What does Mordcha say?"

On cue, Momma took a letter out of her apron pocket. "Everything's all right. He misses us and hopes we'll be together soon." She sighed. "He never writes bad news. In Warsaw, when he was having trouble getting a visa, he'd write 'Everything's all right.'"

Sol said, "From trouble can come a blessing, like Yitzchok helping him find a business."

Momma said, "From my troubles come only more troubles."

Sol asked, "We've survived for over five thousand years!"

Momma looked up at the ceiling. "But with such suffering."

"Remember?" asked Sol, a glint in his eye as his voice deepened. "Oh, God, what an honor You've chosen us from all the nations-'" Momma joined in, "Five thousand years is long enough! Can't You make someone else the Chosen People?" They laughed. Sol turned to me. "That's in a Litofsky play." He pursed his lips. "But Surah, if we didn't suffer so, how would we know we were Jews?"

Momma didn't laugh. She turned on the light. The room had darkened so gradually I didn't notice. "You bring us laughter."

He answered, "If you can't help, the least you can do is sigh with them." The Yiddish *krechts* is a more powerful word than its English "sigh." He kissed her cheek and whispered, "Have patience and faith."

"My patience I wore out waiting in Warsaw," said Momma. "And faith is-" she sighed before using two words I memorized and asked Grandpa what they meant: *mishkoyles* and *rizikalish-*

- "precarious" and "risky." She shook her head. "I never dreamed it would happen here."

Sol said, "Life is inventive."

Momma said, "I don't mind when it's ordinary or boring."

The bell rang--Grandpa! He said he was "taking a walk" and decided to see how we were doing. Sol said he could have driven him, but Grandpa said he enjoyed the walk. Momma served everybody tea and when Grandpa asked how Mordcha was doing, Momma cried. "Everything was going so well with Mordcha working most of the year." When she asked, "Why did he have to jump into this union craziness?" she became angry.

Sol tried to calm Momma by saying, "God's name is *Shalom*, but, alas, man is only man and sometimes not even that."

I was half-listening to the conversation, wondering if Grandpa intended to mention the school play. But it was Momma who said, "Yalka's schoolteacher asked him to be that Christian saint in a play. Can you imagine a teacher asking a Jewish boy to play their God?" She glanced at me. "There'd be a *pogrom!*""

Grandpa said, "Surah, that's the old country. And *Dyed Morozh* isn't a God."

Momma looked at him severely. "Is there a difference between the *old* and the *new* country? I was in the old one for those eight years when you and Mordcha's brothers were here. Yalka will understand when he's older." This was the first time I'd seen her angry with Grandpa. My eyes were stinging when Sol said, "But Yalka is an actor--Paul Muni plays a Christian fugitive in that movie, but that doesn't mean-"

Momma turned to the two of them: "You're ganging up on me! The poor boy doesn't have a father around to make him do what's right--don't undermine his mother." Momma noticed Morris in the doorway. "Don't act the *zakonodatel!*" I didn't need her to translate "an interpreter of the Torah." Despite her anger, she was on the verge of tears. So was I and ran from the room.

That night, when I was in bed, Morris asked, "What did your teacher say about your not playing Santa Claus?"

There was a long pause before I whispered, "I didn't tell her."

His reply was a loud "What!" But he was decent enough not to say another word. I tossed for a long time before falling asleep. And then-

"What?" exclaimed Miss Cleary. "You're telling me ten minutes before the performance that you can't play Santa Claus!" The whole class, dressed in their costumes, looked accusingly at me. Willie, in his Blitzen outfit, threatened to beat me up. Pat flapped her wings as she said, "All the angels in heaven will curse you!" Clarence, dressed as *Donder,* asked, "Why didn't you run away?" Harold said, "I won't be able to be the *Wooden Soldier with the Broken Leg*--you're not my friend!" Above the shouts and accusations, I said, "I can't be Santa Claus because I'm Jewish." Miss Cleary said, "Jews always make trouble!" Momma was right, just wait long enough and a Christian shows his anti-Semitism. Mr. O'Hare came onto the stage. "You're a disgrace! We can't have you stay in P.S. 4!" Then the detectives that visited Momma appeared. The tall one said, "We'll have to ship him back to where he came from." I screamed, "My mother said I was born in Bronx Hospital!" The detective said, "We don't trust your mother. Nor your father--he lied on his citizenship application!" Miss Cleary said, "The Bronx is in Russia, Al said so himself." Willie and several other classmates shouted, "We heard him!" Morgan wrote that down in his notebook. Willie shouted, "Fatso Russian-Bronx, Al!" The whole class burst out laughing.

I woke up in a sweat and was afraid to fall asleep again.

Twelve

Sisters in suffering

I was the unhappiest child in P.S. 4 that next day--or in the entire history of the school. Willie and Clarence could tell from the way I looked. Willie joked, "Did your horse come in last?" Just before dismissal, Harold gestured excitedly toward the door: Morris! Miss Cleary turned in the direction of our stares. Although Morris looked his usual self--round-faced and serious, with his school tie and jacket--I couldn't believe it was him. Miss Cleary gestured him in and he hesitantly entered.

Harold called, "Al's brother!"

The bell rang. Miss Cleary asked Jane to take the class down and me to stay. As the class filed out, all heads turned toward us. When the last pupil was out the door, Miss Cleary gave Morris a *What-brings-you-here?* look. Morris shifted from one foot to the other and she asked that question aloud.

Avoiding her stare, he said, "The Christmas play." Then he glanced at me, but my tongue was frozen.

Miss Cleary said, "I hope your whole family can come."

Morris took a deep breath. "We can't." A quizzical expression crossed her face. "Our mother doesn't want Al playing Santa Claus."

Now she looked confused. "It's the best part!"

"We're Jewish and--and-" Morris spluttered.

She looked at me, but my eyes were on my high-top shoes. Morris regained his voice. "We don't celebrate Christmas. Our mother comes from Russia--on Christmas there were pogroms, Christians killed Jews."

"She won't let Al be in the play?" She looked at me. "Why didn't you tell me?"

My mouth opened but no words came out.

119

Morris said, "Al *wants* to be in the play. We told our mother that Christmas here was different-"

She interrupted with a worried, "There isn't enough time for someone else to learn the part."

Morris explained, "Al hoped our mother would change her mind."

Did you tell her it's a public holiday?" Morris nodded and she shook her head. " How could Santa Claus offend anyone?"

"We have a Jewish holiday that's like Christmas," said Morris.

She interrupted, "Khanukah--you also exchange gifts."

For a moment I was afraid Morris would correct her pronunciation, but he took a paper out of his pocket and hesitantly asked, "If you could add some lines, on page eight, where Santa says-" He read from the play. "Ho, ho, I've brought Christmas presents to all good children of the land, from the first days of that noble Pilgrim band' -- if you could change it to, 'I bring Christmas and Chanukah presents to children of all faiths in the land, from the first days of the noble Pilgrim band-" He looked up uncertainly.

"Christmas and *Khanukah* presents?" It was several seconds before she recovered with, "I've been giving Christmas plays for over twenty-five years and no one has suggested *that*. Another Jewish boy played Santa Claus--I'm *flabbergasted!*" I'd never seen her as uncertain about anything. She asked Morris for his name and where he went to school. After he told her, she said, "You must be smart."

Morris looked embarrassed and mumbled, "I study a lot."

She turned to me. "Do you plan to go to Stuyvesant?" I nodded. I'd never told Morris that. Then, to Morris, "Khanukah is a Jewish holiday--it may be against the law to mention a religious holiday in a public school play." She shook her head. "In all my years of teaching-" Then, glancing at the clock, "Nice meeting you, Morris." Her expression changed when she turned to me. "I wish you told me sooner!"

Morris said, "Glad to have met you. Al talks about you."

I followed Morris out. When we reached Fulton Avenue, I asked, "Will Miss Cleary change the play?"

His, "I don't know," wasn't reassuring.

"Will you tell Momma you saw Miss Cleary?" He gave me the same answer.

Momma didn't say anything about our coming home together. She did ask him about his club meeting. "I didn't go," he answered. Morris missed his Airplane Club meeting! Later that evening, when I was in bed, I told Morris, "I never thought of saying anything about Chanukah in the play."

He answered, "That's what big brothers are for."

I said, "Thanks." Then, minutes later, I asked, "What does *flabbergasted* mean?"

"Je-sus! Look it up in the dictionary!"

The next day, I looked away whenever Miss Cleary glanced at me, which seemed once a minute. I didn't have to guess what she was thinking. Every time she spoke, I dreaded she'd tell the class. Worse was the rehearsal, when I said lines that Miss Cleary also knew would never be heard in P.S. 4's auditorium. Stage fright was difficult enough, now I felt myself an impostor. When I looked at Betty, I saw *Betty,* not Mrs. Claus. Fortunately, she spoke first and all I had to do at the beginning of the scene was stand there, *Looking very tired*, and *holding an empty bag,* "Santa," said Mrs. Claus, her voice unmistakably Betty's, "it's time we had a party at the North Pole for you and all our toy-makers!"

"That's a wonderful idea. My helpers have worked very hard and deserve a party. *Shake empty bag and look upset*, " which I didn't find hard to do. I explained, "I've given away all the presents. What can I give our toy-makers?" Miss Cleary interrupted the play. "We'll stop." Did anyone else notice that she could have let us rehearse another five minutes? As we waited impatiently on line for the dismissal bell, Miss Cleary called, "Al!" This was the moment I had dreaded most, but all she did was hand me an envelope and say, "Give this to your mother." I slipped it into my book bag. As we went down the stairs, Willie whispered, "Al's in trouble! His mother has to come to school."

When I got home, I put my book bag underneath the sofa, with my hidden comic books. I tried to look forlorn so Momma would not suspect anything. Only when Morris came home did I take out the letter. He looked at the school envelope and said, "It's from your school--and it's addressed to Mom."

"I know that! Miss Cleary said you should explain it to her."

"I'd better open it in front of her," he said.

"Can't we open it *now?* You'll have to read it to her."

He shook his head. "It's against the law--give it to her after supper."

I moaned. Supper took a hundred years in coming. Momma was shocked to see me while her first call echoed through the apartment. Although I had little appetite, I quickly downed my food. Morris ate in slow motion, my stares not speeding him up. I left the table and waited for him in the living room. As soon as he entered, I asked, "Now?" He looked at his wrist watch. "Too soon." I groaned. He was following the family rule to the letter: not only to postpone serious news until after supper, but to wait until digestion was complete.

Fifteen minutes later, I followed him into the kitchen, my eagerness now dampened with apprehension. Fortunately, he did the talking. "Mom?" She looked at us, suspicion spreading across her face. She was sitting at the table, re-reading a letter from Poppa. "Al's teacher sent you a letter." He held it up for her.

Always the optimist, she asked, "What's wrong?"

Morris took that as permission to tear it open. "Dear Mrs. Segal," He read slowly, his eyes scanning ahead. My heart thumped at the double suspense--discovering what Miss Cleary had written and Momma's reaction. "It was a pleasure meeting your older son, Morris, who explained your feelings-'"

"Meeting your older son, Morris?" Momma repeated.

Morris ignored her accusing stare and continued, "-about Al playing Santa Claus. I've talked over the matter with Principal Preston and would like to talk to you personally. Could you arrange to come in to see me as soon as possible? Signed, Katherine L. Cleary." He met Momma's stare for the first time. "Al's teacher wants to see you."

After a long silence, Momma asked, "Yalka's teacher wants to see me?" Morris nodded. She asked, "You went to Yalka's teacher?" He nodded again. "Why? Yalka told her he's not in the play." She looked at me. "Didn't you?"

I was grateful Morris continued, "I talked to Miss Cleary about putting something about Chanukah in the play, so it wouldn't be just for Christians."

Momma looked from Morris to me. "Didn't you tell her?"

My silence was answer enough. Angrily, yet solemnly, she said, "I swear to-" That was the beginning of her Oath to God! When she swore to Him, especially reinforcing her vow with a pledge of "Over my dead body!" any retraction was impossible! Even if God was reasonable enough to reconsider, Momma's Oath prevented it. I was too paralyzed to say anything.

"Mom!" pleaded Morris, frantically waving the letter to distract her. "Miss Cleary wants to talk to you!" I don't know whether it was Morris' letter-waving or Miss Cleary's wanting to see her that interrupted her Oath and left the matter in the hands of mortals. "Miss Cleary talked to the principal--the head of the school!"

"The teacher and the principal?" asked Momma, obviously impressed enough not to swear hastily. "What's there to talk about? Yalka can't be Santa Claus!"

Morris read from the letter, "I'd like to talk to you personally. Could you arrange to come in to see me?"

Momma's lips pursed the way they did when she didn't want to do something but hadn't figured out a way of avoiding it. "What's there to talk?"

Momma was on uncertain grounds with the request coming from the school authorities rather than us, a cunning maneuver. Just to make sure, he dangled the official letter aloft and said, "Maybe she wants to find out more about Chanukah." Momma's expression of distrust deepened. Morris guessed another reason for her uneasiness. "Al will be with you." I took the cue, quickly agreeing, "I'll be there."

She looked at me suspiciously. I knew what she was thinking: how could she trust me to translate after my deceit? I blinked and held my breath. This was my last chance, if it wasn't too late. Morris placed the letter on the table and walked back to the living room. I followed. In the safety of our living room, he whispered, "Let her be." Morris knew it best that Momma be left alone to think over this unforeseen turn of events.

I didn't venture into the kitchen until I went for my bedtime snack. Momma quickly put away the letter. I sat with my eyes on my cupcake and milk.

"Yalka," said Momma, "if you told your teacher you couldn't be in this Christian play, I wouldn't have to go to school to see Miss Cory." Her eyes narrowed accusingly. My heart pounded. I had sense enough not to correct her mispronouncing my teacher's name. *One* careless word could reverse her decision. I held my breath as she said, *"If* I go, don't think it's going to change my mind." Before I could leave, she mumbled something about "all the trouble" I caused her, "starting way back."

When I was back in the living room, I whispered to Morris, "She *might* go."

His warning: "Just keep your big mouth shut!" was unnecessary. Only when I was in bed did she come to our doorway. "I wish your father was here. Fathers think all they have to do is make money and the rest is easy. *Gayen tsu kind* was the hardest part I thought, not realizing what mothers had to suffer afterwards."

Morris casually asked, "When will you go?"

She held up the letter. "Tomorrow morning--his teacher wants to see me right away." She kissed me perfunctorily and said, "My mother used to say, 'Little children don't let you sleep; big ones don't let you live.' I didn't understand her when I was small, like you don't understand. Just wait until you have children." Then, to Morris, "Don't stay up late." When she closed the door, I sat up. "What does *gayen tsu kind* mean?"

Morris turned from his desk. "It's when a mother has a baby--don't you know *anything?"* I lay down, relieved, until Morris said, "What I wouldn't give to be there tomorrow."

I sat up in panic. I'd have gladly traded places with him. Later, when Morris got into bed, he whispered, "Good luck! I hope it works out." He knew I wasn't sleeping. I was thinking about translating Momma's Yiddish to Miss Cleary and her English to Momma. In front of the whole class! Apprehension replaced jubilation. I tossed restlessly, angry at Morris for getting me into this predicament.

I did not have to wait until the morning to find out about "the personal talk." When I fell asleep, Momma was sitting at Miss Cleary's desk. The two women could not be more different: one Irish-American and born in this country, tall and authoritative, a college graduate; the other Jewish and born in a Russian *shtetl,* never having attended school a single day, plump and insecure, so short that her feet did not reach the floor. They eye each other warily, then start talking. Miss Cleary speaks first, her voice and facial expressions familiar enough; Momma's mannerisms are equally familiar. First one speaks, then the other, back and forth, no need for me to translate. Each listens respectfully to the other before replying. I can't understand a single word! Each is speaking a *different* language, neither English nor Yiddish. I wonder, *How can they understand each other?* but that doesn't stop their chattering. Willie grins from ear to ear and calls out to me. I know they're taunts despite their being in a third strange language! Miss Cleary ignores him, although he has the whole class laughing. When I open my mouth, no words came out. When they finally do, I talk in a fourth strange language! Everyone bursts out laughing at me--Miss Cleary, Momma, Willie, Clarence, the whole class!

I don't know how many times Momma had to call to wake me. I ate breakfast while she dressed. "We'll be late," she called. I went through all of my morning preparations as slowly as possible, while Momma, in her going out dress, reminded me of the time. I still don't know how she got into her corset without Poppa. Her black wavy hair was carefully brushed, her cheeks rouged and her lips crimson with lipstick. On the way, we met Harold. Of all days. Unable to contain his curiosity, he asked, "You going shopping?" Momma replied, "I'm going to see your teacher, Miss Cory." Harold said, "Parents need a pass." I had forgotten. I told Momma, "Go in the front--room 204. My teacher's name is Miss *Cleary!"* Momma hesitated before heading toward the entrance. I walked on with Harold, wondering if she'd remember the room *and* my teacher's name. Harold waited for an explanation, but I kept looking ahead. He asked, "She's going to see Miss Cleary about your costume!" He sounded pleased to have figured it out. I didn't correct him.

"You're in trouble," said Willie, when he saw me glancing toward the door. If Clarence noticed my nervousness, he didn't say anything. I helped Willie with the spelling and explained my history notes to Clarence, all the while wondering where Momma was. She could easily get lost in any store larger than the small shops on Bathgate Avenue! Was she wandering about, unable to make herself understood? When a monitor entered and handed Miss Cleary a note, my worries about Momma's disappearance turned into a panic that she *would* materialize. And she did, stepping into the doorway and standing there uncertainly. Everyone stared at her.

"Al's mother!" Harold may have thought he whispered, but every eye turned from Momma to me.

Miss Cleary stood up. "Jane, you'll be monitor." Then, to the others, "Your work's on the board. Answer in complete sentences." She beckoned me and I followed. I heard whispering behind me and it was unnecessary for Harold to again announce, "That's Al's mother."

"I'm glad to meet you, Mrs. Segal," Miss Cleary said to Momma outside the classroom. "I'm Miss Cleary, Al's teacher."

Momma, in surprisingly understandable English, said, "I am glad to meet you, too."

I was relieved that Miss Cleary made the introductions and Momma answered in English, but my heart was pounding. Miss Cleary said, "Mr. O'Hare said we could meet in his office." I wondered whether I should walk alongside Momma or Miss Cleary. Or, as a seasoned monitor, lead the way. My indecision settled the matter because Miss Cleary started down the hall with Momma at her side. I hurried after them. Momma was dwarfed next to Miss Cleary, barely coming up to her shoulder. Miss Cleary said, "I hope you didn't interrupt your day," and Momma answered, "No bother." We entered Mr. O'Hare's empty office and Miss Cleary gestured for Momma to sit in the chair beside the desk. After Momma sat down, Miss Cleary settled into Mr. O'Hare's chair. I remained in the doorway and Miss Cleary had to tell me to pull up a chair. I had a full view of Miss Cleary's face above the back of Momma's head.

"I'm glad you came," said Miss Cleary. She took Momma's silence as a signal to continue. "I met your older son--he's a pleasant and bright young man." Momma's head bobbed appreciatively and she mumbled "Morris," as if wanting to confirm which son Miss Cleary was referring to. Miss Cleary glanced over Momma's head at me and said, "Al is one of my best pupils." Momma's head bobbed again and then turned to look at me. I held my breath, fearful she'd call me *Yalka*, a possibility I hadn't considered until then. Fortunately, Miss Cleary leaned back in the swivel chair, which tilted dangerously until she righted herself. The noise drew Momma's attention to Miss Cleary, who recovered and said, "Morris said you were upset about the play." She waited for Momma, who after a long silence, said, "Christmas is not our-" She turned to me and whispered, *"Yom tov."* I translated, "Holiday." Momma continued, "I don't want you to be-" she paused but in perfect English said, "insulted."

Miss Cleary said, "Every year we have a Christmas play that includes *all* the children. You have a holiday like ours."

Momma supplied, "Chanukah."

Miss Cleary nodded. "Yes, I know, Khanukah. You also give presents. I spoke to Mr. Preston, the principal and to Mr. O'Hare, the assistant principal, and we're going to have Al say he's giving presents to children of *all* faiths, those celebrating Khanukah as well as Christmas." She waited.

Finally, Momma asked, "Al will say Chanukah?"

Miss Cleary nodded. "Yes, Al will say-" she read from Morris' paper, "I bring Christmas and Khanukah presents to good children of all faiths-" She looked up at Momma, who repeated, "Al will say-" Momma turned and I read bewilderment in her face. I said, "I'm going to bring *Chanukah* presents." It sounded like a shout in the small office. Momma turned to Miss Cleary and asked, "Al will bring Chanukah presents?" Miss Cleary nodded vigorously. In a loud voice I said in Yiddish, "I'm going to say I give Chanukah presents!" not caring that Miss Cleary was there. Momma, not ready to commit herself, cautiously said,

"If Al says that-" but Miss Cleary smiled and said, "Good!"

I held my breath and blinked, opening my eyes to see Momma nod, her wavy hair rippling. Only when Miss Cleary nodded in synchrony with Momma's, smiled and repeated, "Good," did I really believe what I heard and saw. I don't know who was more elated, Miss Cleary or me.

Miss Cleary leaned toward Momma. "I want you to understand that I'm Irish Catholic, and we've had our share of troubles. My grandfather came from Glencoh in Connemara where a quarter of the population starved or emigrated in the last century because of religious and political persecution." Miss Cleary's expression revealed a pain I'd never seen before and her eyes held steadily onto Momma's.

I didn't see Momma's expression, but she leaned forward and timidly touched Miss Cleary's arm. "I lost most of my family in *pogroms* in Russia before coming to this country. Only my mother and me lived through the pogrom in our town."

Miss Cleary's face was sympathetic. She gripped Momma's hand. "Beneath it all," Miss Cleary said, "we're sisters in suffering." They sat motionless for a few seconds, looking into each other's eyes.

Momma, in a confidential tone, said, "I didn't have the chance to go to school but my father was a learned man, like a rabbi." Miss Clearly listened intently. "He said-" I thought she'd turn to me but she said in English, "There are many religions, but only one God."

Miss Cleary smiled. "That's very wise." She started to get up, but Momma held her arm and whispered, "Maybe you don't know--it's because of the Jews that America was-" she turned to me and said, *"aindekt."* I translated, "Discovered." Miss Cleary looked quizzically at her. Momma continued, "The Jews were chased out of Spain the same year Columbus-" she turned to me but Miss Cleary supplied the word "discovered." Momma nodded. "Torres, a Jew, went with Columbus to find a safe place for the Jews. Without Torres-" Momma's head-shake indicated the perils that would have confronted Columbus had he attempted the voyage without him. She clasped Miss Cleary's arm more tightly. "Some say Columbus was also a Jew, a secret Jew."

"That's very interesting," said Miss Cleary, gently dislodging herself from Momma's grip. "I'm glad you came." She stood up.

"I'm glad to meet you, too," said Momma and shook Miss Cleary's hand. "Al says you're very nice."

Miss Cleary smiled and put her hand on my shoulder. "He's a fine boy. You have two lovely children. You're very fortunate."

Momma smiled modestly. I was terrified that she'd ask Miss Cleary if she planned to get married and have children, but Miss Cleary spoke first. "I've asked the mothers to sew their children's costumes. I've heard about the peasant costume you made for Al in first grade."

Momma beamed appreciatively. "I worked as a dressmaker in Europe and when I first came to this country."

Miss Cleary smiled. "I'm sure it'll be a fine costume."

Outside the office, the monitor was waiting to escort Momma to the front entrance. Momma turned to me and I stepped back. For a moment I thought she was going to kiss me, but she smiled and followed the monitor. On the way back to our classroom, Miss Cleary said, "You have a lovely mother." I tried to think of something to say but couldn't.

When we returned to the classroom, Willie was out of his seat. Miss Cleary punished him with two zeros. Later, Willie whispered, "It's your fault."

I whispered back, "I wasn't here!"

"If your mother hadn't come," he replied, "I wouldn't have gotten into trouble."

I thought, *I'm glad you have a cast.*

Willie muttered, "Soon I'll be out of this cast."

When I got home, Momma was wearing her house dress and slippers as if she hadn't been out. All during lunch I waited for her to say something about her visit. She didn't. Neither did I.

When Morris came home, I told him what happened. He said, "With Miss Cleary saying something about Chanukah, Mom couldn't say No." I didn't mention that he wasn't as confident yesterday. I told him Miss Cleary used his wording. He looked very pleased and said, "That was a stroke of genius thinking that up and writing it down." I couldn't fault his lack of modesty. In fact, I said, "If it wasn't for you-" I told him I was surprised at how much English Momma knew. He whispered, "This morning, before you got up, Mom asked how to say 'I'm glad to meet you, too,' and other words. I reminded her to call you Al- Morris stopped abruptly.

Momma was standing in the doorway. "I'm not sure I did the right thing. What would my father, a religious man think-" She shook her head. "Between you and your brother and Miss Cory mentioning Chanukah-" She shrugged, about to leave, but asked, "What's this costume?"

I didn't give her the letter! I managed to say, "A red suit-"

Momma screwed up her face. "I have to sew a suit for that Christian Saint? On my machine?" She used the idiom, *A bruch iz mir!* meaning either "A disaster!" or "Woe is me!" Then, "Don't think this business is over. I can still go back to school and tell your teacher I made a mistake." She walked out.

Panic spread though me. I turned to Morris, who whispered, "I don't think she'll change her mind after telling your teacher." Then, in an even lower voice, "She does that with Pop when she finally agrees to something she didn't want to." I wasn't as certain until Morris said, "I don't think she wants to speak to your Miss Cory again."

When I was in bed, I asked Morris, "Did you tell Momma about Torres?" Morris looked up. His face was outside the circle of light from his lamp. I said, "Torres, the Jew who helped Columbus discover America."

Morris replied, "Mom told me about him a long time ago."

"Did they really chase the Jews out of Spain in 1492?"

"That, or killed them if they didn't convert."

"That's not in our history book."

"They don't tell you much in school books." He parodied, "In 1492, Columbus sailed the ocean blue-' and Queen Isabella selling her jewels to buy the boats." Much later, Morris asked, "Why did Mom ask me the English for 'There are many religions, but only one God.'?" I pretended to be asleep.

Thirteen

Let Tyrants Remember

While the crisis with the Christmas play was over, at least for the time being, the one with the Chanukah play was yet to begin. We were in the third week of rehearsing the Litofsky play. The politics was complicated: Jason, a Hebrew high priest, helped Antiochus Hellenize the Jews, but some Jews thought Jason too lenient and wanted Antiochus to appoint the more ruthless priest Menelaus. Many Jews remained faithful to the religion of their ancestor but were afraid to do anything. In Mod'in, when a Jew accepted conversion, Mattathias Maccabee slew the traitor and the Assyrian soldiers, starting a rebellion. Mrs. Schwartz chose me to be Mattathias and Lenny volunteered to be the Assyrian captain who enjoyed defiling Jews by making them eat pork. Lenny relished the line, "Kill this pig and eat its flesh," while I preferred, "As a priest and elder of Mod'in, I will not obey your heathen law." During one rehearsal, he was carried away and pushed me. I ad-libbed, "Your king Antiochus is a pig and a *meshugenah!*" While the king preferred the Greek name *Epiphanes,* "Known God," Mrs. Schwartz told us many Jews called him *Epimanes,* the "Madman." Despite Mrs. Schwartz attempts to quiet us, Lenny's soldiers and my sons joined in the shoving match while Mrs. Schwartz pleaded, "Please don't!" Only when she was close to tears did we stop fighting. After dismissal, we lined up outside to continue our struggle. Just then, Rabbi Weiss left the building. As stern and punitive a man as he was, he thought we were rehearsing and complimented us on our dedication. Little did we realize how little he knew about the play.

Later in the play, I was Simon and Lenny was Judah, sons of Mattathias. The play was complicated and several of us played more than one character. Deborah felt that the girls were given only minor parts and Mrs. Schwartz let them be Maccabean warriors as well as wives and mothers. Rabbi Weiss came into observe a rehearsal for the first time, when we were celebrating a victory, but were worried about Lysias, a resourceful Assyrian general. Lenny said, "His army grows." I replied, "Traitors who have adopted Greek ways have joined him." Lenny threatened, "We'll kill the traitors and rouse our loyal brothers to join us!" Jochanan said, "We have no choice." Eleazar said, "We'll retake Jerusalem and our Temple!" We no longer noticed Deborah and Sarah playing the roles of our brothers.

We were doing our best to impress Rabbi Weiss with the play and that Mrs. Schwartz was a good teacher. I sounded as brave as possible planning the defeat of Lysias. Lenny spoke with gusto of the pleasure he'd have in killing the Hebrew traitors and getting others to join our army. Deborah and Sarah were dramatic in words and gestures. Suddenly Deborah stopped in mid-sentence. She was first to see Rabbi Weiss rush toward us. He asked the girls, "Who are you?"

"I'm Jochanan," Deborah answered and noticing Sarah's frozen expression, "Sarah's my brother Eleazar." The rabbi turned to Lenny and asked, "Who are you?" Lenny replied, "Judah." The rabbi, with a shocked expression, asked, "And you're killing Jews?" Lenny looked as if he had been committing murder. The rabbi grabbed the script out Lenny's hand and turned to Mrs. Schwartz. He asked, "Who wrote this?" Mrs. Schwartz barely managed, "Lev Litofsky." He roared, "I wondered who'd make so many Jews traitors? And *force* Jews to join the Maccabees!"

"At this time in the rebellion-" was as far as Mrs. Schwartz got. The rabbi interrupted her with, "Do you want the parents and others in the audience to see Jews killing Jews?" He didn't wait for her answer. "Litofsky makes history serve his politics. *His* leaders are rabble-rousers like himself. Under *God's* will was Jerusalem freed and the Menorah lit. When you said you were doing a play, I thought it would be from the *Bible*,' not from Litofsky!" He commanded me, "Collect the plays!"

I went up and down the aisles, avoiding everyone's eyes. The rabbi grabbed them out my hands and growled at Mrs.

Schwartz, "Step outside!" He walked out and she followed, her face flushed. We remained petrified and had no trouble hearing the rabbi in the hallway. "Did you know he's a Bundist-Socialist? An atheist who makes a mockery of the Bible!" We did not hear Mrs. Schwartz, but his booming rejoinder was, "I didn't think your judgment so poor you'd pick a play by an agitator who'd start a blood bath in Europe! Was it Litofsky's idea to have Mattathias' sons played by *girls?*" We didn't hear her reply, but knew the answer. If we hadn't seen Mrs. Schwartz walk out with him, we'd have thought the rabbi was delivering a wrathful soliloquy, pausing only to answer rhetorical questions. His final pronouncement was not about the play. "I'm very displeased with your class' behavior. You should have better control of those children by now." Rabbi Weiss' footsteps clattered down the hallway. We stared at the door but Mrs. Schwartz did not appear. It was as if she'd vanished before his wrath. Finally, she rushed in, her face turned away. I closed my eyes. When I opened them, she had written Hebrew words on the board with their English meanings. Still facing the board, she said, "Copy your vocabulary, then you may leave." We were the most well-behaved we'd been that term. When we walked out, she was sitting at her desk, facing away. Outside, we scattered. Herschel caught up to me. We fell into step, neither saying a word. He was a tall good-looking boy who said little, yet we enjoyed each other's silent company. When we reached 173rd Street, where he turned off, we gave the Maccabean salute--a gesture we had made up.

I crossed Fulton Avenue to Crotona Park. The fallen leaves crunched sadly under me. The park was a place where I'd effortlessly escape into fantasy, becoming Superman, Running Bear and, more recently, a Maccabee. Rabbi Weiss' anger and Mrs. Schwartz' crying prevented me from conjuring up a fantasy. I didn't then consider the irony of Momma's anger at my being a Christian saint and the rabbi my being a Maccabee. I just started kicking the unfortunate leaves that were the first to fall that Autumn.

The next day, I got to Hebrew school early. Several of my classmates were waiting outside. Deborah expressed our feelings when she said, "He shouldn't have yelled at her like that." We didn't have to speculate on the fate of the play but none of us dared guess what would happen to Mrs. Schwartz. When we entered our classroom, we were relieved to see her. For a moment I thought we had imagined yesterday, but two things were different: she wasn't imploring us to be quiet and not a single pupil even whispered. She greeted us with *"Shalom!"* and in chorus we replied. She asked in Hebrew, "How are you?" and we answered, "We're fine. How are you?" She'd been teaching us Hebrew through conversation. Rabbi Weiss entered to find us completing the conversation part of our lesson and then copying our new Hebrew words without complaint. I was not alone in believing we had proven him wrong about Mrs. Schwartz not being able to control us. He left the room looking disappointed. Mrs. Schwartz took a deep breath as she usually did before telling us a story.

"I've told you about the Book of Genesis," she said, "and today, I'm going to tell you something about Isaiah." We listened attentively. "Before Antiochus, there were other tyrants. When enslaved in Babylon, our people lost hope of ever returning to Jerusalem, but God told Israel they would be His witness before all peoples--'a light unto the nations'--and bring peace to the world." She paused. "This may be hard for you to understand, even grown-ups have trouble." She asked me, "You remember your speech when Antiochus sent 40,000 soldiers against you?"

Of course! She waited and I knew what she wanted. I was more nervous than during a regular rehearsal as I gave the Judah speech: "Our strength is from heaven-" I searched for the words "-they come to destroy us and our wives and children; but we fight for our lives and our Law. It is better for us-" the bell rang. I expected everyone to rush out as usual, but no one moved. "It is better for us to die in battle, than to accept the evil that has befallen our nation." Mrs. Schwartz said, "Though that speech is Litofsky's play, they come word-for-word from the Book of Maccabees. *Shalom.*" We chorused *Shalom* and left quietly. As Herschel and I walked home, we knew something special had happened.

The events at public and Hebrew school had pushed Poppa's

absence into the background of my thoughts. Perhaps I let them because Poppa's absence was so painful. Both Poppa and what made him go to Atlanta were brought to my attention the next morning when I was awakened by Momma's plaintive, "What do you want?" I raced to the doorway and found the reply from a voice I recognized: "Could you let us in!"

I glimpsed the taller detective through the slightly opened door. When he asked, "Want your neighbors to hear?" Momma unchained the door. They stepped inside as arrogantly as the first time. The taller one said, "I have a few more questions."

Momma didn't wait for me to translate. "My husband answered your questions."

He addressed me. "Tell her these are questions for her." He took out his pad and asked, "Are you a citizen?"

Momma said to me in Yiddish, "Next year, I'll apply--tell him." He wrote down what I said. The shorter detective looked uncomfortable as his partner continued his questioning: Where was Momma born, when she came to this country, when she first met the Deutsch and his wife, did she see them only when Poppa was around. He wrote down the answers.

Momma said to me, "Tell him this is our adopted country. We traveled thousands of miles to come here." As I translated as best I could, he looked more and more exasperated. Then Momma asked *him* if he knew what a pogrom was, but he frowned. "Six people in my house were killed, only my mother and me escaped. Just because we were Jews. We were honest, hard-working people-"

The detective interrupted, "These are routine questions, sonny, she doesn't have to get excited. Tell her we know that your father went to Atlanta, but-"

Momma interrupted, "He went to his brother to see about getting a painting business. He'll go wherever he has to make a living for his family."

The shorter one spoke for the first time. "Sonny, tell her not to get upset. Just routine questions in our investigation."

Momma looked from him to the taller one. "What are your names?"

The tall one frowned, then smiled uncomfortably. "I'm detective Morgan and this is detective Cooper."

Momma extended her hand to Morgan and looked up into his face. He was about two feet taller than her and their handshake was awkward. As she stretched out her hand to Cooper, she asked, "Were you born here?" She was no longer using me as a translator.

Morgan replied, "My family didn't come on the Mayflower--shortly afterwards." He laughed. "Don't ask Cooper--his family's shoes are still wet." He laughed but Cooper didn't.

Momma addressed both of them. "We came for a better life. My husband worked from the first day he left Ellis Island. He's honest, never did wrong in his life-"

Morgan said, "Mrs. Segal-"

She ignored him and continued, "This is the *Land of Dreams*. We suffered like everyone in the Depression; now my husband wants a better living-" She turned to me to translate, "We're raising our children to be good citizens, like you-"

Detective Morgan, who'd been nodding, took a couple of steps backward.

Momma asked, "Is he married?" I hesitated, but I asked and then translated for her, "Yes, and he has two children." He took another step backwards.

Cooper answered before I asked. "I'm not married."

Morgan said, "He's a lucky bachelor." He touched the brim of his hat as he said, "Good talking to you, Mrs. Segal." Then he turned to me and after a moment's hesitation, said, "Thanks Yalka." I said, "In school they call me Al."

With his hand behind his back, he opened the door. "You're a good translator, Al."

Detective Cooper nodded and said, "Sorry-"

Momma told me to tell Cooper that he's handsome, that if he doesn't have a girlfriend, he should get one, marry her and have children. I translated that he should get a girl-friend, leaving out the rest. He smiled and as I closed the door, said to Morgan, "She asked more questions than *you!*"

Morgan muttered, "The third-degree!"

I heard laughter through the closed door.

Momma whispered, "Cossacks! especially Morgan." Then, "Sometimes it's best to keep quiet and other times to talk back."

"Let tyrants remember his fate," I quoted in a whisper.

Momma frowned and muttered, "Just when I thought it was all over. If I call your father, he'll say, 'Don't worry-' She shook her head. "My mother had a saying, 'Each day brings its own troubles.' If your father had only listened to me about the union in the first place and-" Noticing my expression, she hugged me and said, "Yalka, why am I bothering your young head with grown-up troubles. Don't worry, everything will be all right." Then she looked at the clock. "Hurry! Dress and I'll make breakfast." Before I left for school, she kissed me and repeated, "Don't worry, everything will be all right."

I was not reassured, but I managed to get through the day. That afternoon, worries about Poppa were displaced with the events at Hebrew School. Mrs. Schwartz' appearance the day after Rabbi Weiss' outburst was too good to be true. Today, after the bell rang, we faced her empty chair. When Rabbi Weiss entered with a bearded young man, I guessed what was up. Rabbi Weiss said, "I'm pleased you're quiet." His smile looked like a sneer. "Mrs. Schwartz is not well." We sat stone-faced. "Mr. Ravitch will be teaching you."

Although we had never seen him, we instantly detested him. If Mr. Ravitch was too nervous to notice, the rabbi wasn't. His squint and tone warned us to behave. "Mr. Ravitch will soon be a rabbi. He'll teach you not only Hebrew and religion, but respect for authority. We'll have our Chanukah play-one we can proudly present to our families and congregation." Our new teacher self-consciously smiled. "Show Mr. Ravitch that you talk only when he calls on you." When the rabbi walked out, his threatening presence remained. We turned our attention to Mr. Ravitch, who was uncertain what to do next, the papers in his hand quivering. We were expert at reading teachers and knew he was inexperienced. He sensed that and was unnerved even more. When Lenny raised his hand--rare for him--Mr. Ravitch asked, "Yes?"

"Where is Mrs. Schwartz?"

"I-I don't know," he faltered. Then, "Let's not waste time--

you have Hebrew words to learn." He turned to the blackboard and looked for chalk. When he couldn't find any, the assurance disappeared from his face. Mrs. Schwartz had learned not to leave chalk on the blackboard ledge--it disappeared only to reappear as missiles. He asked, "Where's the chalk?" Deborah's hand had risen several inches but froze when all eyes turned toward her. Her automatic good-natured response was aborted. Secure no one would tell, we turned to watch him. He walked along the length of the blackboard and back, as if his sheer need for the chalk would make it appear. Then he rummaged through the center drawer of the desk. He pleaded, "Does anyone know where the chalk is?" I felt sorry for him, as Deborah and others surely did, but no hand was raised.

"Mrs. Schwartz didn't give written work," Lenny called out.

"She must have," said Mr. Ravitch. He gestured to Mrs. Schwartz' neat script on the blackboard.

Lenny said, "She told stories and rehearsed the Chanukah play."

Mr. Ravitch took a step toward the door, then stopped. "Someone go to Rabbi Weiss and ask for chalk." When no one volunteered, he looked up and down the rows until his gaze settled on me in the front row. "Go, *please!*" I turned to the others, fearful of disobeying him but wanting their permission. I rose uneasily and Lenny whispered, "Take your time."

The fifteen steps down the hallway didn't take as long as I'd have liked. Rabbi Weiss was annoyed. "What do you want?"

"Mr. Ravitch wants chalk." I quickly added, "He sent me."

"You know where the chalk is!" He was instantly out the door, me following. He turned so abruptly that I nearly ran into him. He bent down so that the point of his beard nearly pierced me and his cigarette breath filled my nostrils. "You are not a *shodad!*" He translated the Hebrew into Yiddish *"Bondit!"* -- *Gangster!* My heart pounded as he continued, "You're a good boy-" his tone didn't endorse his words. "-not like some others. Your grandfather is a scholar." *How did he know?* "I want you to be an example." It was a threat, not a request. He walked into the classroom and I followed. He brushed past Mr. Ravitch, took a piece of chalk out of the side drawer of the desk, and thrust it at

him. Then his eyes pierced us. "I will see *all* of your parents if-"
He didn't have to say more before striding out.

Mr. Ravitch looked gratefully at the chalk in his hand and
wrote a list of Hebrew words and their English meanings on the
blackboard. When he needed more space, he didn't ask us where
the eraser was or pause to look for it. He wiped off Mrs.
Schwartz' writing with his palm. We copied the words in silence,
our hands getting tired, and were still writing when the bell rang.
Mr. Ravitch turned to us, a bewildered expression on his face.
Lenny called out, "That's the dismissal bell." Mr. Ravitch
nodded gratefully, but looked helpless. Lenny was first to stand
up. We exited in our usual disorganized manner, but without
talking. Herschel and I parted with neither of us asking the
question: *Where was Mrs. Schwartz?*

I didn't wait until after supper to tell Momma that I no longer
wanted to go to Hebrew School. She said, "You pestered me for
weeks. Besides, I paid for the term."

I explained what had happened to Mrs. Schwartz and she
said, "You told me there were boys she couldn't stop from
misbehaving. In Europe we didn't have lady teachers no matter
how much they knew. Your Mrs. Schwartz, I'm sure her husband
won't let her starve."

I told her about the play. She asked, "What's this new
interest in plays? You've aggravated me enough with your school
play--I've yet to make your *goyisher* suit."

Morris was unsympathetic for other reasons. "What can you
expect from rabbis who tell you the earth and *everything* were
made in six days." I answered, "Days were longer then and God
can work *very* fast." I thought my answer ingenious, but Morris
shook his head and said, "If you fill your head with nonsense
like that, all you'll ever become is a rabbi or lawyer." Then, to
prove he wasn't prejudiced, he said, "Other religions teach a lot
of unscientific things as well." About the play--he asked,
"Should I visit your rabbi and tell him about the Bill of Rights?"
I wasn't sure if he was joking but I said, "No!"

When Uncle Sol came visiting, I told him what had
happened. He said, "Jews fighting Jews is our misery. If our
enemies don't do us in, other Jews will." Although sympathetic --

"Lev Litofsky's play had the audience cheering like Odets' *Waiting for Lefty*" --he was against my doing anything hasty. "Your father is in trouble enough with his idealism. Where will you run if they come after you?" I replied, "I was born here--I'm an American Citizen." He replied, "So was Joe Hill and a lot good it did him." It was years later that I learned about his fate. Sol concluded with, "Acting is a very *insecure* line of work." He defined *oimzechur* and advised me, "Become a doctor or undertaker--people are always sick or dying."

I made a special trip to my grandparents. Grandpa was in bed. Grandma said he wasn't feeling well and she insisted he stay home and rest. She hadn't wanted him to go to shul the past Saturday because it was cold and he wasn't feeling well, but he had gone because he knew I'd be there. I didn't want to trouble him but he insisted on my telling him. He listened and then shook his head. "I wonder what your rabbi will say about the Jews when God was giving Moses the ten commandments?" I didn't ask but learned later that after Moses had the Golden Calf burnt and ground up, he forced the children of Israel to drink it. Then he ordered the sons of Levi to kill his traitorous brothers and neighbors.

Grandpa said, "I should visit your rabbi," but Grandma said, "You don't need more aggravation--you're sick enough." But Grandpa was optimistic: "Trust things will work out." I didn't tell him I couldn't see how. I kissed him and left.

I wasn't sure if I'd be a coward by staying in Hebrew School or if I'd be one by leaving. If Poppa were around, he could tell me what to do. Or would he tell me I had to make up my own mind? I missed him as much as during the first few days he'd gone away.

The next day, as I walked home from public school, I was determined to convince Momma to let me drop out of Hebrew School. I rehearsed my reasons, including, "Poppa would agree with me." But when I got to my apartment door, Harold's mother was waiting for me. She told me Momma had gone shopping and I'd have my snack with Harold before going to Hebrew School. Despite my Yankee Doodle Cupcake on Mrs. Chernow's kitchen table and my Hebrew books in her hallway, I was suspicious.

Harold's delight at having me for company--Momma left a cupcake for him--was a pleasant distraction.

In Hebrew school we translated Genesis VI-"Therefore shall his days be a hundred and twenty years." I did not want my unhappiness with Hebrew School to squelch my curiosity and asked, "Why doesn't everyone live that long now?" I had asked variations of this question and was surprised when Ravitch smiled. "Good question, Al." Years later, I realized my "Good" questions were answered in the Commentaries. "Adam's 930 years were shortened in later generations to the 600 of Noah. Today only the most righteous live 120 years." He was so pleased with himself that he made the mistake of asking, "Do you have another question?" I did. "Were the Nephilim the 'sons of-" He interrupted with "No more questions!" but I continued, "It says that 'The sons of God saw the daughters of men were fair-" Besides longevity I was curious about sex and wanted to know about the Sons of God taking human wives and their having children.

Rabbi Weiss was in the doorway. "Come with me!" He had been listening outside the door! I followed him into his office. He turned and asked, "Did Mrs. Schwartz encourage such questions?" My instant reaction was to protect her, uncertain if his vengeance could pursue her. I replied, "They come out of my own head."

He sneered, "Then you're very clever--or a troublemaker." He continued, "A fool can ask more questions in an hour than ten wise men can answer in a year!" He glanced at a card on his desk. "I'd like to see your father. What's your phone number?"

"We don't have a phone." I was grateful for Momma's frugality. "My father's in Atlanta."

He eyed me suspiciously. "Does your grandfather go to the *Beth Yakov* shul on St. Paul's Place?"

Did Momma tell him that when she registered me?

"I'll speak to your grandfather instead. This is a matter to be settled with him rather than your mother."

When I got back to the classroom, only Mr. Ravitch was there; the class was dismissed. I hoped he'd intervene with the rabbi, but he kept writing the next day's words on the blackboard. Outside, Deborah and Herschel were waiting. I told them what the rabbi said. Deborah said, "I'm telling my father!" I thought that nice though I didn't know how that would help.

Fourteen

His Days Shall Be a 120 Years

I crossed over to Crotona Park and tried to fantasize a rescue. I didn't want to ask Grandpa to see the rabbi. Then I thought, *Morris?* First as a question, then, *Morris!* Could he figure a way out as he had with the Christmas play?

As if in answer to my plea, Morris was standing outside our building. We ran toward each other, but he spoke first. "What took you so long?" He looked so upset that alarm bells went off, eclipsing my worries about the rabbi. I had forgotten Momma's absence after school and now saw a frantic Morris.

"Come!" he commanded, grabbing me by the shoulder and shoving me down Fulton Avenue. I refused to budge until he told me where we were going. "Bronx Hospital--Grandpa had a heart attack!"

As we ran down Fulton Avenue, Morris told me what happened. Momma got a call from the hospital at Mrs. Stone's; She arranged for Mrs. Chernow to give me my snack but not to tell me about Grandpa. When we got to the hospital, the man at the reception desk told us children couldn't visit. Morris' claim that he was a sixteen-year-old senior in Stuyvesant High didn't convince him. He did tell Morris Grandpa was in room 303, with the warning, "Even if your mother's up there, you can't go." We found seats in the waiting room.

I wondered how sick Grandpa was, but was too frightened to ask. I felt a stab of guilt--had Grandpa's going to shul last week caused the heart attack? Grandma didn't wanted him to go but he didn't want to disappoint me. Morris told me not to move and then joined a group of people walking toward the elevator. He disappeared with them. I felt very alone sitting among strangers and it seemed like hours before Morris reappeared. He gestured for me to follow and we went past the Emergency

Room and up a stairway. On the third floor, he cautioned, "Act like you're supposed to be here." He squeezed my hand as a man in a white coat with a stethoscope poking out of his jacket pocket walked past us. Morris pulled me into room 303. I hesitated before two long rows of beds, but followed him down the narrow aisle where I saw Momma and Grandma. I embraced them and turned to Grandpa. Except for his head, he was covered by a sheet. His eyes were closed and his chest rose and fell irregularly. He looked strange and frightening. I whispered, "Is he all right?" Before anyone could answer, Grandpa's eyelids fluttered. "Yalkala?"

I said, "Grandpa." Noticing his uncovered head, I asked, "Your *yarmulke?*"

He whispered, "God will have to forgive me," and closed his eyes.

I took out my *yarmulke* and placed it on his head. He smiled without opening his eyes. His fingers protruded from the sheet and I gently held them. They felt cold. I said, "I'm sorry you went out in the bad weather on Saturday."

He opened his eyes. "It wasn't the weather, Yalkala, my scholar."

I said, "I'll pray for you, straight from my heart, like the *Midrash* says."

Morris whispered, "He shouldn't talk. We'd better go."

I kissed Grandpa and his eyes fluttered. Momma said she'd soon be down. As we left, I heard a patient moaning from behind a screen. We returned the way we'd come, passing nurses and physicians too busy to notice us.

We met Sol in the lobby. He had been downtown and just got the news. He said, "Your grandfather is a strong and pious man, God will hear our prayers." He went to the elevator. Shortly afterwards, Momma came down. "Sol will take your grandmother home. I'll be back in the morning." As we walked home, Momma asked Morris how they let us in. He made believe he didn't hear. She didn't ask again. A cold fall wind was blowing and I hoped Momma wouldn't say anything about the weather: she had not wanted me to go to shul last Saturday because of the cold and agreed only when I said Grandpa would be waiting for me. She had muttered, "Your grandfather shouldn't go either."

While Momma was preparing supper, Morris asked if Poppa knew. Momma said, "We'll wait till your uncle talks to the doctor." When Sol came, he looked upset. Grandpa had "a setback" and visitors were asked to leave. He tried to be encouraging. "Doctor Astrakhan says *Tata's* a fighter." He told Momma he'd call Mordcha and Yitzchok "right away!"

When I was in bed, I asked Morris, "Did Grandpa's going out in the cold hurt his heart? He went because I-" Morris interrupted with, "Grandpa had heart trouble for a long time." I wondered, *Did he say that to make me feel better?* When Momma kissed me goodnight, she said, "God should hear our prayers." I lay in bed thinking, *Dear God, please let Grandpa live.* I reminded God why: *Grandpa is a righteous man and he isn't 120 years old.*

The next thing I knew, I was in an enormous room lit up more brightly than Orchard Beach on a summer day. A murmur of prayers grew louder and the ram's horn, blown on special holidays, plaintively bleated and echoed through the chamber. The sunlight sparkled the specks of dust with stained-glass light so they formed colorful columns rising higher than in the ante- room of Grandpa's synagogue. My heart beat nervously. Grandpa had once told me about *Shekinah*--the presence of God! The music faded and I was standing on the *bimah,* the platform in *shul* from which services are conducted. I addressed God: "Kenan lived nine hundred and ten years--he was Grandpa's age- -seventy--when he begot Mahalalel. I know people don't live as long today, but Grandpa is righteous and should live 120 years." Just to make sure God didn't think I made that up, I added, "That's in Genesis VI." Then the ram's horn bleated, a signal that my prayer had been heard. The roof of the chamber dissolved and the night sky emerged. The moon smiled, stars glittered, wondrous music surrounded me, and an intense white light glowed brilliantly. I was in the presence of *Ruach Adonoi*-- The Spirit of God! I trembled more in awe than fear and covered my eyes. God was giving me His answer: Grandpa would live! I

145

awakened to see the darkness of the living room, yet I was so relieved I went back to sleep.

When I awakened again, it was light. I ran to the kitchen and shouted, "Grandpa's going to live!"

Momma and Morris turned to me, both looked puzzled. Morris caught on first. "Al was dreaming."

I shouted, "Grandpa's going to live!" Momma held me until I calmed down. I quickly washed up and returned to the kitchen. I was drinking my milk when the doorbell rang. A shadow of fear crossed Momma's face as Morris rushed to the door. Sol came bursting in and hugged Morris, Momma and me in quick succession. He shouted, "Grandpa made a remarkable recovery! Overnight! The doctors can't believe it! A *nisimdik!*" A miracle!

Momma said, "Al dreamt he'd live!" They all turned to me.

I tried to describe the room "All lit up, with music. God-"

Sol interrupted, "When?" I said, "The middle of the night." He looked from me to Momma. "The nurse told Dr. Astrakhan that at four o'clock *Tata's* blood pressure dropped, his heart beat regularly and he breathed easier. The nurse--she's been at Bronx Hospital ten years--also said it was a miracle!" Sol gave me a strange look. "My nephew is like Joseph in the Bible."

I felt as Joseph must have felt. Years later, I could still recapture my feelings of elation and vindication. I can also smile at the timing of Sol's arrival and their expressions of incredulity.

Momma quickly thought of more practical matters. "Did you call Mordcha?"

"Last night with the bad news," he said, "and this morning with the good!" He was returning to the hospital and Momma would go with him. She arranged for me to eat lunch at Harold's and said I could meet her at the hospital after Hebrew School. She warned Morris not to sneak into Grandpa's room again. Before they left, Sol, in good spirits, said, "If you dream about the stock market, call me!" While we dressed, Morris kept looking at me strangely.

For the first time that term, I forgot my Current Events article. Willie shoved his crumpled *Daily News* toward me. He boasted that he swiped his copies from a newsstand, but I suspected he picked them out of a trash can near the train station. Clarence asked what was wrong and I told him. He whispered, "My grandfather has heart medicine." Willie asked, "Indian medicine?" and Clarence's eyes narrowed.

In Current Events, I reported a soccer match between Italian and French teams in a city whose name I couldn't pronounce. The class showed more surprise than interest. Miss Cleary thought it strange, but said, "The game *was* in Europe." All morning I kept thinking about Grandpa and my dream.

I ate lunch at Harold's and after school disobeyed Momma and went to the hospital. I wasn't as lucky as Morris--a guard caught me. I ran to Hebrew School and met Rabbi Weiss in the corridor. Before he could ask, I explained why I was late. His angry expression changed to one of concern and he said, "Let's pray to the Almighty that he recovers." Then, "Before you even told me, I decided your grandfather won't have to come in--I'm giving you another chance." He looked at me sternly. "Remember, In seeking wisdom, the first step is silence." He paused as if to show me what that meant. "The second is listening." In case I didn't know to whom, he enumerated, "God, the Bible, the Talmud, the scholars, your rabbi." He concluded with, "I'll pray for your grandfather at the *maariv* service." He escorted me to class and explained my lateness to Mr. Ravitch. I sat down and copied Genesis VI from the board.

Mr. Ravitch translated that God saw man as wicked and wanted to destroy him and all the animals. I could understand God destroying man but why the innocent animals? I was tempted to ask, but didn't dare. I couldn't imagine God having a tantrum. When Mr. Ravitch left the room for a few minutes, I whispered to Debby that the rabbi said I didn't have to bring my grandfather to school. She whispered, "Last night, my father called the rabbi and read something from the Talmud about scholars asking questions."

After Mr. Ravitch returned, Rabbi Weiss came into the room. He beckoned Deborah and me. The class watched with concern as we followed him. After sitting down in his office, he said to me, "You can become a *Talmud chochem.*" To Deborah, "A girl doesn't need to be a scholar. She needs to be a devoted wife and mother." He smiled. "Your father's dowry won't hurt." Then, to both of us, "Mr. Ravitch will give you the two main parts in the Chanukah play." His eyes narrowed threateningly before continuing. "I want you to cooperate with Mr. Ravitch and be models for the others. I had my doubts about your other teacher from the beginning, but I gave her a chance. You wasted valuable learning time and that play-" He shook his head. "Jews killing Jews." Then, "Being principal of a Hebrew School and rabbi of a congregation are not just a matter of praying and studying the Bible. They taught us little in Yeshiva about pleasing a board of directors or how to raise money to keep a *shul* going." He stood up. "My wife says I can't say two words without giving a sermon." He smiled a rare smile. "Some sweeten learning with honey, but horseradish is often necessary!" He walked us back to the class and announced that our class would be giving a Chanukah play that "our families and the congregation can be proud of." He said we would sell tickets and the money would go to "helping the Yeshivas in Europe as well as our own shul." He nodded to Mr. Ravitch before leaving.

Mr. Ravitch left the door open and told us that Deborah and me would be the parents in the new play and Sarah and Herschel the children. The rest of the class was the chorus. Then he distributed the scripts.

We turned through the pages of *Chanukah, Festival of Dedication,* by Rabbi C. L Balsom. The *Setting* was *The Dining Room on the first night of Chanukah. The Family* sat around the table and *The Father* did most of the talking while *The Wife*, *The Son* and *The Daughter* listened or asked questions. Sitting around the dinner table *talking* about the Maccabees and *The Mother* serving *lotkes*-- "to commemorate the burning oil of the Menorah" was as boring as the stories in our public school *Our Reader.* Instead of the Litofsky drama, the Children asked questions which the Father answered while the Mother served food. The rest of the class sang Chanukah songs.

The bell rang and Mr. Ravitch asked the four of us to stay. I regretted having a part and would have wanted to leave with the others. Ravich told us that since he didn't want the play to interfere with our Bible memorization, he asked if we could rehearse after school. Sarah told him she had to go straight home and the rest of us nodded that was true for us. He asked if we could meet at one of our homes on a Sunday. Deborah said she'd ask her parents. We left. Herschel and I parted without a word.

At Bronx Hospital, Morris was in the waiting room. Momma came down a few minutes later. She was smiling because Grandpa told Dr. Astrakhan he wanted to go home. We left in a light-hearted mood. After supper, Morris made me promise not to tell Momma that he tried to sneak up to Grandpa. A guard caught him. Despite explaining to the guard that he wanted to tell Grandpa about my dream, the guard escorted Morris to the lobby. Uncle Sol was there and took charge of Morris by telling the guard, "If he does that again, *he'll* need a hospital bed!" Sol told Morris he wouldn't tell Momma on one condition. I couldn't guess. Morris looked away as he said, "If I told you."

Fifteen

Poppa's Return

Despite Sol's second call telling Poppa of Grandpa's miraculous recovery, Poppa decided to come anyway. He arrived Saturday afternoon and we hugged and kissed as if we hadn't seen each other in years. After reassuring Momma that he ate on the train, he said he wanted to visit Grandpa. Momma told him visiting hours would start again that evening, but he couldn't wait. Morris and I went with him.

As we walked down Fulton Avenue, I recalled the night that Poppa left for Atlanta, when I couldn't imagine him not being home. While he was not involved with the details of my life like Momma, he provided a presence and security that I had taken for granted. That first excruciating day passed, then another. Although I missed him unbearably at times, I was astonished at how all-absorbing my life was, erasing at times not only the pain of his absence, but the memory as well. Then some reminder--the razor strop that hung in the bathroom, a letter, his empty kitchen chair, Momma's sadness--was enough to pierce the orb of memory and explode reminiscences and feelings that lingered long afterwards. When Momma read his letter or cried, I resonated to her despondency and my own was amplified. One night, suppressing her tears, she quoted an Hasidic saying of her father's, "The person who cannot survive the bad times will not see the good times." I don't know how much that helped her, but it was too abstract for me. Nevertheless, I was discovering ways to survive. Walking together to the hospital, it seemed as if he had never been gone. The hospital waiting room was empty, the man at the visitors' desk gone, but there was a guard near the elevator. Poppa went over to talk to him. When the guard shook his head, Poppa slipped him something that he put it in his pocket. Poppa waved us over. The guard rang for the elevator and told the operator, "This family's come from Georgia to see a patient." The operator frowned, but the guard led us in. On the third floor, he told a nurse we had special permission.

Grandpa was asleep, the sheet covering him rhythmically rising and falling above his chest. When his eyelids flickered, I gently touched his hand and Poppa whispered, *"Tata."* Grandpa's eyes opened and he and Poppa kissed. Poppa helped him sit up and Grandpa asked, "When can I go home?"

Poppa answered, "When you're well,"

Grandpa held my hand and said, "My *Dreamer* healed me."

Morris told Poppa about my dream and Poppa kissed me. A slender nurse, a curl of blond hair escaping her cap, stopped beside the bed and asked, "You all right, grandpa?" They exchanged smiles. She told us, "He had a close call, but he's doing well now." She pointed to his *yarmulke*. "His only complaint was about his grandson's hat falling off. I clipped it on with a bobby pin." She patted his arm and whispered that we should leave in ten minutes--Grandpa needed his sleep. We stood quietly by the bed. Nearby, a patient coughed and the radiator near the window hissed.

Poppa said, "Sleep, *Tata,* I'll be back later."

Grandpa replied, "Tell your mother not to worry." He squeezed my hand and we each kissed him. The familiar brush of his beard and the softness of his lips were reassuring. When we were at the door we waved and he waved back.

Outside, Poppa said we were good grandchildren and to tell Momma that he'd visit Grandma and then come home. Morris went home and I accompanied Poppa. Grandma hugged and kissed him, murmuring, "My littlest one." That was the way Momma often greeted me!

When we returned, Morris told our parents that he was going to visit a friend. Then he signaled me. I followed him into the living room. He asked, "Aren't you going out?" I shook my head. He muttered, "Get lost! They haven't seen each other for weeks." He expected me to understand. "Go play with Harold!"

I answered, "I'm not bothering you."

He hissed, "Don't you know *anything?*" He grabbed my arm and I struggled with him.

Momma was at the doorway. "Your father's hardly home and the two of you are fighting."

Poppa came up alongside of her. "I hope you behaved when I was gone."

Morris, his back to Poppa, his face glaring at me, said, "We behaved. Al is going out with me."

As I walked with him in the street, he asked, "Don't you know about the birds and the bees?" His anger changed to a frown when he realized I didn't. In a softer voice, he said, "They want to be alone. I'm visiting my friend."

"How long should I play outside?" I asked.

Morris hesitated. "An hour-" Then his mouth twisted the way it did when figuring out something. "No, play it safe--an hour and a half."

I crossed the street to the park. *Running Bear* didn't feel like playing cards with Harold. I walked through the trees bare of leaves, careful to make as little noise as possible in my moccasins. Would I kill another bear like on the last hunt? I was beginning a long journey, wearing only a loin cloth, not feeling the cold. With winter approaching our tribe needed food. I headed in the direction of the sun, leaving my village behind. I had the improbable thought of meeting Clarence. Would he be another brave or a black gang member? Would he recognize me? The sun was low in the sky and suddenly I felt cold. I asked a friendly paleface the time in his language. More than two hours had passed. I headed to my village.

I entered the apartment cautiously, wondering if Morris had underestimated how long I should be gone. When I smelled cooking and heard Momma in the kitchen, I was relieved. Poppa was in the bedroom, reading the newspaper. Whatever was supposed to have happened, happened. Now everything seemed no different than usual. Morris came home ten minutes later and we had a chicken dinner.

Poppa ate lustily and exclaimed, "It's delicious!" He paid Momma more compliments than in dozens of meals before he left. Momma still asked, "Doesn't Mondlin's cook make nice meals?" He answered, "Not as tasty as yours." He joked, "If Sol was here, he'd tell you to open a restaurant in Atlanta." Momma looked pleased the whole time, until he told her he'd visit the Deutsch. Momma said, "If it's to thank him-" After the Deutsch recovered, he and his wife visited us. He gave Momma an envelope with a $125 collection from the men. Momma said the men shouldn't have, but the Deutsch said that was the least they could do with Poppa having to leave his job. Only when his wife said, "The men did the same for us," did Momma take the envelope.

While Poppa put on his jacket, she said, "Don't make it a union meeting--my heart can stand only so much aggravation."

I asked if I could go. Momma was about to say "No" but she asked Poppa, "You want him along?"

Poppa looked at me uncertainly, but said, "Why not? I'm not hiding anything."

We didn't have to wait long for the trolley. Poppa let me sit next to the window, but rather than look out, I wanted to talk. I blurted out what had happened at Hebrew school: Mrs. Schwartz being fired, Mr. Ravitch making learning boring, how much I liked the first play and how terrible was its replacement, I left out the rabbi's wanting to see him.

When I finished, he put his arm around my shoulder and said it wasn't "right to fire a teacher like that." I asked if teachers had unions and he laughed. "Teachers are smarter than painters with books, but not in keeping their jobs." He had also seen a Litofsky play on Second Avenue and liked it--"He showed workers can change their lives for the better."

I told him how much I liked being a Maccabee in the play and then blurted, "I don't want to go to Hebrew School!"

He asked, "What would you gain by running away?"

I said, "You ran away from Russia!"

"I had to take your grandmother to America," he said. "Otherwise I might have stayed."

Did Momma know that? I wondered. He was silent for a while and I asked, "Did you run away by going to Atlanta?"

His grip tightened, then loosened. "I'm not saying going away is *never* the right thing." He was silent and then, "Learning is important. I went to school for only a couple of years before the war-and-revolution." I asked about the citizenship test and he said that he took along the books I had helped him with. He tousled my hair. "You remembered."

We got off the trolley at West Farms and as we walked, Poppa said, "You won't give the Litofsky play, but you'll remember it."

What good is that? I thought, but said nothing.

We walked up the stairs of a two story building and Poppa rang a bell. The Deutsch opened the door, shouted in delight and hugged Poppa. He then hugged me, lifting me off the ground. He asked, "How's your father doing?"

"Much better," said Poppa, glancing at me as if to see if I realized they had recently talked to each other.

The Deutsch gripped Poppa around the shoulder and they walked into the living room. I followed. Seated were men I recognized from the union meeting. They enthusiastically greeted Poppa. Then, in a whisper, Poppa asked the Deutsch, "Your wife-"

Just then she entered the room with a pot of coffee and a plate of cheese and crackers. "You don't have to whisper," she said to Poppa.

"We have an agreement," said the Deutsch. "I can be in the union but can't run for office." He winked at Poppa. "Do you let your wife run your life?" The men laughed and his wife shook her head—"A grown man with six children acts like a child." The Deutsch raised his hands. "She frightens me more than the gangsters!" She playfully swatted him on the arm before leaving.

The stocky man who talked as if he were on a soap box said to Poppa, "Glad you could make it." The others nodded.

The stocky man said, as if he were continuing where he left off, "Now that we agreed to postpone the elections, Leon won't agree on a new date." He turned to Poppa. "I told them what you told me over the phone, that it played into their hands."

One of the others said, "Max wasn't here to know how many men wanted out because of the shooting *and* the police investigation."

The stocky man said, "Wasn't Max the prime suspect?" He turned to the Deutsch. "Your best friend wanted the privilege of becoming treasurer." The others laughed. "The police scare made us play into the hands of the bosses and gangsters." Someone muttered, "The police were paid off." Another man said, "Max, you're still the best bet--we need the support of the Jewish painters."

Herman peeked into the room. I was delighted to see him, but I wanted to hear more. Poppa said to me, "Why don't you go with Herman?" I left with him and we played with his toy Indians and cowboys. Katie stayed in the room, but we ignored her until she nearly cried. Then we let her play. Later their mother called us for pie and milk. When Poppa came into the kitchen, I knew we were leaving.

In the hallway, the stocky painter asked, "Which side are you on--the union or bosses?" The others laughed. Even I hear the union song, "Which Side Are You On?" The Deutsch clasped Poppa's shoulder. "Max will always be Max and a friend. If he wasn't a Rank and Filer, he wouldn't be in Atlanta."

The Deutsch's wife kissed me and the Deutsch squeezed my shoulder and whispered loud enough for everyone to hear, "Don't forget your Yankee friends and don't switch baseball teams!" He hugged Poppa. Herman and I shook hands. Katie kissed me on the cheek--I blushed and everyone laughed.

On the trolley ride home, Poppa told me about his *Cheder* in Russia. "We sat on hard benches and repeated what the rabbi said. If we misbehaved or didn't study, he hit us with a stick. What was most frightening was his telling our fathers." I asked if he had gotten into trouble. He looked out the window. "The rabbi warned me, 'With your father off in America, God will watch you more carefully." Poppa paused, as if uncertain whether to continue. "The rabbi caught me before God did." I didn't dare ask what he did and after staring into space for a while, he said, "I went to Cheder after finishing work in the candy factory-" He explained that he worked to earn money for himself and Grandma. "I worked all day." *Why did that get him into trouble?* I didn't have to ask. "I told the rabbi I was sick."

I protested, "You were working to make money!"

His eyes were back in the present. "I hadn't told the truth."

I shouted, "That's not fair!" Then I asked, "What did he do?"

He hesitated, but said, "He hit me with the switch--ten times." *Ten times!* He imitated the rabbi's voice—"Five for your father, and five from me."

I asked, "Where did he hit you?"

He replied, "On my backside. I couldn't sit for a week. But I was lucky." *Lucky?* He explained, "He forgot about God!" *God?* "If he hit me five times for *Tata* and five times for himself, imagine how many more he would have hit me for God!" I tried to join Poppa's laughter, but couldn't.

Then I told Poppa that Rabbi Weiss was so angry at my question about the Gods and their human wives that he asked to see him. Poppa looked at me quizzically and I told him about Genesis VI. He didn't remember that passage but said, "Your rabbi shouldn't stop you from asking questions. Does he still want to see me?" I told him about Deborah's father calling the rabbi and he said, "It's always good to have buddies who stick up for you." I again said, "I don't like going to Hebrew School." He shook his head and said, "That would be running away."

I said, "After the detectives came, you ran away from the Bronx." I leaned away, as if afraid he would slap me. When he didn't, I cautiously looked up. Poppa was looking out the window. Finally, he said, "I have to think not only about me, but also about your mother and my children." He paused. "I give you my word, I won't be angry whatever you do. As for your mother, you'll have to answer to her." Another pause. "Some decisions are hard no matter how smart you think you are."

I asked, "Can't you find a business in the Bronx?"

Poppa smiled. "In the Bronx, I'm a painter and a Rank-and-Filer. In Atlanta, I can be a boss." He made it sound so obvious that I didn't question it, but I really didn't understand.

As we walked home from the trolley, Poppa said, "In Atlanta we'll have a car like your uncles and the Deutsch. Your mother will be pleased to have her own home with servants." Then as an afterthought, "There are nice schools there for you and Morris." I thought, *I don't care about a car or servants--I want to stay in the Bronx!*

When we got home, Momma looked at the clock and asked, "Did they have a meeting at the Deutsch's?" Poppa hung up his jacket. Momma continued sewing as she said, "Your buddies must be upset that you'll become a boss while they remain poor workers." I quickly left the room--too quickly. Momma said, "You've made him a conspirator."

After supper, we visited Grandpa. He was sitting up, looking as if he'd never had a heart attack. Grandma said, "I hope you retire now," but Grandpa didn't answer. I knew he was having a hard time making up his mind.

Later, back home, I joined my parents and Morris in the kitchen. I lingered on my snack to hear the discussion. Poppa said, "I'm close to signing."

Momma said, "I can't wait to leave the union business and police. When can we can move?"

"Perhaps by the middle of December," said Poppa. He took another sip. "I wanted to surprise you."

"*Halevai!*" exclaimed Momma.

I shouted, "That's before the plays!" I ran from the room. Later, Morris said, "Not only won't you be in the plays, you won't be in P.S. 4."

The reality of the move was first sinking in. When Momma said goodnight, I covered my head with my blanket. She pulled it back and said, "Don't you want our family to be together?" I turned face down. Momma said, "What's this craziness with that Santa play? You don't care about the Chanukah play." I refused to kiss her goodnight and she left saying, "I won't kiss you either." I lay there feeling terrible.

Poppa came in and sat on my bed. I uncovered my head. "I wish life was simple," he said, "so *everyone* could always be happy." He patted my shoulder and left. When Morris got into bed, I asked "Can you figure a way we can stay in the Bronx?"

The darkness lengthened the silence but I patiently waited. It took me a while to fall asleep and if he answered me, I didn't hear.

Poppa left the next morning. I was becoming a veteran of his leavings. The first was harder. This was easier because I had survived the other; I also knew being reunited would mean moving. Much as I wanted our family together again, I did not want to go to Atlanta. The guilt stuck in my throat.

"If you want to leave with your father," said Momma, you'd better finish your cereal." Although I had no appetite, I cleaned out my bowl--when it came to food, Momma kept her word.

While Poppa finished his second glass of tea, Momma again asked him how long the trip would take. He told her and she marveled at the size of America, saying, "From my town to Kiev was only two hours by train." Despite Poppa's assuring her that the train had a restaurant car, she filled a bag with sandwiches and fruit. Poppa said it would last a week, but Momma was afraid *his* train wouldn't have a restaurant car; or they'd run out of food; or Poppa wouldn't like what they served. At the door, Momma didn't give Poppa a chance to say, "Everything will be all right." She did, but couldn't hold back her tears. I thought, *Moving to Atlanta will never be all right* but didn't say it.

I walked with Poppa and Morris to the Third Avenue train station that would take Poppa to Pennsylvania Station and Morris to his high school. Poppa was carrying a presentable suitcase Yitzchok had lent him, not Borinka's battered one.

"I want the two of you to behave," said Poppa, "your mother has enough to worry about." We promised him we would. Morris asked if Carl, the Deutsch's son, was home during yesterday's visit. Poppa said he wasn't. Morris said, "I bet the Rank-and-Filers don't want you to leave."

Poppa glanced at me and replied, "We have to think of the family when we make important decisions." At the stairway to the elevated station, I kissed Poppa. He said, "I know you don't like your rabbi, but by staying you'll learn things you wouldn't otherwise."

I wanted to say, "You're not staying in the Bronx with the Rank-and-Filers," but didn't. Poppa turned at the first landing to wave, then disappeared with Morris just as the train was noisily entered the station. I raced down Third Avenue, chased by the trains' rumbling that quickly overtook me. Its roar filled the cavern of Third Avenue and the slats of sunlight coming through the ties above turned to darkness. I kept running even when the sunlight slats reappeared in front of me and the train's rumbling faded away. Breathless, I finally stopped and turned toward school, envying Morris.

Sixteen

The Rehearsals

Poppa's absence slipped into the background and I returned to the routine of my life. One priority was the Chanukah play. Deborah, Sarah, Herschel and I had banded together against the injustices of Rabbi Weiss, just as the Macabbees were united in their struggle against Antiochus. We called ourselves the *Arba,* the Hebrew word for "Four." While we had submitted to his authority and accepted Mrs. Schwartz' replacement--however grudgingly--our resentment smoldered. Morris asked, "How come you keep going if you don't like your new teacher and the play?" How could I explain? I had learned obedience in my family and at school. Despite Ravitch's rote instruction, how else was I to learn the Bible stories? While I detested the play, I had a major part and knew there'd be an appreciative audience contributing money, some going to help the Jews in Europe. I had the fellowship of the Arba. Among these many reasons lurked fear. Some fears were clear: disapproval. Others were vague but palpable. Uncertainty was a side-product of the fear: what would happen if I quit? I had only a vague realization that Poppa was also struggling with his conflicts.

These thoughts were murkily going through my head as I walked to Deborah's for our rehearsal on a Sunday afternoon. Morris had given me directions to get to the Lewis-Morris building, where a high school friend lived and which he described as the "fanciest apartment building in the Bronx." He said, "If she's got a pretty older sister, let me know. The family must be rich." He tried to pass it off as a joke, but I knew that he had become interested in girls. I couldn't understand why.

Before I left, he gave me directions for the last time, warning me not to wander off 174th Street or I'd "get lost in the tunnel." Momma wondered why I wore my school clothes and warned me not to get them dirty. Morris joked, "He's got a date." I must have blushed because Momma smiled. I hadn't told either of them much about Deborah.

I followed 174th Street, leaving behind the familiar streets--Fulton, Third, and Washington. I clutched the Chanukah script and regretted not arranging to have the company of Herschel. When I reached the top of the hill, I recognized the Lewis-Morris building although I had never seen it before. Morris was right: it was the biggest apartment building I'd ever seen and towered over the Grand Concourse, the widest street I had ever seen. Its two tree-lined islands stretched as far as I could see in both directions. When the light turned green, I ran as fast as I could, afraid it would change before I got across.

It was a day of many firsts, including a doorman. He was an imposing uniformed man who blocked my way. He had the authority I associated with the police. When I gave him Deborah's full name, as well as my own, he called on the intercom--an invention I had never seen--and then turned to me. "She's expecting you." My next surprise was the elevator and its uniformed operator. Everything contrasted with my five-story walk-up apartment building. My feet eerily sank into the floor as the operator whisked me up to the fourteenth floor and after letting me out, pointed to the apartment door. The door plate read, "Dr. Jonas Kaplan." Deborah never mentioned her father was a doctor. I hesitated, my heart pounding, but finally pressed the button. I was startled to hear chimes.

Deborah greeted me with a smile and motioned me in. I followed her through a hallway with a ceiling that seemed two stories high and then into a living room that was larger than our whole apartment. It was filled with comfortable-looking furniture, including a piano. Her father sat in an armchair, her mother on a sofa. I wasn't sure who to go to first but Deborah, at my side, said, "Mother, this is Al Segal from my Hebrew Class." Mrs. Kaplan, a slender woman, wore a print dress unlike the everyday house dresses of Momma, or for that matter, the mothers I knew. She wore make-up, while Momma used lipstick and rouge only when she went visiting. Mrs. Kaplan smiled. "Deborah's told me about you."

I nearly asked, "What did she say?" but managed an "Hello." Deborah was half-way across the room and I scampered after her. She introduced me to her father as if he hadn't heard the earlier introduction. Dr. Kaplan extended his hand and smiled. He was a stout man with a round friendly face and a thin mustache. "Deborah tells me you're a scholar and a Maccabee." He had an impish smile and eyes that resembled Uncle Sol's. I barely managed to smile. Mrs. Kaplan addressed Deborah, "Ask Al if he would like something to drink." Their formalities were as natural to them as they were unfamiliar to me. Couldn't Mrs. Kaplan have asked me directly? I said, "No," before realizing how dry my mouth was. But it was too late. Deborah said, "We'll rehearse in my room." I followed, uncertain if I was supposed to say something to her parents. Her father picked up the Sunday *New York Times* and the mother a book. We reached her room when the chimes rang. When Deborah went to the door, I looked about a room she had all to herself: a bed three times the width of my fold-away one and covered with a lace bedspread; a modern desk, unlike Morris'; a dresser with a mirror larger than Momma's; print drapes at her double windows. I heard Deborah introducing Herschel and Sarah to her parents and strained to hear if Dr. Kaplan called Herschel a scholar and a Maccabee. Their voices were inaudible--I was tempted to step out and listen, but I didn't.

I was relieved when Deborah brought Sarah and Herschel into her room. I said hello to Sarah and shook Herschel's hand. I had never greeted either like that. Herschel wore a jacket and long pants. I was self-conscious about my knickers and imagined him comfortable and not nervous like me. Sarah's brown hair was neatly combed and rested on her shoulders. I didn't remember how she wore it before. Of course I remembered Deborah's attractive shoulder-length black hair. Deborah said she'd get drinks and when she returned I was relieved she brought a glass for me.

We started rehearsing, me *The Father,* Deborah *The Mother,* Herschel *The Son,* and Sarah *The Daughter.* I answered the children's questions about religion and history, and Deborah those about the holiday foods. On the first day I explain the

Menorah and its *shamus,* the candle that lights the others. Deborah gives the recipe for *lotkes,* from peeling the potatoes to cooking them until "they're golden brown." I explain the religious significance of *lotkes.* "Since oil burns in the Menorah, your mother, by using oil in cooking your delicious *lotkes,* also celebrates the holiday." The stage directions read, *Mother turns to father and smiles,* which is my cue to say, "Yes, the miracle of oil is part of the festival of the Feast of Lights." When the children play with their *dreidels,* I explain, "The four letters on each side stand for the first letters of the words *Nes Gadol Haya Sham,* which mean, 'A great miracle happened there." When the children quarrel, I *Sternly warn them,* "Children should not argue on Chanukah." Mother says, "If you behave, we have presents for you." After the last line, we looked at each other.

I said, "It doesn't tell much about the Maccabees." The others were as disappointed. I said to Herschel, "You Simon, are a brave brother," quoting from the Litofsky's play. They laughed. I told Deborah how well she played Jochanan and complimented Sarah as Eleazar. Herschel said, "Remember Lenny as the Assyrian General?" He imitated Lenny saying, "Eat this pig, you pig!" We burst out laughing. Sarah pointed to me. "Remember nearly getting into a fight with Lenny and Rabbi Weiss thinking you were acting." Deborah said, "Maccabees, let us overcome Appolonius!" Sarah added, "Judah, lead us to victory."

We looked from one to the other and had the same idea, which I shouted first: "Let's do the Litofsky play!" Herschel reminded us, "Rabbi Weiss took all the scripts." I dramatically gave the first line of the play, "There are tyrants today and there were tyrants in the old days, but never shall the Hebrews forget the evil Emperor Antiochus." The others gave the Macabbee salute. Encouraged, I continued, "I am called Mattathias and live with my wife and five sons-"

Deborah jumped up. "Let's write it down!" She ran to her desk, took out a pad and grabbed a pencil. "Al, repeat the beginning." She wrote it down. Then, "Let's write our parts!" She tore off sheets of paper and got more pencils. We were surprised at how much we remembered.

Herschel, as Simon, gave the next to last speech. "I, Simon, ruler of Judea, in the year 143 B.C.E., remind you that we fought not only for religious freedom but to become a free nation." *Off stage, Voice of Martyred Maccabees* is my cue. "We fought bravely in those ancient times and now you, in the year 1938 (Mrs. Schwartz had crossed out 1936, the year the play was first given) must continue to fight for freedom all over the world." We had the whole play, unsure of only a few lines! Deborah assembled all the pages. "I'll ask my father's secretary to type this."

Her mother knocked on the door and apologized for interrupting. "Your friends are welcome to stay for supper." It was five-thirty. Mrs. Kaplan, still talking to Deborah, added, "They'd better call their parents." The three of us looked at each other. Herschel spoke first. "No, thank you." Sarah declined and then I did. I was relieved. How could I explain my family didn't have a phone?

We went into the living room and Deborah asked her father if he knew the vowel sounds in Psalm 30 from the play. I wasn't sure of the pronunciation. Dr. Kaplan put on his eyeglasses and searched the shelves--there were two walls with books, almost as many as in our school library. He found the psalm and as I copied the vowels, I said, "Thanks for calling Rabbi Weiss."

Dr. Kaplan smiled. "Don't thank me, thank the sages. They say, 'Better one should be a questioner than a fool.'"

"My *Zaidi* also says that."

Dr. Kaplan smiled. "Then he must also be a sage."

Mrs. Kaplan, sitting on the couch, said, "You haven't lost your touch as a Hebrew scholar."

Dr. Kaplan replied, "Studying the Torah is like riding a bicycle, you don't forget. Like you with the piano."

Mrs. Kaplan said, "I get out of tune, just like an unused piano."

I marveled at their talking as if we weren't there!

Dr. Kaplan placed the *siddur* on the table. "When I chose medicine, I didn't forget my Yeshiva education. My father was disappointed that I abandoned Raschi for Hippocrates. Most

Jewish parents want their sons to become doctors, but for my rabbi father, it was a disappointment."

Mrs. Kaplan said, "He appreciated your being a healer."

Dr. Kaplan sighed. "The soul was his deepest concern, the body its temporary courier. For me, it was the reverse." Noticing us, he said, "It was a pleasure meeting Deborah's friends." We chorused good-bys and followed Deborah to the door. She said, "I'm sorry you couldn't stay for supper." Then, "My father liked the Litofsky play." She rang for the elevator and told the operator, "Fred, take my friends to the lobby."

The floor dropped away, but I tried to look casual. Outside, we crossed the Grand Concourse. A block off 174th Street, Sarah turned and said she didn't have far to go. It was dark on this fall night and patches of 174th Street were lit by the street lamps. Herschel said, "Some apartment." I agreed. After another block, he said, "I wanted to stay for supper."

We walked a half block before I asked, "Why didn't you?"

It was another block before he answered, looking straight ahead. "We don't have a phone."

We walked another block before I said, "My brother wants us to get one."

Momma was upset at my coming home late. Morris said, "If we had a phone, Al could have called." Momma asked if my friend had one, expecting that she didn't. When I nodded, Morris smirked. Momma frowned, unsure if I was conspiring with Morris. Later, I told Morris, "The family is rich, but you're out of luck--she doesn't have an older sister."

Preparations were continuing with the "Christmas-Chanukah" play, which is what I called it when talking to Momma. While our class was busy rehearsing, the senior shop class was making scenery and props. It was Willie who suggested to the shop teacher that the sleigh have wheels so it could be drawn across the stage. Mr. Carter frowned, as did Miss Cleary, but the reindeer shrieked their agreement. Miss Cleary said, "We've never had a moveable sleigh." She turned to Mr. Carter. "Is it possible to build one?" Mr. Carter rose to the challenge. "I believe my senior class can." I was skeptical of Willie's motives but when he said, "Maybe Mr. Carter can't make one strong enough to hold fat Santa," I chimed in, "The pillow makes me *look*   heavy." The matter was left for Mr. Carter to think over.

That week, while I was listening to my afternoon adventure programs, Momma interrupted to announce, "We're going shopping." I automatically protested that I couldn't leave without finding out how the Long Ranger survived the episode. That is, until she said, "So I won't make your costume." Now it was me rushing Momma toward Bathgate Avenue. I didn't know if that afternoon was convenient for her shopping or she wanted me to forfeit my afternoon adventure serials just as she was sacrificing her time to make the costume. Almost as exciting as getting the material was the realization that Poppa must have written her that we wouldn't move before Christmas. She wouldn't be making the costume if we were.

We reached the Bathgate Avenue Market, which was a composite of the lower East Side's Delancey Street, an oriental bazaar and a forerunner of the later discount stores. One could buy a banana from the sidewalk "Banana Man," a single cigarette or stick of gum in the candy store, a bedroom set in a furniture store, and live carp or chickens. I didn't glance through the doorway of the chicken market where thousands of imprisoned chickens were in cages along the walls. I had no time for my fantasy of unlocking the cages and leading a gigantic flock of liberated chickens down Bathgate Avenue, rescuing them from the kosher slaughterer who slit their throats in a flurry of feathery protests. We rushed past fruit and vegetable stores whose stands spilled onto the sidewalk, while nearby pushcart peddlers out-shouted competitors to attract customers. We were not only bombarded with sights and sounds, but assaulted with smells ranging from mouth-watering sweets drifting from bakeries to the fulsome odors of butcher shops. Momma deftly made her way through streets crowded with sellers and buyers, I following in her wake. She had lost me once when I chased after a stray kitten and for years afterwards held my hand or kept an eye on me as she filled two bulging shopping bags that danced inches off the ground, all done without benefit of a shopping list.

Today she had only one item to buy, but muttered, "What have I gotten myself into?"

We entered Rosenbloom's Material and Yarn Shop, where Mrs. Rosenbloom smiled from behind the counter and asked, "What are you making now, Mrs. Segal?" She was one of the few merchants who addressed Momma by name. Momma asked, "Do you have plain red material, Mrs. Rosenbloom?" reciprocating the formality but ignoring her question. Mrs. Rosenbloom, her sales skills honed in her many years of experience with Bathgate shoppers, didn't ask again. She emerged from behind the counter and walked swiftly despite being a third more in girth than Momma's ample girth. She stopped in front of a row of bins that went up to the ceiling. She couldn't reach the bolt on an upper shelf and called, "Sol!"--I always expected to see my uncle--and her husband, nearly as large in girth, but several inches taller, excused himself from a customer. He squinted at the bin and asked, "That red?" as if she'd made a mistake. Mrs. Rosenbloom turned to Momma and asked, "Plain red, Mrs. Segal?" She tried to sound as if she was merely requesting information about the color, not expressing curiosity about the material's purpose. Momma nodded and Mrs. Rosenbloom in turn passed the nod on to her husband. He got his ladder, again apologizing to the woman he was waiting on, obviously someone who was not as regular a customer as Momma. As he lowered the bolt to his wife, I noticed his incredulous expression. The garish material had worked its way up the bins to its practically inaccessible height. Mrs. Rosenbloom stealthily brushed off the dust and held it for Momma's inspection. Momma felt the material and glanced at her fingers as if its brightness rubbed off.

"*Kesten broin*," said Mrs. Rosenbloom. "Maroon," although the label read *Prussian Red*. Momma peered at the material, squeezed it and asked, "How much?" Mrs. Rosenbloom asked, "How much?" Momma's lips pursed thoughtfully--"Two yards." Mrs. Rosenbloom said, "Twenty cents a yard," as if the price was clearly marked, adding, "For you, thirty-six cents the two yards." Momma rubbed the material again and made a face--a routine I witnessed with everything Momma bought in the market. Mrs. Rosenbloom was no amateur on her side of the counter and said, "Imported," waiting for that to sink in before adding, "from overseas." She looked away, seemingly unconcerned that Momma didn't want to take advantage of the bargain. Momma asked, "Thirty-six cents?" and Mrs. Rosenbloom said, "Hand-made on the best machine loom." While Momma frowned at the material, Mrs. Rosenbloom said, "It'll wear like iron!"

Her husband walked over, having made his sale with the other customer. He caressed the material and said, "Few customers appreciate quality." He ostensibly addressed his wife and glanced up at the bin, as if they kept exclusive material out of the reach of ordinary customers. Momma's internal debate was evident on her face. At this delicate point in the negotiations, the Rosenblooms remained patiently silent while glancing with approval at the bolt of cloth. I could tell they were curious as to why Momma wanted this red, knowing her usual purchases were practical prints. They wisely held their curiosity in check.

"Thirty-five cents," said Mrs. Rosenbloom and her husband's mouth opened in amazement. His wife tightened her jaw, looking as if she preferred confronting her husband's anger rather than not giving Momma a bargain. But she added, "That's rock bottom. It costs more wholesale." Momma's expression still didn't change. In case Momma didn't notice Mr. Rosenbloom's expression, his wife said, "Anything less and Mr. Rosenbloom will divorce me! You can look anywhere on Bathgate Avenue and not find such material." Mrs. Rosenbloom walked behind the counter, as if she no longer cared to make the sale. During those few moments something transpired between the two women that wordlessly concluded the sale, except for some face-saving formalities. Mrs. Rosenbloom measured the material under Momma's watchful eye and made appreciative sounds while Momma grumbled, "Not even a pattern." Mrs. Rosenbloom gingerly put the material in a bag and Momma paid her.

Outside, clutching the bundle, Momma said, "If she asked me what it was for, I'd have walked out." Then, as if the material were on fire, she thrust it at me. "You carry this!" At the corner of Third Avenue, while waiting for a train to pass overhead, she said, "I don't know why I bargained, your school's paying and Mrs. Rosenbloom could have had those pennies." At home, Momma glared at me. "My father was a scholar, like a rabbi and me celebrating *nitl!*" I didn't have to ask what it meant. That was the first and last time I heard her say *Christmas*.

That night Momma fitted me. She was determined to complete this sacrilegious task as soon as possible. I showed her the sketch, but she waved it away with, "I'm a seamstress!" She draped the cloth around me and when she started inserting the pins, I froze. She accurately but angrily inserted the pins while saying, "My mother kept the most kosher home in Chernobyl. If she saw me now-" I wished she concentrated more on her pin-thrusting rather than telling me things I already knew. I listened attentively, not moving a muscle. "My father studied-" I jumped when the pin pierced my side. I didn't yell, having expected this. Momma kissed me soothingly and warned, "Don't move again." The doorbell rang. Momma's hand froze. I could have been staring into her terrified eyes in the *pogrom*. She dashed to the door and I followed.

She recognized the voice and fumbled with the chain lock. In stepped the agent. Momma asked, "What's wrong?" He looked at me draped in the red cloth and said, "You're busy-" Momma looked at me as if she was shocked at what I was wearing, but managed to say, "A party costume." Then-"News from my sister? I haven't had a letter in over a month." He shook his head. "It's not only the mail that's not been getting through. With Europe upside down and borders closing-" Momma led him into the kitchen. After he sat down at the table and Momma opposite him, Momma asked, "How much?"

Looking away and intertwining his stubby fingers, he said, "Just the other hundred and fifty."

Momma said, "That was *after* you reached them."

He said, "We talk dollars but our agents risk their lives."

"If you came earlier this week, said Momma, "you could have explained this to my husband. He thought you were charging enough."

He nervously explained there were "new troubles in Europe" and "greater risks in travel."

Momma tightened her jaw, but went to the bedroom. She returned and frowned as she counted out one hundred and fifty dollars. He put the money into his wallet more casually this time, talking all the while about how happy Momma would be when her family was rescued.

After Momma closed the door behind him, she muttered, "The gonif! Your father was right--it's like throwing money out the window." Taken aback by what she had said, she asked me, "How could we not take the chance?" She looked into my eyes and waited; she was expecting an answer! I hesitantly nodded. Momma shook her head and said, "See, I'm right!"

Momma completed the fitting, barely paying attention to me. Before she took the material off and as I shrunk to avoid any stray pins, she said, "Your father also said we had to try."

Seventeen

Shlichus

On the first Saturday Grandpa was released from the hospital, I rushed over to see him. At the doorway, I grazed Grandma's cheek and ran to the bedroom, but hesitated outside the door. I peeked in, relieved to see him sitting up. When we kissed, I was surprised to feel the strength of his arm around me. He thanked me for my prayers and dream. Grandma whispered loud enough for him to hear, "Yalkala, tell him that in your dream he stops working."

Grandpa made a face and said, "I'll retire!"

Grandma said, "You say that when you're sick, but when you get better-" She shook her head and left the room.

Grandpa gestured to the straw-bottom chair and I pulled it to the side of the bed. He asked, "How's the question-maker?"

I had already told him that the rabbi didn't like questions and said, "I stopped asking questions."

Grandpa's eyebrows furrowed and he shook his head. "That's how we learn." I brought him up-to-date about the rabbi firing "our nice lady teacher." He sighed and said, "Yalkala, I can't say a good word for every rabbi, but don't run away from learning because of a poor teacher." He patted the prayer book on the table next to the bed. "Some scholars are like donkeys--they *carry* a lot of books. Even if one reads, but doesn't think, that isn't learning. Even when one answers a question, we find another question." I nodded vigorously and he continued, "That is how you discover your *shlichus.*" He explained that meant *Mission.* "Your *Ruach Adonoi* glows more brightly when you have a mission." He paused to make sure I understood. "My father said that there are three ways of living: the lucky know their purpose early in life. Others discover it after they've lived most of their lives." His eyes glazed over. I prompted, "The

173

third?" He sighed again. "Most people live as on a sailboat with broken *kerma.*" He explained that was a rudder "-sometimes steering and other times driven by the winds and waves, once in a while glimpsing their purpose. I thought mine was to be a scholar and I questioned everything like you. I had my doubts." I could not imagine Grandpa doubting. He whispered, "If you pay attention, you can discover your mission." He stared into my eyes and I held my breath. I thought he'd tell me what mine was, but he said, "Only you can discover it."

He talked about many things that afternoon. "Everyone living today came from Adam and Eve, so we're all brothers and sisters." Although Morris didn't believe in Genesis, he also said that. Yet I asked, *"Everyone?"* He answered, *"Everyone!* No matter how different they look." Despite what Grandpa and Morris said, I found it hard to believe that Willie, Clarence and me, way back, had the same parents. When Grandma came into the room, she said, "Give your heart and tongue a rest, as well as Yalka's ears. If you men would *do* more and *talk* less, you'd finish more than the Talmud. And if you would *think* before *doing,* the world would be a better place." Grandpa winked at me and said, "And if men asked women more questions, the world would have better answers."

That evening, Morris didn't take long to answer me. "My purpose is to become a pilot!" He said it with such assurance there was no sense asking him anything else.

I went into the kitchen and asked Momma. She looked up from reading Poppa's letter. "Meaning? Purpose?" I nodded, hoping I'd used Grandpa's Yiddish correctly. She said, "If God had a purpose, he didn't tell me. Whether God meant it or not, I hope His purpose was not to make people suffer. If it was, I'd stop believing in Him."

Later when Momma kissed me goodnight, she whispered, *"My* purpose is to take care of my family. Yours should be to take care of yourself and make my job easier." I was going to tell her that I could take better care of myself by staying in the Bronx. I didn't. I didn't make her life easier that night.

Sleep came quickly. I was Superman's *older* brother. Our parents came rushing into our room, shouting, "Krypton will explode!" They took the small rocket from the foyer closet and Father said, "We can send one of you to Earth." Mother asked, "Which one shall we save?" Father asked me, "What is your purpose in life?" I looked blankly at them. They turned to my brother, who said, "I'll be a champion of the weak and the oppressed." He was only one year old! Our parents turned to me. "We love you, but we have only one rocket." They blasted him off before our planet exploded.

I landed in a field that looked like the one in Tibbets Brook. Jack Armstrong walked up to me. "I'm looking for someone to help me take the Tibetan Monk's message to the boys and girls of America. Are you honest and do you have a Heart of Gold?" I answered, "I hope so." His smile disappeared and he shook his head. "I'll have to find a boy or girl who's more confident." I pleaded, "I eat Wheaties every morning and love America!" but he walked away. *Did he know that I sometimes ate Ralston and Oatmeal?*

A cowboy rode toward me. "Whoa!" It was Tom Mix! I asked if I could be his "side-kick." To convince him I was worthy, I said, "I eat Ralston." He looked down from Wonder Horse Tony. "How many times a week?" I had signed the *Ralston Straight Shooter Pledge of Allegiance*, in which I promised to eat "at least three bowls of Ralston every week." I answered, "Four." I repeated another pledge for good measure: "I obey my father and mother, and eat the food they want me to eat." That was Pledge Number One. I asked "What's your purpose?" He smiled and touched the brim of his hat. "To be a Straight Shooter, arrest Lawbreakers and eat Ralston Cereal *every* day. You can't be my side-kick." I asked, "Why?" As he rode off, he said, "You don't eat enough Ralston!" I shouted, "I saved enough box tops to get your Straight Shooter pocketknife and slide whistle ring!" He rode on.

A rocket ship zoomed down. Out stepped Buck Rogers and Wilma Deering. Buck told me their purpose before I asked. "We want to save the *whole* universe!" Wilma, pulling on a yellow curl that had escaped her helmet, said, "Not everyone is ready to do that." I pleaded, "I'm ready! I can help capture Killer Kane and Ardala and take them to the intergalactic Rehabilitation

Center and-" Buck interrupted, "You have a Disintegrator Gun?" I had wanted to buy one at Alexander's Department Store on Fordham Road, but Momma said they cost too much. Buck and Wilma must have known. Without waiting for my answer, they climbed back into their rocket and took off.

Flash Gordon's rocket landed as Buck's disappeared. He came down the gangplank, Dale Arden at his side. Flash's mission was "To destroy Ming the Merciless and make sure that Zarkov prevents the planet Mongo from crashing into Earth." He smiled at Dale. "And to be true to you." She took his hand and added, "To be true to Fair Play." Flash nodded and they climbed back into their rocket. They hadn't even *asked* what mine was!

A man with a fedora pulled over his eyes walked toward me. I asked, "What's your purpose in life?" Dick Tracy's jaw jutted out further than ever as he asked, "Don't you read the Sunday *News?*" Was that in the comics Poppa angrily tore up when Morris and I had that fight? Dick was nice enough to tell me anyway. "To capture the thugs who killed Tess' father. If you listen to my radio program, you'd have a goal, too." He didn't have to tell me: to rise up in the ranks of the Dick Tracy Secret Service Patrol. I had gotten as far as sergeant, which required five box tops from Quaker Oats Cereal. My further promotions were hindered by Morris' refusal to eat oatmeal. I never got the lieutenant's badge, which required seven. Harold did. But no one I knew ever became an Inspector General--that required *fifteen!* Tracy pulled up his collar and turned on his wrist-watch radio as he walked off.

Whom would I meet next? I heard familiar heavy breathing. Morris! I didn't have to wake him to find out what his purpose was. I lay in the dark, envying him.

Eighteen

The Immigrants

Miss Cleary was as certain our class could not do Committee Projects as Mr. O'Hare was determined that we would. I carried a series of notes from our assistant principal in which he "asked," "requested," "pleaded" and finally "directed" her to do them because "Livingston Street's Committee on Gifted Children" would be "visiting to see *your* class' progress." He had signed his successive notes, "Don," "Donald," "O'Hare" and "Dr. O'Hare." She wrote back that committee work was "impossible," "difficult," "a waste of time," and "doubtful." She was "Kathy," "Kate," "Cleary" and "Miss Cleary." I discovered this by reading their correspondence on the upper landing of the little-used staircase. I also knew of their muttered comments while reading the other's "From the desk of-" notes. He thought she was a "fossilized dinosaur" who should retire while she described him as "dictator" who'd drive her from the school system. I discovered the outcome one morning when she formed Committees for an Immigration Project. Because Willie, Clarence and I were sitting at our table in the back and "worked so nicely together," she made us a committee.

Willie muttered his resentments while Clarence looked impassive. I thought, *I won't be here to give it!* Our presentation date was the second week in January.

Miss Cleary seemed overwhelmed with the addition of the projects to our rehearsals and regular schoolwork. She sent the class to the library where under the stern eye of the librarian-- who inspected our hands before we could touch a book--we "researched" our projects. We gleaned from our school library only a few sentences about Africans, Italians and Jews. Our *Personal Histories* were sparse. Momma told me she was born in Chernobyl and Poppa in Radomysl. Willie's History was, "My mother and father were born in Naples, the most important city in Italy." Clarence's was, "My grandmother way back came from Africa. My grandfather always lived here (he's an Apache.)" Miss Cleary thought we made "a good start," but having only a few sentences in our "Project Books" wouldn't satisfy the Committee. We each added a sentence about the languages in the "Old Countries." I wrote "Russian," leaving out Yiddish. Clarence wrote that the Apache language was "Tinde," and he didn't know the name of the African language. Willie insisted that his parents spoke "American" in Italy, the "same language as here." With Willie's arm in a cast, I did all of his writing. We still had no more than half a page in our project book, which made Miss Cleary roll up her eyes and mutter, "What have you afflicted me with, Don?" I was the only one who knew who Don was.

Shortly afterwards, I carried a note to the assistant principal. It read, "<u>Attention</u>: Don O'Hare, "You'd better postpone the Gifted Committee's visit. <u>You</u> may find 'Projects' easy with your Ph.D., but not my 4-1's. If you insist this nonsense continue, I'll never retire and be here until 1943 or the world blows up!" She signed it, "K. Cleary." Don O'Hare looked up at me and asked if the note deserved an answer. When he saw my expression, he laughed. To this day I don't know if he suspected that I read their notes.

When I returned, Miss Cleary told the class we'd have to go to the public library to continue our Research. Clarence, Willie and I met at the Washington Avenue library, a stately building that was part of the Carnegie Endowment for the education of New Yorkers. Clarence and I arrived first and Clarence applied for a library card. He filled out the application and handed it to the librarian. She couldn't hide curiosity and asked him about the reservation school in Montana. He answered, "I didn't like it." She waited and when he didn't say more, told him "a parent or guardian" had to sign the form. We sat down to wait for Willie and I got up the nerve to ask him about the reservation school. He hesitated then said, "After my mother got sick, the government agents took me away from my grandfather and *made* me go to this school." He watched to see my reaction before he continued. "They didn't let us speak *Tinde* or keep our ways." He had never before told me anything personal and I had never seen him angry. "I only went because they said they'd arrest my grandfather if I didn't." He made a face. "They cut off my long hair and made me wear a uniform. They had boys and girls who were from other tribes--some boys called me names and said I wasn't an Indian." He glanced at his brown arm and his face became impassive again. I had many more questions but even if Willie hadn't arrived I don't believe I would have asked them.

Willie told the librarian that he lost his library card and she checked her file and told him, "You never returned *Golden Fairy Tales* in 1937." He walked over to us muttering, "I'm not paying a dollar!" While he couldn't take books out, he could still read them in the library.

We explained our assignment to the young reference librarian and she led us to a shelf and took out four books. We sat down and read about the Pilgrims and early Dutch and French Settlements. One book had a sentence about Europeans who helped the American Revolution and mentioned Lafayette, Von Steuben and Pulaski. Another, "Immigrants from all over the world came to live in our country." We knew that wouldn't be enough to satisfy Miss Cleary, Mr. O'Hare and the Committee on the Gifted. The librarian showed us another book that said Africans were brought first as slaves. Clarence told her they came as "indentured servants, like other early settlers." Willie agreed with her and Clarence glared at him. We still didn't have enough and she suggested the Forty-Second Street Library, "if we had an older brother or sister" to take us. Willie and Clarence looked at me.

I went home that afternoon feeling the impostor, preparing for a project that I would not be around to give. I wasn't even sure if I'd be around for the Christmas and Chanukah plays! Yet I told no one. I was the Great Pretender, fearful of being exposed and amazed that no one saw through the mask. Perhaps I didn't believe that we would be moving to Atlanta.

Morris was home and I dismissed my worries by asking him about Africans coming here as indentured servants. He frowned and twisted his mouth, the way he did when he wasn't sure of something. I then asked why the English settlers didn't learn the Indian language when they arrived here. Morris had the same expression as the rabbi and the teachers had when I asked some of my questions. I knew not to press him about languages but asked how come someone can have an Indian grandfather and be Negro. He frowned and asked who I was talking about. I told him and he thought for a while and said, "Inter-marriage." His tone showed he would tell me no more. He did ask about "Projects" and I showed him my notes. He said what I expected him to say--that our history book, school and local libraries, "don't have books that teach you *real* history." I innocently asked where we could learn more. Of course he gave the answer I expected, mentioning that he planned to go there soon. I asked if I could go with him, if I wasn't "a pest." I was glad and had only to find out how to get him to take along Clarence and Willie.

Then I thought, *Why do I care about the project when I probably won't be around?* I lived in dread of the letter or phone call that would wrench me from the Bronx. When the doorbell rang, I no longer feared the detectives, but instead Mrs. Stone telling us Poppa was on the phone. Coming home from school, I cautiously opened the front door, afraid Momma would be waving the letter and shouting, "We're moving!" I knew how lonely she was but wanted our move to be delayed as long as possible--if not forever.

One lunch time she was half-delighted as she held a letter she said, "Your father thinks I can come down in a week or two to find a house." Her blissful look contrasted with mine. I knew she'd take me with her, especially when she added, "Yitzchok says there's a nice public school for you in Atlanta." I asked, "What about the plays?" She said, "There'll be other plays." I shouted, "I don't care about *other* plays--I'm staying at P.S. 4 and not moving!" I ran from the living room and slammed the door.

There was no place in the world that I detested more than Atlanta, a city I had never been to. A recurring dream was being alone on a train traveling through a dark tunnel, the hours passing into days. I sat on a hard rattan seat like those on the

Third Avenue El, light bulbs overhead giving off a flickering yellow glow. The car rocked back and forth as the train speedily took me further and further away from the Bronx for an unending ride that never reached Atlanta. *Did that mean we'd never get to Atlanta?* Another night I dreamt I asked Mrs. Schwartz about my train dream. She smiled and said, "When you're in Hebrew II, you'll read about Joseph, but I'll answer your question now. You're going to-" Her smile disappeared. I turned. Rabbi Weiss! He shouted, "No more questions!" I woke up frightened, not having an answer.

What made it harder for me was that I couldn't talk about this with any of my friends, including Harold and Deborah. I knew that our relationship would forever be changed at the telling.

Nineteen

Who Would Want to Live Forever?"

With the upset of the moving and my life uncertain, Grandpa remained a mainstay. I knew he couldn't prevent us from moving or convince Momma to let me stay with them while she found a home in Atlanta. He listened to my complaints and fears with the same earnestness as he did with adults. He didn't dismiss them nor give me superficial reassurances. He listened and nodded thoughtfully so that I believed somehow, with faith and patience, a solution would reveal itself. That was why I was so disappointed at the first snow on a Saturday in the late Fall. As I stood at the window, the swirling flakes obscured the park across Fulton Avenue. "Take a good look," said Morris, who stood behind me. "You won't be seeing snow much longer." I asked, "Doesn't it snow in Atlanta?" The heat from the radiator wafted upwards, bathing the front of my body. Finally, Morris said, "Atlanta is in the tropics." A minute later, from the hallway, I heard Morris arguing with Momma about going to his Saturday job in a Bathgate Avenue grocery. They compromised on his wearing galoshes. I knew that I would have a harder time, but was determined to go because this could be one of the few remaining times I'd go to shul with Grandpa. Volunteering to wear galoshes didn't help. There are several Yiddish words for falling snow, ranging from falling flakes to a blizzard. Momma chose the severest one: "You can't go out in that *zaveruchah!" A blizzard!* I ran back to the window. I told her it was "hardly" snowing and wasn't exaggerating. Occasional flakes were falling on the light coating on the ground. Momma stood behind me and while not confirming what she was also seeing, said, "Your grandfather won't go out in this weather." I was about to object that he'd be expecting me, but Momma continued, "If he doesn't have sense not to go, your grandmother should." I knew arguing wouldn't help so I said, "If you don't want me to pray for the contrabandist finding Avrum and your sister-"

While I ate breakfast, Momma said the storm had lightened up and I could go, "but don't be disappointed if your grandfather isn't there."

I was willing to take that risk and put on my galoshes and scarf without Momma reminding me. I got to *shul* in record time despite being bundled up. I found a hook for my coat and sat down next to Grandpa. He interrupted his praying to whisper, "I wondered if your mother would let you come." With a twinkle in his eyes, he said, "Your grandmother also gave me a hard time." The service dragged on and I couldn't wait for it to end, but enjoyed the sponge cake and juice. Grandpa, sipping his drink, said, "A little brandy warms you in winter." Another man said, "It's good medicine too." They had a second round of *bronfin* and one man toasted, "Today life, tomorrow, who cares." Grandpa said, "Brandy is a funny drink, you pour it into your stomach and it creeps right to your head." As Grandpa put on his heavy overcoat, one of the men helped him. Grandpa asked, "Earning a *mitzvah* by helping an old man?" The man, gray-haired and old in my eyes, replied, "I'm old enough to be concerned about collecting *mitzvahs*." Grandpa said, "It's never too late to impress the Messiah." They laughed and the man said, "I'm younger than you, but I still have aches and pains." Grandpa replied, "Better ten times sick than once dead." They laughed again.

We walked through the slush, slowed down by our galoshes and coats. Although the sun had broken through the clouds, the wind bit into us. Grandpa, as usual, climbed slowly up the stairs, breathing heavily and resting at each half landing. Grandma's *"Gut Shabbes"* greeting was followed with the rebuke, "Why did you go in this weather?" Grandpa winked at me and said, "See, Yalkala did come to *shul.*" Grandma looked at me and asked, "If your grandfather wasn't in *shul,* what would you have done?" I answered, "After the service, I'd have come here." Grandma said, "Your grandson has more sense than you!" I hadn't thought of that until she asked. Eager to change the subject, I said, "I can eat with you!" I was uncomfortable with their arguing, rare as it was. Grandma's chicken soup warmed me and the *kugel* was delicious, but I couldn't wait to go into the living room. When Grandpa settled into his armchair and asked, "What's today's question?" I didn't hesitate.

"I have two of them: Why don't people live forever? Or if they can't live forever, at least as long as Adam?" I figured he knew the Bible said it was 930 years.

Grandpa laughed. "Yalkala, I know why the rabbi gets angry." He quickly added, "Don't be bashful to ask *any* question. There's no *bad* question, only someone who doesn't know the answer." Grandma came into the room and set a tray on the table. "Have some sponge cake for dessert, Yalka." Then to Grandpa, "Drink your tea instead of-" she used the idiom *hakin a chinuk*-- "hitting a tea kettle" which meant talking too much.

Grandpa's eyes twinkled. "Try answering your Grandson's questions." He repeated them. Without hesitating, she said, "With all the trouble and suffering in this world, who would want to live forever? And people suffer more today than they did in Adam's time, so why stretch it out *too* long?"

Grandpa gleefully clapped his hands together. "A *chachem* is your grandmother! No, a *Talmud chachem!* She answered one of the hardest questions just like that. The Talmud hasn't been finished because the rabbis don't allow women scholars!"

Grandma said, "Another reason the Talmud is unfinished is because you men talk too much" and walked out.

Grandpa was still beaming. "Your grandmother is right, if we'd live forever we'd have only more oceans to cross and *pogroms* to live through." He chuckled, although I knew he didn't think that funny. "I'll ask *you* a question. What does living in *Shechinah* mean?" I shook my head. "Living in God's presence, with joy in all that you do, whether learning or playing or working. Then the *Ruach Adonoi* fully lives." He placed a cube of sugar in his mouth and sipped his tea, gesturing for me to have my sponge cake. "When I was a boy, I picked apples for a farmer. I loved to go out into the country, even if it was to work. In the winter, I helped my father fix shoes and studied Torah." From his eyes I knew he was back in those days, but I still

185

couldn't imagine him a boy. "There are experiences in your life that happen once, but are relived again and again in your mind. I remember my wedding day." He paused and I imagined the festivities at the family wedding I had gone to. "Our parents arranged the match, but I was not disappointed-" His eyes twinkled "-maybe I expected worse." Then his eyes became sad. "There were hard days when your grandmother gave birth to our first child, a girl who lived only a week." It was a while before Grandpa saw me again. "But God lets even the poor share in *Shechinah* and be rewarded when the Messiah comes."

That made me think of another question. "If the body returns to dust, what do people look like when the Messiah comes?"

"How do you think up these questions?" His look was one of wonder rather than exasperation, but to make sure I didn't misunderstand, he said, "The sages say, 'Better one should be a questioner than a fool." He sat back. "Your questions wake up an old man's brain. When I was your age I was full of questions, too, studying to be a *Talmud chochem.* I thought being a scholar was more important than being a king or a millionaire. My parents thought so too, but we were nine children." I still couldn't imagine Grandpa a boy. He continued, "I studied but had questions no one could answer. The truth is not simple." His eyes were lost in the past. I waited until he returned. "What was your question?"

I repeated it and he stroked his beard. "Every day we ask God to keep faith with those lying in the dust and to bring them back to life. How He'll do that is not explained. Ezekiel says after the graves open up, the Messiah brings together the body and the soul. He doesn't say how either." He picked up the Bible from the table and I waited until he found the place he was looking for. "Isaiah says, 'The dead shall live, the bodies shall arise--Awake and sing, you who live in the dust.' He also doesn't say how." He closed the Bible. "I can go on, Yalka, but you should be more interested in living, with *Shekinah*--Glory--and *Ruach Adonoi*--the Divine Spirit--and not worry about death. Leave those worries to the prophets or the elderly obsessed with death. Pay attention to life." He closed his eyes and when he opened them said, "Be concerned with two questions God will ask you." I held my breath--I wanted to remember them. "The first is why you haven't enjoyed all of the pleasures He made possible." He waited for that to sink in. "The other question will *not* be if you prayed or if you believed in Him. You *will* be asked if you've been honorable with your fellow man. That's how it's written in the Talmud."

Grandma entered and sat down near the window. "Your grandfather was up late last night, reading his Talmud so he could answer your questions."

Grandpa smiled. "Yalka asks questions that trouble the sages." Then, "The bashful don't learn. A man should never stop asking questions, even on his last day." We sat in silence. I didn't mind--I had no more questions to ask and was groggy from all that I heard, that which I understood and that which I didn't. I was aware of how awash in sunlight the room was and felt my worries lifted like a weight. Yet when I was leaving and kissing him good-by, I asked, "Who's going to answer my questions when I'm in Atlanta?"

With my face pressed against his cheek, he couldn't see my tears. "Some you'll figure out yourself, Yalkala, my little scholar. Others from wise men."

"I want *you* to answer my questions!" Despite my effort to suppress my sobs, he felt me tremble and held me tighter. "You'll hear my voice," he said, "wherever you'll be, just as I'll hear yours."

On the way home, the *kugel* warmed my hands. I still heard Grandma's, "Have a big piece for yourself, after all, you went to *shul.*" The sun had melted most of the snow and it was difficult imagining the storm of that morning. That evening I asked Morris what happened when you die. "You break down into the elements," he said. I wondered if he had been reading up on it as had Grandpa. I discovered I was made mostly of hydrogen and oxygen, the combination being water, along with carbon, iron, copper and other elements. He said the total cost of the elements and chemicals that a person consisted of could be bought for two or three dollars. If I didn't believe him, I could see the exhibit at the Museum of Natural History. I asked, "What about the soul? Do they show that at the exhibit?" He frowned and said,

"Nobody's seen a soul." I replied, "That's because it's invisible!" I ran from the room before he could say anything.

Later, Morris said, "There's another answer to your question about what happens to you after you die." I was surprised that he was going to give me another answer without my asking until he hummed a strange tune and then sang, "Don't you ever laugh as a hearse goes by/ For you may be the next to die-" I covered my ears but still heard, "The worms crawl in, the worms crawl out/ The worms play pinochle in your snout/ They eat your eyes, They eat your nose/ They eat the jelly between your toes." He especially liked my look of disgust when he sang, "A big green worm with glowing eyes/Crawls in your stomach and crawls out your eyes." He did stop then and say, "Don't worry, when you're dead, you won't feel it."

Grandpa's and Morris' explanations of Life and Death were so different. How could two people I loved and trusted have such incongruous beliefs? It was easy believing in God when I was with Grandpa and hard with Morris. When I was with Morris, I doubted God and the Bible. How could I choose without being disloyal to one of them?

When I got into bed I was afraid of falling asleep and dreaming that worms ate my edible parts, leaving only jars of water and nails. Neither did I want to see bodies turning to dust and awaiting the Messiah. The doorbell interrupted my confused thoughts. It was too late to expect anyone. I followed Morris into the hallway. It was Uncle Sol. He'd just found out that his brother-in-law had been beaten and arrested during *Kristallnacht.* He shook his head in disbelief. His mustache, so often twitching mischievously, now hung sadly over his lip. "Innocent people arrested and murdered because they were Jews." Momma said, "Becky's family must leave now." Sol replied, "I hope it's not too late! When they arrested him, they also took away his business." He shook his head and I noticed how gray his hair was. "He didn't leave because he was afraid of losing everything he worked for his whole life. Then, in one night it's stolen from him. Now they'll be lucky to escape with their lives." He shook his head. "From suffering to happiness seems an eternity; from happiness to suffering is but a quick step." Momma wiped her eyes with her apron. When Sol left, he whispered to me, "These are hard times and may even get worse--be brave, like a Maccabee."

He left. I got back into bed. The day had been a long one. More had surged into my child's mind than I could absorb. Sol's news evoked the images of Aunt Becky's family, who stood before me in their studio photo, a young couple and their three children, timelessly frozen in their stylish clothes and smiling proudly at their American relatives. They exuded confidence, prosperity and perfection. The painted background was a ship's deck so they looked as if they were posing on a cruise. I had stared often and enviously at Aaron, the little boy my age, dressed in sailor suit and happier-looking than Avrum. They were two cousins I had never seen and wondered if I ever would. Aaron's mother was plump and had a happy smile. The father sported a trim mustache and his assured expression verged on arrogance. I couldn't imagine him removed from the photo, beaten and jailed. Unimaginable was the full extent of *Kristallnacht,* which was revealed in fragments so that only years later did I realize its sweeping dimensions. The Nazis retaliated for Von Rath's murder by destroying 200 synagogues and 7,500 shops, jailing 20,000 Jews and killing others. The Nazis levied a billion mark penalty on the Jewish community of Germany for all the trouble they had caused.

The day had been long. When I went to bed, I was still thinking about life and death. Uncle Sol's news about *Kristallnacht* capped my anxieties, which pursued me into my dreams. In one, I was pursued by a gigantic green worm and nearly eaten until two angels grabbed him. I awakened before discovering whether they killed him or he ate them.

In the next one, I was the winner of the Jack Armstrong song contest to replace the Hudson High Fight Song *and* had solved Little Orphan Annie's coded message, "D-R-I-N-K O-V-A-L-T-I-N-E." Jack Armstrong had also recommended me by saying "of all the boys in America, you most need the chance to prove yourself." My reward was a secret assignment in Buck Rogers rocket ship. Buck said my mission was "to start a human colony on the Mongo." Wilma Deering said, "You can change your

189

mind. The second-place winner will go." That was Harold, the copy-cat who had also had entered the contests. How could I disappoint not only my heroes, but all the humans on Earth? But Mongo was a planet in another solar system ruled by Ming the Merciless! Wilma said, "Flash is sending Dr. Zarkov to help you." He was the scientist who had gone crazy, but recovered. I couldn't back down. I could do what Torres and Columbus did-- find a haven for the Jews. I had to keep that part of my plan secret from Buck and Wilma, just as Columbus couldn't tell Ferdinand and Isabella. Halfway to Mongo, Emperor Ming's rocket ship fired at us and the explosion woke me up.

Twenty

The Reprieve

On Saturday, Momma brought us a letter from Poppa but refused to say anything. We anxiously hung around the apartment all morning and while I considered myself an expert in reading Momma, her dazed expression gave me no clue. Morris was also at a loss. Momma went through all of her usual activities like a robot. It was a strange feeling to know that our fate was sealed and known by Momma, but all we could do was guess. In the late afternoon she called us into the kitchen. I realized that she had as hard a time *not* telling us as we had waiting. "I hope you're not going to be disappointed-" I blinked, held my breath and thought, "Up-and-away" but still had time to see the panic on Morris' face before she continued, "-but the bank's taking its time lending your father the money. We'll have to wait till after the holidays to move." To confirm the news, she read that part of Poppa's letter and didn't see the elation on our faces. I couldn't help but feel sorry for her, though I rejoiced at the reason for her unhappiness. She hadn't told us sooner because she wanted to spare us the bad news for as long as possible. To our credit, we waited until we were in the living room to rejoice by jumping up and down. Morris, out of breath, whispered, "Maybe I'll finish the term!" I said, "I'll be in both plays!" When Momma kissed me goodnight, the towel around her head broadcast her unhappiness. She whispered, "Every day brings its own troubles." I marveled at what elated us made her so miserable. I was still awake when Morris got into bed. He said, "it's only a reprieve." Although I had never heard the word, I knew what it meant.

The troubled haze in which I'd been living cleared. I no longer had to pretend that I'd be in the plays. Everything became real again and even filtered into my dreams. That night I was in my toy shop at the North Pole when Mattathias entered. I told him it was the Christmas play," but he pleaded, "Something has to be done to save the Jews in Europe. You could help." He pointed to my sled, now as big as a rocket ship! The shop teacher said, "That's the least my shop class can do for the Jews." Mattathias said, "You're the only one who knows how to fly it." A familiar voice said, "You'll need engines." Morris! I said, "I've got something better than engines or rockets." Hitched up to the sled were my reindeer! *Blitzen*, in the lead, shouted, "We're ready, fatso Santa." Clarence, wearing *Donder's* mask, said, "We're off!" Sol shouted, "I always knew a Santa Claus Maccabee would save our people!" I picked up the reins and shouted, "Ho, ho, we'll bring Jews from every European land to join the earlier Pilgrim band." *Blitzen* tried to do a loop--the clouds and blue sky flashed round and round.

I woke up when I fell out of bed and I climbed back without waking Morris.

That Sunday we gave the Litofsky play at the Kaplans. I was familiar with the route to the Lewis Morris Building and routine of gaining entrance. I said, "Deborah Kaplan," to the doorman rather than Dr. Kaplan to make sure he didn't think me sick. I gave the floor before the elevator operator asked me and thanked him when I got off.

Deborah greeted me and led me into the living room filled with grown-ups. I said. "Hello" to Mrs. Kaplan and shook Dr. Kaplan's hand. He asked, "How's the scholar?"

I was prepared. "Asking questions."

He winked. "Good-don't let the rabbi stifle your curiosity." He introduced me to the adults, but I forgot their names almost as soon as he mentioned them. They said they looked forward to our play. Sarah and Herschel arrived soon afterward and we went to Deborah's room. She gave us the scripts--it felt good to hold the script, *Chanukah, the Glory of the Maccabees.* We decided which parts, in addition to our own, we'd play. Deborah suggested we read what we didn't remember. Sarah and Herschel were as relieved as me. As we silently re-read the play, I was surprised at how much I remembered. Deborah's mother knocked on the door and offered us juice as well as reassuring us, "We know you haven't seen the script, so don't be nervous." When I sipped my drink, I realized how dry my mouth was.

The sofas and chairs were all occupied. Dr. Kaplan, sitting in front, whispered to us, "Relax, we're a friendly audience." My heart beat as I cleared my throat and said, "There are tyrants today and there were tyrants in the old days-" My voice steadied despite feeling all their eyes "-but never shall the Hebrews forget the evil Emperor Antiochus." We re-enacted the massacre of the traitor and the soldiers. The audience listened intently as I said, "It's better to die in battle than to look upon the evils of our nation and the Sanctuary." The play went all too quickly and soon we had defeated our enemies and were celebrating with the burning of the miraculous oils in the Menorah.

The adults burst into applause and shouted "Bravo!" They shook our hands and praised us while we beamed our appreciation. Mrs. Kaplan brought out refreshments. Delicious as they were, I was fascinated with the discussion that followed. Years later, I read many of the historical facts they mentioned. Michael, a slender man with a beard, said, "Lev would be delighted with girls playing Maccabees." He turned to the young woman sitting next to him. "Sophie, will the Maccabees become fashionable again?"

She answered, "Not only fashionable, but necessary." She was as young as Mrs. Schwartz and her face lit up when she spoke. "The priests tried to suppress the story of the Maccabean struggle."

Dr. Kaplan asked, "Is that why their rabbi censored the play?"

Sophie explained, "The Books of the Maccabees are not part of the Old Testament--they came down to us in Greek, not Hebrew. The rebellion was a civil war as well as one against an occupying army."

Dr. Kaplan asked, "Why would the priests want to suppress the struggle to preserve Judaism?"

Sophie explained, "Most priests were afraid; others adopted pagan rituals and sacrifices. Don't forget the person slain by Mattathias was a Jew."

Someone said, "What a way for the rebellion to start."

Michael said, "So it was started by fanatics, like the Sons of Liberty."

Sophie nodded. "Lev showed the need to fight traitors as well as foreign occupiers. Priests censored the story because they groveled at the feet of the later occupiers."

Dr. Kaplan said, "Render unto Caesar what is Caesar's-- Christ learned that from the priests!"

Mrs. Kaplan, walking by with a tray of sweets, said, "Christ could have figured that out for himself. Don't forget, he had a Jewish head." The others laughed.

Mrs. Kaplan whispered to me, "Have something for your stomach" and pointed to what looked like a chocolate covered hot-dog. "The éclair is delicious." I was surprised at its taste.

Sophie explained that the *Gomorra* made a fuss over the long-burning oil and didn't mention the civil war.

I said, "That's like the new Chanukah play!"

They turned to me and Dr. Kaplan patted my back. "You're making Al into a radical." They laughed but I wasn't embarrassed. Then, the talk turned to Europe--Chamberlain, Hitler, Stalin, Czechoslovakia. Sophie compared the Popular Front to the Maccabees and the priests to the collaborators. Michael reminded her that the Maccabees became the Hasmonian dynasty and later invited the Romans as protectors. Michael said life has more ironies than the most imaginative dramatist can think of and Sophie said, "Except Litofsky--he saw the parallel before Munich. And he quoted from the sources themselves--the Books of the Maccabees."

I exclaimed, "That's what Mrs. Schwartz said!"

Sophie asked, "Belle Schwartz?"

I shouted her name. Deborah, Sarah and Herschel rushed over. Sophie and Michael knew Mrs. Schwartz! They gave Deborah her address and she said she'd try to call her. We were delighted at the possibility of seeing her again.

I was concentrating on my second éclair while they discussed what a Jew was. Deborah's father got the Talmud from the shelf and read, "When a man appears before the Throne of Judgment, the first question he will be asked is not 'Have you believed in God or observed the ritual?' but have you-"

I interrupted, "-been honorable with your fellow man?"

Everyone turned to me as Dr. Kaplan asked, "Where did you learn that?"

I flushed. "My grandfather. He's Orthodox and goes to *shul* every day."

Sophie smiled. "We need more Jews like Al's grandfather."

Dr. Kaplan said, "And grandchildren like Al."

My face warmed again. They were filling my head with facts and ideas that I would only fully understand years later and read words similar to what was spoken that day. It was getting dark-- Sarah, Herschel and I said we'd have to leave. The grown-ups again told us how much they enjoyed the performance and the Kaplans said we'd have to come more often.

Herschel and I walked Sarah home to an apartment building on Webster Avenue, all the while talking about the play and having Mrs. Schwartz' address. Then, as Herschel and I continued walking, we marveled at the assortment of refreshments. He made a face when I mentioned the éclairs. He thought they were strange hot-dogs and I told him what they were. When I saw his expression, I admitted that I made the same mistake until Mrs. Kaplan told me what they were. We were so absorbed in our conversation that we stopped in front of his apartment building in the shadow of the Third Avenue Elevated Train tracks. I pretended not to notice the shabbiness of the building and knew why he had avoided my walking past his home.

Twenty-One

The Play's the Thing

The only nice thing about the rabbi's Chanukah play was that the Father wore a suit. Momma planned my first pair of long pants for my Bar Mitzvah, a time-span that seemed light years away. While my arguments couldn't revise her schedule, she had no alternative if I was to be in the Chanukah play. How could I appear in knickers? That meant a trip to Sol's store. Momma helped in his search among the unclaimed suits. Her glance and touch judged each suit's style, amount of wear, durability and fit. None that met the first three criteria were anywhere near my size. Did only the mothers of skinny boys leave suits at Sol's or was I the only boy my height who was so fat? Sol had his own theory, which he didn't hesitate to tell. "The mothers who can't pay the cleaning bill also can't afford to feed their boys!" His mustache twitched with delight as he speculated, "With the Depression, some mothers first get rid of the suit, then give away their boy." Sol laughed, but Momma looked shocked. Even in jest she couldn't accept any irreverence toward Mothers.

Momma examined the two most promising suits and finally decided on a dark gray one, handing it to Sol for his assessment. He rubbed the material. "The color's practical and English wool will last forever." Momma nodded her approval. While I could be wearing this suit until my Bar Mitzvah--or beyond--with periodic alterations by Sol, I was merely a spectator. Not only didn't either of them consider asking me what I preferred, *I* didn't believe I had that right. I obediently went into the small bathroom and put on the suit. I was unable to button the waist. When I came out, Sol chalk-marked the pants, muttering, "Either this boy was starving or you've gained weight. Luckily there's material to let out." I squirmed not only at his remark, but also because of the material. I complained, "It itches!" Momma gave me her *Don't-be-ungrateful* look while Sol said, "England has cold winters and the sheep have heavy coats." I said, "It's hot in Atlanta!" Momma said, "You can wear English wool *anywhere!*" When I was all pinned up, Sol stepped back and studied me. "You'll look like Rothschild's son, except there's no money in the pockets--heh, heh!"

A few days later, we came back to try on the suit. Momma said the pants were too tight. Sol looked annoyed and said, "They fit last week." Then his eyes twinkled--You've been stuffing him like a goose for the holidays!" I sucked in my stomach and gasped, "It fits!" Momma, scowled. "He's not fat--just growing!" Sol made new chalk marks and beyond Momma's hearing, whispered, "No eating seconds until after the play."

Two days later, the suit hung in our hallway closet. Morris said, "I'm surprised they make suits like that in Al's size." I didn't like *that,* but enjoyed his aggrieved, "How come I had to wait until I was thirteen to wear a suit?" He deserved Momma's rebuke: "If you were in a Chanukah play, you'd have had a suit." Morris got his revenge: he reminded Momma that she didn't have to make that *other* suit for him, referring to the red outfit Momma banished to an upper shelf in the hallway closet.

We had a last rehearsal at Deborah's and after my boring explanation of Chanukah's origins, I wistfully said, "Couldn't we give the Litofsky play?" The *Arba* reacted with interest, as if I had thought it through. Once mentioned, it became a possibility and I blurted out a plan. I sounded more confident than I felt and they were enthusiastic. While Herschel chattered away on the way home, I was worried. Until we gave the performance, I spent several anxious days and restless nights uncertain if we could carry my plan through. The performance date arrived all too soon. *Everyone* was coming--my family, the Kaplans and their friends, other parents, members of the congregation and people in the community. I hoped that I would have a dream telling me if we should go through with the plan, but the morning of the performance, I awakened with no dream.

At breakfast, Morris glared at the orange box of *Wheaties.* He muttered, "Horse food."

Momma said, "Don't start with your brother, he's nervous enough." She was right and for more reasons than she knew. To keep the peace, she made him a scrambled egg. I'd have preferred one as well, but didn't dare ask. I needed two more box tops for Jack Armstrong's Shooting Plane.

When I was dressed, Momma said, "How my mother and father would have loved to see this." Then, her eyes welled up-- "Better yet, your wedding day--Halevai!" *My* perspective was shorter: surviving the day.

Before I left, Morris asked if we planned to give "that Maccabee play." Although the *Arba* had taken a pledge of secrecy, I told Morris, hoping he'd advise me whether to go ahead. He had said, "Only you can decide." Why was everyone telling me to do things *they* wanted me to do but when it came to my difficult decisions, they left it up to me? However, this morning he saw my expression and said, "I can understand your not doing it." What little confidence I had vanished.

The performance was scheduled for eleven and Mr. Ravitch wanted us to come at ten for a last rehearsal. The *Arba* planned to meet at nine. As I walked to Hebrew School, I barely paid attention to the sunny December Sunday, but I did cross Fulton Avenue to walk along the Crotona Park side of the street. Through the leafless bushes I saw what I first mistook as a squirrel: the cat I had frightened that was struck by the car and then limped away. I thought it died but there it was! It flattened its ears before scampering into the bushes. It limped, but was alive. The omen I'd been waiting for!

I arrived early, but the others were already there. Fortunately, neither the rabbi nor Mr. Ravitch had arrived. After the janitor let us in, Deborah showed us our robes and headdresses. Morris wasn't the only one who was in on our secret. Mrs. Kaplan prepared sheets which we'd wrap around ourselves for robes, along with the *kaffiyehs* for our heads. We hid them in a closet behind the stage. While the janitor finished arranging chairs in the back of the auditorium, we rehearsed the Ravitch play. I burped during the dinner scene and the others couldn't stop laughing. When the janitor left, we rehearsed the Litofsky play, but our excitement made that difficult. I still found it hard to believe we'd go through with it. When the rabbi and Mr. Ravitch arrived, we rehearsed the Balsom play. Herschel panicked--he couldn't remember his lines. Sarah confused hers and I thought I forgot mine. "It's stage-fright," said Deborah. I remembered Miss Cleary telling us that deep breathing helps. We did that and the lines came back.

At ten-thirty, children from our class arrived and we rehearsed our songs. Then the audience trickled in. We watched them from behind the makeshift curtain and stifled our shouts when we recognized our families. We jumped in fright when we heard Rabbi Weiss behind us. He was beaming. "Every seat is filled! I'm having extra chairs brought from the classrooms." He stood next to the closet containing our Maccabean costumes and I was afraid he'd somehow know they were there. When he left, Herschel, trembling, asked, "Should we give the play?" The panic started again. I heard myself saying, "It is better for us to die in battle-" My voice wavered and I was really ready to run, but the others raised their fists in our Maccabean salute.

Deborah saw her parents and their friends, then Sarah and Herschel their families. *Where's my family?* How could I perform if they had vanished en route? The audience became a blur until I saw Uncle Sol leading them in, Becky and Momma on either side, followed by Grandpa and Grandma. Deborah was the first to see Mrs. Schwartz--Michael invited her! She looked as pretty as ever. At five minutes after eleven, Rabbi Weiss welcomed everyone to a "sold out" performance that would help "our school and the Yeshivas in Europe." He boasted about his exemplary instructional program until the audience applauded, impatient for the play. He introduced, "rabbi-to-be" Ravitch, who looked more nervous than he did on the first day of class. Although the audience quieted down, he was barely heard. He mispronounced the author's name, which the audience didn't know but when he called me Al Kaplan, voices corrected him, Sol's unmistakably the loudest. The rabbi rescued him by reminding the audience to have *"latkes* baked by our Ladies Auxiliary after the play." That got the loudest burst of applause.

Two boys pulled back the curtain to reveal us sitting at a table. I stood up and said, "I will extol Thee, O Lord-" and was astonished to see not only the actors stand up, but also the audience! A surge of power replaced my stage fright. "Thou hast raised me up; I cried unto Thee, and Thou didst heal me." I sat down and *everyone* sat down! Then I answered Sarah and Herschel's questions about Chanukah, while Deborah answered those about food. By the time we gave presents to the Children, the audience was restless. They perked up when we sang, *Little Candle Fires*-- "Chanukah pancakes are a treat/Just look at them piled so neat/Sizzling hot/so good to eat/On Chanukah."

At the end of the play the audience kept applauding and we took three curtain calls. When the curtain was closed, we rushed to get our Litofsky costumes. Meanwhile, the rabbi started another speech, something we hadn't expected. I stood frozen, peeking from the side of the curtain, clutching the robe behind my back. When the rabbi smiled at me I felt that if I didn't run off the stage, I'd faint. I took a deep breath, thought *Up-and-away!* and flung the robe around me, pulled the *kaffiyeh* onto my head and stepped out. I looked directly at the audience and in a voice that didn't seem to come from me, shrilled, "There are tyrants today and there were tyrants in the old days-" Rabbi Weiss' mouth opened wide and I was afraid I'd be struck dumb. From where the Kaplans and their friends sat came applause, in which others joined in. The audience thought this was part of our performance! "-never shall the Hebrews forget the evil Emperor Antiochus." That was the cue for the others, but no one appeared. Had they fled and deserted me? Hours seemed to pass before in slow motion the robed figures of Deborah, Herschel and Sarah walked onto the stage. I no longer noticed the rabbi and responded only to my fellow Maccabees. After I killed the traitor and Antiochus' soldiers, Deborah said, "You did the only thing that a righteous Hebrew could do, and I am ready to die with you." Then, worried, she asked, "But what about the children?" Momma called out, *"De Kinder!"* I was reassuring her when I answered, "We'll take the children with us into the hills so Antiochus' soldiers can not harm them." Soon, we were at the end of the play, in unison giving our oath, "They come unto us to destroy us...We fight for our lives and our Law. It is better for us to die in battle, than to look upon the evils of our nation and the Sanctuary."

The applause was thunderous. Dr. Kaplan shouted, "Bravo!" and Sol, "Let the same fate befall Hitler!" Michael called out, "Let us all take the oath!" Other voices chanted, "The oath!" The audience stood up as one person. The four of us repeated the oath, pausing so the words thundered back to us. There was a moment of silence before applause again filled the room. Michael walked onto the stage with Mrs. Schwartz at his side. She carefully walked up the steps--she was pregnant! We hugged her. Holding hands, with her in the middle, the rest of the class joined us as we bowed to the cheers, whistles and shouts of "Bravo!" Rabbi Weiss stepped from behind the curtain and the audience applauded him. Mr. Ravitch joined him and the audience applauded him. The rabbi raised his hands and the applause gradually stopped. My heart pounded when the rabbi started to speak. "Our children-" there was a long pause. "-are our inspiration-" Everyone started applauding and wouldn't stop until he shouted, "We have *lotkes* and drinks!" Rabbi Weiss looked as if he was about to say something to us, but our families came onto the stage. They told him we had performed "two wonderful plays." I introduced Mrs. Schwartz, the Kaplans and their friends to my family. Momma wished that Poppa could have seen me. Sol, clapping me on the back, said, "You were a better Maccabee than a Maccabee! And you don't look bad in the suit." Morris was there! He whispered, "I wouldn't have missed this for anything." I met Sarah and Herschel's family and spent as much time as I could with Mrs. Schwartz. Except for her protruding stomach--she was in her seventh month--she looked as she always did. She told us she was in graduate school and had changed her major from religion to psychology. Her husband was a short, serious-looking man and although I knew little else about him, I didn't think him worthy of her. The rest is vague. I must have had a *lotke* because I remembered Momma giving me a napkin so I wouldn't wipe my greasy fingers on my pants. I did remember Morris saying, "The Maccabee story is the best one in the Bible." I said, "That story *isn't* in the Bible!" I was pleased to show him that he didn't know everything.

That night when I was in bed, he whispered across the darkness, "I know why you have a crush on Mrs. Schwartz."

How did he know?

With the Chanukah play and its worries behind me, I could now concentrate my worries on the Christmas play. Fortunately, there were only five intervening days; unfortunately, there *were* five days. I discovered that peculiar property of time that made each day pass with excruciating slowness while the entire five days passed too quickly. I also experienced my mind's ability to overcome one worry only to have it instantly replaced with the next.

The night before the play, I regretted that we weren't in Atlanta. Morris wondered why I was so nervous. "You did a good job with your Chanukah play." How could I explain what I was discovering: past success didn't make me less anxious. I felt worse, fearful that my Santa performance wouldn't be as good as the Chanukah one. I answered, "Something could happen." He asked, "Like what?" Rather than being reassuring, his question opened the Pandora's Box of possible catastrophes, including ones I hadn't thought of. Morris coached me on how to relax. He'd read about hypnosis and yoga, but they were too complicated to learn the evening before the performance. In order to fall asleep, he said I should count imaginary airplanes taking off. I did but there was no end to them. I resigned myself to just lying there, listening to Morris snore.

An unexpected snowstorm covered my North Pole headquarters. I was prepared to struggle through to my sleigh but Mrs. Claus asked, "How can you go out in such a *zavarucha?*" I explained, "How could I disappoint all the Christian and Jewish children?" I knew the Jewish children would understand, but the Christian ones would have blamed a Jewish Santa. *Blitzen* said, "The Jewish children can't get toys anyway because they don't have chimneys!" I told Willie, "I'll leave them in their foyers." *Donder* said, "For the Indian children we can drop them down the smoke holes." Then *Blitzen* burst out laughing--I was in my underwear! How could I explain that Momma returned the suit to Mrs. Rosenbloom to get her money back?

When I woke up I rushed to the window, but saw no snow, only the eerie glow of the street light. I got back into bed and had another dream which I suppose had to do with missing Poppa. All the excitement about the plays had pushed him into the background. I was in the biggest toy factory in the Universe! Poppa was dressed in his best suit and Sol, a tape measure over his shoulder, was at his side. Sol said, "Your father's the Henry Ford of the Toy makers!" *Poppa owned the factory!* Poppa smiled at me and said, "I was able to buy this factory in the Bronx." *I won't have to leave P. S. #4!* Sol said, "A horse has a big head-" and Poppa, "Everything's better than all right!"

It was daylight and Morris' bed was empty. I wasn't hungry, but gulped down my Ralston to avoid an argument as well as save up for a Tom Mix Decoder Badge. The doorbell rang. It was the *Wooden Soldier with the Broken Leg.* He asked if I was going to wear my costume to school. Momma answered for me: "His uncle pressed it." Momma wasn't the only one who didn't want me wearing it to school. As I carried it in a bag, Harold recited a litany of possible catastrophes. I warned, "If you talk about them, you can make them happen." Of course the other axiom of Momma's was that if you *don't* talk about terrible things they could happen!

Class 4-1 was unrecognizable in their costumes. Miss Cleary let me change in the Boys Bathroom. Momma made the waist loose, as if she expected me to grow into the pants. Miss Cleary suggested I stuff a pillow from her closet into my suit. Willie said something from inside his *Blitzen* mask that I couldn't understand, but I could guess what it was. He fooled around as if Miss Cleary couldn't recognize him. When she threatened not to give him ice cream at our party, he behaved.

Our footsteps echoed through the empty auditorium that would soon be filled with the early grade pupils for the first performance. When we were on stage, Mrs. Santa clutched her stomach. Harold, an expert on such symptoms, warned, "Betty's going to throw up!" Miss Cleary asked Margaret to take her to the Girls Bathroom before the other pupils, nervous enough, became ill. Willie was the only one immune to anxiety. He peered from behind the curtain as teachers led their classes in, the boys in white shirts and red ties, the girls in middy blouses with red neckerchiefs. Each class occupied a rectangle of seats so that the auditorium looked like a checkerboard. Willie called out, "Skinny Gleason" and "Creepy Thompson," his nicknames for our second and third grade teachers whom he blamed for giving him a bad reputation. The rest of us were too nervous for anything but panic. Miss Cleary nearly succeeded in calming us until we heard our Principal Preston address the audience and say he'd remain to watch us perform. Betty had to go to the bathroom again. In the hierarchy of adult power, President Franklin Delano Roosevelt was at the top, Mayor Fiorello LaGuardia next and Principal Stanton Preston third.

As two strong seniors pulled the curtain ropes, I found myself alone in the center of the stage. Despite all our rehearsals, I was petrified standing there before hundreds of children, their teachers and Principal Preston. Even though pillowed out in my suit, I felt too small to contain all of my terror. My feet were screwed into the stage, although my legs felt like putty. Every word I had painstakingly memorized was erased from my mind as the chalkboard after washing. In front of me were dizzying patterns of red and white studded with children's faces. First graders called out "Santa Claus!" reminding me of who I was supposed to be. Hidden behind me were my fellow performers, waiting for me to start the fantasy into which they were to join. I heard the whirring of the fan, which blew leaves across the stage in my direction, the most ambitious leaf finally reaching my shoe. That was my cue to start.

"I see the calling card of Jack Frost." It was my voice, but it sounded strange, as if coming from a body that was not mine. I managed to say the second line of the couplet: "By chill winds idly tossed." I pointed to the leaf, a sturdy maple, one of many I had collected in Crotona Park. "The cold breeze reminds me of my work, Which Santa does not shirk." Morris, when he'd read the play, said, "Frost's 'calling card' was stolen from O'Henry and your teacher's poetry is corny." Although Miss Cleary had her name on the script, she did add, *Adapted from various sources.* While I wouldn't know the reaction of the upper graders and visitors until the afternoon, this morning's audience was more appreciative than Morris.

When I finished my opening couplets, I looked to where Betty was supposed to appear. The spot chalked with an unmistakable X by Miss Cleary was bare! I heard a frenzied voice from back of the stage: Miss Cleary's entreaties for Betty to go on stage. I picked up the front-runner leaf and slowly repeated my opening lines. Stage time was more elongated than off-stage time and I don't know how long it was before Betty wobbled across the stage. Her chubby face was contorted in a terror that I hoped was not visible on mine. Her lips were frozen and I whispered her opening words, using the ventriloquist techniques I learned from watching the Edgar Bergen Show. Betty remained mute until Miss Cleary, from behind the curtain, practically shouted her opening words, jarring her into speaking. After that shaky start, the play proceeded with only minor mishaps until the final scene.

I was fairly relaxed by the time the reindeer pulled me and the sled offstage. Like most disasters, it was the combination of several factors, some seemingly remote. Willie's suggestion to put wheels on the sleigh set the rest in motion, figuratively as well as literally. A second was the shop teacher's accepting the challenge. Another was Miss Cleary's failure to use good judgment. *Nine* reindeer was another--Miss Cleary wanted as many children in the play as possible. No small factor was Willie being the lead reindeer. I admit I wasn't blameless. With great exuberance I not only shouted, "Giddyap! *Blitzen! Donder-*" but swung my whip so that rather than snapping over the heads of the reindeer, it struck *Blitzen.* I never got to name the other seven as *Blitzen* led them off at a speed the axles were not made to withstand. I was quick-thinking enough to let go of the reins or the disaster could have been worse. The reins, along with the front of the my sleigh, obeyed the laws of physics, and were whipped offstage. The rest simply collapsed, leaving me in a shambles of splintered wood. This scene provided more excitement than anyone could have planned. The noise on stage was augmented by shrieks from hundreds of children. We couldn't have planned a more sensational ending, which the children believed was devised for their enjoyment. Shaken, but unhurt, I stood next to the shattered sled until order was restored by the Principal, who told the children, "The play isn't over." He glanced at me and when it became quiet, I ad libbed, "There are so many children in the world to bring Christmas and Chanukah presents to, next year we'll have to build a bigger sled in my toy shop!" Then our class sang the finale, *"Jingle Bells!"* The children wouldn't stop applauding and shrieking, mostly in appreciation of the mishap. We had a half dozen curtain calls. When the teachers finally led the children out, Miss Cleary sent for the shop teacher, who arrived with several seniors. When He assured her that the repairs would be completed for the afternoon performance, she took us to the lunch room. She didn't dare let us return home or even get out of her sight, fearful that we'd not return. Teachers and children came over to compliment us on the sleigh scene. Willie acted as if he made the greatest contribution to the play's success and wasn't angry at me for hitting him with the whip, "-because it made me run faster!"

The afternoon performance was for the upper graders and visiting parents, or rather, mothers. Fathers' jobs were understandably more important than attending their offsprings' school plays. When we returned to the auditorium, the shop teacher was smiling--the sleigh was repaired. The wheels were missing to Willie's regret and my relief. Moments later, our attention was turned to the arriving mothers. Dressed in their best clothes, they were led by senior ushers to a special section in front. From the side of the curtain, we shoved each other looking for our mothers but were considerate enough to allow someone spotting his mother to get a front spot. Harold called our attention to Momma, who followed an eighth grade usher who was a foot taller, despite Momma's hat. Willie was respectful enough not to call out, "There's Fatso Al's Fatso mother in the funny hat!" In those days, mothers of children in P.S. 4 were respected, regardless of how we felt about their offspring.

Then the classes entered, the upper-graders making larger patterns of red and white. As the auditorium filled, our confident, even cocky, attitude dissolved. We realized that rather than being veteran performers, we had gone over big with the "babies." I had used up my quota of luck and was sure there wasn't enough left to see me through the second performance. Momma taught me that the Evil Eye was made vengeful by past success. I tried not to think of that as I listened to Principal Preston repeat what he'd said earlier, except for saying that parents had an opportunity to see that we not only "learned the Three R's, but American culture as well." Nervous as I was, I noted the principal's failure to mention Chanukah, making that responsibility mine alone. As the curtains parted, I went through an even more panicked reaction--however physiologically impossible that was--trying to ignore Momma's hat, which was all I could see of her because of the tall mother in front. The more I tried to avoid looking, the more I looked, interfering with my concentration. When I was ready to say my opening lines, I waited in vain for the leaves. But they--or the fan--were uncooperative. I stared at my toe, where the leaf was supposed to be, unable to start without my cue. When Betty traipsed across the stage, she was as nervously loose-jointed now as she'd been rigid before. Offstage Miss Cleary said, "I see the calling cards of Jack Frost," thinking I had forgotten my line. I bellowed the words, frightening Betty so that she didn't recover when it was her turn. She finally did and the play was off. Years later I realized that many of the glaring mistakes from behind the footlights were unnoticed or overlooked by an audience.

The rest of the performance was relatively uneventful, although I held my breath and thought *Up-and- away!* when Margaret, the visiting angel said, "-if one has faith in God and in Christ." I hoped Momma hadn't heard--or understood--and breathed easier when I saw her remain motionless. In one of my nightmares she had leapt out of her seat and shouted, "Yalka, you didn't tell me they'd say their God's name!"

When Margaret prepared to depart for heaven by flapping her wings--an aeronautical miracle if ever there was one--the wings that had worked so cooperatively this morning fell off, alerting me again to the danger of complacency. The flapping was Betty's cue to say, "Beautiful angels we say good-by, And watch you off to heaven fly," but all Betty could do was stare at the fallen wings, while Margaret remained in a state of paralysis. Miss Cleary called from offstage, "Leave!" For an instant I thought *everyone* would walk off the stage. I scooped up the wings, handed them to Margaret and said, "Good-by, Off to heaven fly," shoving her. Fortunately, she starting walking and the other angels followed. Betty recovered after they were gone and completed her couplet, "See, Santa, If we have faith and pray, The helping angels will make our day." When I climbed aboard the sleigh to deliver my toys, I shouted my lines, hoping they'd more than make up for Margaret's reference to Christ:

"Onto the sleigh I bring my bag of toys,
    To make happy girls and boys,
    Who celebrate Chanukah and Christmas
Which bring them joy and bliss!"

I had made up the two couplets for good measure and Miss Cleary never seemed to notice. That made *two* references to Chanukah. In the final scene, after I said, *"Giddyap!"* I stood next to the immobile sleigh, which was the new cue to bring down the curtains. No one had told the curtain-pullers of the changed ending. *Blitzen* ran around the stage, pulling *Donder* and the others after him. They become entangled in the harnesses. Miss Cleary pulled the curtains herself as I shouted, "We're off!" The applause and cheers stopped only when Principal Preston raised his hands for the third time. He thanked our class again and wished everyone "a Merry Christmas and a Happy Chanukah!" The upper graders broke into fresh applause and shouts that ended only when their teachers led them out.

The mothers came on stage and Miss Cleary said nice things about their children. Willie's mother was as short and fat as Momma, over-dressed, uncomfortable, her accent thick. Mrs. Mangione beamed when Miss Cleary said, "Willie can be a good pupil when he tries," and gave Willie an *I-hope-you-appreciate-my-saying-something-nice-about-you* look. Staring at his shoes, you'd have thought he deserved her compliment. Her praise for me was not as conditional. "Mrs. Segal, I hope you're proud of your son. You sewed a beautiful costume." Momma beamed.

Harold's mother, who wore a coat trimmed with a fox-tail collar, listened to Miss Cleary's complimenting Harold and then said, "Harold is always saying such nice things about you." Clarence explained to Miss Cleary that his mother was working but his grandfather had come. She looked huge standing next to the frail man with a wrinkled bronze-colored face and long white hair. A worn overcoat didn't conceal his wizened body. She shook his hand and said, "I'm glad to have Clarence in my class." Then I saw Morris. Miss Cleary greeted him by name and shook his hand. After saying nice things about their children to the remaining mothers--for some more out of the Season's Good Spirits than earned--Miss Cleary thanked the shop and art teachers and led us to our classroom.

She surprised us by not only splurging on candy and ice cream at our Christmas party, but also by letting us play *Dunking for the Apple* and *Pinning the Tail on the Donkey.* We loudly sang Christmas carols, not only being in the holiday spirit, but also to make up for all the silence we had endured in that classroom. As was the custom in those days, we gave Miss Cleary gifts. Mine was a change purse Momma bought at Woolworth's Five and Dime on Bathgate Avenue and wrapped in a gift box. Miss Cleary said, "That's sweet of you but it wasn't necessary," to me and everyone else as she placed the gifts on the growing pile on her desk.

Willie interrupted to shout, "We didn't do Current Events!" At first we thought he had taken leave of his senses, but then he held up two clippings he'd taken from my desk. We all laughed and Miss Cleary asked if he wanted to give a report. He stuck out his stomach--everyone thought that funny except me--and mispronounced the names of the Russian and German leaders. That made for more laughter, although I noticed that he correctly pronounced Mussolini. Miss Cleary, ever ready to express her opinions, explained, "Maybe Hitler and Stalin could finish each other off and leave the rest of the world in peace." She thought that was a hopeful note "to welcome 1939." I looked at the article Willie didn't parody--Germany ordering all Jews to leave Danzig by April of 1939.

While everyone was elated when we lined up for dismissal, I was thinking that this was my last Christmas in P.S. 4. Miss Cleary reminded us that we should be working on our projects during the vacation--everyone groaned--and that we should exchange addresses with our committee members. Willie, Clarence and I did that on pieces of paper. I told them I'd find out if Morris would take us to the Forty-second Street Library, all the while thinking I'd be in Atlanta by then.

Momma greeted me with a big hug and kiss, which I didn't mind because I was afraid she'd do that on the stage of the auditorium. She didn't say anything about my wearing the Santa costume home, instead--"I hope the Gentiles learned about Chanukah" and "I wish your father could have seen you." When she kissed me goodnight, she whispered, "I'm sure you'll be in school plays in Atlanta." I didn't tell her that I planned *never* to be in an Atlanta school play. When Morris turned off the light and got into bed, I thanked him for coming. He said, "I wanted to hear the Chanukah lines." Then, "I missed the best part--when the sled fell apart!" He wouldn't tell me how he found out about the morning's disaster, but even that no longer bothered me. Both plays were behind me and before me was the Christmas vacation. I fell asleep more peacefully that night than I had in weeks.

The waters receded and there were the generations after Noah, the ones whose names I found so hard to memorize. Terah was the father of Abram, the first Jew, although he wasn't a Jew until there was an "h" in his name. God told Abram to leave his country and go to Shechem and then Beth-el. I heard thunder and lightning and then stared into the darkness.

I shouted, "We're not going to Atlanta!" Morris sleepily asked, "Where *are* we going?"

"Shechem or Beth-el."

He asked, "Where the heck are they?"

I didn't dare tell him they were in Genesis XII.

Twenty-Two

Poverty's Head Is Very Hard

Before the holidays were over we had another snowfall. Morris, standing behind me at the window, said, "You're lucky to get another look."

I watched the swirling flakes and appreciated the graceful beauty I had taken for granted. I asked, "Will it *ever* snow in Atlanta?"

"If we have another ice age, but don't hold your breath--the last one was over ten thousand years ago."

I watched the street and park being coated white and thought, *I'll never see you again.*

The doorbell rang--Mrs. Stone was calling! Morris and I raced up the stairs. *Was this the call we'd been dreading?* Morris barely said, "Hello" before Momma rushed in. She took the phone and asked, "Everything's all right? ... You're sure?" She made a face, listened, again asked if he was all right and hung up. She didn't give Morris or me a chance to talk and just nodded her thanks to Mrs. Stone. We followed her down the stairs.

Once back in our apartment, Morris and I clamored to find out what Poppa had told her. She said, "You'll find out when he comes." I looked at Morris, who asked, "Why is he coming home?" Momma shook her head and mumbled, "He said I shouldn't worry, but how can I not?"

I followed Morris into the living room. He asked what I was thinking: "Either she doesn't want to tell us or Pop didn't tell her." Then he said what I hadn't thought of: "It could take days before we find out!" Morris' expression mirrored mine--it seemed impossible to wait even five minutes.

Morris rushed back to the kitchen--I followed. "Why don't you call Uncle Sol? Maybe he can find out what happened."

Momma nodded. "Yes! Call Sol."

I was dressing as quickly as Morris. We both knew this was a call that could not be made from Mrs. Stone. Momma was so upset she didn't say "No" to my going to the candy store with Morris.

Fulton Avenue was coated white and we left a trail of footprints. In the store, Morris talked to Sol--I listened, shifting from one galosh to the other, a puddle forming under me. When Morris hung up the receiver, he told me Sol would call Yitzchok. We walked home without saying a word, although we knew what the other was thinking.

The next hour passed with excruciating slowness. I went to the kitchen several times, hoping Momma would reveal more of the telephone conversation, but she sat mutely at the table, her glass of tea getting cold. Morris had a book in front of him, but his eyes weren't moving. The bell rang. It was Sol. He didn't get past the hallway before we showered him with questions. He waved us into silence and then said, "I called Yitzchok and all he'd say was, 'Poverty's head is very hard."

In unison, we repeated, "Poverty's head is very hard?"

Sol nodded. "I told Yitzchok, 'Don't give me riddles, I'm calling long distance.' Yitzchok asks, 'You want answers and I shouldn't talk riddles? Well, how's this, 'Poverty and stupidity are brothers."

In unison, we repeated that. Sol nodded. "That's all he'd say, besides, 'He's *your* brother, not mine.' Then he hung up." He asked Momma, "When did Mordcha say he'd be back?"

Momma didn't know, but Morris, calculating quickly, said, "By tomorrow afternoon."

Sol said what we knew, "We'll just have to wait." He refused Momma's offer of tea--"Yussie's alone in the store, but who'll bring clothes in weather like this?" He left.

That day went by in slow motion like the special effects in the movies. The next morning, Morris bought the *Sunday News* and gave me half the comics without my asking. Sol stopped by at eleven, in case Poppa "arrived early." Momma bought a steak in the Kosher butcher shop and rushed home with Poppa's favorite dinner. At one o'clock, Morris and I went to the Third

Avenue train station, as if by waiting there we'd speed up Poppa's return. When Morris said, "Maybe he's coming another way," we ran home. Sol came at two and drank tea with Momma before joining Morris and me at the window. He whispered, "If I drink another glass, my bladder will bust." Momma wondered if "something happened?" She left unsaid the many possible catastrophes. Sol said, "Horses have big heads-" and Momma interrupted with, "I know!" He then said, "Troubles are as plentiful as wood, but they can't heat an oven." Momma ignored him. Her seeds of worry germinated easily in my mind.

The others abandoned the window and I remained the lone watch upon whom Poppa's return depended. I imagined myself with Columbus and Torres, wanting to get the bounty for being the first to see land. Then Poppa entered the courtyard! I waited to make sure he wasn't a mirage before shouting, "Poppa!" Morris confirmed what I saw. The four of us rushed into the hallway and greeted him, Momma hugging him and Morris grabbing the suitcase. Despite the excitement, I noticed it was Borinka's.

Poppa wasn't hungry--he ate on the train. Momma eyed him suspiciously but settled for serving tea and cake. We sat around the kitchen table, our questions written on our faces. Poppa looked tired and had a couple of day's stubble. Finally, after his second sip, he said, "The bank gave me the loan."

Sol interrupted, "That's what you were waiting for!"

Poppa ignored him. The cube of sugar clinked against his teeth. "We were in Yitzchok's office and Benny--he was supposed to be my partner-" *Supposed to be* wasn't lost on us. "Everyone was there--lawyers, the man from the bank-" He paused to let us visualize the scene. "The table was covered with papers--agreements, contracts, provisions-"

In the pause, Sol said, "Partnerships aren't made with handshakes anymore."

Poppa stared at his glass. "A banker brought the loan contract; the papers had to be signed in order. First I get the loan, then I can sign the partnership papers-" He paused. "So I sign for the bank loan-" He gestured signing. "My lawyer says, 'The partnership papers are in order.' Yitzchok opens a bottle of *schnapps*. Benny jokes to Yitzchok, 'If your brother is half as good a businessman as you, we'll make our first million in no time.' Everybody laughs."

Sol said, "When fortune calls, quick give her a chair."

We glared at him as Poppa continued, "Benny says, 'One thing more–" Poppa paused--the kitchen clock ticked loudly. "Benny holds up a paper and nods to this man--he looked familiar, but I thought he was a contractor Yitzchok invited to have a drink with us." Poppa lifted the imaginary paper. "I saw 'Painters Association.' Benny says, 'Contractors with more than five painters sign with them.' I start reading but everybody gets restless. Yitzchok says, 'Sign both papers, Mordcha, Benny's been signing for years. It won't cost you a penny. The men pay a couple of dollars a month.' I ask, 'A union?' They laughed. 'Not a union,' says Benny. I look carefully at this man–" Poppa stared across the table. "He says, 'There are no *unions* here, but we have an association that keeps things smooth between painters and the companies.' His accent is not Southern and he looks more and more familiar. I ask him his name. 'Deniken,' he says. I ask, "Do you know Leon?' He nods but goes on, 'We don't need strikes or unions to settle things." Poppa's eyes narrowed. "He *was* one of Leon's men! They had the same crooked deal in Atlanta that we are trying to get rid of in New York, except there they have no Rank and File."

The blood drained from Momma's face. Poppa avoided looking at her. "I'm ready to be a boss, but to agree to bust unions–"

Sol was first to ask, "What happened?"

Poppa took a long sip of tea. "Yitzchok says, 'Sign, Mordcha, the *painters* join the association. It has nothing to do with you.' I ask Deniken, 'Why don't *you* sign the men up?' He laughs and says, 'It's easier if the bosses do it.' Benny says, 'The association sends us good painters.' I ask, 'Mr. Deniken, were you with Leon three months ago?" Poppa looked at us and said in an aside, "That's when the Deutsch was shot." Then, "His face gets red, and he says, 'I see Leon from time to time.' Then *he* gets angry and says, 'If you want to do business here–' Yitzchok says, 'Mordcha, for God's sake don't be a fool!'"

Sol couldn't restrain himself--"So?"

Poppa's expression was one of surprise, as if the answer was obvious. "How could I sign?" He turned to Momma, who was already crying. She said, "You promised me a home--" she wiped her tears with her apron, "-with a big kitchen and separate bedrooms for the boys-" She ran out of the kitchen.

Poppa looked at Sol. "Don't say it."

Sol shrugged. "Say what?"

"When the Messiah comes, the sick will be healed, but fools will remain fools."

Sol shook his head. "I'm not the fool to judge a man."

Poppa cuddled the glass in his hands. "Yitzchok said, 'Don't make the same mistake your other brother made."

Sol gave Morris and me a *You-boys-better-leave* look.

When we were back in the living room, I asked, "What's going to happen?" Morris shrugged. After Sol left, Poppa remained alone in the kitchen before calling to Momma through the bedroom door, "I'll say hello to my parents." Next I heard the stropping of the razor and the water running in the bathroom. Before Poppa finished shaving, Momma came out of the bedroom and called into our room, "I'm making dinner." Then, toward the bathroom, "You'll eat first." Several minutes later, I smelled steak cooking.

Morris and I were in the kitchen at Momma's first call. Morris got the ketchup--the first time since Poppa left, but I don't think Poppa noticed. I wasn't hungry, but finished every bit of steak and mashed potatoes. The meal was eaten in silence. When Poppa got up to leave, I asked if I could go. He said, "Ask your mother." Before I could ask, she said, "Your father asks my opinion for *that,* but *he* decides the family's life-and-death matters!" Poppa didn't say anything as Momma cleared the table. I took her remark as meaning I could go, but as I followed Poppa out of the kitchen, she said, "Yalka, if you catch cold in this *zavarucha*, it's not *my* fault." I put on *everything,* from galoshes to my woolen hat.

The late afternoon sun had melted almost all of the snow and warmed me so that I had to loosen my scarf. Poppa walked quickly, but I kept up with him. Unexpectedly, he squeezed my shoulder and said that he was sorry to miss my plays. I told him about the Litofsky play and he said, "That was a brave thing to do." I answered, "I had my three friends." Poppa replied, "It's important to have friends." He asked what the rabbi did afterwards. Rabbi Weiss, on the Monday following the play, gave us a long lecture about "obedience" and "respect." He finished with, "Fish die out of water, and people die without law and order." He didn't mention the Litofsky play. Poppa smiled. "See, you did a brave thing and the rabbi didn't punish you. He only gave you a lecture. Don't expect things *not* to work out."

Grandma and Grandpa were surprised to see Poppa. Grandma served tea and Poppa told them what happened. He didn't seem as assured about not signing as he did with us at home. He asked, "Am I a fool?" Grandpa sighed and put his hand on Poppa's. "The Proverbs say that it is better to be poor and walk upright than to be rich and dishonest with yourself." Poppa quoted Yitzchok's, "A heavy purse makes a light heart." Grandpa replied, "No man will bring his gold with him to the Messiah. Both of you are my sons, but you and he are different." Grandpa paused and said, "The truly rich are satisfied with their share." He turned to me and smiled. "The greatest wealth is *Shekinah* and *Ruach Adonoi.*" I was glad I had come and pleased to have them talk so openly with me there. I discovered that Yitzchok had talked Benny into giving Poppa two weeks to change his mind. When we left, Grandma whispered, "Pray that you'll have your Bar Mitzvah in the Bronx." I knew she didn't want another son living far away.

As we walked home, I couldn't help but ask, "Will you go back to Atlanta and sign?"

Poppa took a while before answering. "Your mother will be very unhappy if I don't go into this business. If I do, I will have trouble living with myself." That was all he said the rest of the way home. I stared at Crotona Park's trees with their snow foliage.

Although Momma and Poppa didn't argue, supper was not pleasant. We all knew how unhappy one of them would be with either decision. After Poppa left the table, Momma muttered, "Expect nothing and you'll never be disappointed."

Later, Momma took two headache powders and went to bed. It was the first time she went to bed without kissing me goodnight. Yet I was relieved--how could I have returned her kiss if I wanted to remain in the Bronx? After Morris turned off the light, Poppa came to the door of our room. He whispered, "You asleep?" When Morris and I answered, "No," he entered and sat down on my bed. "How are you boys? I don't like being away from you-" he paused.

Morris, embarrassed at Poppa's display of emotion, answered his question. "I'm okay, in school and everything."

I answered, "Me, too."

Poppa said, "I know it's been hard-" In the darkness, I couldn't see his face. "You may not understand decisions grown-ups have to make-"

Morris interrupted, "I understand!" I wanted to say, "I do, too," but hesitated too long. There was a long silence before Morris said, "You've got to live with yourself."

After another silence, Poppa said, "With some decisions, it's hard to live with yourself either way."

Morris said, "There are principles-"

"Don't! My head is swimming with principles--for the union, for your mother-" He stopped. He had spoken so loud that the silence afterwards sounded strange. Poppa walked over to Morris. "I didn't mean to shout-"

Morris said, "I know Pop. I wasn't trying to tell you-"

Poppa bent over and hugged Morris. In the darkness, I couldn't tell if he kissed him as well. Poppa said, "You decided to go to that special high school instead of the one in the neighborhood and soon will make even bigger decisions."

"I make decisions, too," I called across the room. "About Santa Claus--the Litofsky play."

Poppa walked back, sat down on my bed and hugged me. "I know you make decisions, too. Both of you are growing up--so fast." He stood up abruptly and from the doorway said, "I love you." Then his silhouette quickly disappeared.

I whispered, "Will Poppa go to Atlanta?"

"I don't think Pop knows yet."

"How will he decide?"

"Je-sus! I don't know." Then more softly, "Pop's very upset--he was close to crying."

I had noticed something strange in his voice at the doorway, but said, "Poppa's never cried."

"Go to sleep!" said Morris.

I rolled over. I knew there was no use in asking any more questions. I thought of the possibility of our moving to Atlanta--no matter what, that was not what I wanted. When I finally fell asleep, I was in an Indian Reservation School. Poppa and Momma had sent me there: Momma because I was disloyal to her; Poppa because I had betrayed him. At the school, I knew none of the children and the teachers were mean. I decided to run away and find Clarence. I climbed out of the window and was in Crotona Park. As fast as I ran, the park wouldn't end. I was afraid I'd never get out. I woke up frightened and crying.

No decision was made by the Christmas vacation-- at least as far as I knew. So I decided to go ahead with the project. When Morris was in a good mood, he agreed to take the three of us to the 42nd Street Library--"if none of you are pests." On the last day of school, we had exchanged addresses and I knew where Willie and Clarence lived.

Willie lived in a building on Third Avenue near 168th Street. It was one of narrow dirty-gray brick buildings--very much like Herschel's--that were under the shadow of the elevated train trestle. Luckily, Willie had given me the apartment number since I couldn't find his name on the letter boxes. I walked through the narrow hallway and *down* the stairs. In the sooty basement, after passing smelly garbage cans, I found the door, along with a sign, *Superintendent*. I rang the bell and recognized Mrs. Mangione from her visits to school. Like Momma, she wore a worn house dress and had on no make-up. She shouted, "Willie," and he came to the door. I told him Morris would take us to the library on Sunday and to meet at my house at one o'clock. A man inside shouted, "Who the hell is it? I hope not one of those damn tenants at this hour." Willie's defiant expression was replaced with fear. He called back, "A friend from school." The gruff voice replied, "Shut the door--there's a draft." Willie said, "I'll be over," and closed the door. I stared at the battered door for several seconds before leaving.

Clarence lived several blocks away, off Webster Avenue. I expected an apartment building but found a small wooden-frame house, an oversight when they built the neighboring apartment buildings. Behind a rock wall, a stone stairway led up to the front porch, where his grandfather was sitting. He was bundled up in a long unfashionable coat. His face was shielded from the sun by a wide-brimmed hat. The door had no bell, so I knocked. Clarence was surprised to see me. I told him about going to the library and he nodded. He noticed me glancing at his grandfather, who had opened his eyes and said something to Clarence that I couldn't understand. Clarence replied in what I suppose was *Tinde* and then led me over to him, saying, "This is my friend, Al, from school. He was Santa in the play." He nodded and smiled. Now that I was closer, I saw how much his wrinkled and leathery face resembled the Indian warriors I had seen in old photos. We shook hands, his was hard and callused. Clarence said, "Al's grandfather is the one who has heart sickness." The grandfather said something to Clarence, who said that his grandfather was waiting for special medicine from out west. I said Grandpa was better and thanked him. He nodded without Clarence having to translate. Clarence said he'd see me and watched me walk down the stairs. When I reached the street, I glanced back. Clarence had gone inside and his grandfather had closed his eyes.

That evening I asked Morris if he'd met any "real" Indians. He told me that when he was small, Poppa took him to a circus where he saw Indians having a make-believe battle with cowboys. He told me that Indians had been treated unfairly, robbed of their lands and hunted like animals. That conversation was when Indians were still considered the villains by non-Indians and movie audiences cheered the whites as they massacred them.

Clarence and Willie arrived on time. Momma asked if they wanted cookies and milk. When they hesitated, I answered for them. Momma surprised me by serving Yankee Doodle cupcakes. She kept glancing at them and they at her when she wasn't looking. I was relieved at how well-behaved they were--

especially Willie--and Momma's treating them to a snack. When we finished we walked with Morris to the Third Avenue station, climbed up the stairs and lined up behind Morris at the turnstile. Each of us inserted our nickel and pushed our way through. Then up another flight of stairs to the platform. We watched the toy-size train coming down the tracks, growing in size and roaring into the station. The conductor swung open the gates and Morris led us into the lead car. Willie and Clarence went to the front window, next to the motorman's cab. Though that was the best view, Momma was afraid to let me stand there and I envied the children who did. Without asking Morris, I joined my friends. To his credit, he didn't warn me away. The three of us squeezed together and watched the tracks fly toward us while the adjacent buildings whizzed by. When we crossed the East River, we excitedly looked through the side windows to see a tugboat pulling a barge. Willie asked, "Can the bridge keep us up?" I was pleased to see him frightened and was ready to say that it could fall down. But I didn't.

When we arrived at the 42nd Street Station, we walked down the stairs and through the Manhattan streets. Clarence and Willie stared up at the tall buildings around us. I had never been to this part of the city, but tried to be as casual as Morris. When we reached the library, we followed Morris up the stairs, past the stone lions and into the reading room. Morris helped us use the card catalogue, fill out slips and showed us where to get the books. I don't think he got much of his own work done that afternoon.

With Morris' help, we found information that became fashionable only years later: Jews coming to New Amsterdam despite Governor Peter Minuet not wanting them; Haym Solomon helping Washington supply the soldiers in the Revolution; the first Africans coming to the colonies as indentured servants, like Clarence said; Negroes "mingled with the American Indians" (in a book by Hershkowitz that Clarence looked through and which years later I read); Italians coming in large numbers during the struggles to unify Italy (Morris explained that to Willie). I had to make notes for Willie, but kept them as short as possible.

On the return trip back, Clarence sat next to me. He told me that his grandfather also had a heart condition and needed the medicine for himself. I said, "He's nice." I felt embarrassed saying that, but Clarence nodded and said, *"They* put him in prison." My face showed surprise and he continued, "The Apaches didn't want their land taken and the government didn't keep its treaties with them." He whispered, "He escaped." I thought it only fair to tell him that someone in my family was in trouble with the government, but *they* didn't catch him. Clarence said his grandfather escaped into the Florida swamps. It was there that he met Clarence's grandmother. When the imprisoned Indians were eventually released, his grandfather returned to the reservation with his family, including Clarence's mother. That was another secret I would tell no one. Years later I read about the government's imprisoning in Florida "renegade" Apaches, along with Apache scouts who aided the U.S. cavalry.

That night I found out from Morris what *melazane* meant. He had asked an Italian-American friend of his. Besides meaning Eggplant, it was a racist term for Negroes. While Willie had said that the first time he saw Clarence, I never heard him say that again.

Twenty-Three

Did God Suck the Air Out?

My parents maintained an uneasy truce and I had no idea if our family's fate was decided. After the holidays, I was grateful to be back in school, something I wouldn't admit to any of my friends. Not only did school keep me busy, but I could make believe I'd never leave P.S. 4. My first Current Events article was about Hitler's demand for the return of Danzig to Germany in order not to invade Poland. Miss Cleary said, "I hope he keeps his promise this time." I knew differently: Sol and Poppa said it would only "whet his appetite again."

In Hebrew School, we translated Genesis XII, when God tells Abram to leave Babylon and his father's house so that he can become leader of a great nation. Ravitch told us the commentator Raschi explained that God wanted Abram to leave behind his idol-worshipping family and people. Abram was then seventy five, which impressed me since that was Grandpa's age. When Abram was very righteous, he became Abraham and died when he was 175. Since Grandpa was righteous, I thought that he should live that long.

The bell rang. Outside, someone called my name--Morris! I ran across the street. Instead of walking home, Morris started briskly in the opposite direction. I asked where we were going but he didn't answer. I stopped and only when he said, "We're going to Grandpa and Grandma," did I continue. Morris seemed in no mood to answer any question and I tried to guess why we were going there, wondering if Poppa would tell his decision to the whole family at a special dinner.

I was out of breath when we reached the apartment building, but I ran ahead of Morris. As I raced up the stairs, food aromas drifted by and I was hungry for Grandma's dinner. I paused at the open front door, which was always closed, and peeked into the foyer. The interior rooms were crowded--I recognized relatives whom I saw only on special occasions, several neighbors, and men from Grandpa's *shul*. Everyone seemed to be talking, but in whispers that blended into a strange hum.

I turned, but Morris wasn't behind me. I took a cautious step, searching for my grandparents. As I squeezed through, no one noticed me. I heard a low moan and felt the back of my neck tightening. Momma was with Aunt Becky in a corner of the room. They were holding Grandma, whose moan became a high-pitched wail. Momma and Becky were also crying. *They'll upset Grandpa!* I thought, looking around the room for him. The bedroom door was ajar--candles flickered inside. I thought, *Today isn't Friday!* Besides, candles were never lit in the bedroom. Then I saw Poppa--he was crying! I wanted to shout, "What happened?" but couldn't. I felt terrified in the crowded room and ran to Momma. I pulled her arm to get her attention and my eyes asked, "What happened?" Her hand reached for me, but she didn't turn from Grandma. "Where's Grandpa?" I asked, feeling desperate, but Momma didn't answer. I closed my eyes, wishing for everything to disappear. Then I could enter the apartment again, this time turning the clapper on the door so that its quaint ring would bring Grandma. She'd kiss me and I'd find Grandpa in his armchair. He'd put down his Yiddish newspaper and smile. We'd kiss, his beard tickling my cheek. He'd ask, "Yalkala, what question did you bring today?" What *was* today's question?

When I opened my eyes, the Sabbath candles were not on the foyer table and their glow was coming from the bedroom. I tugged desperately on Momma's arm but it hung limp. Grandma wailed again. I saw Morris in the doorway and dodged through the people to reach him. I asked, "Where's Grandpa?" I wanted him to tell me Grandpa was all right and explain why everyone was here. But when I saw his tears, I knew. I said, "You promised I was going to see him!" I burst into tears and remembered little after that, not even how I got home. I do remember it was Morris who tucked me in bed and asked, "What does Mom tell you before you go to sleep, something her mother told her?" I answered, "Sleep is the best doctor." Morris repeated it before switching off the light.

Next, I saw a flash of lightning and heard an explosion of thunder. Sheets of rain blinded me but I managed to walk up the mountain to a robed figure. I shouted, "Grandpa!" but it was Noah who turned around. Would *he* answer my question? I asked, "How did you live nine hundred and fifty years?" I had last seen him at the time of the flood, when he was six hundred years old. He looked at me quizzically, then smiled, the twinkle in his eyes resembling Grandpa's. "I'm seven hundred years old-- *Kinehorah*-- and don't know how long I'll live. Where have you been the last hundred years?" Rather than answering him, I asked what was bothering me since studying Genesis IX. "Why did you punish Canaan, your grandson, when it was his father, Ham, who saw you naked?" He looked perplexed and I reminded him, "After you drank the wine." His eyes flared and his beard shortened until he became Rabbi Weiss. "I don't answer questions! And you shouldn't ask them! Read the commentaries!" Lightning flashed, thunder roared and a wall of rain blocked out everything, wetting my cheeks.

I was crying but didn't dare fully awaken. I fell back asleep and was in *shul,* listening to the cantor's plaintive chanting. Grandpa noticed my uneasiness and looked up from his prayer book. He smiled, but knowing that was not enough, placed his hand on my shoulder.

"Yalkala, wake up." I opened my eyes but it was Momma nudging me. "Eat breakfast with Morris." I wanted her to tell me I dreamt that Grandpa died, but she said, "I'm going back. Morris will take you later." She didn't have to say where.

Morris was dressing in his good suit. My Chanukah suit was on the couch. We silently ate soft-boiled eggs and buttered rolls that Momma had prepared. Afterwards, Morris walked the familiar route so slowly that I could have easily left him behind. But I didn't. The walk up the worn stairs took longer than usual, although we reached the fourth floor sooner than I wanted to.

The day was shrouded in a haze. The apartment was crowded with relatives, neighbors, men from the synagogue, and others I didn't know. Momma kissed me and asked if I had my breakfast. Poppa, his eyes red, held me and whispered, "Be brave." Sol kissed me and whispered, "Yalka, what can I say?" Aunt Becky said nothing but kissed me; despite being in a daze, I resented the lipstick smear. My cousins Ben and Simon shook my hand. They looked strange in suits. I avoided looking toward the bedroom, where candles still burned, but couldn't help seeing Grandma sitting next to the coffin, surrounded by women relatives. People walked into the bedroom, stayed a few minutes and left. I don't know how long I stood there when Uncle Yitzchok and his family arrived from Atlanta. Yitzchok greeted me with a handshake and Aunt Miriam kissed me politely. I hardly recognized my cousin David, in his early twenties, and Natalie, not quite twenty. I hadn't seen them in over two years. Sol told Yitzchok of the suddenness of Grandpa's heart attack. "He complained of indigestion in the morning, and when *Muter* came back with a glass of tea, he was dead--just like that. At least he didn't suffer." Yitzchok said, "He earned at least that going to *shul* these past few years." I didn't realize the significance of the "past few years" until later.

Uncle Yitzchok immediately "took charge." He complained to the Radomysl Burial Society's representative that the coffin's pine was too knotted. The elderly bearded man, visibly upset, said, "Orthodox rites prescribe the plainest wood-" Yitzchok interrupted with, "I don't need lectures on *Halakha*. Plain doesn't mean inferior or defective!" The man replied, "This coffin is no different from the others." Yitzchok glanced at Sol and said, "I'd buy coffins from a different lumber company." I didn't hear the rest because Morris whispered, "Do you want to see Grandpa?"

See Grandpa? Before I could ask what he meant, he led me to our cousins. David, his face and voice a younger version of his father's, said, "I can't look at dead bodies. The undertaker patched up this friend killed in a car accident-" I didn't listen to the rest. Ben said, "Orthodox Jews don't usually let you look at dead bodies--my father got special permission." Although frightened, I said, "I want to see Grandpa." David said, "Don't let him-he'll have nightmares the rest of his life." I looked pleadingly at Morris. "I *want* to." Simon said, "If he really wants to-"

Morris led me to the bedroom, but I froze in the doorway. Morris whispered, "Do you really want to?" I nodded, but my feet didn't move. Morris took my hand and led me in. Grandpa was wrapped in a white robe and his prayer shawl. I thought, *He's only asleep!* But his chest didn't rise and fall. A voice in my head asked, *If God breathed into man's nostrils to make him alive, did He suck out the air to make him dead?* I thought, "*Good-by, Grandpa*," but may have said it aloud. Everything started spinning.

I came to in the kitchen. David said, "I warned them." Yitzchok said to Morris, "Why did you take him?" I answered, "I wanted to say good-by!" and burst into tears. Momma hugged me and whispered, "Yalkala, Yalkala." Our tears mingled on our cheeks. Poppa came into the room and told the others, "Leave him be."

I can still see the driver leaning against the side of the hearse and smoking a cigarette, but don't remember getting into Sol's car. Only when we started moving did I realize I was squeezed in with Morris, David and Simon. Aunt Becky and Ben sat in the front. At first there was only silence, then someone mentioned the last Passover Seder, when Ben and Simon drank all that wine. David talked about how nice Atlanta was and boasted about managing one of his father's stores. Sol, who was driving, said, "A shame, just when he decided to retire." No one seemed to hear him. David was a fan of a Georgia football team and Ben claimed another team was better. Sol asked, "How will *Muter* get along without him?" No one seemed to hear him. The trivial chatter continued and I stopped listening. I thought, *Why aren't they talking about how much they'll miss Grandpa?* Outside, there were no longer apartment buildings, only bare fields, but I saw images: Grandpa reading the prayer book in *shul,* answering my questions in the living room, playing the practical joke with the tallis. When we followed the string of cars through the gate of the cemetery, I remembered where I was.

Poppa, my uncles and three other men carried the coffin from the hearse. When they lowered it to the ground, I first thought it was too heavy, but they did it several more times. I knew it had religious significance, But who could I ask? They stopped near a gaping hole with a mound of freshly dug soil next to it. I shuddered and looked away. When I turned again, men were lowering the coffin with ropes. It took so long, I thought the grave had no bottom. Meanwhile, Grandma's wails became a shriek. When the ropes stopped moving, Poppa and my uncles had to hold Grandma from leaping into the grave. The rabbi prayed in Hebrew and all I remembered of his Yiddish speech was that Grandpa's soul had returned to heaven. Poppa and my uncles said the *Kaddish,* The men took turns tossing in shovelfulls of soil. The first few landed with frightening thuds that I winced, fearful they were disturbing Grandpa.

After starting the car, Sol said, "His life on earth is over." Although his back was to me, I could hear him sobbing above the noise of the engine. *"Key memenoh lekoht key ohfor atoh vel ohfor tohshub."* I didn't realize I had said it aloud until the others looked at me. Tears were streaming down Sol's cheeks. "Yalka, even a Maccabee can't help us." He turned front and the car lurched forward. Morris gave me his handkerchief and I wiped my tears. Once outside the cemetery, the others resumed their chatter. I wanted to shriek, "Keep quiet! Grandpa's dead!" I didn't. I kept mumbling the Hebrew Genesis III words, "For dust thou art, and unto dust shalt thou return."

We had left my grandparent's apartment and returned to Grandma's. The bare living room table was crowded with dishes of food. It seemed as miraculous to me as manna to the Israelites in the desert. While we were gone, neighbors had prepared the traditional Meal of Comfort. That expressed their compassion and relieved the grieving family from having to prepare food. I watched in amazement as relatives and friends downed tumblerfulls of *schnapps* and ate with hearty appetites. I resented Momma's first suggesting and then coaxing me to eat. My appetite embarrassed me at first and then later betrayed my wanting to feel only grief. Though hunger pangs knotted my stomach, I couldn't approach the table. Momma resolved my conflict by bringing me an egg sandwich. Sitting in a corner of the room, I waited until she left and hoped no one saw me eating. The afternoon dragged on. Grandma sobbed more quietly now, as if she had given up hope of bringing Grandpa back. Momma and my aunts took turns comforting her. I heard a few comments about Grandpa before conversations turned to ordinary topics. I wanted to shout, "What about Grandpa?" When I closed my eyes, instead of seeing Grandpa on his favorite armchair, I saw his coffin being lowered into the ground.

I was surprised when Momma encouraged me to eat again. It was supper time! Neighbors were still bringing in food and Momma prepared a plate of chicken and *kasha*, which I ate when I thought no one was watching. Conversations drifted in and out of awareness the same way I heard radio programs I wasn't interested in. Morris and Ben talked about airplanes, Yitzchok told Sol that the burial society was cheating them, people I didn't know talked about their families. I was pleased to hear two men from *shul* say that Grandpa earned a place in Heaven and would be among the first called by the Messiah.

People started leaving, first neighbors and friends, then more distant relatives, until only the immediate family remained. The exceptions were Aunt Miriam and my cousins Natalie and David, who left early to take a Pullman back to Atlanta. The nearly empty apartment and the darkness outside intensified my gloom. When Momma whispered to Morris while looking at me, I knew what she was telling him. I said good-by to Grandma, frightening as that was.

As I cautiously approached her in the darkened bedroom, I avoided looking at the bed. Grandma was rocking her head back and forth, her stare vacant. I thought she didn't see me when I kissed her cheek, but she wearily whispered, "Yalkala, what are we going to do?" I burst into tears. That was a question I hadn't yet thought of.

I walked home with Morris, the sights familiar but seen through eyes that didn't seem mine. I felt as if my true self had been replaced with an alien who was trying to make sense of what was happening. Everything seemed strange. Fortunately, Morris, although sullen, was still Morris. I wondered if he was as upset and confused as me, but didn't ask. When we got home, he told me to have my snack. Those were obviously my mother's instructions. I shook my head. Unlike Momma, he made no fuss, which surprised me. When I was in bed, I felt hungry but was too embarrassed to change my mind. Much later--I had fallen asleep and awakened several times--Momma kissed me. I made believe I was asleep.

Later, Poppa stood in the doorway. I could barely make him out in the dark. I whispered, "Poppa?" He came to the side of my bed. I asked, "Did Grandpa take his *tallis?*" He knelt next to me and whispered, "His *tallis* goes with him to the other world." He paused and I could feel his breath on my cheek. "Its fringes were cut-that shows he has no more earthly responsibilities. His father--my grandfather--gave him the *tallis* for his Bar Mitzvah." He kissed me and left. Grandpa's prayer shawl would accompany him to the Other World! As it had embraced him in life, it would protect him in his grave. I was comforted by that and surprised that Poppa knew. I closed my eyes and saw Grandpa praying, the striped pattern of his *tallis* swaying back and forth. I tried to picture him at his Bar Mitzvah, but could not imagine him that young or without a beard. I fell asleep seeing him praying in *shul.*

I awakened at Momma's first call. Morris' bed was empty. Although I had not thought of what I would be doing after Grandpa's death, I could not imagine my life continuing as usual. I was shocked to hear that Morris had left for school and that Momma would give me breakfast and expect me to go. I wanted to object, but could think of nothing else to do. As I ate, Momma said Poppa and my uncles were sitting *shiva* and that she would be there most of the day. I said, "I want to go!" Momma firmly said it was only for grown-ups. I knew it was useless to protest. When I left, she kissed me and whispered, "We pray for your grandfather's Soul, as he's praying for us--our lives go on." She gave that added authority by saying, "That's what my mother used to say." Then, "I'll be back for your lunch."

Only after getting to class did I remember that I hadn't brought an absence note. I was actually afraid of being punished. When I sat down, Willie whispered, "Hooky player!" Miss Cleary called the roll and asked for my note. I walked up to her desk and whispered, "My grandfather died."

Her expression changed instantly. She said, "I'm sorry to hear that," and touched my hand. "Will you be able to work

232

today?" I nodded and rushed back to my seat. I hoped no one saw my tears. Miss Cleary started our spelling lesson and the class turned from me. I was fumbling for my notebook when she asked, "Al, please take this to Mr. O'Hare?" She finished writing and put the note in an envelope. There was nothing unusual about making me a messenger, but I waited outside the classroom. From the crack under the closed door, I heard her say, "Al's grandfather died." The news seemed as much of a shock to me as it did to the class, which murmured sympathetic "Ooh's." I next heard Clarence say, "He had a weak heart." I walked down the corridor and brushed away my tears.

As overwhelmed as I was with grief, I automatically went to my stairway hiding place and found myself reading the note. When Mr. O'Hare read it, I tried to look as if I didn't know its contents. He looked at me, his face sympathetic. "I'll need a good monitor today." He nodded to the bench and I sat down. The day passed in a blur. I delivered messages and stopped at my staircase hide-away not to read them but to cry. At the lunch time dismissal, Clarence said he was sorry his grandfather's medicine hadn't arrived. When I walked home with Harold, he told me that before he was born, one of his grandfathers died. I ate Momma's lunch more to please her than being hungry. After the three o'clock dismissal, I had my snack with Harold, who tried to distract me by playing cards.

I purposefully got to Hebrew School just before the class started, but Mr. Ravitch asked why I was absent. I whispered the reason. He said he was sorry. I don't remember how Rabbi Weiss found out but he called me to his office. In a strangely sympathetic tone, he said that Grandpa was a devout man who would be rewarded for his good deeds in the Hereafter. He said I would honor him by being a good scholar and not listening to false prophets. When he said Grandpa would be sitting with God and the angels after the Messiah comes, I thought, *Why can't Grandpa be with me until the Messiah comes?*

The *Arba* waited for me and told me how sorry they were. I welcomed their sympathy but wanted to get away. I walked along the park side of Fulton Avenue and saw the cat. I had named him *Shorid*-- Survivor. That came from the Litofsky play.

Twenty-Four

The Grave Is Big Enough

I don't know how long I felt more an observer of myself than me. It was strange; while I wasn't *me,* I knew I wasn't someone else. It was different from acting Santa or a Maccabee. Then I knew who I was and the role I was playing. I didn't feel as if I were in a daydream, when I *was* Superman but could instantly revert to myself. Neither was it like dreaming, when everything was more real than real. Several days after the funeral I dreamt that I asked Grandpa, who lay in the coffin, why he didn't live to be Abraham's age. He opened his eyes and said, "That's a good question!" I woke up so frightened that I couldn't fall back to sleep. Other mornings, in the hazy boundary between sleep and wakefulness, I prayed that Grandpa's death was a nightmare and that I'd awaken and find everything the way it was. Even during the day I would imagine him alive.

Reality jarred me when I went to Grandma's. Poppa and my uncles stayed there day and night. They didn't sit on the couches or chairs but instead on little cardboard boxes. They didn't shave and wore slippers. I envied their so openly expressing their grief. Despite my pleading, I could only stay with them after Hebrew School. The first two days, the apartment was crowded with relatives and friends. They looked uncomfortable whispering condolences and saying nice things about Grandpa. Then they talked about ordinary things and couldn't wait to leave.

On the first evening after the funeral, Grandpa's friends from *shul* held an evening service. I put on my yarmulke and followed the prayers in Poppa's *siddur.* He kept the place with his finger, just like Grandpa--except Poppa's hands weren't as wrinkled. I wondered if Grandpa had taught him to pray like that, but didn't ask. Morris put on a yarmulke and held a *siddur.* He wasn't on the same page as Poppa and when he saw me notice, lifted the *siddur* out of my view. He mumbled what sounded like a prayer and then whispered, "I went to Hebrew School, too."

Most of the men were as old as Grandpa and resembled him with their beards, gray hair, and wrinkled faces. I thought, *Why are they alive and Grandpa dead?* The fourteen men--I counted them--swayed and chanted with a fervor that threatened to burst open the small living room. They prayed as if Grandpa's entrance into heaven depended on them. In their grim faces and chanting they were mourning not only for a departed friend, but for themselves. How many times had Grandpa been at similar services? Had he imagined his friends being at his? I stared at their *tallises,* all they would take with them to the next world, leaving behind everything else--family and possessions. The worn fabric had witnessed so many of their prayers, its stripes still mourning the destruction of the Jerusalem Temple two thousand years ago. No wonder Grandpa lovingly kissed it each time he put it on and took it off, saying a prayer that was woven into the fabric around the collar. Then he'd tenderly place it in its velvet bag, next to his prayer book and phylacteries.

Grandma stood near the men, not hiding as she did in shul with the other women, invisible in the balcony or behind a curtain. She prayed and sobbed unashamedly. When the men finished and put away their *tallises,* they expressed their condolences to Grandma, Poppa and my uncles. Sol led them to the dining room table laden with food. They ate and drank somberly and then gradually became talkative. Their voices rose to conversational levels, their faces became enlivened and they gestured. They were affirming Life and defying Death, which had just snatched away their friend. At first they talked about Grandpa, even laughing, not at all irreverent. One man quoted Grandpa's, "Better ten times sick than once dead," and the others smiled. Another reminded them of Grandpa saying, "Life is only loaned to us." I hadn't heard, "Ever since dying came into fashion, life hasn't been safe" or "If the rich could hire others to die for them, the poor would make a nice living." A man repeated what I'd heard Grandpa say in other words, "Saloons don't make good men bad, and *shul* doesn't make bad men good." Someone entering the room would have thought they were at a party talking about a living friend. Their words and smiles spun a web that brought Grandpa back to life and stilled their fears. Then the conversations drifted to themselves-- illnesses and aches, families, and politics. Grandpa's presence slowly faded, just as the surface of water gradually becomes smooth after a rock has been tossed in. Unlike the other visitors, they left in a group. Late that night, when I was in bed, Momma returned and came into the living room. She gently kissed me. She must have thought I was asleep, otherwise she'd never have whispered, "All life ends in weeping."

By the second evening, Poppa and my uncles looked haggard with stubble darkening their faces. They were not embarrassed being unkempt, rather it was the symbol of their mourning. Not that they could see themselves since all the mirrors were draped in black cloth. With fewer visitors, I had a chance to observe the three brothers. Yitzchok was portly, Sol flabby and Poppa lean. The differences were more than physical. Yitzchok was domineering, Sol easygoing and Poppa thoughtful. Yitzchok was quick to strike with sharp words, Sol ready to joke, Poppa to defend his beliefs. Sitting in the corner, I not only found out more about them, but filled in gaps about family history.

I discovered what broke up Yitzchok's and Sol's partnership- -they made it sound as if it happened yesterday. Yitzchok sneered, "Why didn't you join me in Atlanta?" and Sol answered, "I had to pay off our debts." Yitzchok said, "But he died," and Sol, "He had a wife." Yitzchok countered with, "He wouldn't have cared for our wives; besides she had sons to support her." They gave good reasons for what they did: Yitzchok threw up his hands when he said, "If a dead man's earthly responsibilities end, why should the living be indebted to one who leaves the earth?" Sol shook his head when he answered, "Keeping one's word is more important than money." They were sharp in their accusations: Yitzchok saying, "You couldn't make a living selling lollipops and newspapers!" and Sol, "Swindling is no admirable skill!"

Yitzchok and Poppa had their exchanges. Yitzchok said to Poppa, "What has your painter's union gotten you, Mordcha?" He didn't wait for Poppa's answer. "A bullet for your friend and danger for yourself, not only from gangsters, but the police and immigration. Even if you get rid of these gangsters and replace them with your reformers, how long will they be honest? Our father had to admit, 'The wicked dwell in this world, saints in the next."

Poppa glanced at me when he replied, "How could I live with myself making money with the help of gangsters who keep workers from making a living. You quoted *Tata*--may he rest in peace--do you remember him saying, 'If you see the wicked doing injustice, don't say, Since they are many, I must follow them?'"

Yitzchok sneered, "One brother swings a paintbrush and quotes Talmud while the other presses clothes and acts the clown." He imitated Sol's "Heh, heh." Not only was I learning about them, but I had discovered my own fate: *We're not going to Atlanta!*

Then Yitzchok, in a tone that was unfamiliar, said, "Mordcha, you took care of our mother those years when we were in America--that's one debt I can't forget." He paused. "I can still convince Benny to go into the partnership--if you come to your senses. Think of your family, not only your useless idealism. Continue with your union reformism and you risk not becoming a citizen--or worse!"

I held my breath. The relief I felt moments before, assured that we wouldn't move, was replaced with fear. Yitzchok's arguments were persuasive, even to me. I thought, *Poppa will go!* I glanced at Poppa--his brow furrowed and eyes narrowed. Then his lips pressed together and his jaw raised slightly. Yitzchok sensed Poppa's indecisiveness and turned to Sol, saying, "Tell him what's sensible! Don't let our brother miss the opportunity of his lifetime." I turned to Sol, my heart beating wildly, but his face was blank. I looked at Poppa, whose lips moved. I made out what he whispered--"If you steal enough eggs, you too, can become rich." Yitzchok shouted, "What?" Either he didn't hear or couldn't believe what he heard. He shook his head and said, "It's useless! All your sacrifice and wisdom, if put into a pot, couldn't feed a skinny chicken. The Jews in Europe had many wise sayings but most of them starved. 'Poverty's head is very hard"

I thought, *That's what it means!*

Yitzchok concluded, "There's no remedy for a fool who wants to forever remain one. And when a wise man argues with a fool, two fools are talking." He stormed out into the kitchen. Poppa just sat there. Sol walked over and without a word, squeezed his shoulder. Then Sol went to the bedroom, where Grandma was. I walked over to Poppa. He looked up and tried to smile. I sat down on the floor next to him and he put his arm around me. We sat there without saying a word.

That night I went to bed with a feeling of relief--although Grandpa could not be brought back to live, I would be spared moving to Atlanta. When Momma kissed me goodnight, I said, "We're not moving."

I immediately regretted revealing Poppa's decision, but she said, "I know." I said, "I'm sorry." She stroked my forehead. "You're happy." I tried to protest but she placed her fingers on my lips. "The biggest *tsuris* is not what your enemies do to you, but what family does. You're too young to understand now." Then, standing up, "Family also give you the *simchas.*" She kissed me and left without telling me if that's what her mother had told her. I lay thinking about *troubles* and *happiness.* I could not hide my elation from myself, despite Momma's unhappiness. I also felt guilty that my happiness at the moment overrode my missing Grandpa.

The next afternoon I took my place in the corner of Grandma's living room. They weren't arguing today, but talking nostalgically about Passovers when they were children. They talked in low voices about Borinka--Yitzchok turned away from them but facing me, I saw his tears. Then they resumed their bickering but I didn't pay attention until Yitzchok said Grandpa "could barely make a living from his leather work and nothing from his study of the Talmud." Sol said Grandpa was "devout and happy." Yitzchok replied, "You can't be happy with an empty stomach on *either* side of the ocean. Who rewards you for your righteousness?"

I knew the answer to that question: "God!" *And I said it out loud!* They turned. I was as surprised as they, but I continued, "God will ask you if you were honorable with your fellow men." Yitzchok nodded toward me but spoke to Poppa. "This *pisher* has big ears and an even bigger mouth."

I didn't know Morris was there until he said, "Al knows it's better to be on the side of Justice."

Yitzchok sneered, "Another county heard from! You his lawyer?" Morris' eyes showed anger, but Poppa spoke: "I'm proud of my sons." Yitzchok said, "You'll have one son a Talmud scholar, the other a lawyer--poverty professions!"

"My sons will not grow up to worship dollar bills," said Poppa. "They'll respect their fellow men and know there's more to life than filling their pockets with silver!"

"You have to have *shlichus!*" I said. "Grandpa said it helps to have a mission in life!"

Yitzchok pointed to me and said to Poppa, "Does your little rabbi know that his grandfather abandoned his faith? And not only once-"

I shouted, "That's a lie!" but was close to tears.

Yitzchok continued, *"Tata* questioned the existence of God."

Poppa said, "That's when Borinka died!"

"There were other times," said Yitzchok, "before you were born, when his first child, a girl, died. And he despaired after the long separation from our mother."

I ran from the room, but not before I heard Yitzchok say, "You all run from the truth!"

I turned to see Poppa rush toward Yitzchok, but Sol stepped between them.

As we walked home, Morris said, "Don't believe everything Yitzchok says."

I replied, *"You* don't believe in God! Why should you care?" I was too hurt and angry to be consoled.

On the next day, I did my homework in a corner of Grandma's living room. I was torn between avoiding Yitzchok and finding out whatever else I could about the family. I overheard them talking about Grandma, Yitzchok concerned that she wasn't eating. Poppa said she was taking food from Momma. Then Yitzchok said Grandma's crying would make her sick, but Sol said, "One has to weep after a death." Yitzchok said, "I tell her, 'Life goes on--don't mourn too deeply'--that's in the Talmud." Poppa said, "Feelings can't be ordered away," and Sol changed the subject, telling Yitzchok how pleased Grandma was to see him and his family. Yitzchok took that as criticism. "My business occupies me." That's when he told them he was not staying for the entire seven day *Shiva* period. They looked surprised and he said, "The Talmud says there should be three days of weeping and then four days of praises for the dead. I can complete the *Shiva* in Atlanta."

Sol muttered, "The devil knows the Bible better than a rabbi."

Yitzchok either didn't hear him or chose to ignore him. He said "Before I leave, we have to decide-" He gestured toward the bedroom.

Sol said, "Mordcha and I talked. She can remain in the apartment. The three of us can give her money for rent and food" Poppa added, "There'll be a check from social security--Morris will find out how much."

Yitzchok, with a dismissive wave of his hand, said, "You plan only as far as your nose! She says she's seventy, but I know she's at least five years older."

Momma entered the room. She was carrying a tray from the bedroom. Yitzchok shook his head to signal his brothers not continue their discussion about Grandma. Yitzchok said, "You're a devoted daughter-in-law." Momma stopped and said, *"Kiddush ha-Shem."* Yitzchok laughed. "Honoring the Lord." Momma said, "Becky also comes." Yitzchok said, "Don't be modest about your helpfulness." Then, "You deserve to be rewarded in this life."

Momma turned. "Don't *you* say anything about Mordcha! We don't have the luxuries that you have, but Mordcha's always provided a roof over our heads and food on our table. Before that, even as a boy, he provided for your mother while you were in America making your fortune." She strode to the kitchen before Yitzchok could answer. Yitzchok did say to Poppa, "Your fortunate in *one* respect--If you don't have a good business, you have a clever wife."

When Yitzchok left, he was shaven and dressed in his suit, a contrast to his brothers. The good-bys were cordial until it came to me. Momma nudged me toward him but I pulled away and shouted, "God doesn't want me to kiss him!"

Yitzchok surprised me by laughing. "I hurt your feelings," he said. Momma said, "Of all his cousins, he was closest to his grandfather and loved him dearly. He alone went to *shul* with him this whole last year of his life! Yalka saw his grandparents-- *your parents*-- every *shabbus!*" Then she turned to me and yanked me forward. "In this family," she said to me, "we show respect!" I reluctantly stretched out my hand and shook hands with my uncle. I regretted it right afterwards when he laughingly said, "Don't be a scholar lost in Talmud that he doesn't see that borscht is red."

I went to bed that night peacefully. I was still in pain from Grandpa's death, but the rest of my life would resume its routine. At school, Willie walked into class wearing only a sling. Miss Cleary had trouble quieting us. Harold looked terrified. I was uneasy myself, but when I brought the attendance book down to the office that morning, I read his doctor's note. His arm needed "further healing" and he "should be excused from writing." I was relieved. Willie wouldn't risk beating *anyone* if that meant Miss Cleary would discover how well he could use his arm. While Harold was cringing upstairs, I knew we were safe.

In Current Events I reported on the German Government's plan to solve the "Jewish problem" by shipping the Jews out of Germany. Miss Cleary asked, "Where will they all go?" I didn't repeat what Sol had said, that the only place accepting Jews without questions was Shanghai. Even I knew that city could accommodate few Jews. I thought about Becky's family for the first time in days, wondering if they were safe. Then about Avrum and his family. Sometimes I forgot to think of Grandpa and when I realized that, I felt guilty and couldn't stop thinking about him.

242

In Hebrew School, Mr. Ravitch asked why Abram's name was changed to Abraham. Not one hand was raised. The class had decided if he didn't answer our questions, we wouldn't answer his. He banged his ruler on the desk but that did no good. We'd *write* answers, compromising on that. Rabbi Weiss decided I was the ringleader and threatened to suspend me. The *Arba* met after class and Deborah suggested we answer his questions, but keep our answers short. We agreed without saying that the real reason was to keep me from getting into trouble.

Poppa returned to work and I visited Grandma on Saturdays. Momma helped her with shopping and Grandma even had *kugel* for me. Life was resuming and the danger of leaving for Atlanta was gone. My wish to remain with my friends and graduate from P.S. 4 would be fulfilled. Grandpa's death was enough of an upset. I thought my world had finally righted itself until one evening I heard Momma shout, "What do you mean your mother will live with us?" They lowered their voices and I stood outside the kitchen doorway to hear Momma say, "We have two sons in folding beds in our living room while Yitzchok has a mansion with enough rooms for ten mothers." Poppa asked, "Who does she know in Atlanta?" Momma replied, "Sol has an apartment over the store here-"

I couldn't help it and I stepped into the kitchen. "Can't Grandma live in her apartment?" They both turned to me and Poppa angrily said, "Don't mix in grown-ups' business." I left but heard Momma say, "He has more sense than you and your brothers! Just because you're the youngest. You already took care of her all those years when they were in America!"

Morris heard everything from the living room. Later, I whispered across the darkness, "Where will Grandma stay?" Morris answered, "Why don't you try to dream a solution?" I sensed the sarcasm, but hoped I could. Not that I could *force* myself to dream. That night I had a hard time falling asleep as our parents argued. I didn't have to eavesdrop--we heard every word through the wall. Momma shouted, "She's a mother with *three* sons! Why don't *they* love their mother enough to beg you to let *them* take her?" Poppa countered, "If you wanted *your* mother to live with us, I'd have agreed." Momma said, "You can risk saying that because she isn't alive--may she rest among the angels." Then she cut to the quick with, "You listen to Yitzchok when he tells you to take your mother, but not when he offers you a business." Although it was late, Poppa stormed out and slammed the door behind him. The apartment was silent, but I couldn't fall asleep. When I finally did, I didn't dream.

Over the next days, my parents alternated between angry quarrels and sullen silences. Only the union had caused such strife. While their arguing upset me, I couldn't help but admire their contentious skills. They were ingenious in buttressing their positions and devastating in attacking the other's. Their arguments, counter arguments and counter-counter arguments-- sometimes carried on simultaneously--would have aroused the admiration of any Talmud scholar or a Supreme Court Judge. Besides reasoning, they used strong emotional appeals, like Poppa's, "How can I turn away my mother?" Ridicule was another method, like Momma's, "You're a tiger with gangsters and a mouse with Yitzchok." When words failed them, Momma went into the bedroom and slammed the door. On his part, Poppa would walk out the apartment and slam the front door.

Sol dropped by. He sat with Poppa in the kitchen while Momma was in the bedroom. They were whispering. I crawled into the hallway. Sol whispered, *"Muter* says, 'I can take care of myself, shopping and cooking, and don't want to be a burden to my sons. Do you want to put me away where I'm not wanted? I have sons, not daughters. How long will a daughter-in-law want me in her house?" A chair scraped and I scampered back to the living room. I sneaked back later and heard Poppa say that Momma was upset--then Sol unexpected had to go to the bathroom and nearly tripped over me. He asked, "What are you looking for in the dark?" I said, "I'm going to the bathroom." He replied, "So am I. But you won't find it in the kitchen--heh, heh."

Twenty-Five

A Stranger in the Land

I dreamt that night that I was Abram's nephew. He got into trouble with Pharaoh. This was long before Moses and rather than this Pharaoh trying to keep us from leaving, chased us out. We started on a long journey, stopping at Beth-el and other places, but the Canaanites and Perizzites who lived there picked on us. I told Abram, "We should never have left Babylon." We had lived comfortably in a big city before leaving for Egypt. Abram said, "We have to do what Yahweh tells us to do." I asked how long we'd have to wander. He replied, "I will be a stranger in the land for four hundred years." I gasped--*Four hundred years!*

When I woke up, I wondered what the dream meant since we weren't moving. I told Momma my dream. She looked at me strangely. "I don't need your dreams to know we'll have troubles. Tell your father, not me." Which is what I did. Poppa frowned at the names of Abram's enemies and said, "Nobody likes to move. But it worked out all right. The whatever-you-call them didn't stop Abram." I replied, "But it took four hundred years!"

I went to Grandma's that afternoon. I was relieved she didn't ask why I hadn't been going to *shul* or visiting her more frequently. The apartment looked strange although everything was same. Grandma went about the kitchen doing what she usually did, as if she would continue living there. I offered to go shopping for her. She kissed me and said, "Grandparents couldn't ask for a better grandson." She rapped her knuckles on the table. "Whatever *they* say, I can still go shopping for the few things I need." From her expression I knew she was thinking of Grandpa. I hadn't thought that with him gone, she'd need half as many groceries. When I left, she gave me a piece of *kugel.*

Walking home, I felt guilty not visiting her often and leaving so soon. I couldn't admit to myself I was relieved to be out of the apartment. It had too many painful reminders of Grandpa. I wondered how Grandma felt living there.

That night, Poppa asked me to help him with his Citizenship studies. He hadn't asked in a long time and I was pleased to help. He was in *Book II, Our American Way of Life.* I asked, "Who built the United States?" Poppa answered, "Immigrants from all over the world." We got as far as the chapter on *Becoming An American Citizen.* I asked, "Who can *not* become President?" Poppa said, "Anyone not born here. You and Morris can." Momma, who was sewing, said, "For a Jew to become President there have to be three Mondays in a week." Poppa said, "It's not likely in our lifetime." That was the first time they agreed about anything in a long time!

That Sunday started ordinarily enough with Poppa getting the *Sunday News* and *Forward* and Momma making pancakes. That is until Momma said Poppa had something to tell us. We dropped the comics and ran to their bedroom. Poppa, sitting in his armchair, put down the *Forward,* indicating he had a serious announcement. He waited so long that Momma said, "Well, tell them!" Poppa cleared his throat--"Your Grandma's going to live with us." I was too stunned to speak but Morris asked, "Where's she going to stay?" Poppa said, "She'll have her own bedroom." He tried to soothe us by saying Morris and I would have our own bedroom--"with regular beds that your mother won't have to fold up every day-" Momma interrupted with, "Don't make out you're moving to make it easier for me!"

Back in the bedroom, Morris said, "I'm glad I'm going to high school--I won't have to switch schools." *Switch schools?* What did Morris mean that *I* would have to go to a different school? Morris explained *elementary* school districts. I was in shock.

I ran back to Poppa and asked, "Where are we moving to?"

Poppa put down the paper. "I'm looking."

I asked, "Can't we find a bigger apartment in *this* building?"

Poppa said, "Rents for three bedrooms are too expensive."

"I *have* to stay in P.S. 4!" I turned to Momma, who was darning a sock.

She didn't look up. "You're not the only unhappy one."

"Can't Grandma stay where she is? I can shop for her."

Momma said, "Ask your father. I don't count in making decisions in this house."

Poppa's answer was to pick up the newspaper.

I ran back to the living room and threw myself on the couch, pressing my face into the cushion. Morris said, "It'll take a while before Poppa finds an apartment. Besides, P.S 4 has a large school district." Was he saying that just to reassure me? While he was sympathetic, he was as powerless as me.

The next day, I asked Clarence how he had run away from the reservation school. "I hid in the back of the maintenance man's pick-up truck. He was a Navajo." I didn't see how that could help me, but I was considering every possibility. That evening, I hid outside the kitchen when Sol visited Poppa. I waited for him to finish telling Poppa his latest joke--It was about Abe and Harry meeting after fifteen years and asking about their children. "Abe asks, 'How's your boy Sid?" Harry says, 'Sidney's *wonderful!* He's a doctor with a new office.' Abe asks, 'And Joe?' Harry says, *'Exceptional!* He's a lawyer who argues cases in the Supreme Court.' Abe asks, And Mutel?' Harry sighs. 'Mutel's Mutel--still a tailor, but if it wasn't for Mutel, we'd all be starving!" Sol couldn't stop laughing. I felt miserable listening to their laughter. They planned to go apartment hunting that week. Even Sol couldn't be trusted!

Before he left, he came into the living room. "You're angry with your uncle?"

My expression was my answer.

He shook his head. "Yalka, you think you have troubles?"

I said, "My name's Al!"

He sighed. "Al, I wish I was either very wise or had a fortune, but I do the best I can. Two brothers couldn't make the decision alone--we needed all three."

"Why did you listen to Uncle Yitzchok?" I shouted.

Sol shook his head. "We need the wisdom of your grandfather to solve this--and he's not here--may he rest in peace."

247

I shouted, "Why did he die?" I buried my face in the pillow on the couch.

Sol squeezed my shoulder. "From misfortune to fortune is a ten thousand mile journey; but from fortune to misfortune is but one step."

Poppa came into the living room. "What's the yelling?"

Sol answered, "Al's upset--I can't blame him."

Later that night, I told Poppa about Clarence. I mentioned that he was sent to a school he didn't want to go to and ran away. Poppa said that the settlers often didn't treat Indians fairly. *That* wasn't what I was trying to get across. He knew what was bothering me because he said, "I didn't want to move after my father left for America."

I said, "But you *had* to bring Grandma to Grandpa."

He said, "Didn't Abram have to move? We won't take three hundred years."

I didn't think that funny, nor did I correct him on the number of years. I was also upset my dream was being used against me.

Angry as I was with Poppa, I went with him to Grandma's. He tried to give her several dollar bills but she pushed his hand away, saying, "I have money." Then, "A worker from Anshul's factory brought me money the workers collected." She was close to tears. "Your father always talked of saving money so he could visit the Holy Land." She shook her head. "When one's alive, the world's too small. After death, the grave is big enough." Poppa held her until she stopped crying. Before we left, he asked her if she was lonely living by herself. She said, "I can take care of myself." To me, "I know you're busy with school, but please visit me more often." I felt guilty.

As we walked home, I wondered if she knew she was going to move in with us. I had listened carefully, but they didn't mention moving. Had the plans changed? I wouldn't have minded.

That night I dreamt I was in *shul* with Grandpa. I watched his finger keep the place in the prayer book and felt the silkiness of the *tallis* and the security of his arm around my shoulder. The cantor sang more melodiously than ever and I felt a tingling through my body. I thought, *Shekinah!* On the way home I asked Grandpa if he would have lived longer had he been a Kohan and knew the secret way they held their hands. He asked, "Do I look dead?" He didn't. I told him about the Indian medicine Clarence's grandfather was getting for him so he wouldn't get sick again. He said, "Thank your friend, but I won't need it." He looked tired and I stopped asking questions. I awakened and stared into the darkness for a long time.

That Saturday, Poppa told us they found an apartment-- "1720 Weeks Avenue." Morris said it wasn't *that* far away and "probably in P.S. 4's district." I'm not sure if he believed that or wanted to give me hope. All week-end I couldn't stop thinking about whether I'd have to leave my school. I was so angry I didn't ask about visiting the new apartment. Anyway, that wouldn't have helped me find out if it was in P.S. 4's district.

Monday morning, Miss Cleary was surprised at how eagerly I waved my hand to be Mr. O'Hare's monitor. She picked me. That was a good omen. All week-end I thought of going to his office where he had the district map. When I arrived out of breath, he joked, "Another fire?" I stared at the placard on his desk that I read for the first time.

"Yesterday is your past; today is your future--
because tomorrow is unknown."

I looked at the map behind him as I said, "A friend of mine is moving to 1720 Weeks Avenue. Can he come to our school?" His brow furrowed up to his hairline. I wondered if he suspected who the "friend" was. He stood up and looked at the map. Until that moment, my fate was undecided--it rested on what he saw. I held my breath, blinked, and thought, *Up-and-away!* "Your friend-" his lips moved in slow motion--"would go to P.S.-" I don't think he paused, but it seemed forever before he said, "70." I repeated, *"1720* Weeks Avenue?" hoping he made a mistake. He shook his head. I took out the slip of paper, just to make sure and read, "1720!"

He shook his head again. *"All* of Weeks Avenue is in P.S. 70's district." He smiled. "Tell your friend P. S. 70 is a good school." He winked. "Of course, not as good as P.S. 4."

Whether I tried to distract myself from his revelation or thought I'd never have another chance to find out, I pointed to the sign. "What does it mean?" He read it aloud and explained, "All you can be sure of is today. No one knows what's going to happen tomorrow."

I was discovering that was all too true. Grasping at straws, I asked, "If my friend wanted very much to stay-" I quickly corrected myself "-to come to P.S. 4, could he?" He pointed to the chair next to his desk that only parents sat in. After I sat down, he said, "The Board of Education is strict about school boundaries. Living on the other side of a street can change your school."

I was in shock the rest of the day, although I did everything I usually did--delivering messages, returning to class, eating lunch, going to Hebrew School, eating supper and going to bed-- but remembered no details. I do remember asking Morris if he could try to convince Mr. O'Hare to let me stay in my school. After all, he convinced Miss Cleary and the principal about the play. He said, "I'd try if I thought it would do any good." I pleaded with him to at least *try,* but he insisted the Board of Education makes no exceptions. I said, "You never help me!" No matter where we'd move, he'd go to Stuyvesant. *That wasn't fair!*

As I lay in bed, I couldn't imagine myself *not* being in Class 4-1 and leaving my friends. I already missed not only Harold, Clarence, Herschel and Deborah, but also Willie! Then I thought of Miss Cleary--if anyone had told me I'd be crying into my pillow at the thought of no longer having her for my teacher, I'd have thought him crazy. Momma came into the room while I was in the midst of my misery.

"Remember," she whispered when she kissed me, "I had nothing to do with this." Although up until then I had in no way held her to blame--I even considered her an ally--I said, *"You* could have kept Poppa from moving!" I burst in fresh crying. She held me but that made me angrier. "You made Poppa change his mind about running for union office!" She couldn't make him move to Atlanta, but I didn't mention that.

Momma whispered, "My mother warned me that one person can suffer more than what ten oxen can carry."

I shouted, "We're not oxen!" Nothing could comfort me.

The next day, I asked Clarence if he had any ideas. "I'll be moving soon myself," he said. "My grandfather is getting old and I'll be going back to live with my mother." He saw my expression and said, "The first few moves are the hardest. After that, it gets easier." I wondered if what he said was really true or if he was just trying to make me feel better. I didn't ask.

I told Debbie and she said, "You can't move!" I wanted her to say that to Mr. O'Hare--she convinced me!

The passing days seemed like a dream. While the minutes crawled, two weeks flashed by. I vaguely remember the good-bys and pledges of eternal friendship. Herschel and I exchanged hand gestures--our friendship was more keeping each other company than with words. Deborah made me promise I'd visit-- her parents invited me to have dinner with them and I certainly intended to go--but I never did. Clarence showed me how to say "Good-by" and "See-you-another-time" in sign language. He whispered that his grandfather said special prayers for Grandpa's spirit. Clarence himself would be moving before the end of the month--that would leave only Willie to give our report! He tried to be encouraging by saying he lost count of the number of times he moved. "The Apaches were always on the move," he said, "especially with the U.S. cavalry chasing them. And we're still around." Willie thought I was moving for two reasons: to escape his healed arm and not to give my Committee Report. He confided what I already knew: the sling hadn't kept him from beating me up--he didn't want me to stop doing his writing. He asked, "Think your Superman *'Up-and-away'* can help you beat me up?" He wanted to test that right there in the school yard! I admitted I could never have beaten him in a fair fight and his face softened. If I hadn't said that, I was certain he would have slipped his arm out of the sling and beaten me up. There was no sense my lying *and* getting beaten up. I hastily shook his left hand and we parted. I was relieved not to have tested our tenuous relationship.

There were other good-bys I didn't mind. Rabbi Weiss said I could still come to his Hebrew School--"I don't have a district like your public school." I said nothing and thought he knew I'd never come back. Mr. Ravitch said the next time I saw him I could ask any question I wanted. I'm sure that was his rare attempt at humor, but without thinking, I said, "I'll ask it now: Why didn't you like my asking questions?" His smile disappeared and he looked flustered. When he recovered, he didn't answer but instead solemnly said he hoped that what he and the rabbi taught me would have a lasting impression. It did, but it wasn't what he thought it was.

Miss Cleary said, "You're joking!" as if I'd ever dare joke with her. When she was convinced I wasn't, she said she'd miss me and that I "was the best Santa ever." I asked, "Will the other Santas bring Chanukah presents?" She tried to hide her smile. "I think Mr. Preston will let me keep those *Kanukah* lines in the play." She bent over and kissed my cheek. I saw it coming but couldn't get away--she was holding my shoulder.

I visited Grandma. Her apartment looked strange with her things packed into boxes and crates. She seemed resigned to move in with us. I asked what made her agree. She sighed, "How long can an old woman, without a husband, hold out against three sons?" She shook her head wistfully-- "If your grandfather were alive, he wouldn't let them do this to me." I thought, *If Grandpa was alive, she wouldn't have had to move,* but I didn't say that. She looked sad in the darkness of the kitchen. Then, "Don't tell anyone, but if I'm not happy, I'll move out and live on my own!" She said it with determination. I admired her spirit and hoped that she'd have the courage to do that. Unfortunately, it didn't prevent our moving now. I sat down in the living room, the way I had with Grandpa, except she didn't sit in Grandpa's vacant armchair--she sat in the one she always used. I pulled my cane-bottom chair next to hers. She held my hand and kissed it. "Too bad your grandfather isn't here to answer your questions."

I reminded her, "Grandpa said you had the best answer to the hardest question--'Why don't people live forever?'" I was immediately sorry I said that, but Grandma looked pleased. Then her face darkened. She said, "There's an even harder question-- 'Why is there such suffering'?" She looked frail and lonely and I wondered if she was asking *me.* After a brief silence, she said, "When we laugh, everyone sees us; when we cry, no one does." I hugged her and wished I had the answer. She whispered, "His suffering is over and soon mine too." I felt guilty that in my anger I had blamed her for our having to move. When I left, she apologized for not having *kugel.* I told her I understood since her pans were packed. She handed me a bag and said, "Since you visited, be sure to eat the biggest piece." After her last hug and kiss, she said, "Soon I'll make *kugel* in your oven." I couldn't imagine her cooking in Momma's kitchen, but didn't say that.

Outside, I looked in the bag. It was honey cake from the bakery. Walking home on the park side of Crotona Park, I saw *Shorid.* She approached cautiously, crawling with little sign of her injury. This time I had something to feed her. We shared the *whole* cake. I didn't have to rationalize not bringing any home. Grandma said I should have the biggest piece and I did.

The morning before we moved, I leapt out of bed. I had the solution! It was crystal clear, as if I had dreamt it. I dressed quickly and ate hurriedly. The most difficult problem can have a simple solution. After Harold opened his door, I practically knocked him down. When we were in his room, I asked, "Can I stay with you when my family moves?" Harold, shocked at my entrance, now looked more shocked. His reaction and the fact that I was whispering so his mother couldn't hear me were two signs of my plan's vulnerability. After he explained that his parents wanted only one child and gave up the chance of having others, I realized the futility of asking his mother. But Harold, a true friend, said he'd ask her. I asked, "When?" After all, I had only one day to make the arrangements. He went into the kitchen. His hallway was different from ours. His mother could see me if I stepped out of the living room. All I heard was whispering. Harold returned and shook his head. I don't know if he asked, but knew the answer would have been the same.

I remember the next morning all too well. I covered myself with my blanket and refused to get out of bed. Momma was unsuccessful for the first time. I ignored Morris' pleas--I considered him a traitor for not resisting. Finally, Poppa appeared. Morris explained, "It's like the sit-downs of the auto workers." Morris' likening my tactic to those used by unions against the auto magnates was not appreciated by Poppa. In fact, when I peeked, Poppa was holding the razor strop. I'm still not sure whether he was going to shave or threaten me with it. I covered my head, but instead of feeling the strop heard Poppa say, "We'll eat without him." When I lifted the blanket, instead of seeing anyone, I smelled scrambled eggs. I covered my head again and after several minutes figured out Poppa's strategy. I was hungry, but debated whether to miss breakfast "to show them." Momma didn't come to get me, but Morris warned, "Mom's going to pack the frying pan."

The passing minutes seemed like hours and my hunger became unbearable. Finally, another lesson was added to those that I learned that year: Hunger can overcome Principle. To my family's credit, when I joined them in the kitchen, they said nothing. Despite the turmoil of our last morning in the apartment, with most of the kitchenware packed away, Momma was serving us a special breakfast, attesting to the sanctity of mealtime and the orderliness of the universe. And this was not a cereal breakfast, but her special breakfast of fried eggs with hot buttered rolls! Poppa, sipping tea, said, "You'll have a bigger kitchen in the new apartment." Momma answered, "The smaller the kitchen, the less I have to walk my feet off." Poppa, not dissuaded, said, "The rooms are painted the colors you picked, and I put up wallpaper that's even brighter than the one in this living room." I couldn't imagine any wallpaper more kaleidoscopic than our red, yellow and purple flowers. Momma's response was, "The paint job here can last another year and I'm satisfied with this wallpaper." Poppa didn't seem to realize that Momma couldn't recognize a single advantage of our new apartment, but to his credit he controlled his annoyance and avoided an argument. After all, Momma was doing what she said she'd never do. When she placed a plateful of eggs in front of me, I lost my appetite: Principle overcame Hunger. If my Lying Down tactic didn't work, I would Sit-and-Refuse to eat. Meanwhile, Morris and Poppa had second helpings. Even Momma was eating. When I realized they didn't notice me or chose to ignore me, I capitulated. After eating a portion, I saw no reason not to have seconds.

After breakfast, I first noticed the chaos. The furniture, covered with sheets for protection, was unrecognizable, while our smaller possessions had disappeared into boxes and barrels. As I dressed, I had one more solution. Living in the Indian cave in Crotona Park! My friends could bring me food--Harold could at least do that. I faced two problems: the winter cold and my never having found the cave. When Momma asked, "Why aren't the moving men here?" I realized something else I had learned that year, although not yet with the poetic, "The best laid plans of mice and men-" The unforeseen play a larger role in our lives than we care to admit. Poppa said, "Moving men are never on time." I shouted, "I hope they never come!" It was an unnecessary display since they ignored me. Morris thought they were late because "they stopped off at a saloon." Momma exclaimed, "I don't want drunkards moving my precious things!" I was amazed at the numerous possible ways our moving could still be derailed or at least delayed. My hopes rose again--until Morris suggested calling the moving company. He couldn't call from a neighbor "who'd know all our business," so he went to the candy store. As he left he muttered, "I hope we get a phone in the new apartment." *That was what bothered him!*

I sat on the couch that Momma had disguised with an old bedspread to prevent its being dirtied by the movers. I stared at the boxes that were piled up or forlornly spread helter-skelter on the floor. I was distracted by listening to my parents' conversation. Their problems left me cold. Yet I felt a malicious satisfaction in knowing they suffered aggravations as well, although I couldn't imagine theirs approached my misery. Poppa tried to calm Momma by saying, "It's not across the ocean we're moving." She replied, "I'm tired of moving. I've lost count of how many times. From my father's *shtetl* to my grandparents', then to my stepmother, who mistreated me so that I went back to my mother. Then to Chernobyl-" She was soon counting on the fingers of her other hand--"Warsaw, then across an ocean to the *Land of Dreams.*" I was nearly knocked off the couch when she grabbed me. I felt her soft sobs. "Yalkala, Yalkala! You don't know how fortunate you are to have known only this apartment your whole life!" My mouth was pressed against her bosom so that I couldn't ask, *Why can't we stay here if you're tired of moving?*

Poppa said, "He was nearly born in this apartment, too. Remember?" *I never heard that story!*

Momma asked, "Do I remember? I wasn't here?" She let go of me to reach for Poppa's hand. "I thought if I didn't have him here, I'd have him on the way to the hospital."

Poppa looked at me. "Your birth certificate address would have been 'Crotona Park.'"

Momma explained, "That's because Morris wanted to walk on the park side of the street. What did he know about labor?" *Morris walked with them?*

Poppa said, "Luckily Bronx Hospital is only four blocks away."

The next part I knew all too well since Momma told it to me whenever she wanted me to feel guilty. "After all that rushing, I was in labor sixteen hours!" She looked accusingly at me. "And second babies are supposed to be easier." Then a worried look crossed her face. "Do you think they'll really be drunk when they get here?"

As if on cue, Morris burst through the door, announcing, "They're here!" He was followed by three burly men, the boss apologizing, "Sorry we're late." They immediately got to work. Momma, knowing my detective skills, whispered, "See if they smell of *schnapps.*" I could have caused trouble by lying to her, but being a truthful detective, I got so close that I nearly got hit with an armchair. I reported they were sober.

I watched in dismay as the furniture and boxes were carried out, as if up until then, there was still a chance for a miracle. Our bond to the apartment was being severed each time they walked out the door with our possessions. Momma followed them to make sure they were "careful" with her "precious" items and in so doing slowed them down. Then she whispered to Poppa, "They're walking so slow--it'll be more than three hours!" That was the deposit they had paid.

The Deutsch appeared with a twirl of his mustache and the words, "Can I help?"

Poppa greeted him with, "Everything's under control."

Momma whispered in Yiddish, "I hope he didn't come to talk about the union."

Poppa said, "Why should he come for that? We worked together yesterday."

I got as close to them as possible without arousing their suspicion and when Momma was in another room, I heard the Deutsch whisper, "Only three locals are not counted. It's pretty sure we won." *I didn't know about the election!* Poppa slapped the Deutsch on the back and the Deutsch playfully punched Poppa's arm. Poppa whispered, "Now that the Rank and File *is* the union, maybe our wives won't think it dangerous that we run for office."

Their grins disappeared when Momma entered the room. She looked around at the remaining cartons. "We've collected so much-" She looked surprised, as if she had nothing to do with it.

Poppa said, "We've lived here ten years, the longest in one place!"

The Deutsch said, "If my children didn't make so much noise--or there weren't so many of them--I'd have had fewer landlords." He and Poppa laughed, but Momma didn't think that funny. The Deutsch, still laughing, pointed to me. "Even Al thinks that funny."

I wasn't aware that I was laughing and immediately stopped. This was one day in my life when I was determined to find *nothing* amusing. The living room was bare when I suddenly remembered! I frantically searched where the sofa had been. Morris asked, "What are you looking for?" I found it under a carton. I carefully straightened the creased covers, not caring if Morris saw. He said, "Your comics were hidden there!" as if he had just made the discovery. I retorted, "You knew where they were--I saw you reading them!" Morris made believe he didn't hear me.

Soon, all that remained were the floors and the walls. I didn't recognize the apartment. The Deutsch said he'd drive us to the new apartment. Momma looked grateful, but said, "I have a new apartment to clean."

Poppa said, "One apartment at a time." Then smiling, "This is one time we're not running away. We're moving *to* a place, not *away* from-"

Momma interrupted with, "You're a philosopher all of a sudden--a philosopher with a paint brush."

The Deutsch thought that very funny. I figured that "philosopher" in Yiddish and German sounded pretty much the same. When Momma went into the bedroom to make sure nothing was left, the Deutsch whispered to Poppa, "Next election, maybe you'll be Secretary-Treasurer." Poppa whispered, "We'll make sure there's no graft or sweetheart contracts."

Morris left clutching his school books and airplane models-- he wasn't going to trust anyone with them. I had put my briefcase into a box and didn't care if it got lost. I whispered to Morris, "Did you take your airplane snapshot?" I don't know why I felt considerate toward him.

He nodded and said, "I guard those with my life-" He read my mind because he whispered, "I did fly! I didn't tell you the pilot's name was Billings and that he was a fighter pilot in the World War. Some day you'll meet him and he'll tell you it's true."

I asked, "Will you teach me how to fly?" Although my skepticism left only the slightest possibility of his telling the truth, I wasn't going to risk losing that opportunity.

He answered, "If you're not a pest."

Poppa waited impatiently for Momma. "Can't you leave this apartment once without checking the gas?" Momma, testing each knob, said, "I don't want an explosion for my old neighbors." Poppa left.

Morris shouted, "The truck's leaving!"

Momma locked the door and asked me to try it. I did, twisting the knob and pushing, knowing it was for the last time. Poppa, near the stairs, asked, "What's there to steal?" Momma ignored him. Harold's mother was waiting near her apartment door and Momma gave her the keys. Mrs. Chernow said, "I won't forget to give them to the super." Momma and Mrs. Chernow hugged each other.

Morris, holding his box, muttered, "Je-sus, it's only ten blocks away." I shouted, "It's not in P.S.4's district!" I hadn't planned to say good-by to Harold after his failure to invite me to live with him. But now, I decided to take my time by shaking hands and hugging him. We were also freed from our inhibitions by the example of our mothers. Harold said, "You're not going to be around for the Committee Reports." I didn't tell him that I didn't care. Only when Morris said, "Do you want to fly?" did I release Harold and wiggle out of his grip. I promised that I would come back tomorrow to visit him. I didn't. In fact, I didn't the next week or the next month. I never saw Harold again and only remembered him from a tattered snapshot of us mugging for the camera.

As I walked through the courtyard, I realized I'd no longer be walking there, as I had since I took my first baby steps. I had taken so many things for granted that I might never see again. Momma and I finally reached the car. She was still clutching her pocketbook, which she hadn't put down since the movers arrived. The Deutsch said I could squeeze in front with Poppa and Morris but I preferred sitting in the back. Much as I wanted to sit in front, I didn't want to give anyone the satisfaction of seeing me having a good time that day. Before we pulled away, Morris asked, "Mom, you want Al to see if the door is locked?" I didn't think that funny. Neither did Momma, who said, "You shouldn't make fun of your mother!" Poppa agreed.

As we drove down Fulton Avenue, I looked long and hard at Crotona Park. Above the noise of the engine, the Deutsch asked Poppa, "You're not sorry about that business deal falling through?" I was surprised he asked that with Momma there.

Poppa answered, "People plan, but fate decides." He turned to Momma, "We've always had enough to eat."

Momma answered, "An ox eats well, but works hard and has few pleasures."

Poppa ignored that and said, "My mother always said, 'A woman prefers poverty with love to riches without love."

Momma answered, "Your mother was married to your father--may he rest in peace. He was special." Although she said that very loud, Poppa made believe he didn't hear. When we turned off Fulton Avenue, Momma said, "I hope we have nice neighbors."

I muttered, "I hope they're Amorites."

Morris asked, "Who?"

I repeated the name of the desert people who plagued Abram for four hundred years. I waited for someone to ask who they were, but no one did.

Momma said, "Yalka has these dreams-" she patted my back "-some of them come true."

The Deutsch glanced at me. "You'd better dream nice things, Al."

Poppa said, "Everything will be all right-" He turned around. "After all-"

Momma interrupted with, "I know, this is-"

Even I joined them in saying, "The *Land of Dreams*."

Epilogue

I don't know how long I'd been standing among the tombstones, but I felt numb. Yet I did not mind, since those below no longer experienced such sensations. The stage before me was silent, all the many actors and actresses entombed. They are gone, along with their momentous dramas. Their lives and visions remain alive only in the memories of those still living. Yet after all these years I still taste Momma's breaded cutlets and Grandma's kugel. I can feel Momma's soft cheek and Poppa's rough hands, Grandma's hard cheekbone, Grandpa's beard and Morris' tugging the comics from me. Standing there, I was the child once more, recapturing the joys and pains of those days. Though I have learned much from life and books, my perceptions then, no matter how naive, were clear and intense. What could be more profound than struggling with the meaning of life, in which we share more childish visions than profound adult understanding. "All are of dust and all turn to dust again." Between two ruahs--the first and last breaths--many dramas are played out. In 1938, I believed I was in two plays, a Santa in one, a Maccabee in another. I didn't realize I was in a third--the drama of my life. I had not yet read Shakespeare's "All the world's a stage." I felt authentic then, but now, standing near whatever remains of Momma and Poppa--realize "We are such stuff as dreams are made on, and our little life is rounded with a sleep." Have they become clichés or do they reveal profound truths? Was my parents' "Land of Dreams" a dream itself? If we sleep in life what do we do in death? Why are our days numbered and why do we suffer? Why are we festive--or vibrate with Shekinah? I've searched for answers in places that Yalka never dreamt of, but have come no closer to the truth. Buddha, when attaining enlightenment, said he attained nothing at all. Does everything disappear into nothingness from which all new things emerge? Adult Yalka asks questions that are as difficult to answer as then.

The End

About the Author

The author was conceived during the week of the stock market crash in 1929 and born nine months later in Bronx Hospital as the nation plunged into the Economic Depression. He was the younger son of Russian Jewish immigrants who had escaped pogroms, World I and the Russian Revolution to settle in the Bronx. His father was a house painter whose economic improvement was marked by the family's moving from apartments in the South and East Bronx to within sight of the Grand Concourse. He went to neighborhood public schools and graduated from the Bronx High School of Science. He left the borough to further his education at the City College of New York, Saint John's University and lastly at Teachers College, Columbia University, where he obtained a doctorate in psychology.

His work career started in the Bronx in the summer he turned sixteen, when he was a messenger for Western Union. In those days, telegrams were delivered by bicycle, and it seemed that most recipients lived on the top floor of five story walk ups. In college he delivered newspapers in the Bronx to earn carfare and textbook money (the City University was free). The college literary magazine published his first story; he was encouraged by a renown English professor to pursue writing. However, as a first generation American he had absorbed his parents' values to pursue a more secure career. But first he left school - and the Bronx - to become a steel worker and union health and welfare officer in Buffalo, New York.

After returning to New York and obtaining his doctorate, he taught at Columbia and the City University. His research was published in national psychology journals and he made numerous presentations at national and one international meeting. He still has a psychotherapy practice in - where else? - the Bronx. While working with today's immigrants, he has been writing memoir fiction about his parents' immigrant generation, which is practically gone, and his brother's World War Two generation, which is fast dwindling. Two short stories were published and he is working on a sequel to *Land of Dreams,* which takes the family through World War Two. He divides his time between his psychotherapy practice and writing about a past generation that except for ethnicity and race confronted problems similar to those of today's immigrants; the saga going back to the time when our earliest Homo Sapiens first ventured from their savanna homeland.

The author still finds time to bicycle in the Bronx and spend time with his wife, grown children, daughter-in-law and grandson.